It's strange enough when Susan Shaw disappears without a trace on a wintry March afternoon. It's stranger still when her uninformative note is found in the hallway of her apartment building, along with a black cat that no one has seen before. And it's strangest of all when she suddenly appears again, wearing clothes that are eighty years out of date, and tells a wild story about an old woman with a fly-away hat, an elevator that travels into the past, and a distressed family that only she can save.

Who is going to believe such a tale? Certainly not her father. But Susan is determined to prove to him that it's all true. And she has other plans for him as well...

Who, in fact, could believe such a tale? Even the author, who takes part in the story, has his doubts. But just as those doubts are all laid to rest, the mystery thickens once more. This time it's a double disappearance...

More books by Edward Ormondroyd

David and the Phoenix
Castaways on Long Ago

For younger readers

Jonathan Frederick Aloysius Brown
Michael the Upstairs Dog
Theodore
Theordore's Rival
Broderick
Johnny Castleseed

Two novels by Edward Ormondroyd

Time at the Top

illustrated by Barb Ericksen

and

All in Good Time

illustrated by Roger Bradfield

Cover by Charles Geer

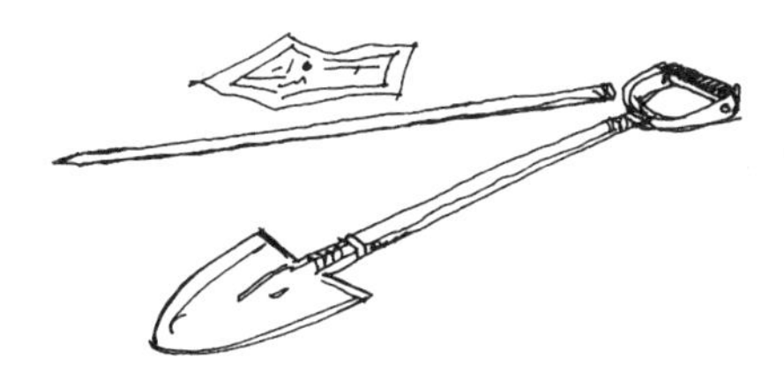

Purple House Press

Kentucky

Published by
Purple House Press, PO Box 787, Cynthiana, KY 41031

Summary: A spunky but lonely girl finds herself transported back in time to 1881, courtesy of her apartment building's elevator.

ISBN-13: 978-1-930900-55-4
LCCN: 2011934308

Printed in the United States of America
1 2 3 4 5 6 7 8 9 10
First Edition

Author's Foreword

Well here it is, *All in Good Time,* the sequel to *Time at the Top*, appearing at last with its predecessor in one volume. And that is where it should be; because the two books together tell a single continuous story.

I never intended to write a sequel to *Time at the Top*. That was a stand-alone book, I thought, and its story was so tidily wrapped up that it seemed nothing more about Susan's adventures could be said. It took me a long time to realize I was wrong. All unknowingly, I had set up in the last few chapters of *Time at the Top* a perfect opportunity for a further story—the success of the plot hatched by Susan and Victoria to combine their two families. The old photograph tells us that it has happened, but we're left without a clue as to *how*. And again all unknowingly, I had given Susan a diary to take with her back to 1881. So I had provided myself with a story—how the girls' plot had succeeded—and a way of telling it, based on the diary. All I needed was the diary itself. The mysterious way it is put into my hands becomes the beginning of *All in Good Time.*

It was a pleasure to plunge in, returning to old scenes and familiar faces. Mrs. Walker and Maggie could now become flesh-and-blood people instead of overheard voices. Jim Perkins and the Hollisters, only names before, could now come forth as real persons too. The embodiment of another name, Cousin Jane, could now burst catastrophically on the scene as that fearsome battle-ax, Jane Hildegarde Clamp. It was a lot of fun to bring her and Mr. Sweeney face to face!

(Oh yes, Mr. Sweeney is back, more of a scoundrel than ever.) And to make the story a cliff-hanger, I put in as many obstacles and disruptions as I could invent.

A warning: you will see that the book ends with a hint that another sequel might be possible. Ignore it, please. One sequel is enough, and the one in your hands is it! My editor was pleased by it, my first publisher was pleased, and I was pleased. It is my sincere hope that you will be pleased as well.

Edward Ormondroyd
2011

Time at the Top

For my daughters Beth and Kitt

What Became of Susan?

One Wednesday in March, late in the afternoon, Susan Shaw vanished from the Ward Street apartment house in which she lived with her father.

The last person to see her was Mrs. Clutchett, a lady of uncertain age but reliable habits, who was employed as a cleaning woman by various residents of the building, and also by Mr. Shaw as a cook. Wednesday was her day to clean as well as cook for the Shaws, so she had been in the apartment when Susan arrived home from school—an arrival, she thought, that was a little later than usual. She reported that Susan had behaved in a moody and restless manner, as if the weather, which was certainly unpleasant enough, had gotten into her bones. The girl fidgeted about the apartment for a while "without a word to say for herself," suddenly muttered something about "going to the top," and went out. According to Mrs. Clutchett, that took place some time after five o'clock, although she wouldn't swear to the exact moment. "The top," no doubt, was the seventh floor, the topmost one of the apartment building, where Susan sometimes went to look out of a window at the end of the hallway.

Mrs. Clutchett had, however, just glanced at the clock when Mr. Shaw walked in, so she could state with authority that his arrival took place at fourteen minutes to six. He was carrying a beautifully wrapped box, and called out as he entered, "Here you are, chick—the loudest one in the whole store!" Mrs. Clutchett gave a small shriek at this announcement, having immediately concluded that the box contained something explosive. Mr. Shaw assured her that it was only an alarm clock for Susan, and asked where she was. He was told of Susan's presumable whereabouts, and sat down to read the paper. Dinner was ready at six-ten. At six-thirty, Mr. Shaw, more irritated than alarmed, took the elevator to the seventh floor to fetch Susan down. She was nowhere to be found.

I first heard of the disappearance around eight o'clock that night, when Mrs. Clutchett breathlessly telephoned me to ask if I'd seen Susan.

"Susan who?" I asked.

"Susan—Shaw—on—the—third—floor. You know, the little girl of that nice Mr. Shaw, with the braids and brown eyes?"

"Oh, yes," I said. I didn't really know Susan, but we had ridden the elevator together once or twice. "What's the trouble?"

"She's *gone*, poor motherless lamb! She's just disappeared into thin air!"

"Oh, she's probably at a movie. I always watched movies two times through when I was her age, to make sure I got my money's worth."

"No sir! That child *never* goes out without leaving a note or saying what she's up to. I wish I could think it was just a movie, but I can't. There's something going on here, Mr. Ormondroyd.

You just mark my words. There's something behind all this."

I had to smile. Mrs. Clutchett cleaned my apartment every other Thursday, and I had come to know her as a curious compound of sentimentality and devotion to mystery. She loved to see in almost everything that happened a huge and sinister plot, suspected by no one but herself. Nearly anyone you could name was probably "up to something" that would astonish the world "if only truth were told." I could see her now at the other end of the line, pursing her lips and nodding with that air she had of ominous satisfaction.

"Oh, nonsense," I said. "She's probably visiting one of her friends."

"Well! I just wish I could think so. I just hope to goodness it's that simple. Poor Mr. Shaw's telephoning all her friends now, and I'm calling all the people in the building—but it won't do any good. We'll have to bring in the police, I can just feel it in my bones. Poor child! It's just those kind that have something awful happen to them."

"Well, I'll have a look around up here," I said. "If I see her I'll send her right home."

"That's awfully nice of you, Mr. Ormondroyd. But I've got a hunch it won't do any good. There's more than meets the eye here, *you mark my words.*" And with that dark utterance she hung up.

I did take a look up and down the hallway of the fifth floor, where I live; but Mrs. Clutchett was right to this extent, that it didn't do any good. There was no Susan in sight.

Next afternoon, Thursday, Mrs. Clutchett boarded the elevator as I was going down.

"Did it turn out all right?" I asked.

"No *sir!*" she said in sorrowful triumph. "What did I tell you! Didn't I say there was something behind all this? That poor child has vanished without a trace!"

"Oh oh!"

"Yes indeed, you may well say 'oh oh!' You'd probably have cause to say more than that if truth were told. Now, I'll tell you what," she said, lowering her voice dramatically and fixing me with her eye. "This whole thing could've been prevented, if you ask me. Nipped right in the bud."

"Really? How?"

"Well, now! It's not that he isn't a good father to her—maybe *too* good, trying to make it up for her, you know. Lucky for him she's so stage-struck that she doesn't think to plague him for things like most girls plague their fathers, because I know he couldn't deny her anything. But if I've told him once, I've told him a hundred times, 'Mr. Shaw,' I've said, 'you ought to marry again. A good-looking, steady man like you. It's not right for the poor child not to have a mother, girls need the influence of a good woman,' I said. Not that I don't respect his feelings. I know what it's like, believe you me. Why, when poor Mr. Clutchett was taken to Heaven I made a vow right then and there never to *look* at another man again, to keep his dear memory ever green, so to speak, and I've kept that vow through thick and thin, believe me, not but what there weren't strong temptations to break it. But *I* didn't have chick nor child like Mr. Shaw has, and that makes a difference, you can't deny it, feelings or not."

"So you think she ran away because of not having a mother?"

"Well, now," she said, changing her tack as if suddenly realizing that such a simple reason didn't have many possibilities for mystification. "I just hope to goodness that it's nothing worse. Not that I'm reproaching him with it now, you understand. Poor man, he's half frantic with worry. I'm staying by his side through thick and thin. I'm just going out now to get some coffee, he's drinking it by the gallon, won't eat a bite. No, I won't say another word about it now, but just you wait till that child comes back, *if* she comes back, won't I just lay into him *then*, night and day, until he finds a good respectable woman to marry and give that poor child a home!"

I went with her to buy the coffee. She talked nonstop all the way to the store and all the way back, veering between real concern and delighted foreboding. The police had been notified and were working on the case under the direction of a certain Detective Haugen. They had searched the building from basement to roof, and had gone over the elevator with magnifying glasses and finger-print equipment, without result. Susan's picture and description had been sent out through the city and to other cities nearby: Missing, Susan Shaw; age, height, weight, etcetera etcetera; wearing a dark coat, grey and red pleated wool tartan skirt, grey pullover sweater, white socks, saddle shoes; reward for information leading to recovery. There were several theories to account for what had happened. She might have run away, she might have amnesia, she might have been kidnapped. Poor Mr. Shaw was still arguing hopefully against all three possibilities. There was no reason, he said, for Susie to run away—she was doing well in school, he had never quarreled with her, she seemed happy enough for a motherless girl. Amnesia wasn't likely; you had to suffer severe strain or shock to lose your memory, and although the death of Mrs. Shaw two years ago had been a terrible blow, nevertheless Susan had come through it very well. And as for kidnapping, what could kidnappers hope to gain by taking such a risk? He was not rich; he was only an accountant with a very small company, and his savings amounted to nothing that the most desperate of abductors would consider worth while.

It was simply a scandal, Mrs. Clutchett went on, the way the tenants were behaving. Well, some of them, anyhow—pretending they had business on the third floor just so's they could walk by the Shaws' apartment and stare in the door. Still, it had to be admitted that most of the people in the building were being just as kind as they could be, offering to cook or run errands, or bringing sandwiches to try to tempt poor Mr. Shaw into eating something to keep his spirits up. Even Mr. Bodoni, the janitor, had come up and had actually (for the first time in his life, probably) taken that horrible dead cigar out of his mouth and put it in his pocket as a sign of respect. He had patted Mr. Shaw on the shoulder, steered him into the kitchen, and whispered solemnly, "You show me anyting here it's outa repair, *any*ting, I fix it right now. No questions asked. Right now—everyting else can wait." Later he came in again with an enormous bunch of daffodils, and, removing his cigar once more, expanded his offer: "You show me anyting here, it don't even *have* to be outa repair, I fix it. All brand-new parts."

"Now wasn't that real sweet?" Mrs. Clutchett said moistly. "It just goes to show you, doesn't it? I'd never have thought it of him in a hundred years—him being foreign-born and usually so mysterious in his ways and all."

"Is there anything I can do?" I asked.

"Well, Mr. Ormondroyd, if you're a praying man as I sincerely hope you are, *most* writers I fear being the contrary, then I guess you better get down on your knees. Police and detectives and all irregardless, I've got a hunch we'll never see that poor child again without Heaven's help. You just mark my words."

Hubbub in the Hallway

The mystery unexpectedly deepened late Thursday night.

Detective Haugen, who suspected that they were dealing with a kidnapping, had stationed a policeman in the Shaws' apartment in case an attempt should be made during the night to deliver a ransom note. At about one-twenty-five A.M. the policeman heard what he thought was a child crying in the hallway. He rushed out to investigate, and found a large black tomcat nervously sniffing the carpet and yowling. On the floor lay a scrap of newspaper with writing on it. 'Ransom note!' he thought; 'Haugen was right!' He wrapped a handkerchief around his fingers, and was stooping to pick up the note when he noticed that the elevator was ascending. (The elevator was on the opposite side of the hallway from the Shaws' apartment, and one door down.) The indicator arrow above the elevator door was steadily creeping around the dial. It had just reached 4 when he looked. He raced into the Shaws' apartment and telephoned the precinct station. "Get hold of Haugen!" he shouted. "I think we've got 'em. They may be going up the elevator right now. —That's right, I said *up*. —That's what the arrow said. —Look, don't argue, get Haugen and some of the boys here, quick. We've got to cut 'em off!"

The building was quickly encircled and all exits covered by armed policemen. Searching parties swept through the building, working their way upward floor by floor—one group up the inside stairs, two up the outside fire escapes.

Nothing. The elevator stood empty on the seventh floor.

"Up to the roof, boys," Detective Haugen ordered. "Don't fire unless they do first. Keep your eye on the hallway here, Murphy."

Nothing!

It suddenly occurred to Detective Haugen as he huddled against the wind on the roof that perhaps the elevator business had been a ruse. You didn't have to be in an elevator to send it anywhere. You could press the button from outside. Perhaps the kidnappers had sent the elevator up to divert attention, while they walked or ran downstairs. They might have been able to leave the building before the police arrived to surround it—or they might have gone on to the basement to hide out until the excitement blew over…

"Come on, boys!"

No one was in the basement.

However, on a dusty part of the floor they found a cat's pawmark. And behind the row of washing machines, by a puddle that had formed there from a leak in one of the hose connections, were several muddy footprints.

"Those weren't here last time we searched," Detective Haugen said. "Look, not even dry yet. Go up and get one of the girl's shoes, Murphy."

The footprints were slightly larger than Susan's shoe. Nevertheless, they were much too small to have been made by an adult.

Since the basement was Mr. Bodoni's particular province, he was seized for questioning as he entered the building a few minutes later. Had he been down in the basement recently?

"Yeah," said Mr. Bodoni.

When?

"Bout half an hour ago, three-quarters of an hour, along in there, I guess."

Had he seen or heard anything out of the ordinary?

Mr. Bodoni looked at the ground and shifted his cigar evasively.

Well?

"Don't tell the tenants, willya?" Mr. Bodoni muttered. "Everyting's under control. I only seen one."

"One *what?*" Detective Haugen shouted. "Out with it, man!"

Mr. Bodoni leaned forward and hoarsely whispered, "Mice!"

Coming home from a late movie, he had entered the elevator and found a mouse in it. He had been fighting mice for three years, and had finally reached the point where he could look any tenant in the eye and say there wasn't a mouse in the house. And now this! He put his foot on the creature, descended to the basement, where he had seen and heard nothing unusual, and collected his mousetraps. Needing bait, he had gone out to an all-night delicatessen for some cheese, and had been grabbed by two policemen on his return. "Whatsa matter?" he demanded. "A man can't buy cheese any more? It's against the law to buy cheese? Buyin' cheese, 'at's all I was—"

"Okay, okay," Detective Haugen sighed. "Forget it."

"That black cat upstairs yours?" Murphy asked.

"What cat? No cats around here. I use traps, see?" He produced one from his pocket. "Don't say nothin' to the tenants, willya? I get everyting under control before they notice."

The piece of newspaper that had been found in the hallway was not a ransom note. The penciled writing on it said:

> Dear Daddy, please don't worry about me. I'm all right. Tell the policeman he can go away, I'm all right. I have to go back for a little while but please don't worry, it's perfectly safe. I'll be home as soon as I can.
>
> Love, Susie

"Careful, Mr. Shaw, don't touch it — there may be fingerprints."

"That's her writing, all right!" Mr. Shaw said. "I'd recognize it anywhere. See that loop on the a's? Thank God she's safe!"

"Well, Mr. Shaw, I don't want to alarm you, but this may be a trick of some kind. They could have forced her to write it, see? 'Tell the policeman he can go away'—that sounds like a fabrication to me. One thing, anyway; if they're clumsy enough to try something like that they're clumsy enough to get caught."

"At least she's safe," Mr. Shaw insisted. "She says she's safe."

"I hope so, Mr. Shaw."

One faint, dusty fingerprint was found on the paper, and identified as Susan's.

I went to the Shaws' apartment Friday afternoon to see if I could be of any service. Mrs. Clutchett told me of the previous night's happenings—she had been sleeping in the apartment on the living room sofa—and introduced me to Susan's father. He looked worn, but hopeful.

"She says she's safe," he said, showing me her note. "I believe her. See how steady the writing is? If anybody had forced her to write it she'd be frightened, and the writing would show it, wouldn't it? But it doesn't even waver. She *must* be all right..."

Meanwhile Mrs. Clutchett was making mysterious signals to me behind Mr. Shaw's back—so mysterious, in fact, that it took me several minutes to interpret them as meaning "Come into the kitchen." I reassured Mr. Shaw as well as I could, pointing out that the last sentence in Susan's note struck me as particularly encouraging, and then followed Mrs. Clutchett into the kitchen.

"Look!" she whispered dramatically, pointing under the sink.

I looked. All I could see was a black cat crouching over a dish of hamburger and making little gargled *rowr rowr* noises as it ate.

"So?" I said.

"If—that—cat—could—talk!" she said, pursing her lips and narrowing her eyes in an expression of vast significance. "Well! Believe you me, that animal's in the thick of this. I've just got a hunch. I'm keeping my eye on it night and day."

"Oh, great!" I said. "Well, when kitty decides to reveal all, just let me know. I'll be right down."

"All right! All right! You go ahead and laugh if it so pleases you. But just you let me tell you something. I used to have a cat, and you may believe this or not but it's the pure gospel—*one month to the day* before poor Mr. Clutchett was taken to

Heaven that cat cried for twenty-four hours without stopping. Now! *Cats know*. You mark my words."

The cat, however, kept whatever secrets it might have had, and Friday night passed without incident.

On Saturday morning a number of people happened to converge on the Shaws' apartment at the same time. Detective Haugen had come to report that nothing had changed, but that his bureau was following up a lead anonymously telephoned in from New Jersey. With him came a young reporter carrying a camera, and a man bearing flowers who was later identified as the vice-president of Mr. Shaw's company. At the same time, four tenants, two men and two women, all acquaintances of Mr. Shaw, approached down the hall from the opposite direction. As everyone arrived simultaneously at the door, it opened to reveal Mr. Shaw and Mrs. Clutchett in the midst of an argument just within. He was insisting that she must go home and get some rest, not that he didn't appreciate her concern; and she was saying that not even wild horses could budge her an inch until that poor child was found. Behind them was the night-guard policeman, stretching and yawning. For a few minutes there was a subdued hubbub at the door, with everyone murmuring "Excuse me. Pardon me." Detective Haugen glanced impatiently at his watch. It was eight-twenty-three.

At that instant the elevator door opened with a sigh, and Susan got out.

She had an odd dress on: it was black, with full-length sleeves, a good deal of material bunched and draped around the hips, and skirts that reached halfway between her ankle and knee. She was also wearing black cotton stockings, and shoes of a strange cut. There were bits of straw in her hair. She was

1 2 3 4 5 6 7

limping, and had dark circles under her eyes. Still, most of the startled observers later agreed that her expression was one of happy excitement; but Mrs. Clutchett immediately diagnosed it as a combination of shock and hysteria.

Mr. Shaw turned pale, and murmured "Susie, Susie!" as she flung herself at him. Mrs. Clutchett shrieked. Instantly there was an enormous uproar. "Susie, Susie! Are you all right, darling? You're not hurt?" "Oh, Daddy, I'm *awfully* sorry if I made you worry. I didn't mean—" "Now, Miss, where did they leave you? What did they look like?" "Hey—smile! That's it!"—and the glare of a flashbulb. "Those clothes!" the women murmured to each other. "Where do you suppose she got those *clothes?"* Doors began flying open up and down the hallway. "Now leave the poor child alone," Mrs. Clutchett shouted, "Can't you see she's *exhausted?"* Within the apartment the cat yowled. "Hold it"—flash!—"one more, now!" "What kind of car did they have? Where did they let you off? Where did that straw come from?"

Susan fainted.

"Now you've done it!" Mrs. Clutchett shrieked. "Get out, get out, all of you! *Hounding* the poor child!" She seized a cushion from the sofa and began laying about her violently, while Mr. Shaw carried Susan inside. "Out! Out! I never heard of such a thing! That child says nothing and sees nobody until she's had a rest and some broth and a doctor. Get *out!* Big grown ignoramuses pestering the poor baby to her death!"

As soon as she had been laid on the bed, Susan opened her eyes and giggled. "Wasn't that a perfect faint? I had to get rid of all those people somehow. Oh, Daddy, you look so tired! I'm awfully sorry if you worried. Did you get my note? No, I *didn't* run away. No, I wasn't kidnapped either. Well, I was going to explain the other night, but there was a policeman—"

"The idea! The idea!" Mrs. Clutchett raged into the bedroom. "Those—those *vultures*! Chafe her wrists, Mr. Shaw. Where's my smelling salts? I'm going to call a doctor."

"No you're not," Susan said. "I'm perfectly all right. I just sprained my ankle a little, that's all. Now please go away, I want to—"

The cat yowled under the bed.

"It's Toby!" She wriggled off the bed and dropped on her knees. "Come on, Toby. Puss puss! I'm awfully glad you're not lost. I promised them I'd bring you back. Daddy! You'll *never* guess how old Toby is, and he doesn't even know it! He's sixty, plus—what's eighty-one from a hundred?"

"Back on that bed, Missy! You're overwrought, that's what you are. Sixty my foot! Although I just *knew* that cat was in the thick of it somewhere. Just wait till I see that Mr. Ormondroyd, thinks he's so smart—"

"Puh-lease, Mrs. Clutchett! I have to talk to Daddy in private. Will you please, please, kindly—"

"All right, all right! I'll go and make some broth. But if you ask *me*, a doctor should—"

"And please shut the door? Please? Thank you."

"Susan Shaw," said her father, clutching his hair with both hands and pulling it, "*will* you please tell me what's been going on around here?"

"Of course, Daddy, I'm going to. Come on, Toby, that's a good boy. Well, it all began—when was it? Wednesday. That horrible day, remember? Oh, I bet you're not going to believe a word of it, it's all so—so *weird!* But cross my heart and hope to die, it's all absolutely true!"

A Day Awry

Wednesday went wrong from the very beginning.

Susan was awakened by a burst of wind that seemed to be trying to rip her bedroom window right out of its frame. Evidently it was going to be another foul March day, the third in a row now, with bitter air, a sunless sky, and an unresting grit-and-paper-bearing wind. She groaned, pulled the blankets up to her chin, and glanced at the clock.

It was seven. She had slept through the alarm again.

"Oh, no!" she muttered, flinging herself out of bed. There still might be time to dress and get out of her room before—but no, she was too late. The television set next door burst into noise. Even the wind couldn't drown out that dreaded greeting. "Yap yap!" shouted Your Genial Breakfast Host, "yap yap yap!" on a soaring note of jollity; and then a crash of applause and whistles and glad cries. Susan huddled her clothes on, trying to deafen at least one ear by pressing it against her shoulder. "No, seriously," the Genial Host shrieked through the wall into her other ear, "isn't life the funniest thing you ever heard of in your *life?*" Laughter, clapping, cries. She slammed her bedroom door behind her.

Mr. Shaw was standing by the window in the living room, looking down at the street as he knotted his tie. "Sounds like they beat you to it again," he grinned.

"Oh," Susan groaned, "I can't *stand* it. My fault for sleeping through the alarm again, I guess…Can I have a new one, Daddy?"

"Alarm clock? Sure, chick. What color would you like?"

"Oh, I don't care. Just so it's loud. All this one says is tinkle tinkle."

"One—loud—alarm—clock," said Mr. Shaw, writing in his notebook, "color no object. Done. Meanwhile, since it's an ill wind that blows nobody good, etcetera etcetera, maybe our friends' antenna will get carried off. Listen to it!"

"Wish it would carry old Yammerface off." Imitating the Genial Host, she cried in a high-pitched voice, "Yap yap a funny thing happened to me on the way to the studio this morning yap yap the wind blew me right into the middle of last week!"

Breakfast was a fiasco. Mr. Shaw started out by spilling coffee on his trousers. While he was changing, the toaster stuck and thoroughly carbonized the two slices of bread in it. Susan burned her thumb trying to pry them out. The second toast-making attempt was more successful, but as she was buttering a slice it slipped from her fingers and fell butter-side down on her skirt. She kicked the table leg, and went to change. Every skirt but the tiresome grey and red tartan was out at the cleaners. "No, seriously," the Genial Host yelled on the other side of the wall, "are you good folks having fun?" Roar. She fled in her slip, and changed in the living room.

The wind was increasing. They picked at their toast without appetite.

"Well," Mr. Shaw sighed at last, looking at his watch, "it's about that time."

"Yes."

"What's the matter, chick?"

"Oh...I have a feeling it's going to be one of those days."

"I *know* it's going to be one of those days. Still, life goes on."

Reaching the sidewalk, they were nearly knocked down by a gust of wind, and as they kissed each other goodbye a sheet of newspaper flew at their heads and wrapped its wings about them like some demented seabird. Mr. Shaw went up Ward Street to the subway, while Susan went two blocks in the opposite direction to catch her bus to school. When she reached the bus stop she discovered that she had no money—it was still in the pocket of her buttered skirt. She had to go back for it, thereby missing the bus and arriving late at school.

There was in her grade a small, leering, unwashed boy who had appointed himself her official tormentor. With proper vigilance she could usually avoid his attentions; but during the first period the class was seated in alphabetical order, which placed him directly behind her. Today, in her preoccupation, she forgot to take the normal defensive steps. Almost instantly her braids were in the hands of the enemy. It cost her a painful wrench of the neck to jerk free. She rounded on him and hissed, "*Stop that!*"

"Susan!" said Miss Melcher.

"But he was—"

"Do pay attention, Susan!"

"Well, I'm trying to, but he keeps—"

"You must try a little harder, Susan."

'All right, you little rat,' she raged to herself, 'just wait till I catch you!' She endured his pestering until the bell rang, then managed to trap him at the door, where she kicked his shin. Miss Melcher looked up just in time to see it.

"Susan Shaw," she said in her high sorrowful voice, "Susan Shaw, why can't you Adjust?"

The Physical Education teacher bellowed, "Doesn't this lovely wind just make you want to shout, girls?" Shivering and sniffling, they were herded out into the elements. A soccer ball came soaring out of the boys' side of the playground and hit Susan on the ear.

She struggled through a particularly difficult set of arithmetic problems, discovering only after she was finished that she had been working on the wrong assignment.

The cafeteria ran out of Swiss steak just as she arrived; she had to take frankfurters, which she loathed.

Her enemy pressed close to her as they entered the first afternoon class. He did not look at her. His face expressed only eagerness to reach his desk and begin his work. She allowed herself to relax. He let fly a backward kick, caught her thwack on the kneecap, and darted out of range. The Problems of Modern Living teacher was staring out the window at the time.

But classes came to an end at last, and Susan's spirits rose as she hurried toward the auditorium for the Thespian Club meeting. Now the whole dismal day would be set right! Yesterday tryouts had been held for "The Lady and the General: a drama of Revolutionary Boston," and she had been at her best. Today Miss Melcher would assign the parts. There was no doubt in Susan's mind who would get what. She was smiling as she took her seat.

Miss Melcher saved the plum until last. "For Lavinia, the feminine lead, Elsie Mautner," she said, avoiding Susan's eyes; and the day's ruin was complete.

Susan boarded the homeward bus and collapsed on her seat in bitterness and despair. "Acting is my *life!"* she frequently told her classmates. At the age of nine she had been a fairy in the neighborhood Little Theatre performance of "A Midsummer Night's Dream," and she had gone on the stage at every opportunity since. She had a flair for thinking herself into a role, and making an audience believe her in it. Furthermore, she had the quick wit that is so necessary when things go wrong. Last year, for instance, she had twice saved the Thespian Club play with her ad-libbing; once when the Chambermaid had burst into hysterical giggles instead of saying, "The King approaches!" and again when the wicked Duke had somehow gotten himself locked in the toilet and missed his entrance cue by half a minute. She loved costumes of all kinds, particularly long, full-skirted dresses that whisper when you walk in them and flare out so beautifully when you make a quick turn. That was the kind of dress this year's lead would have, and Susan had had her heart set on playing the role. Lavinia, a Boston Belle: the part wasn't very well written, but it had possibilities nevertheless; possibilities that Elsie Mautner wouldn't be able to see even if you wrote out a description of them in words of one syllable.

She, Susan, had been assigned the part of a Townswoman, with only one appearance in the first act—"Enter Townspeople, left"—where all that was required of her was to gape at the British soldiers as they marched off to Bunker Hill. When she had complained after the meeting, Miss Melcher said, "Of course, Susan, you did beautifully last year. But, you see, it's very important to let everyone Participate, isn't it?"

"Yes, but it's more important to do the play *right*," Susan argued. "The parts should go to the people that can handle them best, shouldn't they? That's all I—"

"Now, Susan. We must learn to Fit In With The Group. We can't all be prima donnas all the time, can we?"

That was unjust. Susan had no false modesty about her talent, but she was no prima donna. It was just that if they were going to the trouble of putting on a play at all, they should do it as well as possible. It wasn't right for Miss Melcher to regard the play as a Social Experience rather than as an artistic problem; and it wasn't right that Lavinia, a Boston Belle, should be played like a dressmaker's dummy, which was what Elsie would make of the part. And Susan knew, she just *knew*, that the minute something went wrong—and something would go wrong, it always did—Elsie Mautner would freeze up and fumble her lines; while she, Susan, would quietly die in the wings, because she couldn't stand to see anyone, even Elsie Mautner, make a fool of herself in front of an audience…

"Oh, go argue with City Hall!" she muttered savagely as the bus stopped at Ward Street. "Elsie *Mautner!*" Flinging herself down the step, she caught a button in the folding door and tore her coat sleeve.

Gift of Three

"Little girl! Little girl! Yoohoo!"

There was nothing Susan detested more than being called "little girl." Perhaps she was slightly smaller than average, but she was one year ahead of her age group in school; and most of the time she certainly *felt* more mature than anyone seemed willing to give her credit for. 'I'll pretend I don't hear,' she thought, wrinkling her nose. 'Maybe it's not for me, anyway.'

She was on Ward Street, one block from home. Bursts of wind still drove between the buildings, and the clouds that scudded just above the rooftops looked too wet to be able to stay aloft much longer. It was the rush hour. Tension was in the air, as bitter to the taste as the exhaust fumes that swirled over the sidewalks. There was a traffic tie-up at every corner. Above the clamor of the horns Susan could hear the voices of a cabbie and a truck driver inviting each other to "just step out in the street and say that again, wise guy!"

"Yoohoo! Little girl!"

'No,' Susan thought, quickening her pace. But then curiosity got the better of her and she turned.

A strange sight! An old woman, so enveloped in flapping loose ends of clothing that she looked like a dark wind-whipped flame. Her arms were full of unidentifiable objects. She nodded down the street, crying plaintively, "Little girl! My hat!" And certainly there was something—Susan could not recognize it at that distance and in that light as a hat—being harried along the sidewalk by the wind.

'Little girl!' Susan snorted to herself; but the old woman looked so helpless that she repented, and called out, "All right, all right!" and self-consciously set out in pursuit.

It was uncanny how agile the hat was. It dodged between people's legs and shot out from under their hands as they stooped, and twice it actually leaped into the air to escape her clutch. Everyone on the block seemed to be gaping or grinning at her as she hurried along. Her face felt as though it must be glowing like neon. 'Hope it blows into the street and gets smashed by a ten ton truck,' she thought furiously. But just at the corner the wind failed for a moment, and with a great leap she had the thing trapped under her foot.

It was made of green plush, and covered with broken plumes and scraps of fur and glass beads and paper roses and little tucks of chiffon. It was dusty without and greasy within, and smelled of cheap pomade.

Susan picked it up distastefully by the end of one plume, and trudged back up-wind again. She was not eager to meet the owner. Her one glimpse in the failing light had given her the impression that the old woman was one of those crones with safety pins stuck in their ruined coats and packets of newspaper in their pockets, who wander about the city streets mumbling to themselves and poking in trash cans. They are hard to face when you are warmly dressed and well fed. But she was wrong. This woman was not one of those. And yet what an extraordinary creature she was! She had on a shawl and a muffler and three overcoats, one on top of another, and numerous skirts and underskirts and petticoats. Each garment was a different color, each was loose and ill-fastened, and all were making violent efforts to go the way the hat had gone. Her withered hands were encrusted with dimestore bracelets and rings. Her hair was henna-rinsed, and streamed out in loose ends like the thatches that sparrows build behind drainpipes. Her face was covered with white powder, rouge, eye-shadow, lipstick; but everything was slightly askew: one cheek spot was higher than the other, her eyebrows had different slants, her mouth was smeared at the corners.

But her eyes were bright as a lizard's.

"Thank you, dearie," she crooned. "So sweet. Children are so unmannerly these days, usually. Oops, my shawl! Nasty weather. Nicky'll be along in just a minute. Oh dear! Oh my!"

She had been making efforts to shift her burdens, which included an umbrella, a newspaper, and a bulging paper bag. Now as her momentarily free hand clutched her hat, the bag tipped over and discharged a quantity of potatoes.

"Oh my! Contrary things. Help me, dearie, I can't bend over. Lumbago."

The potatoes seemed infected with the same passion for freedom that the hat had shown. They rolled into the gutter and under the feet of the passersby, while Susan scrambled

about on her hands and knees after them. The old woman struggled with the wind and her clothes, saying "Oh my, oh dear, oops" in a quavering, plaintive tone. And when Susan had finally gotten most of the potatoes together, and stood up with her arms full of them, and two clamped under her chin, the old woman's umbrella said *Flump!!* and blew inside out right in her face. Of course she dropped the potatoes again, and the bag ripped open and spilled more. Susan muttered a word that only fathers should use. But the old woman just said, "Hurry, dearie, Nicky's coming," so down on her knees she had to go once more.

"Put the spuds in my shawl, dearie. That's it. Oops, mind the muffler." That raveled length of wool had taken a dislike to Susan, and was flogging her face unmercifully. But this time she kept her hold on the potatoes. The old woman beat the muffler down and got it under control; but meanwhile part of the newspaper saw its chance for escape, and seized it, and went flapping and disintegrating down-wind.

"Oh dear. Well, don't mind it, dearie, all lies anyway, I expect. Just so long as I've got the want ads."

Somehow everything was clawed, clutched or crammed into order again. The potatoes were bundled up in the shawl, the rebellious muffler defeated for good and tucked under the collar of the second overcoat, the shattered umbrella turned right side out and furled with most of its ribs in place.

"Thank you, dearie. *So* sweet. Now then, I'll give you three. No more!"

"Beg pardon?" said Susan.

"Ooh, there's Nicky! Yoohoo! Right over here, dearie!"

A powerful motorcycle had appeared at the curb. Its rider

was dressed in black from head to foot—black boots, black pants, black leather jacket and gauntlets and helmet. The upper half of his face was covered by immense goggles, while the lower half was either lost in shadow or covered with a dense and closely-cropped beard. The old woman hopped briskly on the pillion saddle. "Just three!" she called back, and her cut-glass rings winked as she held up three skinny claws. Then the wind caught her unawares again, the motorcycle blasted away into the traffic, and they rapidly vanished from sight, leaving a wake of bouncing potatoes and newspaper sheets and blue smoke.

"Well!" said Susan. Everything had happened so quickly that only now could she sort out what had been a series of confused impressions and sights and sounds; but, sorting them, she saw how queer it had all been.

'Three?' she wondered, crossing the street to her own block. 'Three what? Potatoes? But she didn't actually hold them out to me or anything. Maybe I was supposed to pick them up when she dropped them from the motorcycle. No, that couldn't be it. Oh, wasn't she a marvelous type! If I ever have to be a crazy woman in a play, I'll try to look just like her—all those clothes and that weird make-up. Funny, the wind never stopped where she was. And that umbrella. Sort of like Mary Poppins. "Just three," she said. Awfully strange. Like a fairy story—oh no! *Oh no!*

Three!

Three wishes?

'Susan Shaw,' she said fiercely in her mind, 'don't be stupid!' But she stopped walking in spite of herself, and her heart tightened. The whole episode had been just strange enough...

She had loved fairy stories in her younger years. But how irritated she had always been at the people in those stories who were granted three wishes only to make a mess of everything! In those days such things still seemed to be within the realm of possibility, so she had decided how she would proceed if it ever happened to her. It was very simple and logical. On the first wish she would ask for something small and harmless, just to make sure she really had the power. Then, very quickly, before she could think of something silly and spoil it all, she would wish that she might never make mistakes, or ask for anything that could get out of control. And then on the third wish she would wish that she could have an unlimited number of wishes. And then—!

"It's all nonsense," she whispered. "I wish—" She looked quickly about her. Her face was hot with shame at her silliness; but her heart thudded with impossible hope. "I wish," she mumbled into the wind for her first, or testing, wish, "I wish there was a ring—let's see, make it a gold ring with a small emerald—in my coat pocket."

Her trembling hands crept into her pockets.

There was no ring.

"I *told* you!" she muttered savagely. "Gosh, what a—oh, honestly, Susan Shaw, they ought to put you in a mental institution!"

It was just the sort of trick you could expect of a day like this. As if she hadn't had sufficient warning from everything else that had happened!

Mrs. Clutchett was dusting when she entered the apartment.

"Well, there she is, home from school. How the day flies! Susie, you should've worn a warmer coat, you could catch your death in this wind. Why, child, what's the matter?"

"Oh, nothing."

"Here, now, you just let me fix you a nice hot cup of cocoa. There's nothing like—"

"*No!*"

"Well, I'm sure!"

"Oh, I'm sorry, Mrs. Clutchett. I mean, no thank you. Really I'm sorry. It's just been such an awful day."

"Hasn't it, though! I never saw such weather. It's those atom bombs, you mark my words. We never had such days when I was a girl, believe me. And you with nothing on your legs and a skimpy little coat! Now, Missy, you sit by the radiator. I'm going to fix some hot cocoa and you're going to drink it. Catching your death! Talk about awful days," she continued from the kitchen, "don't tell me! If my vacuum cleaner didn't go on the fritz *three times!* That Mr. Bodoni stuck his screwdriver in it to see what was the matter, and didn't pull the plug first, and almost got electrocuted and blew the fuse. I don't know about that man. Those slow ones are awfully deep sometimes, you never know what they're really up to. Not that I need the vacuum cleaner here. It's like taking money from a baby to clean here, you keep it so neat. Not like some I could name. You take that Mr. Ormondroyd—socks on the floor, shirts on the floor, cracker crumbs—you wouldn't believe it! Keeps his papers locked up, though, oh yes, tight as a drum, you can't even get a peek at them. I wonder if he isn't up to something. Writers! Mr. Clutchett knew a writer once, this fellow *claimed* he was a writer, but—well, you may believe this or not, but it's the gospel: *that man was a counterfeiter*. Yes sir. They came and took him away one fine day. Twenty-dollar bills, that's what *he* wrote."

The cocoa had a skin on it.

Mrs. Clutchett resumed her work, still talking. As soon as her back was turned Susan poured the cocoa into the rubber-plant pot; cocoa skin made her stomach turn. Mrs. Clutchett rattled on unheeded. Susan kicked her legs back and forth and chewed her knuckle. After a while she tried the television set. Nothing but commercials; toothpaste, breakfast food, scouring powder, smiles, smiles, smiles. She turned it off. The evening paper was on the sofa. She flopped on the floor and began to leaf through it from back to front. The funnies weren't funny—why did she read them any more? The astrology column told her to take her time and to be on the lookout for a great opportunity—'such as three wishes?' she thought, loathing herself. The Hollywood column had an article about her favorite star, a beautiful woman whose roles of courage, nobility and self-sacrifice always left Susan with a lump in her throat. The star was getting her fourth divorce under lurid circumstances. "Citizens Should Support Proposed Bond Issue," said the editorial. She sighed and turned to the front page.

FORTUNE FOUND AT CONSTRUCTION SITE

There was a map, with the caption "Thar's Gold In That Thar Playground, Podner!" Why, she knew the place. It was a few blocks up Ward, around the corner, and down a side street. Her mother used to take her there. Oak Park, everyone had called it, although it was only a small square of asphalt without a tree in sight. With a flicker of interest she read:

"Gold!"

The heart-stirring cry of Sutter's Mill and the Yukon was heard here today as construction workers unearthed a fortune in old U.S. coins in a condemned playground.

The lucky finder was Frank M. Zalewski, 27, a bulldozer operator employed by the Delta-Schirmerhorn Construction Company. The company is erecting a 12-story office building on the 93rd Street site (see map).

"The 'dozer blade lifted it out," Zalewski said. "It was only about a foot under. I saw all this stuff shining in the dirt, and then everybody started hollering 'Gold!'"

The treasure consists of $60,000 in "eagles," or $10 gold pieces. The coins all date from 1863 or earlier. It is believed that the owner may have been killed in the Civil War and thus was unable to reclaim the buried hoard.

Martin Van Tromp, numismatics expert at the

See Page 4, Col. 7

The trouble with treasure, she thought, stifling a yawn, was that it was always found by someone else. Any other news?

MAYOR ASKS BOND ISSUE FOR WATER

A burst of sleet rattled against the window. Oh foo! It was too hot in here. She tossed the paper aside, stood up, stretched, and said, "I'm going to the top."

As she pressed the elevator button the thought came to her again: 'What did the old woman mean by three? Three *what*?'

The Elevator Misbehaves

That elevator always reminded me of a tired old horse. It groaned when it started and groaned when it stopped. It labored up or down the shaft at such a plodding gait that you wondered if you were ever going to arrive. The door sighed when it opened or shut. I once suggested to Mr. Bodoni that we should either put the poor thing out to pasture or have it shot. "Yeah," he said, not getting the joke but willing to be amiable about it.

Around the top of the inside walls was a little frieze of cast-metal rosettes and curlicues. Mr. Bodoni, inspired one year by both the Spring weather and a sudden urge to express himself, had begun to paint these red. I don't know which gave out first, his paint or his inspiration; at any rate he stopped halfway through the fourteenth rosette, and has not finished the job to this day. The rest of the inside was painted buff.

There was the usual bank of buttons—ten of them, including the basement stop, the emergency stop, and the alarm—and a dial-and-arrow above the door to show which floor you were approaching. A yellow ticket assured anyone who wanted to read it that the mechanism had been inspected and found satisfactory by a Mr. Scrawl Blot Scribble, who I sincerely hope is a better inspector than he is a penman. Mr. Bodoni had also hung up a ticket, with *No Smokking in Elvater, Please!* thickly pencilled thereon. (His own cigar was always dead, and didn't count, of course.) Finally there was a metal plate which said *Capacity 1500 Lbs.* I remember that when I first met Susan she was staring at this, moving her lips and ticking off her fingers.

"How does it come out?" I asked.

"I can't make it come out right," she said. "If everybody weighed a hundred and fifty pounds you could get ten people in, but what if they all weighed two hundred pounds? I'm not very good at arithmetic."

"Hmm," I said, and I began to work on it too. But I'm not very good at arithmetic either, and she had gotten off at her floor before I arrived at an answer.

Going up the elevator now, Susan occupied her mind with the usual arithmetical speculations. 'Fifteen hundred ulbs,' she thought. 'Or is it libs? Almost a ton. Or is a ton one thousand? No, two thousand. Suppose everybody weighed a hundred and seventy-five. Let's see, one seventy-five into...um. I wish Mr. Bodoni'd learn to spell. One seventy-five into fifteen hundred, make it nine, nine times five is...um. At least Elsie Mautner's even dumber than I am in arithmetic. Try eight. Eight fives are forty, that's a zero, maybe it'll come out even, let's see, carry the four...um. Wonder how many people *do* weigh a hundred seventy-five? Pretty heavy. Oh well, almost at the top. I'll work it out on the way down.' For the arrow was creeping past six. Too bad there weren't arrows in the classrooms at school to save you when you were stuck on a problem...The arrow plodded up to seven and stopped.

The elevator kept on going.

It was the strangest sensation—as if the elevator were forcing its way up through something sticky in the shaft, like molasses or chewing gum. There was a thin humming noise all around her, and the light dimmed. She was startled, and a little frightened. But of course there were only seven floors, so the elevator would have to stop at the seventh. The arrow must be out of order. She would have to tell Mr. Bodoni. He'd look mournful, the way he always did when something went wrong, as if it were all your fault.

Now the elevator stopped. The door said "Sighhh..." and opened. Susan clutched her hands together and said, "Oh!"

'They must be redecorating,' she thought in astonishment. 'No, that can't be it; you don't redecorate a hallway. Maybe it's a private suite? But why should the public elevator open into a—?'

It was a hallway she was looking into, but it certainly wasn't the seventh-floor hallway of the apartment building as she remembered it. For one thing, the floor, instead of being covered with brown carpeting, was bare parqueted wood, beautifully polished. For another thing, there were no numbered doors opposite; the wall there was solidly wainscotted with oak. Against it stood a marble-topped table with carved lyre-shaped legs, on which were a vase of paper flowers and a stuffed owl under a glass bell. Everything was glowing with—was it sunlight? Sunlight on a March evening like this?

She became aware of sounds. There must be a clock nearby, and a large one too: tock—tock—tock, a stately sound. A bird was singing; not a canary, something richer and wilder and much more inventive. And wait a minute—yes—no—chickens? Impossible! And another sound; a serene whispering murmur, rising and dying. It could only be one thing, a breeze rustling through foliage. And yet only a few minutes ago, downstairs in the apartment, she had heard the rattling gusts of March against the window.

The scent of flowers was very strong.

She stepped out of the elevator in a daze. Yes, there was a clock, a grandfather one, with hunting scenes painted on its porcelain face. The sunlight came through a window to the right of the elevator. It was a funny kind of window, very tall and narrow, with two sets of curtains: straight-hanging white lace framed by drawn-back red velvet. It was open; all the strange scents and sounds were coming through it with the sunlight, irresistibly drawing her to investigate. She leaned her elbows on the sill and stared out, filling her lungs with warm sweet air and murmuring, "Oh my." She had never been any closer to the country than the seaside resort in New Jersey where her father took her during summer vacation. But this was countryside, all right: she could just tell, even though all she could see was a portion of hedged-in garden. The hedge was a tall tangle of roses and privet and honeysuckle. Hydrangeas grew under the window, lifting their pale blue pompons to the sill. The grass was badly in need of cutting, and had flowers growing in it. The base of one of the huge trees on the lawn was encircled by a white-painted iron settee.

'I'm dreaming, that's all there is to it,' she thought. 'I've

fallen asleep over the newspaper. It's like *Alice in Wonderland.* I'll probably try to get into the garden, but the door will be too small, or the golden key will be lost, or something, and there'll be a little bottle with a label saying "Drink Me," and a White Rabbit—no, it's a black cat.' For a large black tom had emerged from the hedge, and was plowing nose-first through the grass like a ship through waves. The bird abruptly ceased its singing, and began to scold: "Mew! Mew!" 'A bird mewing like a cat?' she wondered. 'Maybe the cat sings like a bird...Oh well, pretty soon Mrs. Clutchett'll poke me with her broom and say, "C'mon, Susie, help me set the table." '

"Maw-w-w-!" said a cow in the distance; and she wondered why she should dream that. 'Very realistic of me,' she thought.

The elevator door sighed, and trundled shut.

"No, wait!" she gasped. "*Ow!*" Springing back from the window, she cracked her head against the sash. Her eyes filled with tears. She wasn't dreaming—no dream could hurt like that. Through the blur she saw that the elevator was gone. There was no door in the wall. Solid, unbroken wood paneling!

'Oh no, oh no!' she thought in a panic, searching for the button.

"Vicky!" a woman's voice called. "Vicky?"

Someone was coming. There was no button on the wall, and not enough time to recall the elevator anyhow. But she had no business being here! Quick! Where? The red curtains! She slipped behind the nearest one, and squeezed herself as thin as she could. Fortunately they reached all the way to the floor.

The footsteps came down the hallway, and with them a curious rustling sound as of long skirts. She could not resist a quick peek. What she saw made her catch her breath. It was a lovely, tall, slender woman with masses of rich chestnut hair piled on her head. Susan, always susceptible to beautiful ladies, felt her heart go out to this one at once: 'That's what I want to be like when I grow up,' she thought. And the woman must be an actress, too. Why else would she be in costume? She had on a grey dress whose skirt came down to the floor; it had a lot of material draped around the hips, but was tightly fitted from the waist up. All she needed was make-up to be ready to step out before the footlights.

"Vicky?" she called again, stopping by the grandfather clock.

"What's the matter, Mama?" Now a girl came running down the hallway from the opposite direction. She was slightly taller than Susan; her hair was a dark coppery brown, and fell in waves below her shoulders. She wore a dress similar to her mother's except that the skirt was shorter, and black cotton stockings.

"I just heard the strangest noise somewhere around here!" said the woman in a puzzled voice. "Did you hear anything?"

"No, I was talking with Maggie. What kind of noise?"

"Well, it's hard to say—a kind of rumble, I think it was, and then a thump..."

"Oh, I expect it was just Toby. Shall I look for him?"

"No, I don't think...it sounded like something rolling or sliding. And then a very distinct thump, like—oh, like a bird flying against the window."

"It must have been Toby, chasing that catbird—they hate each other so."

"I suppose you're right...Well, I'm sorry I disturbed you

for nothing."

"Oh, *Mama*. Maggie says supper is almost ready anyway. Doesn't the honeysuckle smell just glorious?"

"Mm, lovely."

They moved off down the hallway with their arms about each other.

"Mama, everything outside is getting so jungly. Why don't we have a gardener in?"

"Well, dear," Susan thought the woman's voice was a little evasive, "suppose we wait just a bit longer. Mr. Branscomb is coming tomorrow afternoon about the investments, and after he's gone I'll think about it..." Their voices faded down the end of the hall.

'Well, that's funny,' Susan thought. 'I never saw either of them before. If they lived up here I would have seen them in the elevator.' It had come to her that part of the seventh floor must have been converted into a very realistic stage set, and that the woman and the girl had been rehearsing their parts in a play. But no, that couldn't be it. No stage set that she had ever seen was so realistic that you could hear cows and smell flowers and feel the warmth of sunlight. And if this were the seventh floor of the apartment building, *why hadn't the woman recognized the sound of the elevator?* That rumbling sigh was unmistakable after you'd heard it once...Well, it was all very queer. Even as a dream it would have been the strangest she'd ever had.

She crept out from behind the curtain and began to look for the button again. If that elevator could come up here once—wherever "here" was—it could come up again. But there was no button. And while she was still peering and poking helplessly along the wainscotting she heard the sound of running feet approaching. This time she lost her head. She darted toward the window curtains, changed her mind and stepped back, glanced desperately about for a better hiding place, and at last, without a second to spare, threw her leg over the windowsill and dropped down the other side—falling through the hydrangeas with a tremendous thrashing and crackling. 'Good grief, what a racket!' she thought; 'like an *elephant!* I hope the bushes cover me.'

Apparently they did, for the girl's voice said, right over her, "All right, you naughty Toby cat! Breaking the bushes! Just wait till I catch you, that's all! And if I don't, Bobbie will tomorrow, and then see if you don't regret the day you were born!"

'Now I've really done it,' Susan sighed when Vicky had gone. 'Although I suppose I could go to the front door and say, "Pardon me, but there's an elevator in your house that you don't know about, and I have to use it." No, no—all that explaining…It's hard enough to explain when you know *what* you're explaining. I certainly don't have any idea of what this is all about. Well, I'll just have to wait till it's dark, and sneak in, and try to get that darned elevator up somehow. Poor Daddy'll worry when I don't show up for dinner. And Mrs. Clutchett will be snorting around and making things worse…How am I ever going to explain this to *anybody* without making them think I've gone absolutely insane…?'

She might as well make herself comfortable for the wait. She snuggled down in the litter of dry leaves, murmuring, "What a day! What a stupid impossible crazy day! I should've stuffed my ears with cotton and gone back to bed and stayed there this morning." Wrapped in blankets, impervious to noise—the idea began to make her feel drowsy. The air was as warm as her own bedclothes; the stirring bushes lulled and hushed, more comfortable to the ear even than silence. 'It *is* a dream, really,' she thought, yawning. 'I hope I can remember it to tell Daddy…'

The Meaning of Three

It was dark when she awakened. 'They've let me sleep through dinner,' she thought. Why should they do that? "Daddy?" she said. There was no answer. Something crackled under her as she shifted.

Then she remembered. It wasn't a dream after all.

She crawled out from under the hydrangeas as quietly as she could, and stood up on the lawn, and then caught her breath with wonder. The sky was ablaze with stars. Where had they all come from? She had never seen more than a few score, feebly competing with the city's neon; here they were beyond imagining in number. 'Why, that must be the Milky Way!' she thought, recognizing that glowing swath overhead from a picture in one of her science textbooks. And in gazing up at it she discovered something else that the city would never have let her find out. The night sky could be *heard*. It was like the sound of the sea in a shell, only much fainter, as though it had come to her straining ears from as far away as the dimmest star.

There were other sounds too. The grass was full of crickets, who were chirping and rustling as they moved about through the stems, so that the whole lawn whispered with them. She was sure she heard frogs nearby. And suddenly in the distance a train said, "Way a *wayyy* oh-h-h-h-h," sweet crescendo, sad diminuendo.

'If I lived here,' she thought, 'I'd never go to bed, never. I'd just sit outside all night and look and listen…'

But she simply had to go back: her father would be worried sick by now, and furious with her for making him worry. All the windows of the house were dark. It was a very large house, she noticed now, tall and narrow and with a profile reminiscent of a castle. She would just have to hope that everyone was asleep, and that she could find an unlocked door. Slowly she began to grope her way through the shadows.

'Wish there was more moon,' she thought after five minutes of blundering. 'There seem to be hedges all over the place. Ouch! Thorns. Well, here's an opening. That sounds like frogs—must be a pond nearby.'

She was right. At the next step there was no ground under her foot; she sprawled forward clutching at the air, and *slosh!*—she was under. Fortunately the water was only waist-deep, and she was on her feet again immediately. The bottom was squdgy. Something cold and soft slithered across her bare knees. She shuddered, and scrambled up the stone bank.

"They'll all be ruined," she muttered, taking off her clothes and wringing them out. "Stupid place for a pond!" But she didn't want to stand about naked while they dried, so she put them on again. They clung to her, and her shoes squelched with every step. It was a good thing that the weather was so warm. What if it had been March here too? The very memory of the wind and sleet she had left behind—how long ago now?—made her shiver.

In another ten minutes she was clear of the hedges and shrubbery, and had found a flight of wooden stairs against the dark bulk of the house. She crept up them one step at a time, testing each tread for squeaks; and thank goodness! there was a door at the top, with a handle that turned easily and quietly.

'Now,' she thought, standing in the interior darkness, 'which side of the house am I on? I'm all mixed up. This might even be the wrong floor…I know, I'll listen for the grandfather clock. It was near the elevator.'

Room after room, all caves of shadow; windows that pretended to be doorways; doors that hid themselves in the darkest corners; sharp-cornered furniture everywhere. She groped along inch by inch, hardly daring to put her hands out for fear of knocking something over, and wincing at every move for fear of striking her face against some unseen projection. She could not hear the clock anywhere.

Eventually she found herself at the foot of a staircase. She felt her way across the bottom stair; encountered the newel post, all knobby with carving; felt her way around that, and met a table top; put her hand on something cold that gave under her touch; and *crash!*—the sound of a metal object bouncing on the floor. Not very loud, actually, but loud enough.

She crouched, suffocating.

A door opened softly upstairs. Pause. Then a whisper: "Toby!"

Pause.

"Toby?"

"Meow!" said Susan, with all the realism she could muster.

A long heart-pounding silence; then the upstairs door softly closed again.

She remained motionless for a few more minutes, to make sure that all was quiet above, then straightened up. Suddenly, somewhere to her left, a sweet melancholy chime struck the quarter hour.

'There it is!' she thought, sagging with relief. As quickly as the dark permitted she went toward the sound, discovered a doorway, and—yes! it was the hallway, all right. Up ahead was the dim patch of light that must be the window, and beyond it she heard the clock solemnly knocking each passing second on the head with its pendulum.

'Now for the button—there *must* be a button.'

She began to run her fingers over the wainscotting. There was no button. The wood seemed to be glowing somehow. Brighter and brighter—her shadow loomed and wavered on the paneling—

She whirled around.

There stood Vicky in a nightgown, holding a trembling candle aloft and staring at her round-eyed with fright. She seemed on the verge of screaming.

Susan hissed, "Now don't yell or do anything silly! I'm not a ghost."

"Are—are you a burglar's accomplice?" Vicky faltered.

"Of course not. I'm just lost, that's all. Soon as I can find the elevator I'll go away. Do you know where the button is?"

Vicky stepped backward. "Button? What button?"

"The *elevator* button. Oh, I forgot—you don't know about

the elevator, do you? Look, I know it doesn't make any sense, but I'm not crazy, really. Why do you keep staring at me like that?"

"Your *clothes*."

"Well, what's the matter with them? They're just wet, that's all. I fell in your pond."

"It's not the wet..."

"What's the matter with you?" Susan burst out after a moment's silence. "You act like I was a freak or something!"

"It's your clothes," said Vicky. "They're the oddest I ever saw."

"Well, that nightgown of yours is pretty hilarious, too," Susan retorted. "And what about those dresses you and your mother were wearing this afternoon? I never saw such funny old-fashioned clothes in all my life."

"Why, they are *not* old-fashioned! Mama just bought that dress a month ago!"

"You mean for a play? Is she going to be in a play?"

"No, of course not—just to wear. Don't you know what people wear?"

"Certainly I know what people wear!" Susan said in exasperation. "And I know perfectly well that people don't wear clothes like that any more. In the Gay Nineties, maybe, but not in 19*60*."

The other girl retreated a step, and the candle shook violently in her hand. "I think you're mad. I didn't say anything about 1960. I mean right now. This year."

"What do you mean, this year?" said Susan, beginning to feel a bit frightened. "I'm *talking* about this year. It's 1960."

Vicky shook her head.

"Well then, for goodness sake, what year *is* it?"

"Don't you really know? It's 1881, of course."

"Oh!" Susan gasped. The shape of the house! The design of the dresses! The funny curtains by the window! All the oddities she had noticed in the last few hours clicked into place in her mind. "Eighteen—eighteen—oh no! What's happened? Where am I? What street are we on?"

"Street? It's not a street, it's a country road."

"All right, all right, but what's it called?"

"Ward Lane."

Well, that sounded right—or almost right. "But where's the city?"

"Don't you know? It's about five miles from here."

"Five *miles!*" Susan moaned, clutching her head. "Oh, am I lost! Am I ever lost! Listen—when I got on the elevator I was *in* the city, on Ward *Street,* and it was *1960!*"

"Nonsense," Vicky said faintly. "Things like that can't happen."

"I know they can't! Look, I don't want to argue: I just want to go back. I'm here whether it can happen or n—" Striking herself dramatically at the word *here,* she felt something hard in the pocket of her skirt. "Look!" she continued excitedly, "I can prove it—about being from the twentieth century, I mean. You know about dimes and quarters, don't you? Well, here, look at the dates. Oh, go on, take them, I'm not going to hurt you!"

Vicky hesitantly took the coins and held them close to the candle flame. "What funny designs they have! Oh! This one says 1953! 1945! 1960—oh, my goodness! 1960! You—maybe you are from the twentieth century. But it's impos—how could you possibly *get* here?"

"I've been *telling* you, I came in the elevator. Do you know what an elevator is?"

"We may live in the country," Vicky said, "but we are not backward."

"All right, I'm sorry. I didn't know whether they'd been invented yet. Anyway, I got on this elevator where I live, just across the hall, and it let me out here instead of where I thought I was going, and then it went down again and I can't call it back. You know, I'm beginning to think the stupid thing wants me to be here."

Vicky gave a sudden start. "*Wants* you to be here?"

"Oh, I know it sounds silly—it is silly. I just can't think why—"

"No," Vicky whispered. "No. It isn't silly." Her eyes were widening again, and the candle in her hand shook so much that it almost guttered out. "I just remembered something. The well! It must be the—yes, it has to be! *It worked!* Look, you don't have to go back right away, do you?"

"Well, I ought—"

"Look," Vicky interrupted with growing excitement, catching Susan by the sleeve, "you *can't* go back now, I simply must talk with you. Really, it's *essential.* Come up to my—are you hungry? I'll get something to eat. And we'll have to get those wet clothes off you. Oh, my heavens, talk about—! I was right, I was right—it's perfectly true, Maggie doesn't know what she's talking about! Here, wait, don't move a step, I'll be right back!"

She hurried soundlessly down the hallway, and returned in

a minute carrying some slices of bread and a pot of jam.

"All I could find in a hurry, I'm afraid. Maggie's hidden everything because Bobbie's coming home tomorrow, and he always—Come on, you *must* tell me all about it, and I'll tell you about—oh, it's just unbelievable!—please be very careful on the stair, we mustn't wake Mama up."

Susan, utterly bewildered, allowed herself to be led on tiptoe up the stairs and cautiously along a second floor hallway.

"Oh, what a lovely bed!" she exclaimed on entering Vicky's room. It was a high four-poster with a frilly arched canopy, and curtains at the head.

"Ssshh! You mustn't talk loud. Mama's a fairly sound sleeper, but Maggie has ears like an owl. Yes, isn't it a beauty? Grandmama left it to me in her will. Here, you can wear one of my nightgowns. Take off those wet things—I won't look. I'll put some jam on the bread. Oh pooh, I forgot the spoon. I guess we can just dip the slices in. Wish we had some tea. Does the nightgown fit all right? I'm a little taller than you."

"Yes, it's fine. Where shall I put my things?"

"Oh, over the back of the chair is all right, they'll dry soon. That's awfully nice material. What funny shoes! Does everybody wear such short skirts in the twentieth century?"

"Yes, why not?"

"It seems so immodest. But I suppose if everybody does it's all right. I don't wear corsets myself, neither does Mama. She says they're such a torture, and there's no sense in it if your waist is naturally slender. Thank goodness ours are! Here, sit on the bed, you can put your feet under the sheets if they're cold. Oh! My manners—you must forgive me, I'm so excited about the magic. I don't care if it *does* sound silly, it *is* magic. I'm Victoria

Albertine Walker."

"Susan Shaw."

" 'Charmed to meet you, Miss Shaw. Isn't the weather delightful?' That's what we say in Deportment Class," she giggled. "Now! Please tell me what happened, and don't leave out *anything*, because it may be of great importance."

So Susan recounted the events of the day. When she got to the part about the old woman with the runaway hat, Victoria's eyes grew rounder and rounder, and she hugged her knees; and as soon as the tale was finished she burst out:

"Yes, of course! The old woman was a witch, a good witch!"

"A witch?" Susan said. "That's craz—" She checked herself. Everything else was crazy—why not a witch? "She didn't look like one, anyway. I thought she might have been a gypsy or something."

"Of course she didn't look like one. They never do, that's just the point. If she looked like a witch you'd do whatever she asked, to get her blessings, and it wouldn't be any test of your character. You see? It's like that in lots of stories. But if they look like someone else, and they're troublesome, and you help them out of the kindness of your heart anyway, then they know that you're worthy."

"Hmm. Well, that could be it, I suppose. But I still can't figure out what she meant by giving me three. Three what?"

"Why, that's perfectly plain. They always give you three of something. She must have meant that you could have three trips in the elevator to here!"

"Ohhhh! That could be it, couldn't it? But why here?"

Victoria gave her a long speculative look. "That's what I wanted to talk to you about. I think I know why."

"Why? How can you know?"

"Because—oh, it's all so spooky! *You were sent here on purpose because I wished you here.*"

Susan felt a shiver race down her back. "Me? How did you know about me?"

"Oh, I didn't wish for you in particular; just—somebody." She hesitated a moment. "Cross your heart and hope to die you won't tell? It's a *very serious* secret."

"Cross my heart three times and hope to die."

"All right. Well, first I wished on a star. You know, 'Star light, star bright, first star I see tonight.' Do you do that in the twentieth century too? Anyway, it didn't work. Then I remembered there was an old abandoned well about half a mile down the lane, and I thought, 'Maybe it's a wishing well.' So I asked Maggie, she's Irish, but she said no it wasn't, that was all blasphemy, only God can grant your wishes and He doesn't do it very often because it's not for the good of your soul. And she believes in ghosts, too, can you imagine? But I don't care, it can't be blasphemy if you're wishing for someone else's sake—can it? So I went there this very afternoon, and I threw in the thing I love best, a little gold locket that Papa gave me when I was ten, and I marched around it three times, and I said, 'I wish someone would come and chase Mr. Sweeney away.' "

"And?"

"Well, I never dreamed it would happen this way—but here you are!" Victoria concluded triumphantly.

"Oh, now, wait a minute!" Susan protested. "I can't—who's Mr. Sweeney?"

"Oh, he's this perfectly dreadful man who's been absolutely hounding poor Mama to marry him."

"Oh! Is your father—?"

"Yes, poor Papa died two years ago."

"Why, so did my mother."

"Oh, I *am* sorry…"

"Anyway," Victoria went on after an interval of silence, "I was hoping some handsome man with a noble brow would come along, and show Mr. Sweeney up for a scoundrel and give him a thrashing. But I'm sure you'll do just as well. You're from the future, after all, you must know an awful lot. Oh no," she added hastily, seeing that Susan was going to interrupt, "I don't mean *you* should thrash him. Maybe you could just—I don't know. Scare him away, maybe."

"Well, I don't know…Why doesn't your Mama turn him down?"

"Oh, she has. But he's so persistent. He's after her money, I'm certain of it, the scoundrel. Poor Papa left quite a lot… Sweeeeeney," she drawled in a savage falsetto. "Isn't that a dreadful name? I couldn't stand having a name like that."

"Why, your Mama could marry anyone she wanted to," Susan said warmly. "She's the most beautiful lady I ever saw. She's as beautiful as a movie star!"

"Oh, how poetic! 'Beautiful as a moving star.' I'll have to write that in my diary. Yes, she is. But, you know, she's been so —oh, resigned since Papa died. She sold our city house and buried herself out here because Papa loved it here so much, and she won't go out in society where she could meet suitable men. And Mr. Sweeney keeps lurking around and forcing his attentions on her and wearing her down, until I'm afraid she'll say yes just to have some peace…Well! We won't have to worry about it until tomorrow. My brother Bobbie's coming home from school

tomorrow. We'll have to consult him first anyway, he's the man of the house now, even if he's only twelve. Robert Lincoln Walker. Don't ever call him Bobolink, it makes him furious."

"Oh, I can't stay till tomorrow. I have to go back."

"But Susan, you only have three trips, it's a shame to waste one."

"Yes, but my father is probably frantic by now."

"That's right, I forgot…But look, it's so late; surely a few more minutes won't matter?"

"Well…just a few."

"Good! Tell me about your Mama. You don't mind talking about it?"

So Susan told her all she could remember. Then Victoria told Susan all about her late Papa. Devouring bread and jam by candlelight, they agreed that two parents seemed to be able to take care of themselves, but that one alone required careful management; which was a great responsibility, but no doubt worth it in the long run. Then Victoria swore Susan to secrecy, and brought out her diary, and read selected parts of it out loud; which proved so fascinating that Susan resolved to keep one of her own as soon as she could begin. (Although she determined that *her* style would be more brisk, and would not run so much to sad pure thoughts, and moonlight on marble gravestones, and noble breaking hearts and so on.) And of course certain passages in the diary brought them around to the subject of Boys; and Susan quite forgot about going home while they pursued that fascinating topic...Gradually their voices began to trail off—they yawned—the silences grew longer; and at last the two friends slept, curled up on the bed, while the candle burned down to a puddle of wax and put itself out.

Hatching the Plot

When Susan awoke next morning she found a note on the night stand, propped against the candlestick:

Dear Susan—Don't make a sound. No one suspects. I'm going to smuggle some breakfast up for you. I'll knock 3-2-1. If anyone tries to enter without the secret signal hide under the bed. Isn't it all romantic?

Victoria

It certainly was, she thought, smiling and hugging herself. It was like living in a stage setting for one of those period plays she loved so much. 'Marvelous props!' she thought, looking around her with a professional eye. But no, she had to force herself to realize that these things weren't here to convince an audience. People lived with them and used them every day. They were *real*; the tall spindle-backed rocking chair, the foot-stool with its carved legs and quilted upholstering, the secretary with its little drawers and cubbyholes and scroll-surrounded top shelf, the tall chest of drawers surmounted by a kind of miniature balustrade, the marble-topped dressing table on knobbed legs. Best of all was the bed. Although the room was warm, she wriggled under the sheets to savor the luxury of being in a four-poster. Tall walnut columns, dark green velvet canopy, curtains drawn back at the head—why didn't they make beds like this any more? They were so much beddier than modern ones. You felt like someone in a piece of furniture like this...

Then her conscience had to spoil it all.

'Better be going back,' it said.

'No, I won't go back for a while,' she answered defiantly. 'I'd just have to explain and explain, and nobody'll believe me. Why should they, I don't really believe it myself.'

'That's no excuse. The longer you stay, the more you'll have to explain.'

'I don't want to go to school,' Susan pleaded. 'Elsie Mautner will just be impossible, going around with her head all swelled up and sort of smiling at me whenever we meet. Thinks she's so wonderful! She can't even act in a crowd scene without looking like a wooden post. Bet if *she* were thrown into 1881 she'd have hysterics.'

'That's no excuse either. Your father's worrying, and you know it.'

Her heart squirmed within her. 'Poor Daddy...Oh, go away!' she raged. 'He doesn't *have* to worry, I'm perfectly safe. It isn't as if I'd had an accident or something!'

But she could no longer enjoy the four-poster. She got out, splashed her face in the washstand basin, and went to the window. The front lawn was below, an immense overgrown space containing circular flower beds and a pair of iron stags. Then came a privet hedge, very shaggy, and a wrought iron gate; then a dirt road on the other side; and beyond that, open fields starred with daisies and Queen Anne's lace; and then woods.

'I can't get over how sweet it smells,' she thought, pushing her conscience aside and breathing deeply. 'That must be Ward—what did she call it?—Ward Lane. Ward Lane, Ward Street, same thing…? Oh! I know what happened—no, wait, it hasn't happened yet, it *will* happen. The city's going to grow out here, there's plenty of time for it; sixty years plus eighty-one from a hundred is…um. Lots of time, anyway, cities grow so fast. And then Ward Lane turns into Ward *Street!* I bet the apartment building will be built right on this spot! And that's where the florist will be, and the five-and-dime; and Benjamin's Men's and Boys' Wear will be right by that tree…And none of the people that run them or shop in them are even born yet. Why, come to think of it, *I'm* not even born yet!' That was such a weird thought, and it gave her such a spooky feeling, that she murmured:

"Weird Street—that's what it really should be called."

There was a quiet knock at the door, three, two, one, and Victoria slipped in.

"Oh, you're up! Good morning, isn't it beautiful out? That Maggie! She has eyes like a hawk. Bobbie steals food all the time, it's second nature for her to keep her eyes on the larder. So this is all I could get," producing from her pockets two hard-boiled eggs and a muffin sliced in half and filled with jam. "Don't worry, when Bobbie's here we'll feed you better, he's an expert. 'Foraging raids,' he calls it: he wants to be a soldier. We're perfectly safe for a while, Mama's writing letters in the sun parlor. Oh, we'll have to hide your clothes. You can wear some of mine, just in case somebody sees us. You are staying just a little longer, aren't you?"

'No!' said Susan's conscience.

"Well..." Susan said.

"You really must, you know," Victoria said. "It's a responsibility. I've thought it all out. You can't accept a piece of magic one minute and turn it down the next without *serious* consequences."

'So there!' Susan told her conscience. "All right," she said, "I'll stay for a little while, anyway."

"Good! You *are* a dear! Now, Bobbie's coming this afternoon right after lunch, the trap'll drive him in from the station. Then we can all think about chasing Mr. Sweeney away. Now please don't frown so, Susan, there's a dear. That's what you're here *for*, you know. I'm sure we'll think of something. Well! We don't have to worry about it until this afternoon, anyway. The main thing right now is clothes. Here, tell me which dress you'd like."

So the problem of Mr. Sweeney was dismissed for the time being; and Susan spent a fascinating morning trying on all of Victoria's dresses, one after the other, in front of a gilt-framed oval mirror, while Victoria fussed around her with the pleasurable little frown of a fashion expert.

Robert arrived—not in a trap, as Victoria had predicted, but on foot—at one o'clock in the afternoon. Very shortly thereafter, while the reunited Walkers were still talking and laughing downstairs, Susan saw a horse and buggy coming up Ward Lane. It stopped at the gate. A tall, thin man got out, threw

the reins over the gatepost, picked up a dispatch case from the seat, and started up the walk. Susan dodged behind the curtains just in time to avoid being seen by him as he glanced up at the house. She wondered if it could be Mr. Sweeney. If so, why should Victoria have such an aversion to him? As far as she could see, he was quite distinguished looking.

His arrival set off another burst of talk below. But soon there was quiet again; then footsteps in the upper hallway, and whispering just outside the door, of which Susan caught three words, "Now behave yourself!" And then Victoria entered with an owlish-faced, rather plump boy. He was dressed in a short-trousered suit, black stockings, and high shoes.

"May I present my brother Robert?" Victoria said in her Deportment Class voice. "This is Miss Susan Shaw, Robert."

"Pleased to meet you," Robert said dubiously.

"Pleased to meet *you*."

They shook hands.

"Isn't the weather delightful?" Susan said desperately after a while.

"I guess so."

"Oh, for goodness sake, Bobbie, stop staring!" Victoria burst out. "Where are your manners, anyway?"

"Well, gosh, Vic, I never saw anybody from the twentieth century before. She doesn't look any different to me. I think you're just telling me a big story."

"Of course she doesn't look any different, why should she? She has my clothes on, not hers. Show him the coins, Susan."

Susan brought them out and handed them over.

"Great Caesar!" Robert said. "1960, 1945, 1953! They certainly *look* real..." He stared at Susan again. "But say, there can't be an elevator by the clock, you know. The wall's too thin."

"Well, that's where I got out," Susan said. "Really."

"But it's only a foot thick!"

"Well, I can't help that. You can watch when I go down again, if you don't believe it."

"Well," he conceded, "Maybe it sort of bulges the wall on the outside of the house...Hey, do they—?"

"Don't say 'hey,' " Victoria broke in. "It isn't at all nice."

"Oh, sisters!" he groaned, making a comic face at Susan. "Always ragging at a fellow! Do they still have soldiers in the twentieth century?"

"I'm afraid so."

"That's good. I'm going to be a colonel by 1910, I've got it all worked out. Hey, Vic, guess what! You know who drove me from the station?"

"Jim Perkins?"

"No—Mr. Sweeney! And you know what he said?"

Victoria pressed her hands to her breast and sank into a chair. "Oh no!" she said. "Don't tell me he—you mean you *accepted a ride* from him?"

"Well, what could I do? Jim wasn't there."

"I can just imagine he wasn't. No doubt Mr. Sweeney saw to *that.* Getting you into his clutches! I thought we agreed that we would not have anything to do with him beyond ordinary politeness. Didn't we?"

"I know we did, Vic, but listen! I don't think we've been fair. He's really all right once you get to know him. Really! You know what he said? He said that if him and Mama—"

"*He* and Mama," she interrupted automatically.

"He said that if he and Mama get—uh—"

"Oh, it's all right," she sighed. "Susan knows the situation. All right, what's the wonderful thing that happens if he and Mama, perish the thought, do get married?"

"He said if they do, he's going to send me to military school!"

"Oh," said Victoria icily. "Now he's an angel. Now he's all right, really, once you get to know him. Of course he's just doing it out of the kindness of his heart! *You* don't have to do anything for *him*, I suppose! *Do* you, Robert dear!"

"Well," Robert said, coloring, "I guess he did mention that it wouldn't hurt if I put in a good word for him when I saw Mama."

"And were you going to?"

"Well, my goodness, Vic! I haven't said anything to her *yet*, have I?"

"Oh, Robert Lincoln Walker, you are the despair of my life!"

"Well, thunderation!" he burst out. "Women just don't understand. I don't know why I don't run away and join the army right now, and work my way up through the ranks! You might take me seriously then. Mama thinks I'm still in *curls*, and you treat me like a six-year-old. Rag, rag, rag! At least Mr. Sweeney knows what a fellow feels. He knows how to treat a fellow. He let me drive his mare two miles, and he gave me a puff of his cigar!"

"He *what*?"

"There! See? That's just what I mean! You don't think a fellow *ever* grows up. What am I supposed to do, wait till I'm *eighty* for my first cigar?"

"Oh, Vicky," Susan broke in soothingly, "don't look so shocked. It isn't fatal. How did it taste?" she asked Robert.

"Well...I guess I coughed a little. But a fellow could get used to it if he tried. And besides," rounding on Victoria again, "I'll bet Papa would have let me do the same, if I'd asked him. Hey, Vic. Hey, wait a minute, don't cry."

"What Papa would have done," she sniffled, "and what Mr. Sweeney does are as different as night and day. Don't you *dare* disgrace P-P-Papa's memory by com-comparing them."

"I'm sorry, Vic, honest. I didn't mean—I guess I got riled."

"Here's a hanky," said Susan helplessly.

Victoria hiccuped once or twice and dried her eyes. "Thank you, Sue, I'm all right now. I'm sorry if I ragged you, Bobbie. I know you're growing up, really I do. But you ought to be grown up enough to see what Mr. Sweeney's trying to do: he's trying to worm his way into your good graces. It's all very well for you to think he's a fine fellow and to fall for his flattery, but don't you see?—it's *Mama* who will have to marry him. It's

Mama we're really talking about, not you."

"Well, why doesn't she send him packing, then?" Robert said sulkily.

"You know very well she's tried. But he'll *never* give up as long as he thinks he has a chance of getting her money. You know that that's all he wants, don't you?"

"You can't prove it."

"*Prove* it! I don't have to prove it, I know it. All you have to do is look at him to know he's a fortune hunter."

"He looks all right to me."

"Oh, what do boys know about these things? Of course he looks all right to you—he makes a special effort to. He wouldn't get very far if he looked like a scoundrel, would he? Listen! Did you ever see him alone when he thought no one was looking?"

"No."

"Well, I did. You know what he did? He looked at everything—the room and the furniture and the rugs and the curtains and the pictures—he simply *devoured* everything with his eyes; and all the time he kept rubbing his hands together. Rub, rub, rub..." As Victoria spoke she mimicked what she had seen. Susan was fascinated. What an actress this girl might have been! Her imitation of gloating greed was as convincing and chilling as the real thing. "And *that*," said Victoria, "is what you want Mama to marry, is it?"

"Well—"

"Rub, rub, rub...?"

"All right, all *right*. But what can we do about it? Listen, you never gave me a chance to tell you. You know the *real* reason why he drove me home? He didn't just drop me and go back to town. He's going to board at the Hollister's. He says he's going to lay siege to Mama, and he won't let up till he's carried the fort!"

"Ahh!" said Victoria slowly. She shot a significant look at Susan. "So—he's right next door. This is our chance, Sue!"

"Oh, that isn't Mr. Sweeney downstairs?" Susan said.

"Goodness, no—that's Mr. Branscomb. *He's* a gentleman."

"He's the lawyer who handles Mama's money," Robert added. "Hey, Vic, what do you mean, this is your chance? What have you two got up your sleeve?"

"Oh, it's just this crazy idea Vicky has," Susan said uneasily. "I don't—"

"It isn't a crazy idea," Victoria said. "We just have to go through with it, now that the witch and the well have gone to all the trouble of bringing you here."

"Well?" Robert asked. "What well? What is all this mystery, anyway?"

"I didn't tell you everything, there wasn't time," Victoria said; and she proceeded to explain the part that she thought the wishing well had played in Susan's arrival.

"You mean," Robert said when she finished, "that Susan was *sent* here to chase Mr. Sweeney off? That's a major campaign! How are you going to do it, Sue?"

"I haven't the faintest idea," Susan said helplessly. "Listen, just because I'm from the twentieth century doesn't mean that I can do *any*thing. I'm still just a girl, not a—a *genie* or something."

"We know that," Victoria said. "We're not going to just drop the whole thing in your lap and fold our hands. It's up to all of us, of course. We have to think, think, think!"

They thought.

"Maybe," Robert said, "if we really have to chase him off, maybe we could play ghosts. You know, dress up in sheets and sneak into the Hollister's after dark and haunt him? Hey, come to think of it, there's some old pieces of chain out in the stable! We could rattle them and groan—"

"Oh pooh!"

"No, listen! Remember when Papa read 'Sleepy Hollow' to us? It worked on Ichabod Crane, didn't it—playing ghost?"

"Oh, Bobbie! The whole point was that there was this *legend* about the ghost on the horse, and Ichabod Crane was half expecting to meet him anyway. Mr. Sweeney isn't Ichabod and Hollister's isn't haunted. It's probably the least haunted house in the whole county, Bobbie."

"Well, it was just an idea…"

They thought some more.

"Wait a minute," Susan said. "You say he's after your Mama's money. What if he thought your Mama had lost it all?"

"Ah!" said Victoria, widening her eyes. "He'd show a clean pair of heels then! But why should he think that?"

"Well, I just thought we could give him the idea somehow. Send him a letter, or—I don't know."

"That just might do it, though," Victoria mused. "If only you were taller, Bobbie! We could put a pair of false whiskers on you, and you could meet him somewhere and scrape up an acquaintance and say"—she jumped up and assumed an exaggerated masculine swagger— " 'Heard about Mrs. Walker? Lost all her money, poor woman. Extraordinary case, sir!' "

"That'd be fun," Robert laughed. "But he'd recognize me, Vic, he's not blind."

"I know…"

There was another interval of cogitation.

"Wait a minute!" Robert suddenly whispered, "*He wouldn't recognize Susan!*"

"Ah!" said Victoria. They looked at Susan hopefully.

"Don't stare at me like that," Susan said. "I'm trying to think." She was ahead of them in realizing that Mr. Sweeney wouldn't recognize her. And it was no use protesting that it was none of her business. The whole course of recent events had made it her business. She was it, willy-nilly.

Ever since Robert's mention of "Sleepy Hollow" her mind had been turning over memories of all the books she had read. There should be an idea somewhere among them...She thought of Mr. Toad, humbugging his way across the country in his washerwoman's disguise. No good in this case...Disguises and acting, though—that was right in her line. "Wait a minute, wait a minute," she muttered. Let's see, there was...Tom Sawyer or—

"Huckleberry Finn!" she cried. "Remember?"

The Walkers both looked blank. "What's that?" Robert asked.

"You know! It's a book—*Huckleberry Finn?* Oh, maybe it hasn't been written yet...Anyway, what was it now? They were going down the river on this raft. How did it go? Huck wanted to keep someone away from the raft, they were in a rowboat, I think...And he—ah! What would Mr. Sweeney do if your Mama had smallpox?"

"Don't," said Robert in a thin voice.

"No, no! I just mean if he *thought* she had it."

Victoria was staring at her open-mouthed. "Susan Shaw," she whispered, "You positively frighten me."

"It worked in *Huckleberry Finn.* Is smallpox serious or not?"

"*Serious?*" Victoria looked at her brother. "Remember Ginny Schmidt?" Robert nodded solemnly. "She *died* of it."

"All right! Don't look so shocked, it has to be drastic if it's going to work at all. It won't chase him away if I just say your Mama's lost her money—he'll only come over to see if it's true. We've got to *scare* him. Now, if I can just get him by himself for a while—"

"Bobbie," Victoria said decisively, "run and see if he's anywhere in sight. Go on, go on, you can look out Mama's window. Susan, that's the most incredible idea I ever heard in my whole life! You should be a magician with a mind like yours!"

"Oh, let me think, will you?" Susan said, chewing her knuckle.

Robert came running back in a minute. "Yes, he's in the Hollister's backyard right now, smoking a cigar!" Then, in a dubious voice, "Listen, I don't know about this. It's a thumping big lie. I don't know whether—"

"It's a stratagem," Victoria said firmly. "It's a kind of test. What would *you* do if you heard that I'd lost all my money and had smallpox?"

"Don't talk that way, Vic."

"What would you do? Would you run away?"

"No, I'd bring you all my money, if I had any, and I'd nurse you back to health."

"All right! So would any real gentleman. Now, if Mr. Sweeney runs away, he isn't *fit* to marry Mama, is he? And if he stays—oh," she threw her hands in the air, "then I give up, he's a better man than I thought. Anyway, we have to know. For Mama's sake."

"I've got it!" Susan said. "I'm going to be a servant girl. Have you got that kind of a dress, Vicky?"

"Umm…I guess you could wear my mourning dress, it's all black. But the material's too good for a—"

"That's all right, it could be a hand-me-down. Now, let's see…I'll need a little trunk or a bundle or something. I'm going to pretend I'm running away."

"Wait a minute." Victoria rummaged around in her chest of drawers. "How about this old shawl?"

"Yes, that'll do. We can wrap a pillow up in it. Do servant girls wear hats? Never mind, I'll pretend I came away so fast that I forgot mine. Does Mr. Sweeney know Mr. Branscomb?"

"I don't know. Do you, Bobbie?"

"I don't know—don't think so. Why?"

"The horse and buggy out front," Susan explained. "If your Mama's supposed to be sick the doctor would be here."

"Dr. Balch drives a dogcart," Robert said.

"Well, does he know Dr. Balch?"

"I don't think so," Victoria said.

"Oh, well, the whole thing's a big gamble anyway. We'll just have to hope. Help me off with this dress, Vicky."

"You may leave the room, Robert," Victoria said. "I know, you can scout the territory. See what Maggie's doing. We'll have to smuggle Sue down the back stairs. Oh, this is all so exciting, I can't *stand* it!"

Susan's Greatest Role

Susan had not noticed Hollister's before; it was on the opposite side of the Walker's house from the garden where she had wandered during the night, and it could not be seen from Victoria's room. It was a little square box of a place, deeply shaded by elms, with a chicken run along the far side.

They crouched by a gap in the hedge, breathing hard and studying the enemy.

"Beast!" Victoria hissed. "Look at him swagger!"

"Here, smudge my face, will you?" Susan whispered. Robert grubbed up a handful of dirt. "Just a smidgen, now, don't overdo it; nothing spoils a performance like a bad make-up job. Wish we'd brought a mirror. How's my hair, Vicky? Muss it up a little, will you? Maybe you can pull some strands out of my braids. I want it kind of bird's-nesty. Do you mind if I make just a little tear in the sleeve?"

"Oh no. I don't know why I kept the dress anyway, it's too small for me now."

"Here, use my pocketknife, Sue."

"Thanks. There, that's it. Now, let's see...some wrinkles in my stockings."

"*Do* look the other way, Robert!"

"There! Now please don't giggle or anything, you'll spoil the whole show."

"Oh, I couldn't! I'm just ready to *die!*"

"Me too," said Robert in a shaking voice.

Susan herself was feeling the familiar pangs of stage fright. 'Calm down,' she thought, 'calm down, it won't be any worse than last year when what's-her-name forgot her lines and had hysterics…' But she knew it could be much worse. This was not an audience already inclined to be sympathetic that she had to convince, but a man who was persistent and perhaps unscrupulous in getting what he wanted; a man, moreover, who didn't know his lines, but would have to take all his cues from her. 'Just feed him a little information at a time,' she warned herself. 'Build it up, don't blurt it all out at once.' She stood up, remembering all the servant girls she had read of in books or seen in the movies or on the stage. She would have to say "sir" frequently. It might be well to whine a bit…

Now or never. She took a deep breath, squeezed through the hedge, and advanced to meet the foe.

Mr. Sweeney was—handsome! She didn't know what she had been expecting, but it certainly wasn't this. She was seized with panic. This distinguished man a scoundrel? Victoria must be mistaken! What was she doing here, what had she gotten herself into? She checked her approach. But no, she must go on—they were watching her; Victoria had said that they *had* to know; if she spoiled it now there might not be another chance.

Her numbed legs would hardly propel her forward again. "Please, sir," she quavered, dropping an awkward little curtsy.

Mr. Sweeney removed his cigar, regarded her for a moment, then smiled. And with that smile Susan recognized whom she was dealing with. 'Oho, you smoothie!' she thought, with a surge of returning confidence. 'I'll bet you've been practicing that in front of a mirror! But if you think it's going to make *me* swoon, you're wrong.' Now that she was closer her first impression of him began to change. Handsome, yes. But he held his cigar in a fastidious way, in a hand that was white and soft. His mustache was clipped with mathematical precision. His derby was tilted slightly to reveal a wave of black hair so perfect that it seemed to have been lacquered in place.

"Ah, my dear," he said in a smooth, low voice. "May I be of any assistance?"

"Please, sir, I'm in awful trouble. I just lost my job —my *position*, I mean—through no fault of my own."

"Ah," Mr. Sweeney murmured, "distressing, distressing." His smile lost a little of its brilliance.

"Please, sir, I just wanted to ask you a little favor, you looked like such a kind gentleman."

"Anything in my power, my dear. But may I suggest that you approach me later—say in two weeks' time? I expect to be in circumstances then that will enable me to consider your application. If your references are suitable, of course."

"Oh, thank you, sir. But I didn't mean you should hire me, though I'm sure it'd be a pleasure to work for a kind gentleman like you. I was hoping for a ride to town, if you'll pardon me, sir."

"My dear, it pains me to have to say no. At any other time I would leap to your assistance. But it so happens that I do not intend to return to town for several days. I am here on a matter of some delicacy." He drew on his cigar with a flourish, and fired that dazzling smile at her again. "A matter—I am sure you will understand—of the heart."

'Oh, you ham!' she thought. 'I suppose you expect me to giggle and blush.' Blushing to order was impossible, but she did manage a fair giggle. "Oh, sir, I'm sure the lady will be the luckiest—"

"Therefore," Mr. Sweeney went on, "if you will be so kind, I will resume those tender reveries in which I was engaged when you first found me. Perhaps one of the agricultural gentlemen down the lane will give you a lift."

The scene was threatening to slip out of control. It was time to offer him the bait.

"Oh, sir," she sniffed, "I hate to go on bothering you, sir, but I don't know where to turn. I *am* in trouble, sir. They turned me away *without my wages*." 'Ask me why,' she prayed.

"Really?" Mr. Sweeney murmured. "It grieves me even to entertain the idea, my girl, but perhaps you deserved it." And with that he turned his back on her and began to walk away.

"Oh, sir," she bleated in sincere desperation, "wait!" She trotted after him, trying to think of what to say next. But all that would come to her was "wait."

Mr. Sweeney swung around on her. "Do not presume too far on my patience, miss! I can do nothing for you. No—stay." He plunged a hand into his pocket, felt about carefully, and produced a dime. "If this can alleviate your distress in any measure I shall be gratified. No, no, do not thank me. Good day!"

"Oh, you are a gentleman, sir, *so* kind of you. But begging your pardon, sir, I didn't deserve to be turned away. I always gave satisfactory service—"

"Good day!"

"Satisfactory service," she persisted, raising her voice. "Mrs. Walker always said—"

Aha! That had hit the target. Why hadn't she mentioned the name earlier? 'He's listening now,' she thought; 'throw out that lead about your wages again.'

"Did I understand you to say Mrs. Walker?"

"Yes, sir. I just came from her house. She was very sorry to turn me away without my—"

But Mr. Sweeney still wouldn't take his cue. "It may interest you to know, my dear," he said in his smoothest voice, "that my connection with the Walkers is on a familiar, not to say intimate, footing."

"Yes, sir," she said warily. What was he driving at?

"Therefore," he purred, "I find myself somewhat at a loss to explain why I never saw you in that household."

She fought down a surge of panic. "I-I'm sure you wouldn't have noticed me, sir," she gulped. "I was—in the—in the kitchen. All the time. Maggie was training me out there." A faint hope occurred to her, and she clutched at it. "Oh!" she exclaimed, trying to make it sound like a cry of pleased recognition. "Why, you must be Mr. Sweeney that they all speak so well of!"

It worked. Mr. Sweeney displayed his smile and gave a little flourish with his cigar. Then his eyes narrowed, and in a silky bantering tone he said:

"So—satisfied with your work, were they?"

"Oh, yes, sir. They—"

"And yet you were discharged from service?"

"Yes, sir. You see—"

"Without your wages, if I understand correctly."

"Yes, sir. Mrs. Walk—"

"Perhaps," Mr. Sweeney said, still smiling, but with a cruel little quirk at the corners of his mouth, "perhaps there was a little matter of spoons disappearing, or something like that, eh?"

"Oh, *no*, sir!"

"Would you still accept a ride from me if I told you that we should go directly to a police station?"

"Certainly, sir. I have nothing to—"

"Oh, well," he said, tiring of his game and turning away. "It's no concern of mine what you've been up to. I have no doubt Mrs. Walker was fully justified, however. Good day."

And here, suddenly, was the chance she'd been waiting for.

"Oh, sir, I wouldn't say a word against Mrs. Walker. I'm sure she would have paid my wages. *If she'd been able to.*"

Mr. Sweeney's cigar was arrested halfway to his mouth. "I do not quite apprehend your meaning, my dear," he said carefully.

"Oh," she gasped, putting her hand to her face. "I shouldn't have mentioned it, I'm sure."

"Did I understand you to mean can't? Or won't?"

"Can't, sir. Oh, but I shouldn't have said it. I'm sure they don't want their troubles talked about."

"See here, my girl, I think you had better explain yourself."

Susan retreated a step, averting her eyes so that he wouldn't see the triumph that was shining in them. It was just like playing the old childhood game of I Have A Secret I Won't Tell. She could tell by the sudden wary tone in his voice that he was hooked.

He was also impatient. Seizing her by the arm, he said, "Now, just what do you mean, trouble?"

"Money trouble, sir," she stammered.

His grip tightened. "All right, out with it. I've got to know—as a friend of the family."

She almost reeled under a burst of inspiration. "Well, perhaps if you were to make it worth my while, sir," she whined.

For a moment it looked as if she had gone too far. Then Mr. Sweeney smiled—a genuine, appreciative smile. "Aha! Artful little sharper, aren't you? I think we understand each other, my dear." He explored his pocket again, pulled out a half dollar, and held it up just beyond reach. "Now—short and sweet!"

"Well, sir," she said in a low voice, keeping her eyes on the coin, "a few days ago Mrs. Walker got a letter. I heard her and Miss Victoria talking about it. Really by accident, sir, I'm not an eavesdropper."

"Never mind that."

"They were crying as if their hearts would break, sir, and Mrs. Walker's been shut up in her room for two days and won't eat anything, and she's crying something awful. So I asked Maggie what it was, and she had hysterics—"

"I said never mind that. *Out* with it!"

"It was a confidence man," she whispered. "He had an invention or a—a gold mine or something, and he talked Mrs. Walker into putting her money in it. And now they've found out he's run away to the—to the Continent."

Mr. Sweeney's voice was thick. "What was the take?" he demanded.

"Beg pardon, sir?"

"The *take!*" he snarled, shaking her. "What was in it? How

much did he get away with?"

"*Everything!*" she whispered, looking him full in the face for an instant. Then she turned on the tears. "Oh, sir, they only owe me for a month, and they can't even pay that!"

Mr. Sweeney's face swelled and darkened. The half dollar dropped from his hand. He whipped his derby off, smashed it with his fist, and ground out a noise, half hiss and half strangled shout, between his clenched teeth.

"Oh, sir!" she cried. "Do me one more kindness, *please*. Take me away from here—"

"Now you cut along!" he grated. "I've heard all I want. Get out." He hurled his cigar to the ground and stamped on it.

"Save me, save me!" she wept, flinging herself against him. "Oh, I'm so scared! I must get away, please help me!"

"Here, what's the hurry? What are you hiding from me?"

"Oh, I'm so scared! Mrs. Walker—oh, it's too horrible!"

"What? What? She kill herself?"

"No, sir, but she's so sick."

"Huh! Don't wonder. Sick myself."

"No, *really* sick! Take me away, I don't want to die!"

"Wait a minute!" said Mr. Sweeney hoarsely. "What's she got?"

"The—the doctor says—if she's lucky enough to live—she'll be scarred—for l—l—life!"

"Great Scott!" Mr. Sweeney choked, hastily backing away. "Smallpox!"

"Take me away!" Susan sobbed, clinging to him. "I was just talking to Miss Victoria, and she—she—she said she felt all over strange herself!"

"*Get away from me!*" Mr. Sweeney shouted. He pushed her

violently, lost his balance, and sat down. "Get away! Get away! Touching me! Breathing on me! You little—" His fingers closed around a fragment of brick in the grass. He scrambled to his feet and raised his weapon. "Get away from me!" he panted.

They both turned and fled at the same instant—Mr. Sweeney toward the house, Susan toward the hedge. She stumbled, for she had actually succeeded in frightening herself, and was still wildly weeping; but in her mind sang the triumphant thought, 'Oh, if only Elsie Mautner could have seen that! She'd never dare walk on a stage again!'

Mrs. Walker's Confession

The violence of Mr. Sweeney's reaction had, in fact, frightened all of them; even Susan had not expected to be *that* successful. A fit of hysterical giggling overcame them as they made their way back to the house, and continued for some time after they had regained Victoria's room.

"My!" Victoria said when they had calmed down somewhat. "That was simply *inspired*."

"Well, I've had some experience in dramatics," Susan said modestly. "You were right, Vicky, you were absolutely right about him. I told him that a confidence man had run away with all your Mama's money, and you should have seen his face!"

"Was that when he smashed his hat?"

"Yes! Oh, he was so mad I thought he'd have ap—ap—what-d'you-call-it."

"Apoppalepsy," said Robert.

"Oh, the brute!" Victoria said, shaking her fist. "I wish he had. Foiled in his villainous plans! I wish you were big enough to thrash him, Bobbie. What are you looking so solemn about?"

"Well, the thing is," Robert said, "we don't know whether it's really worked."

"Of course it's worked! What are you talking about? Didn't you see him run?"

"Certainly I saw him run, but that's *now*. How about later when he starts to think it over? What if he begins to check up? He could ask at the bank about Mama's money, and then he'd find out it was all a big fib."

"Stratagem," Victoria insisted.

"All right, stratagem. But he'll call it lying, and then we'll be in trouble."

"No you won't," Susan said. "*I* did it, not you. He didn't even see you."

"No, but he'll probably suspect we were accomplices if he finds out it wasn't true."

"Well, I don't care," Victoria said. "We've unmasked him now and we know he's a villain. That's all that matters. He can even come back if he wants to—once Mama is warned it won't do him a bit of good."

"All right, but *how* are we going to warn Mama?"

"Oh, don't be so slow!" she cried in exasperation. "We'll tell her that he's just after her money."

"You're the one that's being slow, Vic. The first thing Mama will ask is, *how do we know*."

"Oh my goodness!" Victoria said in a small voice. "That's right…"

"The thing is, we really did lie to him. I don't care what you call it, Vic, we did. And if Mama finds out— well, you know what she'll think about that. It won't make any difference to her *why* we did it."

"Now wait a minute," Susan said. "Let's not get panicky. If it works the whole question will never even come up."

"If..." Victoria said gloomily.

They stared at each other in silence.

"What's that?" Victoria suddenly whispered.

"Horse!" Robert said.

They rushed to the window, but it was only Mr. Branscomb driving away.

"Maybe," Susan said hopefully, "maybe Mr. Sweeney left while we were coming up the back stairs. We couldn't have heard him from there, could we?"

"Maybe he hasn't left at all," Robert said.

"Let's look out Mama's window and see," Victoria suggested.

"That won't do any good. You can't see Hollister's stable from there."

"Let's look anyway—I can't *stand* it any more. Maybe we can see something—"

"Ssh! Someone's coming!" Susan whispered.

There was a knock at the door, and Mrs. Walker's voice said, "Bobbie? Vicky?"

"Under the bed!" Robert mouthed silently. Susan flung herself to the floor and wriggled out of sight.

"Children, children!" said Mrs. Walker, opening the door. "Such a thumping and bumping! You haven't been quarreling, I hope?"

"Oh, no, Mama!" Victoria said in a strained voice. "We were just..."

"Just talking," Robert croaked.

"Well! I hope the time will soon come when you won't find

it necessary to stamp your feet while you talk. What is the matter, anyway? You both look as if I'd caught you with your hands in the cookie jar."

"You—you—you just surprised us, Mama," Robert said faintly. "Here, won't you have a chair?"

"Thank you, Bobbie. They've been teaching you well at school, I see." The chair creaked. "I think you had better sit down, too. You too, Vicky. We have something to discuss."

There was a thick silence.

"Well, children," Mrs. Walker said at last. "I think it's time we had a very serious talk about Mr. Sweeney."

She could not have startled them more if she had fired a gun. Even Susan jumped a little under the fourposter, and felt her face go hot.

"Oh, come, children, there's no need to blush! I think it's no secret, is it, that Mr. Sweeney has been—well, interested in us for quite a while?"

Silence from Robert and Victoria. Perhaps they were shaking their heads.

"In fact," Mrs. Walker went on, "it's no secret that he's proposed to me on numerous occasions. Until now I've thought it best to refuse him. That's no secret, either. But…"

"But wh—wh—what, Mama?" Victoria asked.

"Well…he's made a very handsome offer, my dears!"

"You mean you've seen him already?" Victoria blurted out.

"What do you mean, 'already?' Is he here?"

"He's at the Hollister's," Robert said miserably. "I think."

"Oh. Well, he said he'd be here soon, without mentioning exactly when. No, I haven't seen him since last time; but I had a letter from him yesterday."

"Oh," said Victoria. "Well, what is his handsome offer?" Susan could imagine how Victoria's mouth twisted on the word "handsome."

"Why, he speaks of a military school for you, Bobbie! Isn't that splendid? Just what you've been wanting. And a very well-known finishing school for *you*, dear. I'm very pleased to find that he has your welfare so much at heart."

"What about *your* welfare?" Victoria bristled.

"Oh, I don't count," Mrs. Walker laughed. "I'm just an old woman, Vicky. I've had my life—yours is still ahead of you, and it's yours that I'm thinking of."

"You're *not* an old woman, and you *do* count. Mr. Sweeney—goodness!" Victoria suddenly gasped, "you're not in *love* with him, are you, Mama?"

"Well," said Mrs. Walker evasively, "love seems very important when you're young. But you'll find as you grow older that duty comes first."

"Duty to *him?*"

"No, my dear, duty to you and Bobbie. It's simply not right for two growing children to be without a Papa. I've been very concerned about it for some time, and now that—now that things have reached a certain stage...Well, what I'm trying to say is that I must seriously begin to consider your future."

"Oh, Mama!" Victoria wailed. "I don't blame you for worrying about us, but you could do so much better than Mr. Sweeney! If only you'd go to town a little more often."

"Victoria, are you proposing that I go out and throw myself at men's heads?"

"Of course not, Mama! If you'd just visit friends and—well, there'd be dinners and parties—and you'd—you couldn't help being introduced to—"

"I'm afraid I've lost all my heart for society since your Papa died…And, you see, Mr. Sweeney has been kind enough to come to me, instead of the other way around…I know you're not very favorably impressed by him, Vicky—"

"I think he's horrid!" Victoria whispered.

"Oh…What do you think, Bobbie?"

Robert made some inarticulate, but negative, noises.

Mrs. Walker sighed. "I suppose he is a little—too polished, perhaps…" Suddenly her voice broke. "Oh, children, I'm so tired, so tired! I can't think any more, I don't know what to—" Then she regained control of herself, and continued, almost harshly, with: "Well, no matter. There's nothing more to discuss. My own feelings do not concern anyone but myself, and my duty toward you two is clear. Your duty toward me, as children toward their mother, is to yield to my decision. I shall—I shall accept Mr. Sweeney's offer."

"Mama—"

"Please, Vicky! There is nothing more to discuss."

Victoria's voice trembled with a desperate resolve. "I just wanted to ask a question, Mama. How much money does Mr. Sweeney have?"

"Victoria! I'm shocked at you! That's the sort of thing a lady *never* asks a gentleman!"

"I'm sorry, Mama. But that's the sort of thing a *gentleman* would make clear, isn't it? And he hasn't said anything about it, has he?"

"Mr. Sweeney is always very well turned out, as you know. And I'm sure he wouldn't be speaking of expensive schools for you two if he weren't prepared—"

"—prepared to spend *your* money," Victoria broke in. "That's all he's after, Mama. He doesn't care a fig for *us*. He's a fortune-hunter and a scoundrel, and I'd say the same to his face!"

"Victoria Albertine, that is a very serious accusation. You had better take it back and apologize for it, or explain yourself."

'Oh oh!' Susan thought, clenching her hands until they ached. 'Now it comes out…' She knew that Victoria would not back down, but would confess what they had done rather than see her mother make the fatal mistake; and she realized that at that point she herself would be honor-bound to come out from under the bed and take the blame. The ensuing complications would not bear thinking about.

"Well, it's true, Mama," Victoria began bravely. "You see, about an hour ago we—"

There was a knock at the door.

"Come in! Yes, Maggie?"

"Note for you, Mum," said a hoarse voice.

"Thank you, Maggie. Does it require an answer?"

"No'm. Mrs. Hollister brought it. Queerest thing! Herself's not the kind to be passing notes. She always spoke right out before."

"Thank you, Maggie."

The door closed. There was an unbearable silence.

"Well," Mrs. Walker said at last.

"What is it, Mama?" Robert croaked.

Mrs. Walker's voice was flat. "It seems, my dears, that we have been worrying ourselves to no purpose. Mr. Sweeney has changed his mind."

"Mama, what does he say?"

"He says that he has received certain information that makes it necessary for him to withdraw his offer."

So—their scheme had worked. But Susan felt no triumph in the thought. Confession was inevitable now; and that being the case, she might as well come forth at once and tell Mrs. Walker that she was the one who had supplied Mr. Sweeney with his "certain information." She was just about to roll out from under the four-poster when Mrs. Walker stopped her dead by saying quietly:

"I owe you an apology, Vicky. It seems you were right."

"I—I—I—" Victoria stammered, evidently as astonished as Susan was by this unexpected turn.

"Apparently he *is* a fortune-hunter," Mrs. Walker went on. "I don't know how he got his certain information so quickly; but then they do say that bad news travels fast..."

"What bad news?" Robert whispered. "Why are you crying, Mama?"

"I hoped I wouldn't have to tell you, children. I was praying that Mr. Branscomb could set things right—it's been coming a long time, I'm afraid—we've done everything we could—dear Mr. Branscomb has been moving heaven and earth to help us—oh!" she sobbed, "Mr. Sweeney was my last hope for your future! We're ruined, children—we haven't a penny left in the world!"

Quest for a Map

Susan could not see what effect this announcement had on Robert and Victoria, but she could imagine it from the state of her own feelings. She could not have been more shocked if her own father had announced his ruin.

Robert, as befitted a soldier and the man of the family, was the first to recover. "Don't worry, Mama," he quavered. "I'll go to work. I can be an office boy, or work for a newspaper, or something…"

"That's my brave Bobbie."

There was a confused moment of sobbing and murmuring and back-patting, which, as it turned out, was fortunate; because at that very moment Susan said "Oh!" rather loudly, without being able to help herself, and she would have been heard if the Walkers had not been so occupied. It was Robert's mention of the word "newspaper" that did it. Newspaper! She had been looking at one just before getting on the elevator…

When Mrs. Walker had regained some measure of control over her voice, she said, "It's far from hopeless, children. We'll—we'll sell the house. Mr. Branscomb says it will be hard to find a buyer, it's so far from town, but we'll be able to borrow something on it meanwhile. I'm going to write to Cousin Jane; she'll be willing to take us in for a while, and then we can—we can look about us and see what's to be done. Vicky, dear, you're so pale! I'm sorry I frightened you, but the thing has to be faced. We'll just have to be brave, that's all. The Walkers may be down but they've never been out!"

"I'm not out," said Robert.

"You're being wonderful, dear. But then I knew you would be. Well! Come along, we'll all have some hot tea. Remember what your Papa always said: 'Never make an important decision without drinking a cup of tea and having a good night's sleep.' We'll just pretend that he's still with us, and behave as he'd expect us to; and everything will turn out all right, I'm sure."

"We'll be down in a minute, Mama. I want to talk to Vic—privately, please."

"All right, dear. Come as soon as you can. I'll have Maggie put the kettle on."

The door had no sooner closed than Susan was scrambling out from under the bed. "Listen!" she hissed excitedly. "Listen, I—"

"Gosh, Sue, did you hear that?" Robert said. "We've lost all our money—really lost it!"

"Listen, don't worry! I know where—!"

"It's a judgment on us!" Victoria whispered. Her face was very pinched and white. "We told a big lie, and it's coming true, to punish us. Oh!" she cried, throwing herself across the bed and bursting into tears, "why didn't I listen to you, Bobbie? You said it was wrong. Now it's coming true, it's coming true! Oh, if Mama gets smallpox now, I'll just kill myself!"

"Don't talk that way, Vic. It couldn't be our doing. Mama said it's been coming for a long time."

"Oh, listen, both of you!" Susan cried, dancing up and down. "*Listen.* You don't have to worry about a thing! *I know where a treasure is buried!*"

"What?" said Robert, turning to her with a stupefied air.

"Treasure! Thousands and thousands of dollars, just up the street from here!"

"But how do you—how do you—?"

"Oh! Whew, let me catch my breath!" She sat down on the bed beside Victoria, who was gaping at her incredulously. "I read about it in the paper, it was all over the front page—"

"But if it was in the paper that means it's been found already," Robert said. "Anyway, I didn't read anything about—"

"No! Will you please just listen? It was in a 1960 paper. I read about it just before I came here. It hasn't been found, it won't be found for years and years! It's there right now, waiting for us to find it first. The paper even had a map showing where it is!"

"Great Caesar! How much did you say it was?"

"Oh, I forget exactly, but it was thousands. Enough to save you and your Mama, anyway. We're going to find it—I'm going right down the elevator as soon as I can and bring back the map. So don't let your Mama do anything yet. Don't let her sell the house or write to Cousin Jane—"

"Children?" came faintly from below.

"Coming, Mama!" Robert shouted. "What are we going to tell her, Sue?"

"I don't know, you'll have to think of something. Just try to get her to put everything off until we can find the treasure."

"Susan Shaw," Victoria whispered, "I think you came from heaven!"

"Oh, don't be mushy, for goodness sake! Go on, go on. I have to think."

As soon as she was alone she kicked off her shoes and padded silently up and down the room, chewing her knuckle. It was all very well to put up a confident front for Robert and Victoria, but now that they were gone doubts began to creep in. She could get the map, all right—but would it be of any use? There was a vast difference between the city streets of 1960 and the open country of 1881. The whole thing depended on where the Walker's house stood—that was the only point of reference they had to start from. *Was the house standing on the same spot that the apartment building would some day occupy?*

'Well, it just has to be,' she thought. 'The elevator didn't go sideways or back and forth—it *felt* as if it went straight up, anyway. Ward Lane out there does look a little farther off than it should be, but then they could have widened it toward the house when they made Ward Street out of it. It just *has* to be in the same place, that's all...'

Early in the evening Robert returned to the room. With an expression of studious innocence he came up to the bedside stand, and proceeded to unload from his pockets a large quantity of bread-and-butter sandwiches, cold lamb chops, cold boiled potatoes, cookies, and nuts.

"I usually can't do this well," he said modestly, "but Mama

and Vic couldn't eat much at supper. I can always eat. I guess if tomorrow were Judgment Day I could still eat. As a matter of fact..." he added delicately, staring at a cookie.

"Help yourself," Susan said. "I couldn't possibly eat all this. Thanks for bringing it up."

"Welcome...Sue?"

"Mm?"

"Do you really think it'll work?"

"Sure it will," she said, with more conviction than she felt. "Why not?"

"Well...there's something wrong somewhere. I can't put my finger on it, but it bothers me."

"Look. The money was buried sometime around the Civil War. Nobody's dug it up yet. So it's still there. What's wrong about that? All we have to do is find the place."

"Well...When are you going down in the elevator?"

"Soon as it's dark."

"That's an odd thing. I should think you'd go *up* in the elevator. You know, you sort of think of old time on the bottom and new time piled on top, like a—like a—" He waved his cookie helplessly, swallowed it, and selected another. "I don't know. It's awfully strange any way you think of it. Can I watch?"

"Of...course," she said, yawning until her ears cracked. The late conversation of last night, this afternoon's performance for Mr. Sweeney, the strain of worrying about finding the treasure, and now all this food....She crawled into the four-poster, numb with fatigue.

"Wake me up when it's dark?" she mumbled.

"Sure, Sue. Don't you want this chop?"

"Mm-mm…"

Robert happily fell to. Susan slept.

"Sue. Sue. Susan!"

"Urrmmf?" she said. Victoria was an indistinct shape bending over her in the dark. "Time is it?"

"Shh! It's after twelve, I think. I was going to wake you much earlier, but I didn't dare till Mama fell asleep, and then I dropped off myself. Here, while you're waking up I'll go get Bobbie, he'll be furious if he misses it."

Susan stretched and scrubbed her face until she was awake. Victoria returned with Robert, who glimmered ghost-like in his nightshirt.

"We have to be extra quiet," he whispered. "Mama's still tossing around. Hey, Vic, don't light the candle yet."

"Please don't say 'hey,' Bobbie," Victoria sighed.

Robert, as foraging expert, took the lead. They crept down the back stairs, paused to light their candle in the kitchen, and proceeded more quickly to the hallway. The clock said twenty to one.

"It was right here," said Susan, pointing to the wainscotting. "But I don't know where the button is. Do you see one?"

"Button?" Robert said. "What's the button for?"

"You push it and the elevator comes up."

"Oh. Is it like a shirt button or a shoe button?"

"Neither—it's a black knob. Help me find it, will you?"

They searched the paneling inch by inch, holding the candle close, but could find nothing.

"What if I *can't* go back?" Susan said in a small voice.

"Nonsense!" said Victoria. "The old woman gave you three trips, didn't she? Try pushing the place where the button *should* be."

"Well, that might do it. About here, I guess." She pressed her thumb against the wood. "Doesn't feel like—" she muttered. "Wait a minute." She put her ear against the wainscotting. Ah! Faintly, as if from the depths of a canyon, came the sound of mechanisms stirring to life.

"It's all right!" she said. "Whew! It may take a while, though, it's the slowest old elevator in the world."

"Shall we wait here for you, Sue?"

"Well, I don't know. I'll have to explain to Daddy, that'll take some time; and then I'll have to persuade him to let me come up again, that'll take a while—"

"Hey!" Robert said faintly. "It's making a noise!"

"Of course it's making a noise, it always does. Here it comes."

"Sighhh!" said the wainscotting. "Rummmble." It split into two sections that folded back to the right.

"Great Caesar!" The candle in Robert's hand made a wild dip as he clutched his sister's arm. "It's—it's deep in there," he whispered.

"Same old elevator," said Susan, getting into it. "Now listen, I'll come back as soon as I can. You don't have to wait if you don't want to, I can find my way up to Vicky's room by now. Don't worry about me, it's perfectly safe. Bye."

She pressed the third-floor button. The wainscotting sighed and began to close.

A scrabbling noise suddenly made itself heard in the shadows of the hallway. "Oooh!" Victoria squeaked, jumping into the air as something black hurtled past her legs and into the elevator.

"Stop that!" Susan cried. "Get out of here!" But it was too late—the door closed, the elevator began to groan its way downward.

"Here, you—*stop* that—oh, poor mousie! Drop it! *Drop* it!" She slapped with all her strength.

"Mrrowr!" said Toby, flattening his ears. The mouse shot from his jaws and took refuge in a corner.

"Come *here*, you nasty old cat, let it alone! Now I'll have to take you back—no, I can't, it'll waste a trip. Here, behave yourself! Ouch!"

Toby had suddenly discovered that his world was not only too small, but disconcertingly in motion. "Wow!" he said, using his claws.

"Stop it!" she panted. "You're tearing my dress! Oh, I still have Victoria's clothes on! What if anybody sees me? I'll just have to pretend not to see them—hold still! No, I'll pretend I'm rehearsing a part in a play. *Ouch*, you—"

She and Toby battled all the way to the third floor, both of them becoming considerably disheveled in the process. Toby could draw blood, but Susan had size and strength on her side, and was determined to save the mouse from destruction. By the time the door opened again she had managed to get an arm-lock on the cat and one hand clamped around his chops.

How strange the hallway looked, with its rows of doors and the dim night lights! And how strange it smelled—as if the air, tinctured with cigarette smoke and Mr. Bodoni's carpet shampoo, had not been in circulation for a long time. She had only been away since Wednesday, and yet it felt like years. 'Well, it has been years, in a way,' she thought; 'almost a century!' What was that odd voice vibrating in the stillness? It was tiny and metallic, wailing behind one of the closed doors:

Yew broke mah hear-r-r-rt
When yew went uh-way-y-y...

A television set! But of course there were television sets—she was in the twentieth century again.

Toby had calmed down now that his horizon had expanded and the floor was steady again. She kept her grip on him, however, just in case, and peered out cautiously. No one in the hallway! Swiftly she tiptoed to her apartment door and opened it.

'Oh oh!'

The table lamp was lit. There was a policeman sitting in the armchair. His blouse was loosened, his chin rested on his chest, and he wheezed faintly in his sleep. Mrs. Clutchett, mummied in blankets, snored on the sofa.

'What...?' she thought, closing the door again with exquisite care. 'What's going on here? A policeman in the apartment? Has there been a burglary? But why should Mrs. Clutchett—? Oh! It must be me! They probably think I've been kidnapped! Or that I ran away! Oh, poor Daddy. I'll have to tell him at once—'

'But I can't,' she thought, arresting her hand on the knob. 'Maybe I could explain to Daddy, but the policeman will never believe me. And if they think I ran away once they won't let me go again—and if I don't get back soon Mrs. Walker will start selling the house and writing to Cousin Jane, and Bobbie and Vicky'll think that I've deserted them just when they need me most...What to do, what to do?'

"Yew broke mah hear-r-r-rt," whined the television set.

'Oh, be quiet!' she thought. 'What a mess...Why didn't I think that they might—? I know, I'll write a note. Daddy'll recognize my writing, he won't have to worry any more. Let's see—paper, pencil...Basement, that's it. I can get the map there, too.'

She and Toby had another fight on the way down. The clawing and squirming put her in a rage; and when they reached the basement she hurled the cat out the door without even bothering to see if the coast was clear.

Mr. Bodoni made a little extra money by collecting old newspapers from the tenants and selling them, when he had gathered a large pile, to an acquaintance of his in the junk business. Susan hurried to the pile, and searched through the top paper until she found a fashion advertisement with enough blank space to write a note on. There was a stump of pencil in the drawer of Mr. Bodoni's workbench.

'Mmm,' she thought, chewing on it. ' "Dear Daddy, please don't worry about me. I'm *all right.*" Now, let's see—the policeman. "Tell the policeman he can go away," that's so he'll know I'm not kidnapped.' She thought for a moment, and added "I'm all right." 'I'll say it twice in a row, just to make sure...Better tell him what I'm going to do, so he won't—' And she wrote rapidly, "I have to go back for a little while but please don't worry, it's *perfectly safe*. I'll be home as soon as I can. Love, Susie." 'No use saying *where* I have to go back, he won't believe it anyway.'

"Yow," said Toby, nervously sniffing at a valve on the oil furnace.

"Oh, stop that! You make me sick. Now, where's the paper

with the—?" She began to dig down through the stack. "Gosh, what if he hasn't collected the new ones yet—ah!"

FORTUNE FOUND AT CONSTRUCTION SITE

She tore the front page off, folded it small, and thrust it in her pocket. All set!

The elevator door sighed, and trundled shut.

'Oh oh!' she thought. '*Why* can't people go to bed early? Now I'll have to wait until—'

She ran over to the elevator door to see what the arrow was doing. It crept to 1 and stopped. Then it began moving to the left, back to B.

'Oh, someone's coming down!' Aloud she called, "Toby! Come here! Puss puss?"

Toby was vanishing under the oil tank. She got there just in time to seize the tip of his tail. His muscular protest quivered through her hand like an electric current.

"Oh, come *on!"* she sobbed. Dragging him backwards, his claws scraping across the concrete, she rushed for shelter behind the washing machines. There she crouched in a puddle, holding the cat between her knees and stomach and squeezing his jaws shut with both hands.

It was Mr. Bodoni who emerged from the elevator. He was holding something cradled in his palm, and staring at it with infinite bewilderment.

A long silence.

"Mice," said Mr. Bodoni sorrowfully through his cigar.

A long silence.

"Mice," he repeated. "After all I done."

A long silence.

'Oh, get a *move* on, will you?' Susan raged to herself. Toby's hind claws were sinking into her thigh.

"Traps," said Mr. Bodoni at last, with an air of decision.

He carefully put the dead mouse in his vest pocket, ambled over to his workbench, and began to search for mousetraps in the drawer. There were many to be found, and he had to inspect each one with minute care before putting it in his pocket.

At last he was finished. Now he was going. No, he wasn't. He stopped, turned around, came back to the workbench; brought the stumpy pencil out of the drawer; reached over to the calendar on the wall above the bench; and, muttering each letter aloud, laboriously wrote "Mise" under the date.

Halfway to the elevator he stopped again, and stood a long while vaguely patting his pockets.

"Cheese," said Mr. Bodoni.

He entered the elevator, and was gone.

"Woo-oof!" said Susan, shaking the cramp out of her legs. "I never saw anybody slower in my whole life. Ow, let go of my dress! Honestly, Toby, if you weren't the Walkers' cat I'd just leave you here...Well, he has to go out to get the cheese, so we won't have to worry about him any more...There, the elevator's free. Now, if you give me any more trouble I'll strangle you."

He did. They grappled all the way to the third floor; and when the elevator door opened, he raked her forearm with his claws, twisted away from her agonized clutch, and bounded into the hallway.

"Toby!" she whispered.

"Hurry!" the television set was shouting tinnily. "This offer will positively not be repeated! This is your last chance! Hurry!"

"Yow!" said Toby, sniffing the carpet. "Wow? *Wowww!*"

There was a muffled snort behind the door of the Shaws' apartment, and the scrape of a chair being thrust back.

'Good grief!' she thought. 'I can't—' She hurled the note into the hallway, and leaned her whole weight against the seventh-floor button. 'Move!' she prayed. 'Move!'

The elevator door closed just in time.

Susan Despairs

Robert and Victoria were still waiting for her, sitting on the floor with the candle between them. They looked worried about something.

"Got it!" Susan whispered triumphantly. She pressed the seventh-floor button to send the elevator back, and got out. "I almost didn't, though. There was a policeman in the apartment and Mr. Bodoni almost found me in the cellar. And oh, I am sorry, but Toby got away from me, and I had to leave him behind or get caught."

"Poor old Toby in the twentieth century!" said Victoria. "Could he tell it was different? How did he like it?"

"He didn't. Look, he ruined your dress with his claws. Don't worry about him, though, Mrs. Clutchett likes cats, she'll take care of him. I'll bring him back the next time. What are you looking so down in the mouth about?"

"Well," said Robert, "I told you I thought something was wrong, only I couldn't put my finger on it—remember? It finally came to me while you were gone. I—I don't think we're going to find that money."

"Why not? Look, here's the map!"

"Oh, I guess the map's all right, but—Well, look. They found it in 1960—I mean they will find it. That means that we can't find it. See?"

"What do you mean, we can't find it? We'll get there years before they do."

"No, look," he said patiently, drawing circles on the floor with his finger. "It's really very simple—if we find it they can't. Because if we find it, *it won't be there in 1960*. Only it is—was—will be. So that means..."

"Ohhhh..." All the air seemed to go out of Susan with a rush. "Oh, good night!" She dropped to her knees beside them. "I never thought about that."

"So I guess it's all off," said Robert. "It was a good idea, Sue, but—"

They were silent for a while. The clock discreetly said "Whirrr," and chimed the quarter.

"So we'll all end up in the poorhouse," Victoria murmured, rocking herself back and forth. "Cousin Jane isn't rich, she can't keep us forever..."

"Don't talk like that," said Robert. "I told you I'm going to get work."

"Well, so am I—I can sew or something. But my goodness, an office boy! A 'prentice seamstress! We won't be able to make anything—"

"Don't forget the house. It's a good house, it'll bring in something."

"I can't *stand* the idea of anybody else living in this house," Victoria wept. "Nobody could love it the way I do. They'll probably put up horrid new wallpaper, and tear out walls, and—"

"Now listen!" Susan said, thumping her fist on the floor. "This is ridiculous! We know exactly where that treasure is—well, almost exactly. We've got a map! There's absolutely nothing to stop us from finding it. Now, here's what I bet happened—will happen. We'll find it, only there'll be an enormous big lot of it, so we'll just take what we need and *we'll leave the rest to be found in 1960!*"

"Ahh!" said the Walkers in one hopeful breath.

"So I'm going to look for it. And I'll go on looking for it until I find it, even if it takes me *months*. So do I have to do it alone, or are you going to help me?"

"Great Caesar! *Are* we! That must be it—we'll leave some! Let's start right now!"

"Not in the dark. First thing tomorrow, though!"

"First thing! Hey, I'm hungry. Let's make a foraging raid!"

"Oh, Robert, please don't say 'hey.' "

"You hungry, Sue?"

"Ravenous!"

"Come on!"

"What will Maggie say?" Victoria sighed.

It rained next morning.

Susan sat by the window chewing her knuckles with frustration, while Robert and Victoria distractedly popped in and out of the room with the latest reports from below. Mrs. Walker, it seemed, was determined to proceed with her plans, and they were powerless to dissuade her.

First it would be Victoria, wringing her hands: "I can't do anything with her, Sue. She's writing to house agents! But what can I do? I can't say anything definite until we actually find the treasure. Oh, this rain!"

And then Robert, who could make biting into a slice of bread-and-butter look like an act of desperation: "Mama's still at it! She says she's had her cup of tea and her night's sleep, and it's no use putting it off any longer. This rain could go on for a week!"

And then Victoria again, thrusting a tragic face around the door to announce, "*She's writing Cousin Jane.*"

By ten o'clock Robert had worked himself up to such a pitch that he proposed intercepting Mrs. Walker's letters.

"We couldn't!" Victoria gasped. "Why, that's a crime! It's interfering with government business!"

"Well, we wouldn't destroy them," Robert argued. "Besides, it isn't government business until the mailman has them—is it? What we do is, we take them out of the mailbox and keep them until we find the treasure, and then Mama won't have to send them anyway. Or if we don't find the treasure, we'll post them again, and no harm done."

"We'll find it," said Susan. "Look! Isn't that the sun?"

It was. Their spirits immediately soared.

"Wait here a minute," said Robert. "Have to make arrangements."

In ten minutes he was back. "All right! I told Mama we could face our troubles better if we communed with Nature, and Maggie's making us a picnic lunch. Don't worry, Sue, there'll be enough for you too." He patted his pockets. "I'm bringing a little extra, just in case."

Half an hour later they were in the stable at the back of the property. Susan was delighted with its cool shadowy dimness and the sharp compound of straw, manure, leather, and old wood smells it contained. Swallows were nesting in the rafters; iridescent blue and russet-breasted, they flickered in and out the doorway, calling to each other with a rolling squeak. Twice they came so close that Susan felt the wind of their wings on her face.

Robert was busily rummaging about. "Rope—won't need that, probably. Spade. How many spades, Sue?"

"What?" she said, tearing her attention away from the swallows. "Oh. Just one. What we should have is pointed sticks—you know, to feel down through the dirt with. It's easier than digging."

"Hey! That's a good idea. Never thought of that. Stick. Stick..."

"Oh, my goodness!" Victoria gasped, putting her hands to her face. "I just thought. If the treasure's on somebody's property it'll belong to *them!*"

"Oh oh," Robert said.

"Well, let's look at the map," Susan said. She took the newspaper page out of her pocket and unfolded it. "Which way is north, Bobbie?"

"That way."

"All right." She oriented the map, and they all crouched over it. "Yes, that must be right—see, Ward Street goes the same way as Ward Lane. I'm counting on your house being in the same place as the apartment building. The apartment is here—so, one, two, three blocks up Ward, then around the corner and down 93rd. Right here. Where would that be?"

"Knutsen's pasture!" Victoria said in a stricken voice. "It has to be if your blocks are as long as ours. That's Mr. Knutsen's land, so it's his treas—"

"Now that's just where you're wrong!" Robert said triumphantly. "That's county land—Mr. Hollister told me. Somebody had it and lost his money before he could farm it, and now the county holds it for delinquent taxes, and all Mr. Knutsen does is pay them something to run his cows on it!"

"Oh. But then the treasure belongs to the county..."

"It belongs to whoever finds it," Susan said firmly. "The county didn't bury it, some man did, and it says here that he probably died in the Civil War. Anyway, he never dug it up again, so we don't have to worry about *him* either."

"Well, I suppose it's all right, then," Victoria said.

"Sue, what's an H-bomb?" said Robert, pointing to another part of the page.

"Oh, never mind." She hastily folded up the paper and put it back in her pocket. "Come on, let's go."

"Have to find a stick first," Robert said. "For probing. Should be metal so it won't break."

Their searching finally uncovered a three-foot piece of brass curtain rod. Robert insisted on sharpening it; and the girls, hopping with impatience now, had to hold it across the manger while he scraped away with a file.

"Oh, come *on!*" Victoria said. "That's enough—the ground will be all soft with the rain anyway."

At last they were ready to start. Robert took the picnic hamper, Victoria held the probing rod, and Susan carried the spade.

"Now," Susan said when they reached the road. "Let's see..." She consulted the map, looked about her, and shrugged her shoulders. "I guess the only thing to do is just walk down the lane and pretend I'm on Ward Street. If I can remember all the buildings and pace them off right, we'll end up pretty close. Your house is where the apartment building is" — 'I hope,' she added privately. "So, here's the dry goods place next door... we'll just take a few steps for it, it's only a hole in the wall. Now the stationery place. Um. What's next? Oh, Wilson's Market, a

lot of steps for that...Now the cigar store...and here's 95th! Isn't it wonderful, no traffic lights! Watch your step at the curb," she giggled.

"Where did you meet the old woman with the potatoes?" Victoria asked.

"Oh, down the road the other way—past Hollister's place."

"You'll have to show me some day, Sue. I want to put a marker there to remember all this by."

"A big stone," Robert said. " 'Sacred to the memory of Fortune-hunter Sweeney,' " he declaimed, " 'whose fate was decided—no, sealed, on this historic spot.' And hey, we could put dates on! 1960-1881: that'd make everybody sit up and wonder!"

"Don't say 'hey,' Bobbie."

"Stop talking a minute, will you?" Susan said. "I'm trying to think. Oh yes, Rumpelmayer's, that's a department store. It's huge, takes up almost half the block. Then there's a florist, I think—no, a bakery, and then the florist, and then a bank. Come on."

But when they reached what should have been—or was to be—94th Street, they were brought up short. Ward Lane angled off to the right here.

"Is this on the map?" Robert asked.

"No, Ward Street's supposed to be perfectly straight. Hmm. I think we'd better keep on in the same direction we've been going. That means we'll have to cut into the field."

But first the fence had to be negotiated: a split-rail zigzag fence, overgrown with honeysuckle and blackberry and sumac.

"Watch out for poison ivy. Remember when I had it last summer, Vic? I thought I was going to die!"

Victoria had become entangled with a blackberry runner,

and was feeling uncharitable. "Serves you right," she sniffed. "Papa always said you didn't have to worry if you kept a sharp lookout."

"Well, I was looking for a bird's nest. You can't keep a sharp lookout everywhere at once. Ow! Look out, nettles."

The field seemed to be miles in extent. Some distance ahead of them stood a vast tree, with black and white cows lying in its shade.

"Won't they object to us being in their field?" Susan asked nervously.

"Oh no, we're friends," said Victoria. "Bobbie and I feed them apples in the fall."

It was rougher going now. The grass was hip-high and heavy with rain; walking through it was like wading in water. Their legs were soaked in an instant, and the damp heat made them sweat. Worst of all, Susan, now that she was off the road, forgot what buildings were supposed to be on this last and crucial block. Try as she might, she could conjure up no more than a vague memory of a red-brick insurance building and a jumble of show windows. In the end they had to guess the distance by compromising their three various notions of how much walking constituted a city block.

"Sharp left now," Susan said. They trudged a little further in silence.

"Well, whereabouts, Sue?" Robert asked.

She took out the map and looked at it helplessly. "I don't know, it could be anywhere around here...Maybe there'll be a little hump over it. Or a hollow."

"You couldn't see a hump or hollow in this grass," Robert said. He thrust the rod into the ground. "Well, this isn't the place, anyway."

"We can't just go wandering around with that rod," Victoria said. "We'll miss some places and go over others twice."

"No, it's all right, Vic. Thing is to keep together. See the trail we make in the grass? We'll know where we've been. We'll go in a straight line and then double back right beside it."

"One thing, anyhow," Susan said. "The playground wasn't very big. It won't take long to cover it." She kept to herself the nagging suspicion that they weren't even on the playground—or what someday would be the playground.

They set out hopefully, keeping close together and trying to walk in a straight line. Robert jammed the rod into the ground at every step, grunting as he did so. It did not seem to Susan that the rod was penetrating very deeply.

"Thirty," said Victoria after a while.

"Thirty what?" Robert said, wiping his sleeve over his face.

"Thirty probes with the rod. I've been counting."

They looked back over the short way they had come, and then at the immensity of meadow all about them.

"Rome wasn't built in a day," Susan said faintly.

Twenty minutes later the rod grated against something.

"Here it is!" Robert shouted. "Give me the spade!"

He attacked the turf furiously. The earth was soft enough, but the grass roots were tough and thoroughly intertangled. There slowly came to light two pink worms and a small stone.

"Oh, pooh!" he groaned, flinging the spade down. "Here, one of you work the rod for a while. I'm done in."

An hour later they had dug up three more stones and a rusty plow point—to say nothing of worms, grubs, crickets, and other assorted specimens of soil life.

"I'm hungry," Robert said. "Let's eat."

"Oh, honestly!" Susan snapped, turning away.

"Isn't he impossible?" Victoria said.

"Well, who's doing most of the work? Look, I've got blisters on both hands! Even a horse would get fed by this time. All right, all right," he added feebly under their glares, "one more try."

They trudged off again, probing with the rod.

"OW!" Robert shrieked, soaring into the air like a kangaroo.

"What?" said Susan.

"Look out! Yellow jackets!"

"*Run!*" Victoria screamed.

Suddenly something that felt like a white-hot needle stabbed into Susan's leg. She screamed and fled. Another needle! She screamed again, and beat her arms about wildly. She never knew she could run so fast. For a tired and unfed treasure seeker, Robert was also doing superbly; while Victoria turned into a very deer, and outdistanced them both.

Puffing and blowing and rubbing their wounds, they gathered together at a safe distance from the humming nest. Only Victoria had gotten off unscathed. Susan had two stings, and Robert three.

"This is too much!" he said. "I don't care, *I'm* going to have something to eat. You two can suit yourselves. Let's get out of the sun a while, anyway."

They picked up their scattered tools and the picnic hamper, and headed wearily for the tree. The cows under it looked huge to Susan, and she began to drag her feet nervously; but Robert and Victoria made soothing noises of "Soo, boss boss, soo bossy," and the beasts merely looked on with mild interest as the three of them entered the shade and sat down.

"Wouldn't surprise me," Robert said gloomily, as he opened the hamper and fell to on the provender within, "if those yellow jackets weren't nesting right on the spot. Right in with the gold. Be just our luck."

Victoria groaned and rested her chin on her hands. "We might smoke them out," she suggested without conviction.

Susan was too discouraged to say anything. She sat down on a large flat rock and scuffed in the earth with her feet. Acorns were scattered all about in the litter. She picked up a few and rolled them between her fingers to feel their smoothness. Then, although she knew it would do no good, she took out the front page again.

FORTUNE FOUND AT CONSTRUCTION SITE

'Oh yes,' she thought savagely, 'it's all very well for Frank M. Zalewski. *He* had a bulldozer...Wish we did...Couldn't get it up the elevator, though. Some sort of electronic gadget? A what-do-you-call-it counter? No, they're only good for radioactive stuff. Is gold radioactive? Where would I get one anyway? Oh, golly, we'll *never* find it! How nice to be a cow...No worries; just lie in the sweet grass, looking into space, chewing, switching your tail...'

Hesitantly she put out her hand. The nearest cow licked it with a sandpapery tongue. The warm pressure of tears began to build up behind her eyelids. 'We'll never find it,' she thought again, 'we'll never find it.'

Changing History

"Ah!" said Robert, a considerable while later. "Well!" He rubbed his hands together in an offensively cheerful manner. "Shall we look some more?"

The girls stood up without a word and followed him into the field.

"Now, where were we?"

"Little further on," Susan sighed.

"More to the right, wasn't it?" said Victoria.

"Could've sworn we left off about here," Robert said minutes later. "Anybody hear the yellow jackets?"

"No," said Victoria. "We should be over *there*."

"Isn't this it?" said Susan a few minutes later. "What's happened to our trails, anyway?"

The meadow appeared everywhere as unruffled as it had when they first set foot on it. They looked at each other blankly as the realization came to them at last: there was no way of telling where they had already been. During their rest under the tree the grass had sprung erect again, obliterating all traces of their passing through earlier.

That was the last turn of the screw for Susan. She threw herself weeping to the ground. Robert and Victoria patted her back and dabbed at her face with their handkerchiefs, but it did no good; a conviction of the hopelessness of the whole undertaking crushed her. For her own sake she might not have minded so much; but she had as good as promised that the Walkers would be saved, and it was unbearable to have failed them so miserably. "It's just a wild goo-goose chase," she sobbed, "and it's all m-m-my fault, I wish I was *dead*."

When she had no tears left, Robert said gently, "Come on, Sue, don't give up yet. *I'm* not going to give up. Vic isn't either, are you, Vic?"

"No...At least, not if Sue doesn't."

"But I don't know where we are," Susan sniffled. "It's all just guessing. I don't know if your house is really where the apartment will be, and I don't know if we measured the blocks right or—or anything. I don't know *any*thing." Her voice broke. She pulled her crumpled handkerchief from her pocket, and two acorns fell to the ground.

"Here," said Victoria, picking them up. "Don't cry any more, Sue." She gave an encouraging little smile. "You know what they say about acorns and oaks."

"Oaks?" Something stirred in Susan's mind.

" 'Great oaks from little acorns grow,' " Robert said. "It's something like Rome not being built in a day. It means don't get discour—"

"Wait a minute," Susan said. "Is that tree an *oak?*"

"Yes," said Victoria. "But what's that got to do with—?"

"Oh, how dumb can you get?" Susan exclaimed, smacking her forehead. "Of course it's an oak! Here I had these acorns right in my hand, and I never made the connection!"

"What connection?" said Robert.

"Acorns and oaks! Listen, do you know what they used to call the playground? *Oak Park!*"

"Ah!" Victoria said. "And that's the only oak tree for miles."

"So maybe we weren't so far off after all!"

"For that matter," Robert said thoughtfully, "it's the only real *landmark* for miles. You have to have a landmark when you bury something, if you want to find it again."

"That's right!" Victoria said. "Ninety paces due west from the old oak! Or south—"

"Or east or north—or any point between. Or any number of paces, for that matter. Thunderation! I wish we had his map instead of the news—"

"Listen!" Susan cried, seizing them both so suddenly that they jumped. "What if you were going to bury something and you didn't want to fool with any map?"

"Well," Robert stammered, "you—you could write down the number of paces and the direction."

"No, no!—too dangerous—somebody might find your note. No notes, no maps! Think!"

"You could just remember how many paces—" Victoria offered hopefully.

"No!" Susan shouted. "Why try to remember anything? You'd do the simplest thing you could think of! *You'd bury it right under the tree!*"

A shocked second of silence.

Robert whispered, "That must be it!"

"Come on!"

How they ran! The great yellow jacket escape was nothing

compared to this sprint. "Boo!" Robert yelled at the cows. "Yah yah! Yoo hooooop!" The animals snorted and heaved themselves upright and shied away.

"Spade!" Robert panted. "Give me the spade!"

"Wait a minute," Victoria said. "We ought to—"

Robert stabbed the spade into the ground with all his strength. "Here!" he shouted. "Something solid! No rock, either!" The crumbly leaf mould gave way as easily as sand under his attack. "There it is—it's wood!" He rammed the corner of the spade against the dark surface. It glanced off, leaving a moist white wound.

"It's only a root," Victoria said. "Now be sensible, Bobbie. We'll only wear ourselves out digging at random this way."

"I guess it doesn't matter where we start," Susan said faintly as she looked about. "Under the tree" had sounded simple enough when she said it, but now she saw that the words could mean anywhere in an area of hundreds of square feet—or possibly (it was a huge tree) thousands of square feet…

"It might matter," Victoria said. "Now, if *I* were burying something I wanted to find again, I'd pick some sort of mark on the trunk and dig by that."

They circled the tree slowly, studying every foot of trunk.

"That bump is the only real mark," Robert said.

"Except for that smooth place," said Susan, pointing.

"That's just where the cows rub themselves—it might not have been there when the man buried the money."

Susan gazed up into the branches. "Know what I'd do? I'd pick the biggest branch and dig under it. Which is the biggest—this one or that one?"

"This one," said Victoria. "I think."

"Look!" Robert said. "That one's got a crook in it! That's where I'd dig, right under the crook. You couldn't possibly miss a mark like that."

"Well, you couldn't miss the bump on the trunk, either. One's just as good as the other."

"No it isn't, Vic. You can dig right *under* the crook, but you can see the bump anywhere from here on out."

"We'll have to try everything," Susan sighed. "*Any*thing could be a mark, actually. The thing is, we'll have to be systematic about it."

"Around and around," said Robert. "Bigger circles each time. Let's start under the crook, though—just in case."

"How about roots?" Victoria asked. "The ground will be full of them."

"That's all right," said Susan. "Every time the rod hits something we'll mark the place with an acorn. Then if we end up with a line of acorns we'll know there's a root underneath, and we won't have to dig there."

"That means we'll have to pick up all the acorns first," Robert said dubiously. "So we won't mix up the markers and the other ones."

"There must be millions of them," Victoria murmured, scanning the ground.

At that instant Susan gave a shriek and jumped.

"It's only a cow, Sue," Robert said. "It won't hurt you."

"Well, why does it have to sneak up from behind and blow in my ear?"

"Just curious. Oh, thunderation!" he went on angrily. "Here come the rest of them. How are we going to keep track of where we've probed with *them* trampling around and lying down on top of everything? You can't *keep* a cow out of the shade on a day like this. They just keep coming back as fast as you chase them."

Susan quavered. Her legs were shaking with the fright the cow had given her, and despair was closing in again. Under the tree, indeed! They were no better off than before. She was going to cry again...

Blindly she turned away and sank down on her former seat.

"The rock!" Victoria cried.

"What?"

"Under the rock!"

"Come on!" Robert shouted.

"But—but—" Susan stammered as they yanked her to her feet and turned her around.

"Got your fingers under?"

"Grab that edge!"

"Ready? Heave!"

"Heave!"

The rock was large and flat and heavy, but it stirred slightly. Three small grey furry things darted out from under.

"Ooh!" Victoria squeaked. She let go her grip and jumped back. The rock fell.

"They're only mice," Robert said disgustedly.

"I don't like them running over my feet. If you don't *mind*."

"Did you hear how the rock fell?" Susan whispered. "It sounded hollow underneath!"

"Oh, come *on*, Vic!"

"Got it?"

"Heave! Heave!"

Their legs and arms trembled, their spines cracked. The

rock suddenly tore away from its bed, and lifted, and toppled over. The earth underneath was crisscrossed with mouse tunnels.

"It sounded hollow," Susan insisted. "Listen!" She stamped on the bare earth. "There! Did you hear that?" She stamped again, harder, with the point of her heel. There was a soft, punky, crushing noise. Her foot vanished. Something clinked as she pulled it out of the hole.

They dropped to their knees, plunged their hands into the hole, and brought them up heavy with slithers of coins. "Oh!" they breathed, "ah!" as they let the golden eagles sift through their fingers with a slide and a clink and a glitter…

"Let's count them!" Robert said.

"No!" said Susan, suddenly dropping her handful and straightening up. "We must be crazy! Right out in the open, where anybody that wants to can come along and see us! Let's cover it up, quick! We can come back and get it tonight after dark."

Her panic was infectious. They all jumped up and looked about them. Except for themselves and the cows the world appeared empty of life; but at any moment— "Come on!" said Robert. They struggled and grunted until the stone was back in place, settled it down as naturally as they could and brushed the grass and fallen oak leaves around its edges. Then they dropped down at full length and relaxed again, letting a quiet gloating feeling take possession of them. There was a long silence. The cows drifted back into the shade, one by one, swishing their tails.

"I'm hungry!" Victoria suddenly announced. "How about you, Sue?"

"Oh, yes!" said Susan, suddenly rediscovering an appetite that she had thought was lost forever.

"Listen—" Robert began uneasily.

But Victoria had already found out. "Robert, you *hog!* You didn't leave a thing! Oh, you—you *Bobolink!*"

"Well," he protested, dodging out of her reach, "I kept offering you some. You wouldn't even *listen*. What's a fellow supposed to do, anyway? Waste it all? Here, you can have these. I was saving them for later on."

So the girls had to make do with three rather battered sandwiches from his pockets.

"I wish we could've counted it," Robert said, when it seemed safe to speak again.

"Good thing gold isn't edible," Victoria sniffed, "or there wouldn't be any *left* to count."

"All right, all right. I said I was sorry, didn't I?"

"No, you didn't."

"Well, I am, so there…I still wish we could count it. How much does the paper say, Sue?"

"Sixty thousand."

"Sixty thousand!" he whistled. "You know what, that's a huge amount to leave for the twentieth century…Come to think of it, why should we leave any? Are you sure it's that much?"

"See for yourself," she said, giving him the front page.

Robert unfolded it, looked at it, turned it over, turned it over again, and said, "Wrong page, Sue."

"It can't be—I only had one."

"You sure?"

"Well of course I'm sure! I just tore off one page."

"Great Caesar! Look—it's—it's *different!*"

Susan felt her scalp tingle as she examined the page. Most of it was exactly as before. But the headline was now

MAYOR ASKS BOND ISSUE FOR WATER

In the column where the treasure story had been there was an account of a press conference at City Hall. The map now showed the whole city, with three black X's distributed over it; and the caption said, "New Reservoir Sites Proposed By City Engineers."

"You know what?" Victoria whispered after a while. "They never found the treasure in the twentieth century after all!"

"But they *did*," Susan said. "That's why it was in the paper."

"But it's not in the paper any more. It won't be in the paper. It's just as Bobbie said—if *we* find it they *can't*."

"Yes, but—" Susan began. She appealed helplessly to Robert. "What does it mean?"

"Well," he said, rubbing his head slowly with both hands. "I guess it means that they *did* find it until you came up the elevator and *we* found it, and from then on they *didn't* find it. If that makes any sense."

"That's it," Victoria said in awe-stricken tones. "Do you know what we've done? *We've changed history!*"

"Which means we don't have to leave any for the twentieth century after all," Robert said. "When we come back for it tonight we can take every last penny of it."

Night Alarms, Morning Thoughts

"No!" Victoria said. "It would show through the water. What we should do is bury it in the garden somewhere."

"Trouble with that," Robert said, "is that I'd have to do the digging. It'll be all right in the pond, Vic—the water isn't clear enough to show anything on the bottom."

"But then one of us would have to get all wet pulling it out again."

"Well, *I* don't mind getting wet."

"And besides, a lot of it could get lost in the mud. You know how deep it is."

"Well, I guess it is pretty deep…What do you think, Sue?"

But Susan wasn't listening. Every muscle she had ached, her eyes were gritty from lack of sleep, but she was filled with a dreamy, yearning kind of happiness.

She lay in the grass with her hands under her head and gazed up at the Milky Way. Victoria and Robert rested in the dark beside her, their backs propped against a wheelbarrow. In the wheelbarrow lay a potato sack, bulging with gold pieces. Crickets trilled and rustled about them. A nearby cow worked through the grass with a juicy crunching rhythm.

"Sue?"

"Mm?"

"Where are we going to hide the treasure when we get home?"

"I don't care," she murmured.

"You have to care, Sue. It's your treasure!"

"No, it belongs to all of us. You did as much work as I did."

"He's right, though, Sue," Victoria said. "If it weren't for you we'd never—"

"Oh, be sensible! What could *I* do with it? I can't take the time to spend it here, and there's no use taking it to the twentieth century because we don't use gold money any more—it's illegal or something. I couldn't carry it anyway. And why do we have to hide it? We'll just give it to your Mama. That's why we dug it up in the first place."

"I don't know how we're *ever* going to thank you," Victoria said.

"Oh, nonsense," Susan said. "I don't want any thanks. I just want to look at the stars for a while."

There was a long silence.

"Sue?" Victoria said.

"Mm?"

"I've just been thinking...How are you going to give it to Mama? Are you going to tell her about everything?"

"Goodness, no! All that explaining? It's going to be hard enough just to explain to my own father where I've been and what I've been doing."

"Well, how, then?"

"I don't know, I haven't thought about it. Just leave it on the doorstep, I guess. What do you think?"

"Well," Victoria said slowly, "I don't know if that's the best way...It'd be a dreadful shock to Mama. I mean—*sixty thousand dollars* out of the clear blue sky! How are we ever going to make her believe that it's really for *her*?"

"We can pretend it's from a rich uncle in Australia," Robert said.

"Oh, pooh! You know perfectly well we haven't got any uncles in Australia."

"I see your point, though," Susan said. "Hmmm...How about giving her just a little to begin with? Anybody can believe in a *hundred* dollars, can't they?"

"I know!" said Robert. "There can be a note with it that says, 'From the Mysterious Stranger'!"

"How about 'From a Well-Wisher'?" Susan suggested.

"That's it!" Victoria cried. " 'Do not despair,' it'll say. 'To dash the tear from your cheek, to make the smile appear—no, bloom—to make the smile bloom on your lips has ever been the—wish?—no, make it desire—ever been the desire of' and then we sign it 'One who wishes you well.' "

" 'More to follow,' " Robert added. "Just to prepare her for the rest. Sue'll have to do it, though, Mama knows our handwriting. Will you, Sue?"

"Sure."

"How romantic!" Victoria sighed. "Mama will be so mystified! She probably will think it's from some distinguished gentleman with grey hair who's been hopelessly in love with her ever since he saw her in the park one day when she was but a girl."

"Oh—listen—to—*that!*" Robert groaned.

"You're an unfeeling brute, that's what you are. The only thing *you* can get sentimental about is *food*."

There was another silence.

"Anyway," Robert said at last, "we're right back where we started. If we're going to give Mama a little bit at a time we still have to hide the rest somewhere."

"All right," Victoria sighed. "Anywhere but the pond."

"Anything but digging another hole, too. What do you think, Sue?—Sue?"

"Oh, good grief!" Susan said. An idea was struggling to be born in her mind, but how could she think with all this talk going on? She stood up and stretched her aching arms. "*I* don't care. How about the stable? Couldn't we just hide it under the straw?"

"Hey!" said Robert. "That's it. Why didn't I think of—"

"Well, let's go then," Susan said. And then, to make up for the shortness of her tone, she added, "It must be getting awfully late."

The Walkers got up groaning. Robert took the shafts of the wheelbarrow in his grip and heaved upward with a terrific grunt.

"Oh, no! It must weigh a *ton*—I can hardly budge it."

"You take one handle and I'll take the other," Susan said. "Then Vicky, when one of us gets tired."

They soon discovered that the wheelbarrow was more easily pulled than pushed; but they were worn out, and it was too dark to pick the best way across the field, so that even with two of them pulling they could not proceed more than a hundred feet at a time. It took them nearly an hour to reach the far corner of the field, where there was a gate that opened on Ward Lane.

"At least," Robert panted, "it'll roll easier on the road."

It did. Now they could go several hundred feet before stopping to rest and trade off places. But when they had covered only half the distance between the gate and the Walkers' house, the wheel of the barrow began to chirp. Each chirp grew louder and longer, until the "*weeeet weeeet weeeet*" was almost continuous.

"Stop, stop!" Susan cried. "I can't stand it. It's worse than fingernails on a blackboard."

"That'll wake up everybody at our house and Hollister's too," Robert said. "Why didn't I think of oiling the—"

"*Listen!*"

They froze. Susan, straining her ears, could hear a faint rhythmic sound far down the lane.

"We've got to hide!" Robert muttered. "That bush—" He ran to a looming shadow by the roadside, rustled about in it, and came hurrying back. "All right—no thorns. Ram the wheelbarrow right into it."

"*Weeeeeeet!*" shrieked the wheel. The bush crackled and snapped like a falling tree. "Get behind!" Robert whispered. "Down! Hug the ground!"

They lay with their faces pressed into the weeds, scarcely daring to breathe. 'Good night!' Susan thought; '*no*body could have missed hearing that!' The sound came steadily on toward them, resolving, as it grew louder, into the clopping of hooves, the singing crunch of wheels, the creak of harness. Louder and still louder, until it was upon them, a shadow horse, a shadow buggy, a shadow driver huddled on the seat; the horse whickered softly, the huddled figure snored; and they were past, melting again into the dark, clop clop rumble and creak.

"Asleep," Robert breathed. "We're in luck!"

"Asleep!" Susan said in a shocked voice.

"Why not?" said Victoria. "The horse knows the way home."

"I'm going to go get an oil can," Robert said. "If you two stay quiet behind the bush you'll be all right."

"Well..." said Victoria.

"Has to be done, Vic—we can't let the wheel make all that noise without waking everybody up."

"Oh...all right. But *please* hurry, Bobbie, and do take care."

"Oh, girls!" he grumbled. "You'd think I was going through the enemy lines or something..." His voice faded in the dark.

Susan edged closer to Victoria, trying to make it appear as if her real intention were to get comfortable. Somehow the night was not as beautiful as it had been. The shadows seemed blacker all of a sudden, and sinister in shape; yet the one they were sitting in did not hide them very well. The pale oval that was Victoria's face stood out much too clearly...

At the end of ten minutes Victoria whispered shakily, "Sue? Do you—do you believe in ghosts?"

"No!" said Susan, much more loudly than she had intended. They both jumped, then cowered with hearts thudding. "No," she whispered.

"Neither do I—in the daytime."

"Stop it. It's all nonsense."

"Maggie said she saw her brother once seven months after he was drowned at sea! There was seaweed in his hair and his face was all blue—"

"*Stop* it."

Five minutes later Victoria whispered, "I wish Bobbie would hurry."

"So do I."

"What if something happened to him? What if he met a *tramp?*"

"Will you *please* stop that?" Susan whispered.

"I can't help it," Victoria moaned. "He's been gone much too long, and there are tramps on the road—"

"Listen!"

Footsteps were approaching in the dark. Robert—or someone else? They clutched each other, suffocating with terror.

A light bloomed on the road. Behind it a voice shakily enquired, "Vic? Sue?"

"Bobbie!" they screamed. They were up and running. The bull's-eye lantern winked out, and Robert's white face loomed out of the dark. Susan screamed again and went sprawling.

"Sue! What's the matter? Sue?" They fluttered anxiously around her.

"Ankle," she sobbed. "Oh, oh..."

"Which one?" The bull's-eye winked on again.

"Left one. *Ow!* Don't pinch it!"

"Oh, Sue, I am sorry."

"Think you can stand on it?"

"No," she wept. "Can't even wiggle it."

"Wheelbarrow!" Robert said. "It's all right, Sue, we'll get you home. Just let me oil the wheel."

The barrow was trundled out, its wheel lubricated, and Susan hoisted on board. Victoria and Robert took the handles, struggled a few feet, narrowly avoided a tip-over, and collapsed.

"Too heavy!" Robert gasped. "We'll never do it."

"One thing after another," Victoria quavered, wringing her hands. "What're we going to *do*?"

"Dump me off," said Susan. "I can hide under the bush again. Take the treasure home and then come back for me."

"Leave you here *alone?*" Victoria cried. "Never!"

"It's all right, Vicky, I can—"

"No!"

"All right, then, we'll have to leave the treasure here and take *me* home."

There was a glum silence.

"Well, come on!" she cried. The throbbing of her ankle made her savage. "Me or it. We can't stand around all night making up our minds."

"I know!" Robert said. "We can hide it in the fencerow." He opened the shutter of his bull's-eye, went over to the fence, and began to explore along the overgrowth. "Here we are! The blackberry runners make a kind of tunnel. Plenty of dead leaves to bury it under, too."

"Don't forget to keep some out for your Mama," Susan said.

Robert and Victoria had an exasperating time of it, struggling with the weight of the gold, and getting ripped by thorns at every move. They were not speaking to each other by the time they were through. Susan, wrapped in her pain, had nothing further to say either. The long journey back seemed more like the retreat of a beaten army than the triumphant homecoming of successful treasure hunters.

Carrying Susan up to Victoria's room was out of the question. Robert fetched a blanket, and Susan was bedded down in the stable on the very pile of straw that was to have hidden the treasure.

She was awakened in the morning by a fly running over her face. She did not open her eyes at once, but lay there for a while, warm, drowsy and comfortable, thinking how nice it was not to have to worry for once about the Genial Host and his screaming audience. She could loll there until she was *ready* to get up…Still, she would have to go back today—there was no longer any excuse for staying. Ankle? She wiggled her foot cautiously. Still painful, but much better; she'd be able to hobble on it, anyway.

No excuse for staying.

She sighed, and opened her eyes.

There had been a heavy dew-fall during the night, or perhaps another shower of rain. The weeds and grasses by the stable door were covered with drops, all adazzle in the slanting sun. What

she could see of the sky was covered with little quilted clouds. They had a pearly glow as if each bore its own light within it. Hollisters' chickens clucked and crooned in the distance, other bird voices were raised in various song. A small spot detached itself from the lintel, dropped, paused, hung in mid-air silhouetted against the clouds, dropped and paused again; 'a spider,' Susan thought; 'Charlotte, making Charlotte's web!' A swallow shot through the doorway, arced upward as if to burst through the roof, checked, turned, darted out into the sunlight again like a small blue explosion. Charlotte dropped three more inches and waved her legs. Susan's heart filled; she sucked in her breath. The thought she had been struggling with last night was sharp and clear in her mind.

She wanted to live here.

Well?

No excuse for staying; she *had* to go back. And yet...And yet...

She was still deep in thought an hour later when Victoria burst in.

"Sue! How's your poor ankle?"

"Hi, Vicky. Still hurts, but I think I can walk on it."

"Good! I'm so glad! Wasn't it a nightmare last night? They never tell you about these things in stories—the people find the gold and live happily ever after—no mention of having to hide from people and being frightened out of your wits and spraining ankles. Or being so stiff you can hardly move next day."

"Oh, well, everything's all right now."

"I wish I could think so! You know, Bobbie and I simply didn't have the strength to go back after the treasure last night.

It's still in the brambles!"

"Oh? Well, it's hidden, isn't it?"

"Oh, yes, it's hidden all right—leaves all over it and brambles in front of the leaves. But I'm not going to feel safe until we get it home."

"You did remember to take some for your Mama, didn't you?"

"Yes, Bobbie's got it, twelve eagles. But we can't do anything until we have the note. So could you please?" And Victoria drew a sheet of note paper and a pencil from her pocket.

Susan had not cared much last night for the idea of dashing tears from cheeks and making smiles bloom; and now, before Victoria could mention them again, she scribbled, "Do not despair. From a Well-Wisher. More to follow."

"There!" she said. "Now, I have to go back."

Victoria's face fell. "Oh, *Sue*—"

"Now wait a minute. I've got one more trip here, and I've—well, I've been thinking..." Suddenly the enormity of what she had been thinking struck her, and she broke off, chewing her knuckle and staring at Victoria's waiting face. "Well," she went on lamely, "it's probably crazy..."

"*Nothing* you think of is crazy. Please tell me!"

Susan, with some hesitation, told her.

"Oh!" Victoria breathed. "How romantic! Oh, Sue!"

"It's going to take some doing..."

"*You* can do *any*thing! Are you going right now?"

"Yes, if you can keep them all away from the elevator for a while."

"All right! Let's see. I know, I'll pretend I just found the money and the note on the front doorstep. Mama usually goes into the sun parlor when there's a crisis, and I can have Bobbie bring Maggie in, and then I'll wave my handkerchief—come here, I'll show you."

She pulled Susan to her feet and supported her while she limped to the door.

"Can you manage?"

"It's all right. It just twinges when I put my weight on it."

"Don't go out! Just put your head around the door. There, do you see that row of windows? That's it. I'll wave my handkerchief out of the one to the far left."

"Got it. Oh! The picture."

"That's right, I forgot. How about a locket?"

"Perfect!"

"All right. I'll leave it on the table across from the elevator. Anything else?"

"No, I can't think of anything else."

"Well...good luck, Sue."

"It isn't luck so much," said Susan, "as management."

"*I* know."

They exchanged a secret smile. Victoria squeezed Susan's hands and left her. Susan, her mind churning, her heart pounding, her stomach quivering with excitement, waited...waited... waited...Ah! There was the signal! She hobbled from the stable as fast as she could for the back door, the elevator, and the twentieth century.

Mr. Shaw Humors his Daughter

There was a long silence when Susan finished recounting her adventures. Mr. Shaw's expression was one of incredulity, bafflement, concern, and even fear. He stared at her, twisting his hands slowly in his lap.

"I knew you'd find it hard to believe," she sighed.

"Fantastic!" he murmured. "Fan*tas*tic!"

"Well, I know it sounds that way, Daddy, but it's all true just the same."

"I don't know, chick, I don't know. You…"

"I what?"

"Well, you've always had a vivid imagination. Now don't misunderstand me! I think imagination is a fine thing, and I've always been glad that yours—"

"Oh, Daddy," Susan said reproachfully, "you don't think I'm making it up, do you?"

"Well, Susie—old women with potatoes! 1881! Buried treasure!" He waved his hands. "Suppose *I* disappeared for three days and came back with a rigamarole like that, would *you* believe it? Now, I'm not for a minute implying that you're deliberately trying to deceive me."

"What are you implying, then?"

"Well," he said cautiously, "I think you've had a—a shock of some kind."

"Like what, for instance?"

"*I* don't know, chick—that's what I'm trying to find out. You're the only one who can tell me."

"I've *been* telling you, Daddy. I've told you every single thing that's happened to me."

Mr. Shaw gently shook his head. "I'm afraid it's all hallucinations, Susie. I know they can seem very real for a while, until you think them over."

"Look at my clothes," she demanded. "Are they hallucinations? Look," pulling down her stocking, "yellow jacket stings, two of them! Could I make *those* up in my head?"

"Well, the clothes are real enough," he admitted, "and those certainly look like bites or stings of some kind..."

"Well?"

"So there must be some explanation."

"Of *course* there is—what have I been telling you?"

"No, no, Susie—I mean a *real* explanation."

"Oh, good grief! Here," she said, taking an eagle out of her pocket. "Is *this* an hallucination?"

"Where did you get *that?*"

"Oh, honestly!" she cried in despair. "Toby, what can we *do* with him?"

Toby gazed up from her lap with slitted eyes, and purred.

"Well, chick," Mr. Shaw said hesitantly, after turning the coin over in his hands for a time, "this is all...Look, I have an idea. Let's go and see a doctor. Anyone you want—some nice kind understanding man. Just to talk things over?"

Tears of vexation spurted to her eyes. "No," she wept. "What good will talking to anybody else do if my own *father* won't believe me?"

"Oh, Susie," he said, hugging her tight, "don't cry, don't cry. I'm sorry, honey. I don't want to fight with you. I'd really like to believe you, you know. It's just that…"

Suddenly she saw the way.

"Daddy," she murmured against his vest, "will you promise me something? Just one little easy thing?"

"Sure, chick. What is it?"

"Will you go up in the elevator with me? Just once?"

She felt him stiffen a little. "Why?" he asked cautiously.

"So you can see for yourself."

"But, Susie, we've been in the elevator together hundreds of times."

"We never went to the top together."

"But there's nothing to see at the top—"

"*Please*, Daddy. Just once? Just to humor me?"

"Oh, all right," he sighed. "I guess it can't do any harm."

"Promise? Cross your heart and hope to die?"

"It's a promise. Want to go now?"

"No, I want to talk with you about something else first."

"All right." He sat down again, still looking at her a little warily. "Fire away."

She chewed her knuckle for a moment, wondering how to begin. "Now this is serious, Daddy, extremely serious. I can't stand it if you laugh or anything."

"I'll be solemn as a judge! Go on."

"Well," she said, blushing, "it's just an idea I had. I—I think you ought to get married again."

"Oh my!" he cried, throwing up his hands in mock despair. "Do I detect Mrs. Clutchett's hand in all this?"

"She's got nothing to do with it. Why do you mention her?"

"Because getting me married again has been her constant and unwearying idea for the last year. Whenever she can get me alone she talks of nothing else."

"Well, she's perfectly right, then. Why not?"

"I know, chick, I know—don't bite my head off. She *is* right, I guess. So are you. But...Well, how can I explain it?" He thought for a moment, and continued, "You see, sometimes when a person has loved another person very much, and the other person dies...well, sometimes it's very hard to get interested in anyone else. Or even to think about it—"

"Oh," she interrupted impatiently, "that's just what Mrs. Walker said. My goodness, why can't parents be sensible? Look, I loved Mother just as much as you did, but that doesn't mean I have to—well, just scrooge up inside myself and never love anyone else again. Never even *try*."

Now it was Mr. Shaw's turn to blush.

"Honestly, Daddy, I know how you feel. Really I do. I suppose it's natural to feel that way for a year or so, but not *forever*."

"Well," he said with an embarrassed laugh. "I guess I stand corrected...May I ask what brought all this up?"

"I just want to have a Mama again, that's all."

"Just any Mama?"

"No—o—o, not exactly."

"Aha!" he teased, "I thought not. I know that look in your eye! I'll bet you've got a candidate all picked out, haven't you?"

"Yes," she giggled. "That's why we're going up in the elevator—you promised, now!"

"Oh? Someone on the seventh floor?"

"No—Mrs. Walker."

"Who?"

"Mrs. *Walker*. The lady I've been telling you about."

Mr. Shaw leaned back and closed his eyes. "Now wait a minute," he said faintly. "Wait a minute. Let me get this straight. This dream of yours seems so real that you are not only proposing to take me into it, you are also proposing that I should get *married* in it? Is that it?"

"That's it," she said cheerfully. "Now please don't look at me that way, Daddy, the idea will seem perfectly sensible as soon as you get used to it."

Mr. Shaw rubbed his face and groaned.

"Well, I can't *make* you believe me," she sighed; "you'll just have to see for yourself. It'll be simple. We'll go up late at night, and sneak out of the house, and spend the night in the stable. Vicky's going to smuggle blankets and pillows out there for us, and Bobbie'll see that we have something to eat. And then next morning we'll just stroll up to the Hollister's and ask for room and board. You can tell them that you're vacationing and that some friend recommended the country hereabouts, and that you've already sent the trap back to the—well, I'll coach you in all that. Then I'll pretend to make Vicky's acquaintance—of course she wants to see you before she gives her final approval, but that's nothing to worry about. And then we'll introduce you to Mrs. Walker, and then—well, then the inevitable will happen. You don't have to worry about a thing, Daddy, you are awfully handsome, you know. And you'll be rich, too!"

"Incredible," Mr. Shaw said. "Incredible."

"Well, aren't you going to thank me? I'm giving up my career for you!"

"Your what?"

"My stage career. I'm sure I won't be able to go on the stage when we're there. It wasn't respectable in those days, was it? I think I read something about it once. I'm just teasing, though. Really I'm being very selfish. I want to live in a big house, and I want to live out in the country where it's so quiet and pretty, with birds singing and all those stars at night and room for everybody and sweet-smelling air. I want to wear long dresses that go *swish*, when I grow up, and big flowery hats. I want a brother and a sister to play with and fight with and have secrets with. And most of all I want a Mama like Mrs. Walker—I want *her*, I mean. Daddy, she's so beautiful you won't believe it! I only saw her once, and I love her as much as I love you, only in a different way, of course. And she's good, and—I don't know. I want to be like her when I grow up…Look, here's a picture of her. It doesn't really do her justice, but it gives you some idea."

She gave Victoria's locket to her father.

"And you know, Daddy, if the inevitable *isn't*—well, inevitable, we can always come back. But if we do come back it'll be for always, because this is the last trip I'm allowed."

There was a long silence while he studied the picture. "That," he said at last, "is a lovely woman. Where did you get this, Susie?"

She could see that there was no use insisting on the truth of the matter. "Oh, never mind," she sighed. "You don't have to believe me, Daddy, it doesn't really matter. The main thing is going up the elevator, that's all I really care about right now. You did promise me that."

"Yes."

"Tonight?" she insisted.

"Yes, tonight."

"Good! Let's have some breakfast, and then I want to go out and buy a diary like Vicky's. Oh, I almost forgot! We'll have to get you a costume."

"A *what*?"

"A nineteenth century suit. Now don't *look* like that, Daddy, I'll get it with my own money."

"But whatever for?"

"To wear when we go up the elevator."

"Now wait a minute!" Mr. Shaw said, slapping his knee. "This is too much! I promised I'd go up the elevator with you, and I will. But I will *not* make a fool of myself by getting into fancy dress to do it!"

"But, Daddy—"

"No!"

"But, Daddy, you can't go into the nineteenth century with twentieth century clothes on! It'll spoil everything!"

"We're not *going* to the nineteenth century!"

"Well, then, do it—just to humor me."

"Oh, Susie, don't cry—I can't stand it! All right, all right, all right—*on one condition*."

"What?"

"You'll have to promise me that the *minute* we come back from this—this masquerade, you'll come with me to see a doctor."

"You mean a psychiatrist, don't you?"

"No use pussyfooting with you, is there?" he said wanly. "Yes, I mean a psychiatrist."

"All right," she said, smiling again. "*If* we come back I'll go see anyone you want. I'll cooperate one hundred percent. You can even make the appointment now, if you want."

He looked so relieved and hopeful that her heart went out to him. "Poor Daddy," she murmured, kissing him. "You're in for an awful shock, I'm afraid. But you're going to love it when you get used to it."

An Old Photograph

I heard Susan's story from Mrs. Clutchett that afternoon. In retelling it I have supplied many details, but have changed nothing essential. Mrs. Clutchett heard the whole thing by simply and frankly eavesdropping. The good woman had thought herself entitled to some explanation, after having stayed by Mr. Shaw's side night and day since Wednesday; so as soon as she had shut the bedroom door on Susan and Mr. Shaw, she knelt down and applied herself to the keyhole. Like a tape recorder, her ear had soaked up and permanently stored everything Susan had said; and, again like a tape recorder, she faithfully relayed it all to me.

She didn't believe a word of it.

"1881!" she snorted. "Did you ever hear such raving nonsense in your life? Now, the minute I saw that poor child step out of the elevator this morning, I said to myself, 'Well! If ever I've seen hysteria, *this is it.*' Oh, that smile of hers didn't fool me for a minute. I've seen shock before, that's just the way it takes people sometimes. Why, poor Mr. Clutchett was hit on the head once by a boxful of old magazines and went around for hours with such a smile you'd think somebody'd given him a hundred dollars; but it was just daze all the time. Now, if you ask me, that story is pure invention. What's *really* bothering people always comes out in the end. All you have to do is be patient and wait, and the story behind the story comes out."

She fixed me with a significant look and pursed her lips.

"All right," I said, "what was the real story?"

"Asking her father to marry again!" she cried triumphantly. "What did I tell you just the other day! Did you mark my words? Wasn't I telling you the pure gospel, believe it or not? Here that poor motherless lamb had it bottled up inside her until she had to run away and make up this *fantastic* story just to try to convince Mr. Shaw how important it was to her."

"Wait a minute," I said. "How about her dress? You said she was wearing an old-fashioned dress."

"Why, that's nothing! She was always playing these parts in plays. I saw her myself last year at the school. She was so *natural* up there on the stage, it took my breath away. No sir, she could get any kind of costume she wanted at school. It was all just part of the hysteria."

I didn't know what to believe myself. Susan, although I'd only seen her a few times, hadn't struck me as the hysterical sort. Still, there was plenty of evidence that she had a vivid imagination; and something might have happened to unbalance it temporarily. Her story was certainly queer enough. I wanted to hear it again from Susan herself; but I had no right to ask her to tell it, and doubtless her father's disbelief would make her shy about discussing her experiences with a comparative stranger. The only thing to do, then, was to make what investigations I could on my own.

So as soon as Mrs. Clutchett left my apartment (with a sniff at its disorder, and a promise to set me to rights next week), I took a trip in the elevator. Not having met the old woman with the potatoes and the fly-away hat, I expected nothing of this venture—and nothing was the result of it. The elevator laboriously carried me to the seventh floor and stopped.

Next, I went down to the basement to check up on the week's newspapers. I expected nothing to come of this, either. If Susan and Robert and Victoria *had* changed history—which was ridiculous on the face of it—the front pages of each and every newspaper for Wednesday would be changed, and there would be no mention of treasure; and if Susan were making the whole thing up, there would still be no mention of treasure. But the idea must have come from somewhere, so I went through Mr. Bodoni's stack of papers to see what I could find.

MAYOR ASKS BOND ISSUE FOR WATER

was the big local news for Wednesday. There was no mention whatever of the 93rd Street playground. I did find a copy of that day's paper with the front page torn off; but there could be more than one explanation for that.

So it was with a feeling of going on a fool's errand that I walked up to the 93rd Street playground next Monday morning. Construction was indeed going on there. There was no playground any more, only a vast hole fenced off with boards and full of the Delta-Schirmerhorn Construction Company's machinery. I went into the foreman's shack. The foreman himself was seated behind a table, yelling into a telephone, while a short, stocky workman stood by with a yellow slip in his hand.

"Iron pipe!" the foreman was bellowing. "Six-inch iron pipe! All right, what's this four-inch plastic stuff doing here?

No it doesn't. Look at the specs again, for Pete's sake! I don't care, get it here right now! Look, I got a whole crew of plumbers here sitting around and drawing pay for nothing. Don't gimme that! Get that pipe here!" He slammed the phone down and growled, "What d'*you* want?"

"Sorry to bother you," I said. "I was just wondering if you found anything out of the ordinary when you were bulldozing here last week."

"Nah; dirt, stones, tree roots—usual stuff. Smatter, you lose something?"

"No, I—ah—just wondering. Thanks."

He seized the yellow slip out of the other man's hand, looked at it incredulously, and began screaming into the phone again. It seemed like an excellent time to get out. As I was leaving, the other man hurried out after me, calling, "Hey, Mac!"

"Yes?"

"What didja have in mind? Like finding something, maybe?"

"Oh, in a way," I said, feeling like an idiot. "I just had an idea that maybe this ground had never been dug up before—you know."

"Yeah? C'mere a minute."

He beckoned me around the shack to a private spot.

"Matter a fact, I found something here last Wednesday. I'm a 'dozer operator, see? I always keep my eye open. Ya never know what the blade's gonna turn up. Get a load of this."

From his pocket he produced a gold coin.

It was a shock to see it—a pleasurable shock. I suddenly realized that I had wanted to believe Susan all along.

"At's a collector's item, betcha anything," he gloated. "1862, it says on it. Hey, you a dealer? Wanna make me an offer?"

"No, thanks," I said. "I couldn't even afford it at par. Thanks for showing me, anyway." It seemed wiser not to mention that if three children had not gotten there first he would now have thousands of collector's items instead of just one.

'I'll have to see Susan tonight,' I thought. 'She might like to know that at least one person believes her.'

When I arrived at the Shaws' apartment that evening I found it occupied by an exasperated Detective Haugen, a tearful Mrs. Clutchett, and a bewildered Mr. Bodoni. From them I learned that Susan and Mr. Shaw had been missing ever since Saturday night.

Mr. Bodoni had been the last to see them. About ten o'clock Saturday night he had been torn away from his television set by an emergency call from a seventh-floor tenant who was having a lively time with a clogged tub drain and a ruptured hot water faucet. Having averted the flood and calmed the tenant, Mr. Bodoni decided that since his evening's entertainment was ruined anyway he might as well turn the time to account by working his way down floor by floor, checking his mousetraps and collecting newspapers. He reported that he met the Shaws as he was coming along the third-floor hallway.

They were dressed "kinda funny." When pressed for details, he could only state that their clothing struck him as very old-fashioned—"sorta like, well, the Gay Nineties, I guess." Naturally he was a good deal surprised by their appearance; but after staring at them for a while as they waited for the elevator, an answer suggested itself. He grinned around his cigar and said:

1 2 3 4 5 6 7

"Fancy dress party, hah? Costoom party?"

Mr. Shaw muttered something indistinguishable. He had an air of acute embarrassment. Susan, on the other hand, looked radiant with happiness. She smiled at Mr. Bodoni, who remembered thinking, 'That's a good-looking kid. Wonder where she's been last coupla days? Didn't hurt her none by the looks of it.'

The elevator arrived and the Shaws got in. Susan called out, "Goodbye, Mr. Bodoni!"

"Yeah," he answered. "Have a good time."

It wasn't until a few minutes later that he had second thoughts about his costume party theory. For one thing, the elevator arrow showed that the Shaws had gone straight to the seventh floor. Having just come from the seventh floor himself, he was sure that there was no party going on there. For another thing, Mr. Shaw had been carrying a large black cat, and Susan a book bound in blue leather—neither of them an appropriate object to take to a party…

"It don't figure," said Mr. Bodoni, noisily scratching his head. "It just don't figure."

"We'll be lucky if we ever see them again," Mrs. Clutchett sniffled. "You mark my words."

"This checks with Bodoni's story, anyway," Detective Haugen said, showing me a pink slip of paper. It was a receipt from Ace Theatrical Costumers for '1 Victorian gent's outfit.' "You know anything about all this?" he asked me.

I started to tell him what I knew, but he cut me short.

"Okay, okay—I already got the girl's story from Mrs. Clutchett here. Hysterical fantasy, that's plain enough. She must have had some kind of traumatic shock. Or else it was a cover-up story for something else. Somebody could have scared her into telling it. Wish I could have questioned her personally, but she kept putting me off." He pulled a small glass vial from his pocket. "Look at that—straw! The girl was shedding straw when she got out of the elevator Saturday morning. Nobody packs things in straw any more."

"She said she was sleeping in a stable," I volunteered promptly.

"I checked on that. The nearest stable is two and a half miles from here, over in the park. Nobody saw her there. The next nearest source of straw is the zoo. Nobody saw her there, either... Well, the laboratory boys'll tell us where it came from. Now, do any of you know if Shaw had any enemies?"

Mr. Bodoni, Mrs. Clutchett and I shook our heads. "He looked like the kind of man who wouldn't have an enemy in the world," I said.

"Ahh, you can't go by looks. It's the quiet ones that surprise you. But he's all right with the company he works for—no embezzlement or anything; no apparent worries... On the face of it it looks like they were trying to make a getaway. But why they would put on disguises that stick out like sore thumbs, and why they would go *up* the elevator—"

"Yeah," Mr. Bodoni interrupted helpfully. "No party up there, that's for sure."

"—*up* the elevator instead of down, is more than I can figure out. Plus the fact that the girl was missing before... I don't know. I can't work out a theory to fit the facts."

"Look," I said, "why don't you proceed on the assumption that they really did go back into the past, just as the girl claimed? That would solve everything."

It was an interesting look they all gave me.

For all I know, Detective Haugen is still trying to work out a theory to fit the facts. You may remember (if you live in this city) that the newspapers had fun with the case for several days. You may even remember that some solemn crank wrote to the editor to state that Susan and her father had been kidnapped by the crew of a flying saucer "for experimental purposes prior to a mass invasion of the major Continents of the Earth." Mrs. Clutchett, finding this hypothesis much more horrendous than anything she could have invented herself, seized upon it as pure gospel. In fact, she has entered into correspondence with the author of it, a retired plumber named Whipsnade; they have given up hope of ever seeing the Shaws again (as I have myself); and nothing that I or anyone else can say will shake their happy conviction that cataclysm from the skies is imminent, and that they are the first to know.

So there the matter stood until a few days ago, when a friend of mine, an officer of the local Historical Association, invited me to have a look at the Association's new headquarters.

Someone had left the Association a large sum of money, which had been used to build a meeting room and a suite of offices. The little library-museum was a particularly pleasant room, with its leather-bound books, a genuine Colonial fireplace and mantel, exhibit cases full of pewter, and a Confederate cavalry officer's uniform in an excellent state of preservation. But what drew my special attention was a framed sepia-toned photograph on one wall. It showed a tall narrow house, with towers, and pointed windows, and iron railings around the roof, and gingerbread work everywhere. There was a group of people on the verandah steps, and something about them caught my eye.

"Marvelous old horror, isn't it?" my friend said. "The architecture buffs here practically worship that house. Perfect example of the Hudson River Bracketed style."

"Have any idea where it stood?"

"No, not much. It could have been in your part of town, though, up near Ward Street. One of our oldest members thinks he recalls a house like that out there when he was a boy. Of course it was still open country then."

"Hmm. Is the picture dated?"

"I think so. Eighteen eighty—oh, eighty-three, eighty-four; thereabouts. Here, I can look it up in the catalog."

"Don't bother," I said, "that's close enough. Have you got a magnifying glass around here somewhere?"

"Sure. Just a minute."

He came back with a reading glass, saying, "Have a good look at the scroll-work around the porch. It's priceless."

I am no connoisseur of scroll-work, but I looked at it to please him, and duly pronounced it priceless. But of course it was the people that interested me. The photograph was very grainy; but if I held the glass right and narrowed my eyes, quite a bit of detail could be made out. Here is what I saw:

On the left-hand side of the group stands a boy. He wears a kind of military uniform, and his arms are folded. There is a terrific scowl on his face, which I suppose is intended to quell a whole army of hardened veterans; but a certain well-fed plumpness of feature renders the attempt unsuccessful.

Next to him stands a woman. She is extraordinarily beautiful. There is a bundle in her arms, a great swaddle of blankets and lace concealing what is inside; but from the way she smiles at it there must be a baby—a very warm one, no doubt—under all that covering.

A man stands in the middle of the group. There is something familiar about him, but I cannot and will not swear that it is Mr. Shaw. You must remember that I met him only once, and he had no mustache then. This man does have a mustache, a very imposing one; and behind it is the happy but faintly bewildered expression of one who has been led against his better judgment to the foot of a rainbow, and has found, contrary to all common sense and education, a pot of gold there.

Next to him stands a lovely girl, evidently the woman's daughter. She has the faraway musing look of a confirmed romantic.

With the last figure in the group I am on safe ground. It is Susan, all right. She has not yet graduated to long dresses that go *swish*, but to judge by her figure that happy day is not far off. Looking at her face, I remembered her voice saying to me, when we once went up the elevator together, "I can't make it come out right." But she is no longer puzzling over how many two-hundred-pound people can safely ride in an elevator of 1500 lbs. capacity. She has the rather smug little smile of a girl who has undertaken something much more difficult than an arithmetic problem, and has seen it through to her perfect satisfaction.

"I know where that is," I said, giving the glass back to my friend. "You can tell your architecture buffs that that picture was taken on—what did she call it?—Weird Street."

He smiled uncertainly. "What's the joke?"

"Oh, never mind—you wouldn't believe me if I told you."

“Come on,” he insisted. “Grinning like a Cheshire cat. What have you got up your sleeve?”

“Patience, patience!” I said. “Maybe I’ll write a book about it.”

All in Good Time

For Joan,
and the anonymous toucans who started it all.

Susan Shaw Again

One Friday in August, late in the morning, Susan Shaw came into my life again, more than a year and a half after she had vanished from Ward Street and the twentieth century.

It had been a phone call that told me of her disappearance, and it was another that served to bring our paths so curiously together again. But this time I had no inkling that she would be involved; her name wasn't metioned, and what I heard on the phone was mostly noise. It was the kind of call you can't take seriously. If I hadn't been in trouble with my work, nothing would have come of it. But I was in trouble. I had been trying to write for two hours, without any success whatsoever. When the idiot phone began to ring, my first impulse was to tear it off the wall and throw it out the window into Ward Street; and when I finally answered, it was in a very surly fashion.

There was a moment of silence at the other end, followed by a thin, tremulous gasp, as though someone very far away were trying to catch a breath. And then I jumped. Out of the receiver came a *BL-L-LA-A-AAATT BL-L-LAAAAMMBRM-RMRM* that nearly ruptured my eardrum. It sounded like some fool revving up an engine without a muffler. I was just about to slam the phone down when a little quavery feminine voice began to talk through the racket. I heard the word "books."

"What?" I yelled.

"Books," the voice doddered. "A box of—"

BLAHAHAHAAAAMMM!

"Can't *hear* you!"

"At the" *brmmm*-rm-rm "Historical Association" vroo*oooo*OOOM! "very important" *blat-blat*-blammm.

"Are you sure you've got the right number?"

She mentioned a number. It came through a lot of *rrrrrr* and *fap fap fap*, but it was mine.

"Who is this, please?" I asked.

She gave a wavery little gasp, and then there was such an insane crescendo from that motor that I had to jerk the phone away from my ear; and when I was ready to listen again, there was only the sound of the dial tone.

Some kind of dumb practical joke...

I went back to my desk. It was hot outside; a heat wave had been predicted. It was even hotter inside. For half an hour I waited for the next word to come, and then stood up again with a sigh. It was going to be one of those days...Well, sometimes when my head is stuck I can get it moving again by taking a walk. And now that the place had been mentioned, why not drop in on the Historical Association? It was the right distance, and I hadn't seen Charles for a while. He is Vice-President of the Association, and a good friend of mine.

I headed for the elevator—the same elevator in which Susan and her father had disappeared. But I didn't give them a thought as the old machine groaned its way with me down to the first floor. Why should I? That affair was over and done with.

The headquarters of the Historical Association is a solemn old brownstone house. The hush of the past falls over everything as you step inside. Even the air has a kind of antique taste to it —much more breathable than the yellow-tinted stuff out in the streets.

"Edward! Good to see you again. Did you drop in for another look at your favorite mysterious picture?"

"Hello, Charles. No, not really—just out for a walk to clear my head. But now that you've mentioned it, I think I will."

And while he regarded me with an ironic air, I went over to the reading room wall where an old dark brown photograph was displayed. It showed a Victorian family group standing in front of a tall, narrow, much-decorated house. The group, from left to right, consisted of a boy in uniform, a lovely woman holding a baby, a man with a mustache, and two girls. The girl on the far right had a satisfied little smile on her face; and as always, I found myself smiling back at her.

"By the way, Charles," I said, turning back to him, "there wouldn't happen to be some books here for me, would there?"

"No, not that I know of. Why?"

"Oh, somebody called me up, and imitated a little old lady in the middle of a motorcycle race, and said there was a box of books here."

"Oh? I'm the only one here who knows you—and I don't do imitations."

"Well, it must have been somebody trying to be funny, then."

"People do dump books on us, though—old junk from attics and so forth. Want to see if any have come in recently?"

"Oh…" I began to shrug, but he had already turned away; so I followed until we came to a room in the back of the building, where boxes and manuscripts and pictures and bundles of letters and antique household articles and weapons were stacked all over.

"Well!" he said. "How's that for a coincidence?"

On the floor stood a breakfast-food carton heaped with dingy volumes. We picked them out, one by one: sixty-year-old novels, a book of verse entitled *Heart Throbs*, Stodgeley's *Lectures,* little green Latin textbooks…At the bottom of the heap a battered blue leather volume caught my notice. There was no title on the spine, none on the front cover. I opened it: lined pages; handwriting—a fast loopy scrawl. Some kind of journal or diary…On the first page—

"Hey!" Charles cried. "Are you all right?" He swept a pile of letters from a chair and pushed it toward me. I sat, or rather fell, on it. He hovered over me, saying, "Glass of water?"

"No," I gasped. "It's all right—just shock. Oh, good lord! Oh, my word! Charles I—I want this book."

He took it from my shaking hands and riffled through it. "Hmm—an original document. Well, I don't know, Edward, I don't know. Mmm…" A little curl appeared at the corners of his mouth. "I might consider it."

I reached for the book, but he put it behind his back. "Not just yet," he said. "I'm going to blackmail you a little. You want this book. *I* want an explanation. Ever since I first showed you that old photograph out there you've been acting like the cat that swallowed the cream. You know something about that picture that I don't and I want to know what it is."

"Charles, I told you I was going to write a book about all that, and I did. It's coming out next month, as a matter of fact, You can read—"

"I don't want to wait another month. I've already waited more than a year."

"Well…you're not going to believe any of it."

"I want to hear it anyway."

"Oh, all right," I sighed. "Brace yourself."

"Let's see, now…I guess I'd better identify everybody first. The name of the family in the photograph is Shaw. The woman with the baby was a widow when she married Mr. Shaw—her name before all that was Walker. The boy in the uniform and the tall, dreamy-looking girl are her children, Robert and Victoria. The girl on the right with the little smile is Susan. She's Mr. Shaw's daughter. Got it all straight?

"It looks like a typical nineteenth-century family, doesn't it? Well, it is—and it isn't. The fact of the matter is that Mr. Shaw and Susan come—came—from the twentieth century. They were living in my apartment building on Ward Street not two years ago. Don't make those faces, Charles; you asked for this. Mr. Shaw was an accountant for a firm in the city, and Susan went to school somewhere in this part of town.

"One day in March last year she was coming home from school when she met a strange old lady in the street. The old lady asked for help, and Susan gave it to her, and the old lady thanked her by saying, 'I'll give you three.' She was a witch, you see. Don't look like that, Charles. It turned out that she meant three rides on the elevator in our apartment building—rides into the past. Susan took the first one when she got home, although all she intended to do was go up to the seventh floor, the top, to look at the view. What happened was that the elevator kept on going past the seventh floor; and when it stopped, and she got out, she was in a hallway of that house in the photograph, and it was early summer of the year 1881.

"She landed in an interesting situation. A beautiful widow named Mrs. Walker was living in the house. She had a daughter, Victoria, who was Susan's age, and a son, Robert, who was younger. There was also a servant named Maggie, and a cat named Toby. Mrs. Walker was being courted by a man named Sweeney. She wasn't in love with him, but she was on the point of accepting him because her money was almost gone, and she wanted to secure a future for her children. Victoria was sure that Mr. Sweeney was a scoundrel who was only interested in her mother because he thought she was rich. So Victoria had gone to a wishing well and dropped her locket in and wished for someone to come and chase Mr. Sweeney away. That's apparently why the witch had sent Susan there.

"And she did chase Mr. Sweeney away, too. She and Victoria and Robert made up a story that Mrs. Walker had been robbed of all her money by a swindler, and had just caught smallpox as well. Susan pretended to be a servant girl who was running away from all this disaster. She met Mr. Sweeney in the back yard of the house next door, where he was boarding with some people named Hollister. She was an excellent actress, and convinced Mr. Sweeney that the story was true. He took to his heels at once, proving that Victoria's suspicions had been correct.

"Well, the children didn't know it, but Mrs. Walker really had lost all her money. She told them—Robert and Victoria, that is—she never did learn about Susan until much later—she told them what the situation was, and started making plans to sell the house, and wrote to her Cousin Jane for advice and help.

"But Susan thought she could save the situation because she knew where a treasure was buried. Just before she'd come up the elevator she had been reading the newspaper. There had been a front-page story about a bulldozer operator who had uncovered thousand of dollars in pre-Civil War gold coins at a construction site not far from the apartment house. There was a map with the story. Susan's idea was that she would go down the elevator to the twentieth century—she had three rides through time, remember—get the newspaper with the map, take it back to 1881, and then she and Victoria and Robert could find the treasure themselves. And that's what happened. It was all open country back then, you see, following the map and pacing off what would someday be city blocks, they found the place and dug up the treasure. It was a lot harder than I'm making it sound, or course."

"Hold it—hold it!" Charles interrupted. "If they dug up the treasure in 1881, how could a bulldozer operator dig it up again last year?"

"Well, as it turned out, he didn't. He couldn't. After the

children found the treasure, they happened to look at the newspaper—and there was no longer any such story on the front page. It hadn't happened after all, because now it couldn't. The kids called it 'changing history.' "

"I don't get it."

"It's what's known as a time paradox, Charles. All it means is that if you can travel in time, you can, oh, sort of erase things that *have* happened where you came from so that they *won't* happen when you go back. For all I know, you might even be able to do something in the present that could change the past.

"Anyway, they had the treasure, and they were bringing it back that night to hide it in the stable when Susan sprained her ankle. They couldn't carry her and all that heavy gold too, so they hid the treasure under a bramble bush by the roadside. Next morning she had an idea. She loved Victoria and Robert, and she thought Mrs. Walker was marvelous. Her own mother had been dead several years. Why couldn't she go back to the twentieth century and bring her father up the elevator? She and Victoria thought that if Mr. Shaw and Mrs. Walker met, they would fall in love and get married, and then they could all live happily ever after in the nineteenth century. If they *didn't* fall in love, then Susan and her father would come back to the twentieth century. At least the Walkers would be saved from their predicament, because the treasure would stay with them.

"She thought it was worth trying, anyhow. So she came down the elevator, and found that she had created quite a mystery by her absence. She'd been gone from the apartment building for several days, you know, and everyone thought that she'd been kidnapped. There was a detective working on the case, and her father was half crazy with worry. So there was quite a hullaboo when she suddenly appeared again wearing nineteenth-century clothes. When she was finally alone with her father she told him the whole story. There was a snoopy cleaning woman, Mrs. Clutchett, who had been in on the mystery from the beginning, and she listened to Susan through the keyhole and told me—that's how I know about it. (Mrs. Clutchett married a flying saucer crank last year and moved across town, but I can put you in touch with her, Charles, if you want to hear all this from another source.)

"Nobody believed Susan's story, including me at first. Her father thought she had had some sort of mental breakdown, and he was determined to get her to a psychiatrist. She made a bargain with him; she'd go to the psychiatrist if he would first go up the elevator with her to see for himself whether or not her story was true. She didn't hide anything from him, either. She told him frankly that she intended to arrange a meeting with Mrs. Walker, and that she hoped they would fall in love and get married. He agreed to go because he was afraid her madness might become worse if he refused. She even talked him into wearing a nineteenth-century costume for the occasion. They went up on a Saturday night. Our janitor, Mr. Bodoni, saw them getting into the elevator. He thought by the way they were dressed that they were going to a costume party. He was the last person ever to see them. They vanished without a trace. That's a fact, Charles. Whatever you think of the rest of the story, Susan and her father did disappear. I've got newspaper clippings to prove it."

"All right, I'll take your word for that part of it. But the rest—!"

"I know it sounds crazy. But after I did a little checking up, I decided that *I* believed it, anyway—maybe because my taste runs to that sort of thing. The clincher was when you asked me over to see the new Historical Association headquarters, and I saw that old photograph on the wall. I knew it was true then. I mean, there they all are! It's obvious that everything turned out the way Susan hoped it would."

"Are you absolutely sure that those are the people you think they are?"

"Well, I'm sure about Susan."

"Mmm..."

"You're an awful skeptic, Charles. Well, nuts to you. I've given you the explanation you asked for. Now may I have that book?"

He made no move to hand it over. "You know, I thought you were going to pass out when you looked into this book. Now tell me what *that* was about, and it's yours."

"Oh, all right. I'm finding it a little hard to believe this part myself... Well, when Mr. Bodoni saw the Shaws getting on the elevator he noticed that they were both carrying something. Mr. Shaw was carrying a black cat—Toby, the Walkers' cat, who'd come to the twentieth century by mistake with Susan. And Susan was carrying—brace yourself again, Charles—Susan was carrying a diary. A blue leather book. The book you're holding right now."

"Oh, come on!"

"I know, I know! But just read the first sentence will you?"

He read aloud, " 'Daddy and I went up the elevator last night.' " His voice trailed off on the word "night," and he let out a long whistle.

"See what I mean? Now may I have it?"

"Incredible..." he murmured. "Yes, you may have it. Just one more favor, though? Will you read it here so I can read along with you?"

Mr. Shaw at the Top

Daddy and I went up the elevator last night. Poor Daddy—he was in a state. We'd had a terrible day. Everybody kept interrupting, and he tried to get an appointment for me without any luck, he was embarrassed by his costume, and when we finally got there…

"Hallucinations," Mr. Shaw said into the telephone. "She thinks she's gone into the past, and she says she wants to go back again and take me with her.—No. First time anything like this has happened.—No, she's acting normally otherwise. —Well, she looks—she looks happy."

"I am happy," Susan said.

"Thursday!" Mr. Shaw went on. "No, I'm sorry, it really has to be sooner than that.—Oh." He banged down the receiver, wiped his hand over his face, and burst out, "What's the matter with these quacks, anyway? Just because I can't tell 'em that you're rigid as a board and foaming at the mouth, they won't take me seriously. 'Nothing to be alarmed about,' he says, 'I can see you Thursday.' "

"I can't wait till Thursday, Daddy."

"We're seeing somebody today, or Monday afternoon at the latest. Let's see, who's next?" He ran his finger down a column in the telephone directory.

She wanted to say, "We won't be here Monday," but she refrained. He was doing what he felt he had to do, and once an appointment was be made he would feel better. The main thing was that he had agreed to go up the elevator with her to meet

Mrs. Walker. She had agreed, as her side of the bargain, to see a psychiatrist. Maybe it was unfair of her to make such a promise, knowing that she would never have to keep it.

Oh, dear, he was slamming down the receiver again…

"Daddy, why don't we have some lunch now, and then you can try again when you're a little more calm?"

But he was already dialing the next number. 'Please,' she prayed, 'let it be somebody who isn't busy.' She *had* to get her father calmed down soon, because there was still the matter of his costume to take care of. She was all set with the dress and shoes Victoria had lent her, but he had nothing. It was unthinkable that they introduce him to Mrs. Walker in his twentieth-century business suit, or the grey chinos that he had on now. He had agreed under duress to wear a costume, but she knew it was going to be difficult to get him right down to it; and they had to go buy one before the stores closed.

The doorbell rang. "…hallucinations," Mr. Shaw was saying into the telephone for the twentieth time. He motioned toward the door with his eyes. She didn't want to open it. The bell rang again before her reluctant hand turned the knob.

It was the man who had started to pester her with questions that morning the minute she had stepped out of the elevator.

"Hello, Susan," he said. "How are you feeling now?"

"Oh…all right," she answered, not stepping aside to let him in.

He pushed in anyway. "Susan," he said, "let's sit down and have a little heart-to-heart talk, shall we? My name is Mr. Haugen. I'm a detective."

Oh, good grief…"I'm all right," she said. "Nothing happened to me. Really."

Her father put down the receiver and said, "Another quack trying to tell me everything can wait. Hello, Mr. Haugen."

"Hello, Mr. Shaw. Susan and I were just going to get it all straightened out, now that she's feeling better."

The doorbell rang. It was the couple from next door, the ones who always turned on their television set to full blast the first thing in the morning. Ugh! Their tongues were practically hanging down to their waistlines with curiosity. Oh yes, she was fine, everything was all right, she's just been staying with friends, there'd been a little mix-up, pardon me, busy right now. She shut the door on their gleaming eyes.

"You can be perfectly frank with me, Susan," Detective Haugen said. He wasn't going to believe the truth any more that her father did...It was time to put on an act. She made her chin tremble, and said in a wavering voice, "Can I talk about it—later?"

"She's still kind of distraught," her father said.

The doorbell rang. Mr. Shaw grabbed his hair and pulled it. "I'll drop by later," Detective Haugen said, easing himself out the door. "Oops! Pardon me, ma'am."

Mrs. Clutchett came down on them like a tornado.

"Merciful heavens, what're *you* doing up, child? You ought to be in bed with a nice hot cup of cocoa. And limping—still limping! D'you mean to say she hasn't been taken to the doctor *yet,* Mr. Shaw? Why, goodness, don't try to tell *me* it isn't anything, missy! Believe you me, you neglect something like that and the first thing you know complications can set in! And you, sir, standing around like a bump on a log or I don't-know-what while this poor motherless child wastes away from neglect and misunderstanding!" She emphasized the word "motherless" with a little shake of her head. "Well, Mr. Shaw, I don't care if heaven itself falls, I *will* speak my mind concerning a subject of which you know very well what I'm speaking about. Not that I don't respect your feelings, but things have come to the point of no return, as they say, so *if* you will be so kind as to give me a few minutes of your valuable time—alone."

He threw one agonized look over his shoulder at Susan before Mrs. Clutchett swept him into the kitchen and shut the door.

'Trying to talk him into marrying someone again,' Susan thought. 'Poor daddy…and I'm doing the same thing. But I won't have to do any talking, he'll just look at Mrs. Walker and she'll look at him—and pow! Good grief, look at the time! I'm going to have to get his costume myself, or we'll never make it…Oh, and a diary! Vicky's diary was so much fun…'

She scribbled a note: "Dear Daddy, I haven't disappeared again, I just have to buy some things. I'll be right back," and dashed out of the apartment.

"I feel like an idiot in this get-up."

"It's late, Daddy, nobody's going to see us. Here, hold Toby, will you please? I can't handle him and my diary both." She peered out the door. "All clear! Come on!"

They hurried across the hallway. Susan pressed the button, and somewhere below the elevator groaned into action.

"Oh, good night!" Mr. Shaw muttered. "Why did he have to pick *now?*"

Mr. Bodoni was ambling down the hallway, chewing his cigar and carrying a bundle of newspapers under his arm. He stopped when he saw them, and began to grin.

Susan didn't care. Her project was launched now, and joy was bubbling inside her so strongly that she felt as though she could soar like a balloon.

"Fancy dress party, hah?" Mr. Bodoni said. "Costoom party?"

She smiled at him, loving him. There, he'd given them the perfect excuse for looking as they did. Her father didn't have to feel embarrassed now. Why should he mutter like that?

The door wheezed open and they got in. Oh, she was going to float, she'd have to hold on to something to keep her feet on the ground! "Goodbye, Mr. Bodoni!" she called, pressing the seventh-floor button.

"Yeah," he said. "Have a good time."

"Flaming moron!" Mr. Shaw muttered; and then the door closed, and they were on their way.

Toby, who had been growing tense ever since leaving the apartment, moaned as the elevator heaved itself into motion.

"OW!" Mr. Shaw roared.

"Oh, Daddy, I'm sorry! He's such a brute when he gets in here; I forgot. Let me take him."

Toby's claws had sunk deep and he would not turn loose. The three of them struggled for several floors, panting and *ow*ing and yowling.

"I've had it!" Mr. Shaw cried. "This—blasted—animal—gets—*out!*" He reached for the buttons.

"No!" she yelped, throwing herself against him. "We have to take him back! I promised Vicky."

"We can come back for him later when we—ouch!—have a box to put him in."

"Why can't you understand, Daddy? When we get there, there's only half a trip left. If we come down again we'll never be able to get back." She had one of Toby's paws loose now. He said "Ow-w-w-w!" blowing his fishy breath on her.

"Hey!" Mr. Shaw said—but not to her. He was staring over her head. She glanced up. The arrow had come to rest on 7, but the elevator was still rising. There was a sensation of thickness in the air.

"It's all right!" she said. "That's the worst part, that sort of ooshy feeling when it goes through."

"There's something wrong with the mechanism. I'm going to speak to Bodoni about this—it could be dangerous."

The elevator stopped, and the door trundled open. There was a sound of tearing cloth as Toby twisted free, leaped to the floor, and vanished.

"Hey!" Mr. Shaw said again. "What's the matter with the—?"

"*Sssh!*"

Her hiss was so urgent that he lowered his voice. "The lights," he continued, *sotto voce*. "Look, they're practically out. They are out. This whole place goes to ruin while that idiot Bodoni fumbles around with his newspapers!"

"Sssh!" she whispered again. "We really have to be quiet, Daddy. Don't worry about the lights, there aren't any up here. I wonder where Vicky is—she was supposed to meet us. Well, she left us a candle anyway. Come on."

They stepped out into the hallway. Susan turned and pressed the first-floor button. The elevator door sighed and trundled shut, eclipsing the electric light within. They were left in the soft orange glow of candlelight.

"Say," Mr. Shaw murmured, "it really is different up here now, isn't it? Wasn't like this a few days ago. Somebody's been doing a lot of fast work." He gazed about at the oak wainscotting, the dark velvet curtains, the grandfather clock, the little marble-topped table on which stood a stuffed owl under a glass bell and a bowl of paper flowers and a half-consumed candle. "Antiques!" he exclaimed. "They could get stolen, lying around like this."

"Daddy," she whispered, "come on, we really have to go.

You can look at all this later." She took his sleeve in one hand, picked up the candlestick in the other, and began to pull him toward the back of the house. She was wondering if something had gone wrong. Victoria should have been waiting for them. Well, the best thing now was to get out to the stable and wait for Victoria there…

"Ssst!" she hissed, tightening her grip on his sleeve so suddenly he jumped. She looked back over her shoulder. He turned to look too. There was nothing at that end of the hallway but dark shadows.

Somewhere in the front of the house there was a muffled sliding sound, and a heavy thump.

"Vicky?" Susan whispered.

Silence.

"Maybe it was Toby," she murmured. "Come on."

"Susie, I am very tired. I've been under a terrific strain since you disappeared Wednesday night. I think maybe I'm beginning to understand why you're having the kind of hallucinations you have—I mean, obviously there's something out of whack in the elevator, and that fool Bodoni has let all the lights up here burn out, and there's been some redecoration. All right. But the answer is, so what? We're still on the seventh floor. Now let's go down and go to bed."

"Daddy, will you please please just come outside for a minute before you make up your mind? Please?"

"What? My dear child, it's under forty degrees out there, and the wind's blowing!"

"Well, can't we just stick our noses out, then? I'll tell you what; if it is under forty degrees and the wind is blowing, I promise we'll go back right away."

"Oh...all right. Good night, you're a stubborn one! Where are we going, the fire escape?"

"No."

They had reached a door; she wasn't sure, but hoped it was the door to the kitchen. She opened it with care. A little draft burst through and extinguished the candle, but not before she had seen that it was the kitchen on the other side. They were all right, then. She pulled her father in and shut the door behind them.

"Susan!" he whispered, clutching her shoulder. "We shouldn't be sneaking into somebody's apartment like this!"

"It's all right, we're just going to zip through."

They zipped through. She opened the back door, and they stepped out on the porch.

The sweet summer smell of damp earth and grass enveloped them. Frogs were shouting "Brrreep brrreep!" in the pond nearby. The sky glittered with stars and moonlight from horizon to zenith. The shrubbery-dotted back yard, the stable, the surrounding fields and the woods, were drawn in charcoal and silver.

"O-h-oh!" she sighed, taking a deep breath.

Mr. Shaw made a shuddery noise and staggered against her. "I want to sit down," he said in a choked voice. She helped him down. "Where are we?" he whispered.

"Oh, Daddy!" she sighed. "I've told you and *told* you." She sat down beside him and squeezed his trembling hand. "You're going to love it in a minute. You'll see."

. . in the stable. Daddy didn't say anything for so long that I began to worry. Then Vicky and Bobbie came out. They hadn't been able to meet us because Maggie had been prowling around. Daddy made a hit with Bobbie, and Vicky approves of him too. They had some bad news, though. We'll have to work fast. . .

"Sue?"

Straw rustled as Susan and Mr. Shaw gave a start in the darkness.

"Is that you, Vicky?"

"Yes! And Bobbie." The forms appeared in silhouette against the stars in the doorway, and vanished again as Robert and Victoria came into the inky shadows of the stable. "Thank goodness!" Victoria's voice went on. "It *was* you, then! We couldn't tell whether you or Maggie had taken the candle, so we had to come out and see."

"Maggie?" Susan said.

"Yes. Oh, the suspense was dreadful! You see, we left a lighted candle for you on the hallway table, in case you arrived before it was safe for us to come down. We waited and waited, and finally we crept downstairs, and heavens!—there was Maggie in her nightgown, standing in the parlor!"

"I think she was trying to catch me," Robert said. "There's a new cake in the pantry, and she knows I'd like to forage a little of it."

"Anyway, we had to retreat upstairs again and wait for*ever* until Maggie went back to bed, and when we came down the candle was gone; and we didn't know if you'd come or if she'd taken it."

"It was us," Susan said. "Thank you for the candle. Come here, Daddy, I want you to meet the—oh, how am I going to introduce you all in the dark?"

"A soldier is always prepared," Robert announced. There was a click, and a beam of light pierced the darkness. He had opened the shutter of his bull's-eye lantern.

"Victoria Walker, Robert Walker," Susan said, suddenly feeling awkward and shy. "Mr. Shaw, my father." Her heart began to pound. It was so important that they like each other…!

"Pleased to meet you, sir," Robert said, putting out his hand.

"My pleasure," Mr. Shaw said, shaking it.

"Charmed to make your acquaintance, Mr. Shaw," Victoria said. "Did you not find today's heat somewhat fatiguing?"

Mr. Shaw was not prepared for her Deportment Class voice. He mumbled, "Well, ah, yes, I mean no, actually," and then something got caught in his throat and he doubled over trying to *harumph* it clear again.

"Oh dear me!" Victoria cried. "I do hope you are not indisposed, sir?"

Mr. Shaw rallied. "No, no, thank you, frog in my throat, I'm all right. Really pleased to meet you, too. I'm ah—it's just that—oh, look here, I'm having a hard time taking all this in. I mean, Susan's told me an incredible story about herself and you—"

"Oh, it's all true, sir," Robert said.

"Well, it's hard for me to—look, is it really the—? I mean,

what year *is* it, actually?"

"1881, sir."

"Ah," Mr. Shaw said faintly. "I see...Who's President?"

"Mr. Garfield, sir."

"Mmm...1881...I can't seem to get my bearings. Is the, ah, Franco-Prussian war on? Or hasn't it begun?"

"Oh, no, sir, it's been over for some time now—ten years, as a matter of fact. There's no fighting going on anywhere now, I regret to say, except maybe the Transvaal."

"You *regret* you say!"

"Well, you see, sir, I have a professional interest. I want to be an officer in the Army when I grow up."

"Oh. Well, I guess these things seem different when you're young...I was an officer in the Army myself, and it was the happiest day in my life when I got my discharge."

"You were an officer, sir?" Robert said eagerly. "May I ask what rank?"

"First Lieutenant."

Robert's owlish eyes grew even rounder. "Did you see any action?"

"A little. Enough to last me a lifetime."

"Oh, come on, Bobbie," Susan interrupted, "you can talk about all that later. We have our own campaign to think about now. I mean," she checked herself, "*if* it's all right with both of you to—go ahead..."

"Oh, yes!" Robert said. "I should say so!"

"I am sure," Victoria said in her Deportment Class voice, "that there can be no impropriety in arranging a meeting between our mother and Mr. Shaw."

She had been covertly studying Mr. Shaw all during his

conversation with Robert. There was a hesitancy in her manner now that made Susan ask, "What's the matter, Vicky?"

Victoria clasped her hands and lowered her eyes. "I fear it is dreadfully presumptuous of me," she murmured.

"Oh, Vick, for heaven's sake! What is the matter?"

"Well, you see—it's—I'm afraid that—Mr. Shaw's clothes—" and she finished up in a rush, "are-not-quite-the-thing," blushing so furiously that it was noticeable even by the light of the bull's-eye.

The Shaws burst out laughing. "Just what I thought myself," Mr. Shaw said. And Susan threw her arms around Victoria and said, "Oh, Vicky, why did you think we'd care if you told us?"

"Well, I was afraid that you might have gone to a lot of trouble."

"Oh, no—I just went to a theatrical costumer and asked for something suitable for the 'eighties. I never thought about men's styles changing form year to year, but they do, don't they?"

"I think they gave you the wrong period altogether, Sue. I mean, those lapels and the cut of the shoulders and that cravat—goodness, no one wears clothes like that now. It looks as strange as if he were to wear twentieth-century things."

"All right, we'll have to get something fashionable, then. What do you suggest?"

"There's Bardwell's," Robert said.

"Oh..." Victoria made a little face, "But it will have to be something like that, I'm afraid. Bardwell's Haberdashers and Gents' Outfitters," she explained to Susan. "They have ready-made clothes, but their taste leaves much to be desired...Well! I'm sure you can find something wearable there. A light-colored suit would be right for this time of year."

“We concluded that you ought to go into town anyway,” Robert said. “It would look more real if you came to Hollisters’ from town. What we thought was, you could find Jim Perkins at the railroad station, and ask him to recommend a place to stay in the country—”

“You have come to the countryside to take the air,” Victoria said. “You’re travelling for your health. Do you think you could manage to look pale?”

“Oh, we’re both perfectly healthy,” Susan said. “Why can’t we be coming to the country for a vacation? It’s better to keep things simple, you don’t have to explain so much.”

“I expect you’re right,” Victoria sighed. “It’s just that a person

recovering from a long illness is so—interesting. Particularly if the illness was connected with a broken heart."

"Oh, listen to that, will you?" Robert groaned.

"You have no more romance in your soul than a *toad,"* his sister sniffed.

"Anyway, we ask Jim Perkins where to go—?"

"He's sure to recommend the Hollisters," Robert said. "I think they have a little agreement. He'll drive you out in his surrey for fifty cents—"

"And then when you're all settled in," Victoria went on, "you could happen to be walking about in the Hollisters' garden, Sue, and Bobbie and I could just happen to be out strolling ourselves, and we could happen to meet each other, and our acquaintance could ripen into friendship with extraordinary rapidity—"

"Oh!" Robert said. "It had a better be extraordinary rapidity! I just remembered—there isn't much time." He gave his sister a look.

She gasped, putting her hands to her mouth. "There's so much to think about, I quite forgot!"

"What is it?" Susan asked in alarm.

"It's Cousin Jane," Robert said glumly. "Oh, I wish Mama had never—"

"Now, Bobbie, you know Mama would never have written to Cousin Jane if the rest of the family weren't so far away. And she never asked Cousin Jane to come here—she only asked if we could go—"

"Well, it doesn't matter what she wrote or why. The thing is, Cousin Jane *is* coming here. Day after tomorrow, in the afternoon."

"But," Susan said, "didn't your Mama get the money and the note from her unknown admirer that we made up? I thought that was going to keep her from making hasty decisions."

"She'd already written," Victoria sighed. "And it wouldn't have made any difference anyway, as it turns out."

"What happened?"

"Why, we pretended that we'd found the money and the note on the doorstep," Victoria said. "She read the note several times and then she said, 'Well! Some eccentric and *anonymous* person wished to make us the object of his charity,' and she put the money on the table. And I could tell by the way she did it that she would never touch it again…But you know, now that I think about it, I can't blame her. I mean, goodness, it might have been form some terrible person like Mr. Sweeney! I'm afraid I was so carried away by the romantic aspect of the idea that I didn't think."

"So the upshot is," Robert went on, "that Cousin Jane…" His voice trailed off.

"But what's so terrible about Cousin Jane?" Susan asked.

Robert and Victoria looked at each other and sighed.

"She's—a Tartar," Victoria said.

"I'd rather face a regiment of Prussian cavalry than Cousin Jane," Robert said.

"But what can she *do*?"

"She can Disapprove," Victoria said.

"Do you think she's going to disapprove of Daddy?"

"I'm afraid so…In fact, I know she will."

The three of them turned their troubles faces toward Mr. Shaw. He was leaning with folded arms against a post.

"It's nothing to do with you, sir, personally," Robert

explained. "She disapproves of men in general."

Mr. Shaw gave a little smile and said, "I see."

"Good grief!" Susan sighed. "It's beginning to sound so complicated...I'm sorry, Daddy, I thought everything would be simple and straightforward."

"Well, it is, as far as I can see," Mr. Shaw said. "You kids arrange a meeting, and we meet, and—" he lifted his shoulders "—there we are."

'Darn you, Daddy!' she thought. 'Can't you at least *act* as thought you're looking forward to it?' "Yes!" she said, too loudly and too quickly, to cover up her embarrassment. "Have we forgotten anything?" she hurried on. "I guess not. Oh, wait, yes! Money! All I've got is an eagle. We'll need more for Daddy's clothes and something for the Hollisters."

"Totus dexter," Robert said, raising his finger.

"What?"

He grinned. "That's what a fellow in my Latin class always says. It means 'all right.' " He took some gold coins from his pocket and handed them to Susan.

"Fine. I guess we're all set, then. We'll go first thing in the morning. Oh!—which way is it to town?"

"Opposite the way we went to find the treasure," Victoria said. "Good night, sir, I hope you sleep well."

"Good night, sir," Robert said.

"Yes, good night, good night, thank you," Mr. Shaw said.

Robert closed the shutter of his bull's-eye, and he and the girls went outside. Victoria said, "Go on ahead, Bobbie, I want to speak with Sue privately a moment."

"Oh," she went on when Robert had left, "he *is* handsome! I do wish I could go with you when we buy his new clothes—we could make him so nobby! But, Sue...he seems—a little..."

"Unenthusiastic," Susan sighed. "I know. I could just choke him! I guess it's because he's having such a hard time believing what's happening. Grown-ups don't adjust very easily."

"No...Mama's going to be difficult too, I'm afraid. This afternoon I was sounding her out, very delicately, of course; and she as good as said that no man could ever interest her again. I think her spirits were dashed when she discovered the truth about Mr. Sweeney."

"That's understandable...Still, though, I don't think Daddy and I are up here for nothing. The witch gave me three trips on the elevator, after all; and so it couldn't have been *just* to chase Mr. Sweeney away, because we managed that on my first trip."

"That's so. We are dabbling in magic, aren't we? Oooh, it's so—shivery! I keep forgetting because it's all mixed up with real everyday things."

"Yes. Well, Daddy and your Mama can think what they want to think now; but I'm sure that when they meet each other, things will begin to happen. I wish I knew what time we'll be ready, but it'll all depend on how long we're in town. Could you just keep a lookout, and come outside when you see me?"

"Yes! And then when we've all had a chance to become acquainted, we'll persuade Mama to come out and meet the nice gentleman and his lovely daughter—"

"Oh, foo!" Susan said, giving Victoria a little push.

"And then as you said, things will begin to happen! Oh, I declare, I'm not going to be able to sleep a *wink* tonight!"

A Familiar Face

...didn't sleep either, but later we took a nap on the way in. Daddy got a whole new outfit and looks very "nobby" as Vicky would say. An awful thing almost happened while we were waiting at the railroad station...

They were comfortable enough in the stable. Blankets and pillows had been smuggled in during the day by Robert, to spread over the straw. It was dark and quiet and warm. But they couldn't sleep.

Mr. Shaw shifted, and sighed, and shifted, and yawned, and shifted again. Susan lay staring into the dark, feeling as though she were stuck on an emotional rollercoaster. Everything was going to fail. Everything was going to go like a dream. It would be a flop. It would be lovely...She chewed her knuckle until it was sore.

They started as a nearby rooster raucously predicted daybreak. Already? Yes, the stars were growing dim. A bird began to carol. Above her head the swallows stirred and squeaked in their nest.

Ah, well. They had to be gone before anyone else was up, and since they couldn't sleep anyway…"Come on, Daddy," she sighed. "Time to go."

He got up with a groan. Stiff-legged and yawning, they skirted the house, reached the dusty lane, and began to plod town-ward.

"That's Hollisters'," she murmured. "That's where we'll be staying." Mr. Shaw took a brief look and grunted. She could not feel any enthusiasm herself at the moment. The house looked dingy and forlorn next to the grandeur of the Walkers'.

They trudged about a mile in glum silence. The unfolding glory of sunrise only hurt their eyes. They were city people, unused to walking, and their legs quickly wearied. Susan's recently-sprained ankle throbbed. When they reached a little wooden bridge over a stream, Mr. Shaw leaned on the rail and croaked, "I need a rest." They stumbled down the bank to the water's edge and bathed their eyes. The buttercup-spangled grass on the bank was thick and soft. They sank down on it. The stream murmured over its pebbles; heat gathered in the air. They slept.

The sun was high overhead when they woke again.

They splashed water on their faces and looked about them with revived spirits. "First good sleep I've had in several days," Mr. Shaw remarked. "I'm hungry!" she said, "Are you?" He clutched his midriff and groaned. "Come on," she cried, jumping up, "let's get to town quick and have something to eat! Oh, goodness, what a mess we are!" She began to brush bits of straw and grass form Mr. Shaw's rumpled clothes. Of course she had forgotten to bring a comb. Her father was going to need a shave soon, but neither of them had thought about bringing a razor.

How could she have spent so much time considering the right kind of diary, and none at all thinking about necessities like combs and razors? They were going to have to outfit themselves from the ground up!

"Best foot forward!" Mr. Shaw said, and they set off again.

The first house appeared around a bend in the road, and beyond it a scattering of others. And now there were people ahead. Mr. Shaw stared. Susan found that she was staring too; she wasn't as used to nineteenth-century dress as she thought. "It's real, Daddy," she murmured, more to reassure herself than him. Her eyes darted everywhere: she was taking a crash course in contemporary fashions. 'I'll have to get a bonnet,' she thought.

The road turned into a tunnel under a vault of elms, and led them to the town square. "Can't be real," Mr. Shaw murmured; "must be a big movie set." There were formal rosebeds, a white bandstand as decorated as a wedding cake, some cannons on stone pedestals, a fountain, wooden plank sidewalks, stone hitching posts with iron rings.

A mouthwatering smell led them across the square to a bakery, where they bought half a dozen doughnuts. Munching these, they ambled along the plank sidewalk past a bank, a hardware store, a saloon, an aromatic livery stable, a carriage-maker's shop, and so on around two sides of the square until they came to Bardwell's Haberdashers and Gents' Outfitters.

"What is it I'm supposed to get, now?" Mr. Shaw asked.

Susan had drawn some conclusions from her crash course in styles. "Everything," she said firmly.

They went in. A young man with crisply-curled blond hair bounded forward with a glad cry of "Yes, sir!"

Mr. Shaw cleared his throat. "Ah...a new suit—"

The clerk looked Mr. Shaw up and down with an expert flick of his eyes. A puzzled look came over his face. Susan saw that it was time to clarify matters.

"My father and I have just returned from abroad," she said. "From...Prussia. Now that we're back, we think American clothing would be more suitable."

"*Of* course!" cried the clerk, his expression clearing at once. "You've certainly come to the right establishment, sir, if I may say so. Let me show you a cut, sir, that is highly recommended among the better element in these parts."

After a good deal of picking and choosing, Mr. Shaw was outfitted in a fawn-colored checked suit; a cream-colored waistcoat with gold buttons; a snowy shirt with a stand-up collar; a rich maroon cravat; and a straw hat. The clerk was entranced. "Capital, sir!" he cried. "Why, I guess the best concern of the city couldn't turn you out any better. But I might say, sir, that those, ah, Prooshian, ah, slippers—" He frowned at Mr. Shaw's twentieth-century shoes. "May I sud-gest, sir, that the bootmakers across the square, Jackson and Son, can furnish the genuine American article?"

"You do look marvelous, Daddy," Susan said as they came out into the sunlight again. "So young and elegant. And now for the genuine American article!"

Leaving him at the bootmakers', she hurried around the shops until she had acquired a blue bonnet and a tortoise-shell comb for herself, shaving equipment for her father, and toothbrushes for both of them. These purchases, on top of Mr. Shaw's clothes and boots, reduced their funds to a few dollars. Susan looked down at her—Victoria's—dress and sighed. She had hoped…

Ah, well—maybe Vicky could come back to town with her tomorrow and help her choose a whole wardrobe. They would have a lovely time of it together…

Jim Perkins was nowhere in sight at the railroad station.

"He's at a business meetin'," the ticket-seller told them, giving Mr. Shaw a solemn wink. "Next train's due in five minutes; guess he'll be on hand for that—if he ain't been *liquidated.*" They sat down outside the stationhouse on a green bench. Mr. Shaw suddenly looked happy. "I just thought!" he said. "It's going to be a steam locomotive! It'll have to be if we're really… here. Wow! I haven't seen one since I was a kid." Susan had never seen one at all.

The station began to come alive. Wheels and hooves could be heard on the other side of the building; there were voices in the waiting room; people began to stroll up and down on the platform. Then the faraway sound of the whistle, like the one Susan had heard on her first night in this century; bustling sounds from the baggage shed; horses whickering and stamping out front. Then the locomotive was bearing down on them, black and smoky, filling the air with its hissing and the rumble of steel wheels on steel rails and the *ping* of its boiler. Mr. Shaw's eyes shone. Susan, feeling a mixture of fright and excitement, grabbed his sleeve and shouted, "Oh, Daddy, let's go somewhere on a train as soon as we can!" People began to move toward the cars. Among them she noticed a man who wore a derby tilted to reveal a wave of shining black hair, whose mustache was trimmed as if with a ruler, whose white hand fastidiously held a cigar…

Her heart turned over.

It was Mr. Sweeney.

He hadn't seen her. He was strolling toward one of the cars, valise in one hand, cigar in the other. He wouldn't see her if... There was a shout from the other end of the platform where men were handling the baggage. Mr. Sweeney's head began to turn. She doubled over and began to fiddle with her shoe. It was a buttoned one—she couldn't pretend to be tying it. Well, she was checking the buttons, then...Good grief, she wouldn't be able to straighten up again until the train was gone. Mr. Sweeney might happen to sit down by a window just opposite her...She was having trouble breathing.

"Daddy!" she whispered.

"What are you doing?" he asked.

"Daddy, stand in front of me! Bend over and look at my shoe."

"What's the—?"

"*Please!*" she hissed. She heard him grunt, and his puzzled face came level with hers. "Between me and the train!" she said. "Pretend you're looking at something that I'm showing you on my shoe." Her eyes darted right and left under her lowered lids. She could no longer see Mr. Sweeney. Her father's troubled gaze searched her face. "What's all this about?" he murmured.

"It's Mr. Sweeney! Come closer. Keep looking down at my shoe—pretend there's a hole in it or something."

"Who?"

"That fortune-hunter who was after Mrs. Walker! The one we scared away!"

"Oh! Hey, my back's getting tired, can I—?"

"*Don't move!* Not till the train goes."

"But why? What can he do if he does see you?"

"I don't know, but I don't want to find out!"

At last the cry of " 'Board!" sounded, the bell began to ring, the engine huffed, wheels skreeked; and the Shaws straightened up, gasping for air like swimmers who have surfaced just in time.

Plotting

...I got to Hollisters' all right. We had lunch and Daddy took a nap. I went out and "met" Vicky and Bobbie, and we tried to make plans. The big problem was how to get Daddy and Mrs. Walker to meet a second *time. Vicky decided she would have to do something improper and desperate...*

"Woulda been here sooner," Jim Perkins said, "but I had to see a feller." He lowered his voice. "Business praposition," he confided. The Shaws recoiled from a strong smell of beer.

"We're vacationing in the country," Susan said. "Do you know anyone nearby that offers room and board?"

"Eee-yep. Know a place that will meet your requirements in every par-tickler. Cool breezy location, a view equalled by no other in these parts, *and*—" he paused to worry at a twist of tobacco "—victuals of the highest class. Hollisters'. Where's yer baggage?"

There was a moment's pause. "Uh, it's coming later," Susan said.

"Mix-up at the other end," Mr. Shaw added. And to prevent any further discussion he thrust two quarters at Jim Perkins, said, "Up you go, my dear," handed Susan into the surrey, and got in himself.

Jim Perkins projected a stream of tobacco juice over the left front wheel, tilted the remains of a top hat forward at a desperate angle over his forehead, hunched over as if to meet the onslaught of a heavy wind, and flicked the reins. The horse broke into a creaking amble. The Shaws leaned back with a sigh.

Mrs. Hollister, a faded, shy woman, said yes, she guessed they could have two rooms upstairs.

"Reckon I could pick up yer baggage when it gets in," Jim Perkins said.

"Ah—no," Mr. Shaw said, "Thank you, but it's taken care of."

"Wouldn't be no trouble—"

"Can we see our rooms, please?" Susan said. "Thank you, Mr. Perkins, goodbye," and they made their escape into the house.

The rooms were small and untidy and needed dusting. 'Wouldn't Mrs. Clutchett love to give this place a going over!' Susan thought. At the sight of his bed, Mr. Shaw yawned and remarked that he didn't know which he wanted more, lunch or a nap. "How about both?" Susan suggested. Mrs. Hollister produced cold chicken and bread and butter, which they fell upon like wolves. Then Mr. Shaw went to his room, laid himself down with a groan, and fell asleep.

Susan was too keyed up even to consider a nap. A rickety little writing desk by one of the windows in her room reminded her of something. She sat down and brought her diary up to date, scribbling fast to get everything in, and glancing outside every few minutes to see if Victoria or Robert were about.

As soon as she was through, she ran outside. For the first

time since her adventures had begun she could appear in full sight of the Walkers' house without worrying about being seen. She hurried toward the hedge that separated the two properties, muttering to herself, "Come on, you two, we're supposed to—oops!" She slowed down, remembering that she and the Walker children were "meeting" for the first time.

Ah, here they were!

She gave them a grave look over the privet, and said in Deportment Class tones, "How do you do? What a lovely house you live in!"

"Why, thank you," Victoria answered in similar tones. "I don't believe I've seen you before. Are you taking the air in this vicinity?"

Robert's face was twitching. Susan and Victoria, despite her heroic efforts, burst into giggles.

"It's totus dexter," Robert laughed. "No one's watching. Come on over, Sue—we've met now. There's a place up here where you can go through the hedge."

"Let's sit in the swing," Victoria said.

In the Walkers' back yard, under a weeping willow's cascade of foliage, was a wooden swing—the kind with two facing seats and a floor, suspended in a frame. Susan was enchanted by it. She sat opposite the Walkers and watched dragonflies quartering the pond nearby. Robert pushed on the floor and started them swinging.

"Did everything go all right?" Victoria asked.

"Oh, yes, we got Daddy a jazzy suit—oh, pardon me, I guess I mean nobby—and he looks just marvelous, and then we went to the station and oh my goodness! I thought I'd faint—there was Mr. Sweeney!"

They looked at her with startled faces.

"Oh, it's all right, he didn't see *me*. I ducked down and Daddy stood in front of me. But I wanted to go right through the floor."

"But it's been—" Robert ticked off his fingers "—gosh! It's been four days since we chased him away. I wonder why he stayed in town so long?"

"He was getting on the train, anyway," Susan said. "If he'd been getting *off* we might have something to worry about. Now we know he's really gone... Well! Daddy's taking a nap. I'm kind of worried about him. He has this funny look as though he doesn't believe anything that's happening. Or as though it's happening to somebody else... He's in a better mood now, but he's just not involved yet. How're things at your end?"

"Oh, Mama's involved, all right," Robert said, frowning. "That's our trouble—she believes everything that's happened. It's fixed in her mind that we're ruined."

"She's going through her papers and making lists of things that have to be done," Victoria added. "She's really wonderful, you know—so brave and—and resolute. But I declare, she's carrying it too far. Maggie isn't making anything easier, either; she's looking glum and muttering about how her second sight is bothering her. Only she won't say how."

"Second sight?"

"Yes. She claims that she sees—oh, visions. Remember I told you that once she saw her brother seven months after he'd been drowned? Anyway, she's hinting that something dreadful is going to happen soon. She says," Victoria lowered her voice, "she says that she's seen a sign."

"What kind of sign?"

"She won't tell us. All she says is, 'I wouldn't be wantin' to make your flesh creep!' "

"Oh, foo!" Susan said, trying to ignore the little shiver that had run down her spine.

"Something dreadful *is* going to happen," Robert said. "You don't need second sight to know it, either. Cousin Jane arrives tomorrow on the one-thirty-seven."

They all sighed.

"Well," Susan said, "we'll just have to get Daddy and your Mama together as many times as we can before that. Now, what I'm going to do in a little while is this: when Daddy wakes up, we're going for a walk and I'm going to show him the treasure—"

"We really ought to move the treasure to a safer place," Robert interrupted.

"We will, when there's time. But I want to show him now—it might jolt a little belief into him. And anyway, we need some more money for current expenses. Then we'll walk back by your house. Can you bring your Mama out then?"

"We'll try," Victoria said. "It would be easier if she weren't so busy and preoccupied."

"Trust us, Sue," Robert said. "We'll have her out if we have to *dragoon* her into it."

"Fine! Now, just in case they need a little more encouragement, how can we get them together this evening?"

Victoria gave her a worried look. "That's the trouble, Sue. It will be up to your Papa to make the next move, but it would be *much* too hasty of him to call that soon."

"Oh. Well, how about tomorrow morning?"

Victoria began to twist her hands. "Well, you see, Sue, it's not that Mama is stuffy, because she isn't; but she does believe in propriety, and—well, the proper time for making a call is between two and five in the afternoon."

"Oh, good grief, Vick! We don't have *time* to be proper!"

"I know, Sue. But on the other hand, if we allow your Papa to commit social blunders, Mama will be put off—and then we'll lose even more time."

"I've got it!" Robert said. "Maybe we can arrange an accidental meeting. Or an emergency. Nobody bothers about what's proper in an emergency."

"What kind of emergency?" Susan asked.

"Something dangerous that would throw them together. Something dire."

"Mmmm!" Victoria said. A dreamy smile came across her face. "Oh, wouldn't it be splendid if we were picnicking somewhere and a dreadful tempest suddenly sprang up and flood waters were rising by the minute and your Papa dashed up on a wild-eyed steed crying 'By the Heavens, Madame, there is not a second to spare!' and swept Mama up in his—"

"Vi-ick!" Robert protested.

"And what would be wrong with that, you unfeeling brute?"

"Come on," Susan said. "It has to be something that can really happen. That we can *make* happen. Think!"

They thought.

But nothing seemed workable. An accidental meeting could only happen if Mrs. Walker were out-of-doors for some reason. Victoria and Robert agreed that tearing her away from her work once would be hard enough; twice would be impossible without some compelling excuse. Such as? Well...After a long silence Robert suggested a fire in the stable. The girls shuddered—much too dangerous. Victoria came back to her wild-eyed steed; it was hard to discard something so attractive. In novels, the hero and heroine were frequently brought together by a runaway horse. Imagine Mr. Shaw being thrown from his panic-stricken mount right in front of the house, and Mama rushing out to kneel by his insensible form—"Daddy doesn't know how to ride, he wouldn't even get on a horse," Susan said. Another long silence. Then Robert offered himself as a sacrificial victim. He could fall out of a tree. Mr. Shaw, who would just happen to be passing by at that moment, could carry him into the house.

"That would be pretty good, actually." Susan said. "If you didn't hurt yourself."

"Oh, I'd have to hurt myself, Sue. Then your Papa could call as often as he liked, to see how I was mending."

"No," Victoria said, "that would just be too hard on poor Mama, to have you hurt on top of everything else."

Once again, a long silence, broken only by a little crunching noise each time the swing passed a certain spot.

At last Victoria said, with an expression of desperate resolve, "I—I believe it is going to be up to me."

"What? What?" Susan and Robert asked.

"I'm going to force Mama's hand during the first meeting. I'm going to suggest that we invite you and your Papa this evening for—oh, I don't know what, I'll think of something. I'll suggest it while we're all talking together, so it will be very awkward for Mama to say no. Too awkward, I hope...You'll have to second me, Bobbie."

Robert nodded with a troubled look. "Totus dexter. But

there'll probably be a blow-up afterwards."

"I know," Victoria said, shivering. "It *is* a dreadfully ill-bred thing to do, and she'll be so vexed…I wouldn't do it under any other circumstances in the world!"

"And if that doesn't work?" Susan said, chewing her knuckle.

Victoria threw up her hand. "Oh, goodness!" she cried. "I don't know. Perhaps we'll all have to fall out of a tree!"

Meeting

...we went to see the treasure. And then came the Big Event. It was terrible—he looked at her and she looked at him and—nothing! They were going to say goodbye again almost right away, but Vicky forced Mrs. Walker's hand and I had to force Daddy's so we could get them together again next morning. I thought the situation was saved, only it wasn't...

Susan waited, fidgeting, for her father to wake up. He lay on his back, breathing tranquilly, his hands folded over the gold buttons of his waistcoat. He looked as though he could sleep that way for hours. She knew he needed it; but on the other hand, here was the afternoon wearing away, and the great encounter—the whole point of being here, after all—hadn't happened yet...Finally she could stand it no longer, and shook him awake.

"Come on, Daddy. I want to show you something. Remember I told you you were going to be rich? Now I'm going to prove it!"

For the second time that day they set off down the road—but this time in the opposite direction.

"Now we can see the Walkers' house from the front," she said. "Isn't it gorgeous? Don't you love these iron stags in the yard?"

"Mmm," he said. "Pretty impressive. When do I meet Mrs. Walker?"

She glanced at him to see how he meant this. There was no eagerness in his face—he just wanted to know. She sighed and said, "Soon now. Bobbie and Vicky are going to bring her out when they see us coming back."

They walked on.

"Daddy," she said after a while, "if you happened to be going along this road by yourself, would it ever occur to you that there was a treasure hidden somewhere along here?"

"Nope."

"Here, stop. Look around, now. If you *did* suspect a treasure, would you know where to look? Do you see anything unusual?"

"Can't say that I do," Mr. Shaw said after a close scrutiny of both sides of the road. "Looks to me like plain ordinary bushes along a fence."

She smiled with relief. "It's safe as a bank!" she said. "I don't know what Bobbie's so worried about. See that dead stick with the fork at the end? That's the mark." She glanced up and down the road to make sure it was deserted, and said, "Are you seeking your fortune, Mr. Shaw? Try looking here."

They crept on their hands and knees under a tunnel of arching canes. Here it was—she could tell by the feel. "Look!" she said. She brushed away a carpet of dead leaves to reveal the coarse weave of gunny sacking, and pulled aside a fold of the cloth.

"Holy smoke!" Mr. Shaw said.

"Feel it! Isn't it a marvelous sensation?"

They lifted handfuls of gold coins and let them slither through their fingers.

"Good night!" Mr. Shaw murmured. "It this *real?*"

"Oh, Daddy, you're enough to drive me to distraction! Can't you *feel* what's real?"

"Okay, chick, don't bite my head off. I handle thousands of dollars in a week, you know—only it's all pieces of paper and numbers. This—Is it really ours?"

"Yes. Yours. Here, put these in your pocket for—for whatever we might need them for."

She covered up the hoard again, and they backed out of the tunnel.

"All right! Or 'totus dexter', as Bobbie says. Now to meet Mrs. Walker! Ready?"

"I guess."

She brushed a few bits of leaf from his coat, and straightened his cravat. "Remember, you're wearing a hat," she warned. "You're supposed to lift it when you're introduced."

"Right." He practiced a few times. "What am I supposed to say, anyway?"

"Oh, you're not *supposed* to say anything—you're not speaking lines. You're just a person meeting another person—all you do is talk together. I'll help you if you get stuck."

They dawdled along the whole width of the Walker property without any sign of life from the house. 'Oh, good grief!' Susan thought, applying her teeth to her knuckle, 'something's gone wrong.' She steered her father into the Hollisters' yard, and they sauntered alone the hedge that divided the two properties. 'Anyway,' she thought, 'we can walk back and forth here as much as we want. We're here to take the air, after all.'

And then, oh relief!—the front door of the Walkers' house opened, and here came Mrs. Walker at last, being herded across the lawn by her children. 'Oh,' Susan thought, her heart beating high, 'how could Daddy *possibly* not fall in love with her?' For Mrs. Walker was even more lovely than she had remembered. She was wearing a simple white muslin dress. Her chestnut hair gleamed in the sunlight. There were shadows under her eyes—no one was sleeping well these days!—but they added to her beauty rather than detracted to it. Susan gave her father a quick glance. Good!—she could see that he was favorably impressed.

"Susan!" Victoria called out. "How nice to see you again so soon!"

"Hello, Victoria, hello, Robert! Papa and I are taking a stroll. Papa, these are the new friends I told you about: Victoria Walker and her brother Robert."

"Delighted to meet you, Mr. Shaw," Victoria said, with only a slight touch of Deportment Class. "May I introduce you to our mother? This is Mr. Shaw, Mama."

"How do you do, Mr. Shaw?"

"Pleased to meet you, Mrs. Walker," and 'Oh, good for you, Daddy!' Susan thought as he lifted his hat and inclined his head with as much ease as if he'd been doing it all his life.

"And his daughter, Susan."

"How do you do, Susan," Mrs. Walker said, turning to her with such a lovely little smile that she thought she would melt into the ground with pleasure.

There was a moment of silence. They were all looking at

Mr. Shaw. He flushed, but made a gallant try. "The, ah, weather was so beautiful we had to come out and—look at the flowers and so forth."

"Yes," Mrs. Walker said, looking about and breathing deeply, "it is beautiful, isn't it? I've been so busy lately that I've quite neglected the out-of-doors. Why, I might have missed today's sunshine altogether if my children hadn't insisted on my coming out."

"We, ah," Mr. Shaw plowed ahead, "we've been, ah, walking up the road—" He froze, then shot a desperate glance at Susan.

"We've been admiring the countryside," Susan said. "Such lovely flowers and birds."

"I'm so glad you are enjoying it. I understand that you will be vacationing here for a while?"

"Well, actually," Mr. Shaw said, "I don't think we can— "

"Our plans are flexible," Susan interrupted. Good grief, did he really mean what he had started to say? She hurried on: "We find life in the city very tiring—indeed, there are days when I can hardly stand it. Coming to the country is like coming to a whole new world."

"Yes—the loveliest of all worlds," Mrs. Walker said, looking around her again. Her face grew sad, and her eyes brightened with tears. 'Oh, you dumb cluck!' Susan raged at herself. 'That was the wrong thing to say. She thinks she has to lose all this and go live in the city.'

Mrs. Walker's back stiffened, and she turned again to the Shaws with her face composed. "Forgive me, Mr. Shaw. You find us at a difficult moment, I'm afraid. Our circumstances have altered, and we are all a little upset."

"Oh. I'm sorry," Mr. Shaw said. "If there's any way I can help—"

"Thank you, no. I appreciate your concern, but we have matters well in hand, and assistance will be arriving soon... Well, I do hope you have a pleasant vacation, and that you may go back to the city refreshed. It was a pleasure to meet you, Mr. Shaw; and you too, Susan."

'No, wait!' Susan thought in a panic. 'We can't say goodbye now! *Nothing's happened yet!'* But Mrs. Walker was turning to go, her father was saying "My pleasure," and lifting his hand to tip his hat again...

Susan shot a desperate glance at Victoria.

Victoria's face turned scarlet. She said, "M-Mama?" It came out in a strangled beat.

"Yes, dear?"

"Could we not—invite—Mr. Shaw and Susan over this evening—to—to—to look at our magic lantern pictures?"

"Oh, yes, Mama!" Robert put in with feverish brightness. "I believe Susan told us that Mr. Shaw was in the army. Perhaps he'd like to see my views of the Great Battlefields of Europe!"

"*Children!"* Mrs. Walker froze for an instant, then turned back to the Shaws. Her cheeks were pink. "Do please forgive my unruly brood, Mr. Shaw! They sometimes allow their impetuousness to overcome their good breeding."

"Oh, I understand," Mr. Shaw said, smiling. "Susan sometimes does the same. *I* know what it is to be a parent."

She gave him a grateful smile and said, "Children, if you wish to see more of Susan, you have my permission; provided, of course, that she has her Papa's permission to see more of you."

"Oh, absolutely," Mr. Shaw said.

"Mama," Victoria said, turning if possible even redder than before, "could we—invite them—tomorrow morning for—for?"

"For tea?" Robert croaked.

Mrs. Walker was so thunderstruck that she seemed for an instant to forget the Shaws. "*Tea?*" she asked. "In the *morning?*"

"Cousin Jane will be here in the afternoon, Mama," Robert faltered, "and then..."

Victoria burst into tears. "Oh, Mama," she sobbed, "I know it's dreadfully improper, but our poor dead house *deserves* to have one more happy scene in it before we—before we have to—oh, oh, oh, oh!"

"There, there," Mrs. Walker murmured. She put her arms around Victoria. Her own eyes were brimming again. "I seem to have to ask your forgiveness very often, Mr. Shaw! My daughter is strongly attached to our house, and—well, you see, we are forced to give it up."

"Oh!" Susan cried. "How dreadful for you. I'm so sorry."

Mr. Shaw murmured, and looked at Mrs. Walker with an expression of troubled concern.

"I believe," Victoria hiccupped, "that I could—rest content if we could—offer the hospitality of our dear house—once more before we—leave it forever."

A musing look came over Mrs. Walker's face. "Yes," she said, half to herself, "we have been very happy in our house...Perhaps we *could* express our gratitude by—" She gave a wry little smile. "Mr. Shaw, Susan, pray do not think us absurd or forward. If you can countenance the impropriety of it, please come and take tea with us tomorrow morning. The afternoon,

I'm afraid, will be taken up with business. Shall we say ten-thirty? Think of it as a kindness to us—helping us to say good-bye."

"I'm awfully sorry about your house," Mr. Shaw said. "It must be a terrible blow. And I appreciate your very kind invitation. But the fact is—"

Good heavens—*he was going to refuse!* She had to act fast.

"Oh, we'd just love to come!" Susan cried. Hoping that the hedge would hide the gesture from Mrs. Walker, she reached out with her foot and pressed down hard on her father's toe. "I don't think it's absurd or improper or anything like that."

"But really," Mr. Shaw said, sliding his foot out from under hers, "I'm afraid—"

He was going to ruin everything! She couldn't let him do it.

She screamed.

They all jumped and looked at her with startled faces. She twisted her mouth into a grimace of pain, clutched her knee in both hands, and began to hop backwards. "Yellow jackets!" she shrieked. "Look out!"

She could see understanding flash into Robert's face. "Great Caesar!" he cried. "They're swarming in the hedge! Run, Mama! Run, Vick!"

Susan grabbed her father's hand and yelled, "Run, Daddy!"

As the Shaws and Walkers fled in opposite directions, Victoria called back over her shoulder, "Ten-thirty tomorrow morning!" And Susan answered, "We'll be there!"

The Shaws came to rest on the Hollisters' veranda.

"Good night!" Mr. Shaw panted. "We'd better get a cold wet cloth. Does it hurt bad?"

"Hurts," she said, bending over and hugging her imaginary

sting. She was having trouble suppressing a triumphant giggle. "It's—hoo!—all right, Daddy, really. I can stand it."

"What a devil of a time for yellow jackets to start acting up! I was just about to turn down her invitation."

"Why?"

"Because we can't accept it, that's why. We're going to send her a note, or go back over and make our apologies."

She pretended amazement, but her heart was contracting with dread. "Why can't we accept it?"

"We're not going to be here."

"But—"

"No ifs, ands or buts. We're going back to the twentieth century as soon as we can possibly get to the elevator. Tonight."

Mr. Hollister Discourses

...had a discussion. Daddy was right in a way—he had done what he had said he'd do, since Mrs. Walker hadn't bowled him over, why shouldn't we go back? I could tell, though, that all we needed was a little more time. Mr. Hollister gave us the time, but he almost killed us doing it...

"Oh, Daddy," she moaned.

"Now, look here, chick," Mr. Shaw said, "it's time we got things straightened out." He sat down on the veranda steps, took off his hat, and mopped his brow. "I've been very patient with you so far...We had a bargain, remember?"

She had sunk down on the steps beside him. She nodded her head, too miserable to speak.

"Your part of the bargain was that you'd accept some professional help as soon as I could get an appointment. Well, maybe we can forget that. My part of the bargain was that I agreed to come up the elevator with you in costume to meet a certain lady. And I've done it. I did *not* agree to lose another night's sleep and walk my legs off and go through a lot of folderol with new clothes and hide-and-seek at the railroad station and so forth and so on. But I've done all that too. Now I want to go back."

Sussna shook herself free of the numbness that was threatening to settle over her.

"Daddy," she said, "when you saw Mrs. Walker, didn't—didn't anything happen? Didn't you *feel* anything?"

"Well, you were right about her—she is a beautiful woman. I felt the usual amount of interest and attraction that I feel when I'm talking to a beautiful woman."

"Was that all?"

"Well, I felt admiration for her—I think she's very gallant. I felt sorry for her because she's feeling bad. I felt—oh, well, I'll be honest with you. What I was feeling most of all was, 'I'll be glad when this is over.' "

"Oh…"

"Oh, Susie, you look so crushed! Did you really think I was just going to up and fall in love? Like that?" He snapped his fingers.

She gulped and nodded.

"You've been watching too many movies on that television set, chick. That's not the way things happen in real life."

"But they could happen that way, couldn't they?" she insisted.

"Oh, I guess so…I'll concede the point that I could possibly fall in love with her. She *is* gallant and beautiful and appealing, and if she belonged to my own time, I—But that's the thing right there, Susie: time. You and I belong to the twentieth century, not here."

"Do you really *like* the twentieth century, Daddy?"

"It's not a question whether I like it or not. It's our time. It's our place. It's where we know what to do and what to say. It's where your school is and where my job is."

"Oh, school!" she snorted, waving her hand. "And you're not all that crazy about your job, either. Are you?"

"Well, it's not the most exciting job in the world, no. But I know how to do it, and a lot of people rely on me to do it, and I do it well."

"Oh, Daddy…"

"I know, I know," he said with a rueful little laugh. "It must sound very uninspiring…I guess it's the difference between being young and being grown up. When you're young, you think everything you want to happen, will. When you're grown up you learn to accept the fact that most of it won't. I'm sorry that's the way it is, but it is."

"But, Daddy, if—"

"So to get back where we started from: we had a bargain. I've fulfilled my part of it. As soon as we can get back to the elevator tonight we're going home."

Well, maybe he thought the subject was closed; but as far as she was concerned, it wasn't. She had recovered from the initial shock by now, and hope was beginning to reassert itself. He had said so many things that hope could fasten on! "A beautiful woman," he had admitted without hesitation. "Gallant," he had said. "Very appealing. I could very possibly fall in love with her…" His exact words!—well, almost exact. 'Good grief!' she thought, 'he's right on the edge already. He's not willing to recognize it, that's the trouble. Why, I bet the real reason he's so eager to get back is because he's running away! He's making up all those fuddy-duddy excuses about school and his job and "our time" because he's *afraid* of falling in love…Oh, there just has to be way to keep him here a little longer, so things can have time to develop!'

There was.

She almost fell off the steps as the solution hit her. It was so simple and so foolproof! They couldn't go back to the twentieth century if the doors of the Walkers' house were locked. All it required was a word to Victoria or Robert…So they *would* be here tomorrow, after all; and being here, they could accept Mrs. Walker's invitation to tea; and for an hour at least (maybe more!) Mrs. Walker's beauty and gallantry and appeal could make headway against her father's reluctance. And if still *more* time were needed—well, she and Victoria and Robert would think of something.

A lathered horse appeared out on the road, drawing a dilapidated buggy. It turned in through the gate and headed directly toward them. The driver had a familiar appearance.

"It's Uncle Sam, right out of a cartoon!" Mr. Shaw said in a low voice. "A seedy Uncle Sam." The resemblance was so comic that Susan burst into giggles.

Mrs. Hollister emerged from the house, wiping her hands on her apron. "There's the mister," she murmured.

He drew up by the veranda, threw the reins around the stone hitching post, and came toward them, wagging his grey goatee and emitting loud nasal sounds.

"These're the new boarders, Hiram," Mrs. Hollister mumbled.

"N-yas!" Mr. Hollister brayed, displaying large horsey teeth and bearing down on the Shaws with his hand extended.

"Mr. Shaw," Mrs. Hollister murmured at the ceiling. "Miss Shaw."

"A very rare and welcome privilege, sir! And this little lady!" Mr. Hollister's voice dropped four whole tones. He whipped off his mangy stone-pipe hat, pressed it against the frayed edging and food spots on his waistcoat, bowed over it and intoned, "A radiant vision of—ha—budding young womanhood."

Susan curtseyed. Her face was red with the effort of keeping her embarrassed laughter down.

Mr. Hollister's voice resumed it's original pitch. "I sincerely hope and trust, sir, that you propose to stop in these parts for an extensive length of time."

"I don't know," Mr. Shaw said. "Probably not very long. I—"

"Grieved to hear it, sir, acutely grieved. Let me entertain the idea, sir, that further acquaintance with this vicinity will lead you to revise your plans. I believe there is more opportunity here, sir, then is to be found anywhere in the United States. Why, the very air you are now breathing, sir—" his voice performed its four-tone plunge "—the—ha—salubricity of this air, sir, is a matter of record at the State capitol itself. Fact. The fertility of the soil hereabouts—"

"Hiram," Mrs. Hollister murmured. "Supper."

"N-yas. *If* you will pardon me for a brief interim, sir." Wagging his goatee and braying through his nose, Mr. Hollister went off to stable his horse.

"If you want to wash up," Mrs. Hollister mumbled. The Shaws followed her to a lean-to shed in back of the house, where they washed their hands with yellow soap under a pump, and tried to dry them on a dank roller towel. 'I'll have to see Vicky and Bobbie right after dinner about locking up,' Susan thought. She felt a twinge of conscience. Was it right to prevent their return? Her father *had* done everything she had asked… Ugh, this towel! She dropped it, and wiped her hands on her dress. 'It's only for one more day,' she promised that nagging voice within. 'Just to make sure.'

Dinner was a plentiful amount of roast beef, potatoes, onions and gravy, all glistening with grease. In a while Mr. Hollister returned, smelling very horsey and braying. He took up his oration exactly where he had left off.

"The fertility of the soil in these parts, sir, is nothing short of phenomenal. A bumper crop is guaranteed each season. The water, sir, has a balanced mineral content that ensures health of man and beast. The local climate is equalled by none. In short, sir, the spot has been chosen by—ha—Providence. A man of means, sir, could do no better than to invest those means right here. And consider this, sir." His voice dropped. "Progress, sir. Growth." He pointed a knobby index finger over his left shoulder. "The city, sir, is extending its enriching boundaries in this direction. If the currency question, sir, were to be settled as every right-thinking citizen of this Republic knows it should be settled—" He suddenly paused with upraised hand. "But, perhaps, sir, I am treading on delicate ground. May I ask, sir, where are you—ha—political sympathies lie?"

"Now, Hiram," Mrs. Hollister murmured.

Mr. Shaw roused himself. "Well, ah," he said. He looked at Susan. She looked back. He shrugged. "Last election I voted Democratic, for all the good it did me."

"N-yas!" Mr. Hollister brayed. "I had only to look at you, sir, to divine that you were a man of sound politics! The name of Democrat may have its ups and downs, sir, but show me a man that calls himself Republican, and I'll show you either a misguided fool or a scoundrel. The Republican machine, sir—"

"Now, Hiram."

"—is the most devilish engine ever constructed for the oppression of mankind. The vast majority of the populace of this continent groans under its yoke, sir, while a handful of thieves and parasites battens on the lifeblood of—"

The Shaws' eyes glazed. Their dinner settled heavily in their stomachs; a foggy torpor overcame their spirits. In some rapidly dimming corner of her mind Susan recalled that there was something she wanted to do after dinner, but what it was she could no longer remember. Mr. Hollister contrived, without a second's interruption in the flood of words, to light a powerful stogie. Its fumes finally roused them sufficiently to push back from the table and stagger out to the veranda. He pursued them, relentlessly braying. They fell into a prolonged stupor, from which Mr. Shaw at last rescued them only by a superhuman recovery of will.

"Bedtime," he mumbled, struggling to his feet like a man who has been repeatedly knocked down with a club.

"One more point, sir," Mr. Hollister trumpeted, thrusting

the glowing tip of his third cigar at them through the dark. "The recent merger of the telegraph companies is but one more sinister straw in the wind. You may count on it, sir, that the foul hand of the Republican machine was tightly grasping the controls. I have no hesitation in asserting—"

"Goo'night," Mr. Shaw croaked. He grabbed Susan's hand pulling her from her wicker chair. Numbly they crawled up the stairs. Mr. Hollister's denunciation flowed on behind them, unabated.

"Remember," Mr. Shaw muttered thickly, nodding in the direction of the Walkers' house.

"Mm-mm," she murmured, feeling too bludgeoned to know whether she was saying yes or no.

They crawled into their respective beds. 'Daddy can wake us up,' she thought, falling instantly asleep. After an interval of darkness she found herself in the elevator with him, going down, sinking away from the ruin of her hopes. She raised her face to cry out. The light bulb in the ceiling blazed so brightly that she had to throw her hand to cover her eyes. The movement woke her up. Her room was golden with sunshine, and outside a rooster shouted that she had been reprieved.

Singular Behavior of Maggie

...saved for another day, and I thought it was a good omen. Daddy said yes we could go back to the Walkers' for tea now, but we would take the elevator first chance we got. I decided not to let there be a chance. We went over at 10:30. Vicky and Bobbie opened the door and the minute I saw them I knew something awful had happened...

"It's fate, Daddy! Supposed we *had* been able to stay awake last night until it was safe to take the elevator—think about how worn out we'd be now! I'd be falling asleep in class, and you'd be making such awful mistakes at work that your company would lose thousands of dollars!"

He was not amused. But she was too happy to care. It did seem that fate was intervening in their favor, and if her father couldn't see it that way, it was because he hadn't realized yet what was good for him.

"Well, anyway," she went on, "since we are still here, and since we didn't get a chance to refuse Mrs. Walker's invitation, we might as well go there for tea, don't you think?"

"Yes," he answered, so readily that she was startled. Had he changed his mind? "And," he continued, "if there's any chance of getting to that elevator while we're there—any chance at all—we're going to grab it."

"Oh," she said.

"As a matter of fact, I don't see why we even have to wait for a chance. Why can't we just make our apologies and say goodbye and *go?"*

She was aghast. "You mean right in front of everybody?"

"Sure, why not? Robert and Victoria know all about it—they've seen it in operation, haven't they? They could explain it to Mrs. Walker. *We* could explain it to her, for that matter."

"Oh no!"

"Why not, for heaven's sake?"

"Be-be-because," she stammered. Her mind was racing to think of some way to cut off this dreadful line of reasoning. "Because...I mean we just *can't.* It's her house, and she—she... Would you really be cruel enough to give poor Mrs. Walker that kind of shock? 'Oh, pardon us, Mrs. Walker, we have to go now,' and then a wall *in her own house* opens up and swallows us alive. That's what it would look like to her, even if we explained it to her. Why, Daddy, she's under such a strain already, something like that could drive her right over the edge!"

"Oh, all right, all right," he said, rubbing his face. "Not in front of her, then: I'm willing to spare her feelings. But if she leaves us to ourselves for any reason, or if we can think of any excuse to leave her—down we go!"

She sighed, hoping that he would take it as agreement on her part, and they were silent for a while. "We'd better get ready," she said at last. "Oh, I got you something yesterday, Daddy, let me show you." She went to her room and brought back the shaving things: a deadly-looking straight razor, a soap mug, a brush, and a honing strop. They were a great success, particularly the razor.

"Oh, wow, thank you, chick! This is really beautiful. My grandfather had one like this."

"Do you know how to use it?"

"Oh, I have a good idea—I used to watch Grandpa." He pinched his nose and twisted his mouth halfway around his face.

She giggled, and said, "I'll get some hot water."

Mrs. Hollister apologetically pointed out the kettle simmering on an enormous black range. On a nearby shelf a porcelain clock with cupids and roses painted on it said 9:23. Not much more than an hour until…'Something's *got* to happen this time,' she thought.

She hurried back upstairs with the kettle, and they had a good morning wash-up. While Mr. Shaw plied his new razor, Susan went to her room, tore a piece of paper out of her diary, and wrote on it: "Don't let your Mama leave the room under *any circumstances.* This is *very important.*" She folded it small and put it in her pocket. 'I'll just slip this to Vicky or Bobbie as we go in,' she thought. 'We are *not* going down that elevator until I'm convinced the whole thing is absolutely hopeless.'

"Only one nick!" Mr. Shaw announced. "Not so bad for a beginner, eh? Say, chick," he lowered his voice, "you didn't see anything of Uncle Sam Windbag downstairs, did you?"

"No, I think he's gone."

"He'd better be! I must say, though, he's as good as a handful of sleeping pills. I slept better last night than I have in years."

They went down to a welcome breakfast of ham, eggs, fried potatoes and biscuits.

At twenty-five minutes after ten they strolled over to the

Walkers'. Susan drew the mild summer air deeply into her lungs. This was it! Her heart was beginning to thud, and she had to suppress a desire to bounce at her father's side like a rubber ball. Dignity, dignity! Bouncing could come later...

The double front doors were of varnished oak, with stained-glass windowpanes. The knocker was a feminine bronze hand delicately holding a ball between its thumb and two fingers. Susan lifted it and rapped once. There was a sudden murmur of voices within, a sharp exclamation, the sound of running feet. The door swung open to reveal the Walker children.

"Good morning, good morning!" the Shaws began, but their voices died at the sight of the stricken faces confronting them.

From inside the house an unfamiliar voice cried, "Robert! Victoria!"

"*She's here!*" Victoria mouthed. Aloud she said, in a Deportment Class voice that was badly cracked around the edges, "Oh, good morning, Mr. Shaw. Good morning, Miss Shaw. Won't you please come in?"

"Who?" Mr. Shaw said.

"Cousin Jane!" Victoria groaned in a whisper.

"But," Susan murmured, "I thought she wasn't—"

"She came by the eight-forty-seven instead of the afternoon train," Robert whispered. "We've been outflanked!"

"Really, Isabelle," the voice went on, "I am at a loss to understand this behavior in your children. You have a servant, I believe. It should be her duty to answer the door."

With despairing glances at their guests, the Walkers ushered them in and turned toward the parlor. Susan was so numb with apprehension that she forgot the note in her pocket. Her father seemed to have something stuck in his throat. Stiff-legged, they advanced to meet the owner of that voice.

She was sitting rigidly upright on the edge of a dark green plush sofa. Her eyes transfixed them—wintry grey eyes that glittered behind steel-rimmed prince-nez glasses. Her stout figure was dressed entirely in black. Her hair was black, too, drawn tightly into a bun.

Mrs. Walker, very pale but composed, also sitting stiffly upright on the edge of her chair, said in a low voice, "Ah, there you are! So nice to see you again, Mr. Shaw, I would like you to meet my cousin, Miss Clamp."

"A pleasure, Miss Clamp." He tentatively offered his hand and then dropped it again as Cousin Jane inclined her head a quarter of an inch forward and said, "How do you do." Her mouth tightened and her brows twitched together.

"Daddy!" Susan murmured out of the corner of her mouth. "Hat!"

"Oh! Ahhrrrem! I, ah—" Mr. Shaw snatched his hat off, and turned red.

Mrs. Walker didn't seem to notice. She went on, "And this is Mr. Shaw's daughter, Susan. Susan and my two have become great friends."

Susan curtseyed. Cousin Jane said, "Indeed?" and gave her an arctic stare.

"Pray be seated," Mrs. Walker said. "Maggie will be in soon with tea."

All the available chairs were in the line of fire of Cousin Jane's eyes. Aware that every movement was being watched, the Shaws and the Walker children sank into their seats.

"Do not loll, Victoria," Cousin Jane said after a moment of silence. "It is not only ill-bred, but also has a detrimental effect on one's carriage."

Victoria blushed and jerked rigidly upright. Susan felt her own spine stiffening. Mr. Shaw, meanwhile, was having trouble deciding what to do with his hat. He threw a quick questioning

glance at Susan. She signalled back that she was uncertain as he was. His chair had carved wooden arms; and after fumbling with his hat for a moment, he hung it on the end-knob of the left arm. Susan glanced at Cousin Jane, and saw her mouth and brows tightening again. "Oh, good grief!" she groaned to herself; 'everything we do is going to be wrong…'

"Mr. Shaw!" Cousin Jane said. "You are vacationing in this vicinity, I believe."

"Yes, ma'am," Mr. Shaw said, jumping a little and knocking

his hat on the floor. He bent over and picked it up again, turning redder than before.

"It's quite all right to leave your hat on the floor, Mr. Shaw," Mrs. Walker said with a faint but encouraging smile. Mr. Shaw, his face purple, laid his hat on the floor. He raised himself again to find everyone looking at him. "Beautiful day," he said, apparently squeezing the words past a grape-sized obstruction in his throat. "The *aherrrrem* sun—the sun's out."

"Yes!" Mrs. Walker said. "Such lovely weather lately. Early summer is one of my favorite times of year."

"Clement weather is never to be trusted," Cousin Jane said. "I expect it will rain soon.—Cease that fidgeting, Robert! Put both feet on the floor and keep your hands in your lap.—This area is noted for its high rainfall and the severity of its electrical storms. I wonder, Mr. Shaw, that you did not choose to vacation at the seaside or in the mountains. Most people resort to one or the other, I believe."

"Well, I, ah, *like* the country," Mr. Shaw said. "It's so restful and...quiet."

"There is a good deal of talk about the so-called virtues of country living," Cousin Jane said with a little sniff. "I believe it is sentimental twaddle. What is worse, it is pernicious twaddle. There is a dangerous relaxation of standards in the country which encourages bad manners in the young, and eccentricities in their elders."

Mrs. Walker turned a shade paler, but answered in a steady voice, "I realize that tea in the morning is—unusual, Cousin Jane. But the heart, after all, has its reasons that—"

"The heart, Isabelle, is the most unreliable organ in the human frame. Consulting it can lead only to sentimental excesses and improprieties—if not worse."

"Mama is not to be blamed, Cousin Jane," Victoria said in a low voice so low that it was nearly a whisper. "It was really my idea."

"In-deed?" Cousin Jane said slowly swiveled her head toward Victoria, who, without relaxing her backbone or indeed moving a muscle, shrank. Susan felt her face growing warm with anger. Mr. Shaw cleared his throat loudly and said:

"Oh, come now, Miss Clamp, it wasn't such a horrendous idea! I think it was…charming."

Cousin Jane closed her eyes. "The whimsies of unformed minds may seem charming, Mr. Shaw; but to indulge them is to invite the gravest consequences."

Mrs. Walker said, "Well, that's for a parent to judge, Cousin Jane. The consequence in this case is that the Shaws are here—and I don't find that such a *grave* matter." She smiled. Susan melted inside. 'How could Daddy not be devastated by that smile?' she thought. Mrs. Walker hurried on before Cousin Jane could interrupt, "I hope you passed a restful night, Mr. Shaw."

"Oh, yes, absolutely, thank you. I slept like a log. Uncle S—I mean, Mr. Hollister put us both to sleep with an endless lecture on politics."

"Oh, Mr. Hollister!" she laughed. "He is a dreadful filibusterer, isn't he? He dabbles in land speculation, you know, and tried to get into local politics, and comes to grief in nearly everything, and then blames it all on the Republicans. One must be very firm with Mr. Hollister. I feel sorry for his poor wife."

"Most unsuitable neighbors," Cousin Jane said. "They are

the vulgarest of the vulgar. Of course, the whole idea of moving here was a mistake, and I was opposed to it from the first. But naturally the late Mr. Walker would not listen to *me*. He was a stubborn and misguided man."

"You are speaking of my husband," Mrs. Walker said quietly.

"I apologize, Isabelle. I did not mean to single him out for any special opprobrium. All men, after all, are stubborn and misguided—when they are not merely weak and misguided."

A pall of silence settled over them. Robert's face wore a look of stoic blankness; he sat like a ramrod, staring straight ahead, as though he were on parade. Victoria's expression was so miserable that Susan couldn't bear to look any more. She glanced about the room, half-seeing things which in happier circumstances would have delighted her: a white marble fireplace; a glass case containing—jewels?—no, stuffed hummingbirds; a massive mirror whose frame was decorated with gilt bunches of grapes and carved leaves; a vase full of peacock feathers...

"Mr. Shaw!" Cousin Jane said, so suddenly that they all jumped. "May I enquire as to your line of endeavor?"

"Ah—I beg your pardon?"

Cousin Jane closed her eyes. "What do you do in the city?"

"Oh! I'm with Dexler and Feldman. We make—"

"Papa is in finance," Susan plunged in, just in time to prevent him from saying "radio and television parts."

"That's right," he said, recovering from the near-fumble. "I take care of the, ah, financial end of the business." His face turned red.

"In-deed?" Cousin Jane said. She opened her eyes again and brought them to bear on Susan. "In *my* day, children never spoke until spoken to."

"Well," Susan muttered, "things are changing."

"They are indeed—and changing steadily for the worse. One's duty to maintain the highest standards becomes more burdensome every day."

There was another silence, which was broken at last by a relieved cry from Mrs. Walker:

"Ah! Here comes Maggie with the tea."

Mrs. Walker was looking over her shoulder. Following her gaze to a corner of the parlor, Susan noticed for the first time a tall doorway draped in green velvet portieres. She still had only a hazy notion of how the house was arranged, but it seemed to her that this doorway must open into the hall where the elevator was. A tinkling sound on the other side announced Maggie's approach. And here she was, a plump little woman maneuvering a tray past the velvet fringes. The tray was piled high with cups and saucers and the tea pot and silverware and napkins and sugar and cream and butter and rolls. Maggie's round freckled face was set in a frown of concentration. She advanced into the parlor step by step, her eyes fixed on the floor just ahead of her, the tip of her tongue thrust out between her tightened lips. Susan found that she was holding her breath. Everyone else seemed to be doing the same…

Ah! Maggie was going to succeed. She had reached the center of the room. Her tray hovered over the delicate cherrywood table by Mrs. Walker's side. She lifted her face with the beginnings of a triumphant smile on it, turned as if to receive everyone's congratulations—and caught sight of Mr. Shaw.

She gasped. Her face went white. "Mer-r-rciful hivens!" She moaned. Her eyes turned up in their sockets. The tray fell from her hands, slithered over the edge of the table, and precipitated its load to the floor with a crash. There was a second crash as Maggie fell over backwards in a dead faint.

Cousin Jane Prohibits

...happened again, and Cousin Jane used it as an excuse to throw us out. We took a walk because we didn't know what else to do. I began to hope again that there was still a chance, but when we got back Cousin Jane smashed my hopes probably forever...

They were all paralyzed for a moment with shock and surprise. Then Mrs. Walker jumped out of her chair. A fragment of porcelain crunched under her foot as she hurried around the wreckage to kneel by Maggie.

"Bobbie, quick! Fetch my smelling salts. I think they're in my reticule up in my room."

Robert dashed off, throwing one frightened glance over his shoulder as he went. They heard his feet thundering up the stairs.

Victoria leaped up and ran over to her mother, who was now rubbing Maggie's wrists. Mrs. Walker waved her off, saying, "No, dear, I can manage for a moment. Bring a towel, will you? The tea is soaking into the rug." Victoria darted away, wringing her hands.

Cousin Jane closed her eyes and said, "Really, Isabelle, this is distressing. That chinaware was very costly, I believe. I remember Mr. Walker's Aunt Sophronia telling me that she had gone to a great deal of trouble to find that particular pattern."

Mr. Shaw half rose form his chair and asked, "Can I help in some way?"

"Oh, no, thank you, Mr. Shaw, I—Please remain seated. I do hope you'll forgive us for this little—contretemps."

"This sort of thing," Cousin Jane pronounced, her eyes still closed, "does not occur in well-regulated households."

Susan jumped out of her chair, knelt on the other side of Maggie, murmured, "Please let me help," and began to rub Maggie's free wrist.

Mrs. Walker said, "Thank you, Susan," and gave her a smile that had made her glow with pleasure. But pain was mixed with her feelings, too, now that she was close enough to see how hollow Mrs. Walker's eyes looked, and how drawn her face was.

"Having an ill-trained servant is more trouble than having no servant at all," Cousin Jane said.

A flush came over Mrs. Walker's cheeks, and her mouth tightened; but before she could answer, Victoria and Robert came rushing back into the room. Victoria began to sop up the spilt tea and pile the broken china on the tray. Robert, with a shaking hand, thrust a tiny unstoppered vial under Maggie's nose.

"All right!" Mrs. Walker said, attempting a cheerful air. "We'll have her around in no time now," and she rubbed briskly away at Maggie's left wrist, while Susan, who had never done this before and was only imitating her, did the same on the right. "Maggie? Maggie? There's a dear!"

Maggie stirred, and her eyelids fluttered. "Oh, Mum," she muttered in a hoarse undertone, "am I still alive, then?"

"Of course you are, silly!"

Maggie's eyes opened. She looked at Mrs. Walker with a puzzled, apologetic expression. "Oh, I'm so sorry, Mum. I thought it was the last minute of me mortal life."

"What was it, Maggie? You frightened us all half to death!"

"Frightened, is it? Sure, Mum, I saw a sign that would make the very flesh of you melt away from your bones with fright."

Cousin Jane sniffed.

"Sit up, Maggie dear, it's all right now. How *could* you see any such thing right here in our own parlor?"

Maggie struggled into a sitting position. "Our own parlor or not, Mum, me second sight sees what it sees. I jist lifts me eyes from me tray and turns me head—" She demonstrated, with the result that she now saw Susan for the first time.

Her eyes widened with horror. She uttered a dying scream and fell backwards. Mrs. Walker seized her just in time to prevent her head form banging on the floor.

Susan dropped the wrist she had been rubbing, and fell back on her feels in bewilderment. Mrs. Walker cried, "Maggie! What *is* the matter?" Robert began to wave the smelling salts again. Victoria scurried across the floor on her hands and knees and began to rub Maggie's cheeks. Mr. Shaw jumped up, stepping on his hat and crushing it, and cried, "Let's get her into a chair!"

Cousin Jane was the only one who was paying no attention to Maggie. Her eyes were fastened on Mr. Shaw, and they glittered with suspicion.

"Mr. Shaw!" she said like the crack of a whip. Everyone fell silent and turned to look at her. "This is a most peculiar circumstance, is it not?"

"It certainly is! I never saw anything like—"

"Perhaps you are prepared to offer some explanation."

"Who, me?" Mr. Shaw cried. "I have no more idea—"

"Were you acquainted with this unfortunate woman?"

"No! I never saw her before in my life."

"In-deed? I had the distinct impression that she was made insensible by the shock of seeing and recognizing you. I was going to overlook that impression. However, the sight of your daughter has had the same unhappy effect on her. The coincidence seems to me too pointed to be ignored. It was my hope that you could enlighten me."

The coincidence was not only pointed, it was dumbfounding. Mr. Shaw and Susan gaped at Cousin Jane, and at Maggie, and at each other. "I—I don't know what to say," Mr. Shaw finally stammered.

Cousin Jane compressed her lips and turned to Mrs. Walker. "Isabelle, in view of the fact that Mr. Shaw and Miss Shaw have such an unsettling effect on Maggie, do you not think it would be wise if they were elsewhere when she comes to?"

Mrs. Walker flushed, and raised her eyes to Mr. Shaw with an agonized look.

"Mrs. Walker," he said, "I'm sorry. I really am. I don't know why we have such an effect on Maggie, but since we do, we had better go. Thank you for your hospitality, and..."

"Oh, Mr. Shaw, I—I am devastated." Mrs. Walker made a helpless little gesture. "I'm sorrier than I can say that things have—Let us hope that we can meet again under happier circumstances."

Cousin Jane stood, and stared at Susan while she scrambled to her feet and joined her father. Then she advanced on them, making them fall back toward the door. Everyone was murmuring "Goodbye, goodbye." Susan and Robert and Victoria exchanged despairing looks. "Good day, good day, most regrettable," Cousin Jane said. A gleam of malice shone briefly behind her glasses as she held the door for the Shaws. It closed after them with a thump.

Stunned, they walked down the path to Ward Lane. There Mr. Shaw suddenly hurled his ruined hat into the dust and kicked it. "Good *night!*" he ground out through his teeth. "What a poisonous woman!"

Susan looked back at the house where her hopes lay in shambles, and choked down her tears.

There seemed to be no point in going back to the Hollisters' merely to sit around. They began to trudge down the lane.

"Well," Mr. Shaw said after a while, "Looks like we're not going to get to the elevator until tonight. But tonight is *it*. We're going to stay up and watch until it's safe to go, and go."

"All right," she said dully.

"Listen, what *was* that business with Maggie, anyway?"

"I don't know. Maybe we look like somebody else that she—I don't know."

"Somebody else who scares the living daylights out of her, then. Was anybody threatening her or anything?"

"No...Oh! Vicky did say that she's been talking about 'signs' or something like that. She's awfully superstitious. Maybe we look like somebody she used to know who died, and she thinks we're ghosts."

"Hmm... Wish we could throw that kind of scare into that cousin of theirs! Poor Isabelle!"

"Oh, Daddy!" she said, turning to him with desperate appeal. "Isn't it awful? We can't go away without doing *some*thing to help her out."

"Right!" he said, nodding his head. "Absolutely right."

Her heart leaped up. "Oh, Daddy, it would just solve everything if you—"

"Come on, Susie," he broke in with a short laugh. "Will you just drop that idea, please? I'm sure we can help her out and still go back to the twentieth century. Let me think a bit..."

But hope, that tiny, stubborn flame, was alight in her heart once more. There was still the rest of the day left...And he had called her by name—not "poor Mrs. Walker," but "poor Isabelle!" Surely that meant something; some change of attitude that he might not even be aware of himself yet. And she, Mrs. Walker, had *actually said*, "I hope we meet again under happier circumstances." Well, there was still the rest of the day to get them together again somehow. She and Victoria and Robert would have to have a council of war as soon as possible. The main problem now was how to get around Cousin Jane...She shivered. No wonder the Walkers had shown such gloom at the mere mention of her name! But still, dragon though she was, she couldn't be everywhere at once, could she...?

Thus preoccupied with their thoughts, they walked almost as far as the stream where they had napped yesterday morning, then turned around and went back.

Mrs. Hollister met them at the door. She murmured, "Oh, Mr. Shaw," and began to writhe.

"What's the matter?"

"It's," Mrs. Hollister gasped. "I mean—she's—" She signalled toward the parlor with her eyes, twisted her hands, and fled to the shelter of the kitchen.

"Mr. Shaw!" snapped a familiar voice.

There, in the doorway of the parlor, bonneted and clasping a tightly-furled black umbrella, stood Cousin Jane.

Mr. Shaw's nostrils turned white. "Ah," he said in a stiff voice.

"My business is brief," Cousin Jane said. Her eyes glittered at them. "I shall detain you no more than a minute. Mrs. Walker's servant has revived, and I have been questioning her very closely."

She paused to see what effect this announcement had on them, and seemed disappointed that it had none. She continued:

"I do not know what to make of her story. One must consider that she is ignorant and filled with superstitions; on the other hand, her sincerity is beyond question. She claims she fainted because she believed you to be supernatural figures, a 'sign' or some such rubbish—apparently she is given to hysterical notions of that sort. But I cannot lightly dismiss her reasons for so believing. She has an unshakable conviction that at midnight of the night before last, she saw the two of you, surrounded by a ghostly glow—in the hallway of the Walkers' house."

Susan hoped that she was successful in suppressing her gasp. *That* was it! She stared hard at a highlight flashing from one lens of Cousin Jane's prince-nez, and tried to keep her face expressionless.

"Ridiculous!" Mr. Shaw said in a convincing tone.

"Indeed?" Cousin Jane sniffed. "Perhaps. It is not for me to say without further evidence whether the woman's 'vision' was the product of her feverish imagination, or something more, shall we say, *substantial.*"

Cousin Jane paused, and compressed her lips.

"Now look here!" Mr. Shaw said. "Are you implying something?"

"I imply nothing, Mr. Shaw, that a clear conscience would find offensive. Let me continue. I discovered almost as soon as I arrived this morning that you and your daughter had succeeded within a *very* short space of time in exerting a peculiar influence over Robert and Victoria. I discovered that you had exerted that influence in order to scrape an acquaintance with their mother. Now I have just discovered from Mrs. Hollister that you came here, and are staying here, *without baggage*. You travel light, Mr. Shaw—for a person 'in finance.' One cannot help wondering what kind of 'finance' you actually deal in."

Mr. Shaw clenched his fists and said, "What are you getting at?"

"Very well, Mr. Shaw, I will not mince words with you. I find everything about you irregular—highly irregular. I have no option under the circumstances but to forbid you to see or speak to my kinswoman, Mrs. Walker, any further. As for you, Miss Shaw, I forbid you to have any further connection whatsoever with Robert or Victoria."

Mr. Shaw took two steps forward, and said, "Who the devil are *you* to go around saying who we can or can't see?"

"I believe you to be a thoroughgoing scoundrel, sir! I warn you that if you give me the slightest pretext, I shall report you to the nearest police station!"

"You can report me wherever and whenever you like. And if it's the pretext you're waiting for"—Mr. Shaw snapped his fingers an inch from Cousin Jane's nose—"I hope that will serve!"

She fell back a step. Her face went crimson, and her pince-nez dropped off her nose. Half raising her umbrella, she said in a voice that shook with fury, "Do not press me too far, my man! I have said what I came to say, and I am now leaving. Stand aside!"

"Go around, blast you!" he roared.

They stood their ground for perhaps a quarter of a minute, glaring at each other. Then Cousin Jane stabbed the tip of her umbrella into the floor, and, uttering little huffs and groans of rage, walked around Mr. Shaw and stamped out of the house.

Susan at the End of Her Rope

...no more hope for getting Daddy and Mrs. Walker together, as far as I could see. Daddy didn't seem to mind so much but I was sick. He meant it about helping her, though. He had figured out a plan while we were walking. We started to carry it out and ran smack into another disaster...

"By George!" Mr. Shaw gasped. He wiped his forehead with his handkerchief. His face was white, and his hands shook. "Whew! Boy oh boy, how I'd love to—!" He clenched his teeth and rubbed his hands together as though demolishing a noxious insect. "Hey, chick, what's the matter? Come on, it's all right; it's all over now."

"We won't—we won't get to see—Mrs. Walker—again—will we?" she wept.

"Anh-h-h! I've got half a mind to go over there right now just to show that flaming rhinoceros that she can't forbid *me* anything! If I didn't think she'd make ever more trouble for poor Isabelle, I'd—oh lord, I don't know what! We *have* to get the Walkers out from under before we go—and I think I know how to do it."

He led her over to a moth-eaten purple plush sofa, and they sat down.

"It's nothing new," he went on. "It's just a way to get Isa—Mrs. Walker to accept the treasure. When you were telling me about your adventures here, didn't you mention a lawyer who was handling Mrs. Walker's investments?"

"Mr. Branscomb," she said in a dull voice.

"That was it—Branscomb. Wait here a sec—I have to talk to Mrs. H."

His voice and Mrs. Hollister's murmur sounded for a while in the kitchen. Then he was back.

"All right. She doesn't know his address, but he's in town and I'll find him. What we'll do is put the money in a bank under Branscomb's charge. He can tell Mrs. Walker that she hasn't lost everything, as they previously thought—one or two of her investments are rallying again. It's as simple as that. And of course, when she's on her feet again, she can send Cousin Jane back to wherever she came from.

"Now, Mrs. H. says there's a farmer named Knutsen near here who can give us a ride, so I'm going to go and arrange for one. While I'm doing that, you get a sack from the stable and bring back as much gold as you can carry by yourself. Whatever you can bring we'll take into town in Knutsen's buggy, and use it to set up the bank account. We can bring a trunk or chest back with us, and tonight before we leave we'll put the rest of the money in it. Branscomb will have instructions to pick it up here tomorrow and deposit it. Okay?"

"Okay..."

"Honey, I'm sorry, but it's really all I can do."

"I know."

They went out on the veranda.

"All right, chick. I'll see you here in a while. Just bring back what you can carry without a struggle." He squeezed her shoulders, kissed her on the forehead, and set off.

She lurked along the hedge for a while, waiting to see if Victoria or Robert would manage to slip out. She was going to have to tell them that their plan had failed. She was going to have to say goodbye forever, unless they could think of some desperate last-minute plan to—what, what, what? Her vision blurred with tears.

Victoria and Robert did not come out.

She sighed, and went into the Hollisters' stable. There was a pile of sacks draped over the frame of the grindstone. She picked one, folded it, and trudged out to the road.

It was another one of those beautiful days: bright blue sky with pillowy clouds, a mild sweet-smelling breeze, birds everywhere, butterflies wavering from flower to flower. She looked at it with anguish in her heart. Goodbye flowers, goodbye fields and woods and singing birds...Oh, if her father would just—A feeling of intense anger suddenly welled up inside her. He was so blind, so stupid, so stick-in-the-mud! Couldn't even see the fantastic gift that was being laid at his feet! Didn't *want* to see it!

She was still muttering to herself when she came to the forked stick, although part of her mind was trying to tell her that it really wasn't his fault. If nothing happened when he looked at Mrs. Walker—well, nothing happened. And that was that.

She sighed, looked up and down the road to make sure it was clear, and crawled into the thicket.

A burning, copper-tasting sensation clamped down on her tongue. Yesterday she had left dead leaves spread over the sackful of treasure. Now the leaves were all pushed aside, and there was nothing before her eyes but the tunnel's bare earth floor.

When the sick dizzy feeling cleared from her head, she realized that of course it must have been Robert and Victoria. Robert had been worried about the treasure's safety. They had probably moved it last evening, intending to tell her this morning; and they had forgotten, in the shock of Cousin Jane's unexpected arrival.

She trotted back, trying to ignore the pain in her ankle. Good grief, this complicated the situation…! She would have to see them somehow, Cousin Jane or no Cousin Jane, and find out where they'd put it, so that her father could—

But how to do it? Disheveled and panting, she stood by the Walkers' front gate and stared at the house. She couldn't just wait around for them to come out…

"Meow!" Toby said in the hedge.

She looked. A hand appeared over the top of the foliage, beckoned, and vanished.

Ah! She hurried around through the Hollisters' gate. Robert and Victoria were huddled over the hedge.

"Sue!" Robert whispered before she could say anything. "Cousin Jane doesn't know we've escaped yet—I hope! We're not allowed to see you any more. We're not even allowed out of the house. We have to set up a communication post somewhere, quick."

"She's made us start to pack up our clothes and belongings,

Sue!" Victoria said. "We only managed to slip away because she's in Mama's room. Oh, I hate her!—I don't care if it *is* wicked, I hate her! She's picking out all the furniture to be auctioned off, and poor Mama—"

"*Listen,*" Susan broke in, "where is it?"

"Where's what?" Robert asked.

"The treasure, the treasure!" she almost shouted. "Where did you put the treasure?"

Their silence and their puzzled eyes told her that the unimaginable worst had happened.

"Oh," she moaned.

"What's the matter, Sue?" Victoria whispered.

"It's gone," she choked. "It's *gone*!" She collapsed with her head in her arms, sobbing. They patted her back and murmured.

"I ought to be drummed out of the regiment!" Robert muttered after a while. "It's my fault—I knew it wasn't safe out there, but I didn't do anything about it."

"But how could anyone find it?" Victoria said in a cracked voice. "Who would *ever* look in a place like that?"

Robert sighed. "Well, boys would, for one—if they were bird's nesting. Or a tramp's dog...Oh, thunderation! I can't bear it when you cry, Sue, please stop."

"It's not just the treasure," she wept. "It's everything. Our whole plan's a failure. Daddy *won't* fall in love with your Mama and he—he insists on going—back tonight, and it's all over!"

At last Robert said in a faraway voice, "Don't feel bad, Sue. I think we've kind of known since yesterday afternoon that it was going to be a frost. Mama...I don't know, she—"

"Her heart," Victoria gulped, "also remains—untouched.

Oh, I can't understand it!" She began to cry too.

"I feel like I'm leaving you in the lur-ur-urch!" Susan wept.

"Don't feel that way, Sue," Victoria sobbed. "You did everything you could."

"It's really totus dexter, Sue," Robert murmured. "I mean, we're just where we were anyway before you came along. In fact, we're better off, because if you hadn't chased Mr. Sweeney away—"

"Oh!" Victoria gasped. She straightened up and wiped her eyes with the back of her hand. "*Oh!* Before you came along—! Sue! Before you came along, I went to a wishing well, and I wished—and I got my wish! *Why wouldn't it work again?*"

"But the witch is in the twentieth century," Susan said hopelessly, "and we're all here."

"Oh, pooh! What difference does that make? She's a witch, she can do what she want. Oh! Bobbie! Let's both sacrifice something this time and *double* the power of the wish!"

"Hey, that's a capital idea, Vick!" Robert said. "There's a strategic problem, though—we have to do it so Cousin Jane doesn't know we're doing it."

"Oh, mercy, that's right…! I know—you go back and fetch the sacrifices, Bobbie. You're the expert forager, you'd have a better chance of getting past Cousin Jane than I would. I'll go to the stable and watch your back bedroom window. You can drop the things out the window into the bushes. Then even if Cousin Jane catches you, I can still get the things and make a run for the well myself."

"That's it—divided forces! Gosh, Vick, you'd make a great general—if they allowed girls in the Army."

"Pooh! Girls are too sensible to *want* to be in the Army.

Now! We have to decide what we're going to sacrifice. Remember, it has to be something you really love, or it won't have any effect."

Robert considered. He frowned, bit his lip, looked away from his sister, looked back, and slowly stiffened his spine. "Very well, I'll—" He faltered an instant, then went on with a rush. "I'll give my arrowhead collection."

"Oh, Bobbie, that's noble! I'm going to give my little silver mirror that Mama gave me."

"That belonged to Great-great-great-grandmother Wayne," Robert whispered. "Back in the *Revolution*."

"I know," Victoria sighed. "But this is more important than—"

"Wait!" Susan said. "Don't—" She was going to say, "Don't throw away your treasure for nothing," but Victoria stopped her by gently laying her finger against Susan's lips. Perhaps she could see that Susan was at the end of hope. "Ssssh!" she whispered. "Don't say anything. Remember, it's always darkest before dawn."

"It's our campaign now, Sue." Robert added. "You did everything you could. Now it's up to us." He squeezed her hand. "Nil desperandum! We'll see you again when we can. Let's go, Vick!"

"Goodbye, Sue. Don't worry—*please.*—How are you going to get back into the house, Bobbie?"

"I think that window is still open in the sun parlor."

They crawled away along the hedge, talking in low tones, and vanished into the neglected tangle of shrubbery at the back of the Hollister property.

Susan watched them out of sight. Her heart felt like a

chunk of iron. She was convinced that this was the last she would ever see of them. And she had been so numb she hadn't even said goodbye...

The Shaws waited in their rooms for night to come.

Mr. Shaw, not wanting to hear any more about Republican villainy from Mr. Hollister, told Mrs. Hollister that he was feeling unwell, and asked for a light supper that could be sent upstairs on a tray. As a matter of fact, he was feeling unwell. The loss of the treasure, and hence his inability to help Mrs. Walker, had thrown him into a depression. When the tray came up neither he nor Susan could look at it.

Time oozed on. They endured as best they could. Mr. Shaw leafed through a stack of newspapers. Susan tried to write a goodbye letter to Victoria and Robert. After many false starts and long periods of staring into space, she produced a note that said:

> Dear Vicky and Bobbie,
> Goodbye. I have to go back. I'm sorry our plans failed. I don't think I will ever be happy again.
> Love, Susan

She thought she had run out of tears, but she hadn't.

Her father came up behind her quietly and put his hands on her shoulders. "Try to look at it this way, Susie," he pleaded. "This all happened a long time ago, really. It just *seems* to be happening now. But we're really twentieth-century people, honey. All this—" he waved a hand to include the fields and woods, and the nearby town, and the Hollister and Walker houses, and their inhabitants "—all this is *gone*. It was all over and done with before we were even born."

She knew, in a sense, he was right, but she could not be convinced. He didn't sound fully convinced himself.

Mr. Hollister came home and brayed at his wife. She murmured back. The catbird that Susan had heard when she first arrived in the nineteenth century sang, and scolded *mew, mew,* and sang again. A golden evening declined into dusk. Mrs. Hollister brought candles up, and took away their untouched food.

To help pass the time, Susan brought her diary up to date. She wrote at the end of her last entry:

...afraid that the idea wouldn't work. I just had a feeling that something like that doesn't happen twice. Or maybe Vicky and Bobbie never got to the well. Anyway, nothing has happened. Nothing is going to happen. There isn't enough time left to change anything now. We're going back to the twentieth century and I am absolutely in despair.

"Hey!" Charles said. "Is that the end of it?"

After the word "despair" in Susan's diary there was more than half a page, all blank. The facing page was blank. I searched through the rest of the pages to the back cover. They were all blank.

"Oh, no," I groaned.

"But the Shaws *didn't* come back to the twentieth century, did they?" Charles asked.

"No! I'm positive they didn't—I would've heard about it, I would've seen them around the apartment building. And listen, there's that old photograph—they're all in it, Shaws and Walkers both!"

He got that look on his face again. "Edward, the fact is that you never saw Mrs. Walker and you never saw Victoria, and you never saw Robert. For that matter, how well did you actually know the Shaws?"

"Oh—slightly."

"Slightly...Besides which, it's a very grainy photograph. I wonder if you haven't jumped to some mistaken conclusions. The people in that photograph may have nothing to do with people in this—this story of yours."

"*Story!* Blast it, Charles, didn't I tell you about Susan before we read the diary? And wasn't everything in the diary absolutely consistent with that I told you? Story! It's *real,* man!"

"Mmmm..."

"And another thing: I'm the only person in the world except Mrs. Clutchett who could have any notion of what this diary is about. And it falls into my hands *because someone calls me up to tell me where it is*. How do you explain *that*?"

"Well...I don't. But there must be some simple answer. Hey, calm down! It can't be worth getting so excited about."

"What d'you mean, calm down? It's *maddening* not to be able to know what happened!"

"Let me take you to lunch," he suggested soothingly.

"No, thanks. I'm not hungry."

At the front door he said, "Listen, if anything else turns up about this business, keep me posted, will you?"

"Why should I keep *you* posted, you skeptic?"

"Oh, I'm a skeptic, all right; as an historian I have to be. But it's never prevented me from enjoying a good yarn."

A good yarn, forsooth! There are times when I could kick Charles with the greatest of pleasure. That superior, common-sensical air of his! I was being unfair, I suppose. But it irked me beyond endurance to be confronted with this mystery. Here was the diary, ending in the Shaws' total defeat. Here was the photograph, showing the Shaws and Walkers triumphant. How had they ever managed to overcome all the obstacles in their way?

Or—I kept pushing away the dreadful thought, and it kept coming back—or *had* they? Was Charles perhaps right about the photograph? *Was* it just wishful thinking and self-delusion

on my part to see Susan and Mr. Shaw and Mrs. Shaw and Robert and Victoria in those grainy, time-darkened, nineteenth-century faces…?

Oh, blast Charles, anyway!

I looked up, and saw that I was one block from home, and that a crowd was collecting on the sidewalks of Ward Street.

And good reason for it, too! Despondent as I was, I felt my heart lifting at the sight before me. There was the most gorgeous old-fashioned automobile standing by the curb. It was taller than I am, and nearly as long as a fire engine, and only the back part was enclosed; the chauffer's seat was open to the weather. Its condition was perfect. It was blue, so dark as to look almost black, and polished like glass. Silver trim dazzled in the sun, and there were varnished wooden spokes in the wheels.

I pushed through the crowd to get a closer look, and suddenly the chauffeur had me by the arm. He was a swarthy individual in a uniform of impeccable black, including polished black leather puttees. He murmured to me in a lisping foreign accent:

"Yes, sir, very opportune, sir, I beg your pardon, but as you see, a slight mishap, sir, the lady requests your assistance, sir."

The right front tire was flat.

"You mean—?" I began.

"Yes, sir, a trifling matter, sir, she will be most grateful, I have the tools all ready, sir."

I hesitated. I wanted to go home and think, and I am not very mechanically inclined anyway, and there were plenty of other men in the crowd who looked more competent than I; and besides, I had always thought that such matters were the chauffeur's job.

"If you will be so kind, sir, the lady is most anguished, sir."

I saw a tiny fragile white-haired woman in the enclosed part of the car. She was wearing jewels and silvery furs (furs! in August!) and her withered face did have an air of vague, I could almost say absent-minded, distress.

"Oh, all right," I said—I'm afraid with ill grace.

The chauffeur murmured, "Yes, sir, much obliged, sir, here is the jack, sir," and I knelt down to a half-hour of frustrating labor and sweat. Everything went contrariwise. The chauffeur hovered over me, murmuring in an encouraging tone, but refusing to touch anything himself. Men in the crowd made comments and suggestions, but whenever someone stepped forward to give me a hand he would be politely turned back by the murmuring chauffeur. I really don't know how I succeeded in figuring out the jack, and wrenching off the nuts, and extricating the spare wheel from its well in the front fender, and getting the job done. But I did, and then stood up, dripping and grease-stained and in a savage humor.

"Thank you, sir, well done, sir, the lady would like to express her gratitude, sir."

She had pulled a little folding walnut writing desk from its compartment behind the chauffeur's sear, and was writing with—so help me!—a goose-quill pen. 'Is she making out a check?' I wondered. Whatever it was, she put it in an envelope; and the chauffeur, cranking down the window between his seat and the rear compartment, took the envelope from her skinny claws, and handed it over to me.

Then he saluted, leaped into his seat, started up the motor with an incredible blast of noise that made the whole crowd jump; and that vast, stately automobile darted away through the traffic with all the agility of a sports car.

"Boy, they better get that muffler fixed," one of the bystanders said. I agreed, with my ears ringing.

The envelope was made of beautiful thick creamy paper. My fingers had smudged it with grease already; and although I was twitching with curiosity to see what was inside, I decided that I could wait until I had washed up. I was only a block away from home.

There was a new message on the back wall of the elevator. It was written in black crayon, and it said, "Bodoni couldn't fix a roller skate."

Poor Mr. Bodoni! He had been getting a lot of insults like

that lately. The elevator, which had been slow and noisy before the Shaws had disappeared in it, had steadily gotten slower and noisier ever since. Frequently these days it lurched from side to side in the shaft and came to a shuddering near-halt between floors. I think perhaps its travels through time had put too much strain on the mechanism. The increasingly nervous tenants showered Mr. Bodoni with complaints. He could be seen nearly every day poking around in the works with wrench, oil can, and responsible frown—but to no avail. One day someone wrote in red chalk on the back wall of the elevator, "Is this an elevator or a hearse?" The idea caught on, and similar messages began to appear as fast as Mr. Bodoni could scrub them off: "Greased Lightning," "Please replace squirrel in motor," "I'm too young to die!" and so forth.

Nowadays when Mr. Bodoni even suspected that you were going to complain about the elevator, he would back away with a hunted look in his eye, waving his hands and saying, "Not dangerous! Don't you believe! A little slow, maybe, but not dangerous, don't worry!" I guess I am the only tenant who didn't complain; knowing, as the others couldn't, what the elevator had been through.

But I felt like complaining now. It was taking forever to get to the fifth floor where I live, and my impatience to see what was in the envelope was growing. "Come *on*, old horse," I muttered, patting its flank. It responded by giving another earthquake-lurch and a groan, and slowing down.

Eventually the arrow shuddered to a stop on 5, and the door sighed and rumbled open. I dashed to my apartment and scrubbed my hands at the kitchen sink. The grease was as stubborn as a second skin, and in the end I just wiped off what was left on the dish-towel. Now at last I could open the envelope.

It was not a check inside, but a note on the same kind of thick beautiful paper as the envelope was made of. All it said, in tiny wavery spider-web-thin letters, was:

> *Reservations for this year are filled, but you may send a message. I suggest a Special Notice.*

I sat down.

Nothing today was making much sense…

For the next hour I puzzled over it all without reaching any conclusions, except the very tentative one that the lady who had phoned me was the same person I had seen in the automobile. All I had to go on was the fact that the automobile's roar had sounded like the noise on the phone; and the fact, or impression, that the handwriting on the note *looked* the way the voice on the phone had *sounded*, if you see what I mean. Pretty thin evidence, I admit…But wait, there was another similarity. They both—or she, if it was the same person—had singled me out. The voice on the phone had definitely mentioned my number, and the chauffeur had seized my arm as though he had been instructed to wait for help until I came along. Well, all right—but what did it mean? Had I been called out because I was the only person who could know what Susan's diary was about? Maybe. But surely I hadn't been picked by the chauffeur because I was the only person who could change the wheel…As for the note, which I now read for the twentieth time—my mind knocked against it with all the effect of a moth trying to go through a windowpane.

There was a rap on my door.

It was Mr. Bodoni, his face shining with perspiration and

his arms laden with newspapers. He collected these from the tenants to sell; there was an enormous stack in the basement.

"Gotny noospapers?" he said around his dead cigar.

"Nope," I sighed. I had given up telling him that I don't subscribe to a paper and rarely buy one.

"Yeah. Okay," he said. He shifted the bundle in his arms, and said, "Hot, hah?" and turned to go. Two words leaped out at me from the densely printed grey page on top of his load.

"Wait, hold it!" I cried. He turned back. "Can I have that page?"

"Hah?"

"That page there on top. Can I have it?"

"Yeah," he said, staring at me with puzzlement.

It was half a page, actually—the lower part. I tore it off, thanked him, and closed the door.

Did you know—I never did until that moment—that the want ads in the newspaper begin with Legal Notices and continue with Special Notices?"

Special Notices...I stood there, swallowing hard, and reading as fast as I could.

Blood plasma donors wanted...

I will not be responsible for debts incurred by anyone other than myself. Three of these, signed respectively by—well, no matter.

We have room to accept the dumping of approx. 3000 yds. of fill dirt...

NOTICE OF LIQUIDATION...

Oh, my word!

REWARD for info. leading to contact with Jane Hildegarde Clamp. Call TEM-8118.

Jane Hildegarde Clamp? *Jane Clamp*? Of course there could be no connection, but—

I reached for my phone and dialed. A professional, airline-stewardess kind of voice crooned, "Good afternoon, Tri-City Guaranty and Trust Company, may I help you?"

"Ah—?" I said. I hadn't been expecting that. I don't know what I had been expecting. "I'm calling, ah, about that Personal Notice in the paper—"

"Just one moment, sir, I'll connect you with Mr. Thornley."

Some bloops and bleeps and *sotto voce* mumbling and then another professional, deep, money kind of voice said, "Thornley here."

"I'm calling about Jane Hildergarde Clamp."

"Ah! You have some information?"

"No, I want some. Can you tell me what this is all about?"

A slight pause, and then, "I'm sorry, sir, but the matter is confidential. I'm sure you'll understand."

"Can't you tell me anything? Is it Miss Clamp or Mrs. Clamp?"

"I'm sorry, sir, the matter is confidential. May I ask you why you called?"

"Well, the name seemed—I just heard of a name like it this morning."

"I see. Well, there are other names like it in the city. We are *not* referring to—just a moment, please." Sounds of papers rustling. "We don't want to hear about Mrs. June Hilda Clamp of 2637 Larch Street, or Miss Joan H. Clamp of 1178 West 97th Street, or J. Helga Clamp of 21219 New Zealand Avenue. I might also say, although I'm sure I needn't warn *you*, sir, that we can make it uncomfortable for crank callers if we catch them. What we want is bona fide information about the whereabouts of Jane Hildegarde Clamp. We want to get in touch with her."

"I see... Well, thank you."

"Thank *you*, sir."

Well, so much for that. Another coincidence, no doubt. And yet...and yet I had the nagging suspicion that everything was pointing in some particular direction, and that I could make sense of it if only—if only—

But I couldn't make sense of it. I spent the rest of the day alternately trying and giving up, drinking coffee, pacing about, cooking dinner, going to a disappointing movie...

Late that evening I sat down with a sigh to read Susan's diary again. It had occurred to me that perhaps I had overlooked something in it that might give me a clue. I was right. As I neared the end of it, and again read that scene where a despairing Susan crouches under the hedge with Robert and Victoria, and Victoria proposes one last measure to save their plan from total ruin, and Susan says that even that measure is hopeless, because here they are in the nineteenth century whereas the witch is in the twentieth—as I read that for the second time my heart began to thud, and the hair on the back of my neck prickled.

That wavery voice on the telephone! That ancient creature in the huge automobile! Eureka!

The Elevator's Last Trip

Of course I hadn't recognized the witch.

How could I? Whenever I thought of her at all, it was as Susan had described her: an eccentric, garish old woman with an umbrella, a newspaper, a sack of potatoes, and a vague manner, who was driven about on a motorcycle. Whereas *my* lady in distress—Well, no matter. She had changed her appearance and her mode of transportation, but the old vagueness was still there, and her way of doing things was the same. You helped her out, and she gave you something. But what she gave you was a mystery, a hint, a possibility. From there on, you had to figure out her meaning for yourself.

Well, now that I knew who she was, everything clicked into place in my mind. She *was* going to answer the Walker children's plea; and because I was the only person in the world who knew—and accepted—where the Shaws had gone, she had chosen me to carry out her plans.

The first phrase of her note was so roundabout that it took me a while to interpret, but I finally guessed it to mean that I could not go back to 1881 myself. The rest was straightforward enough. I could send a message to the Shaws. The means of sending it would have to be the elevator. The message itself would have to be the Special Notice.

But wait—I'd better be careful about that. Just because I'd found a Special Notice with a familiar name didn't mean that it was the one to go. I took the elevator down to the basement, and spent an hour rummaging through Mr. Bodoni's heap of newspapers. There were some pretty odd Special Notices to be found, but none that seemed closer to the purpose than the one I already had. That one, by the way, appeared in every paper I looked at. Tri-City Guaranty and Trust Company had been seeking contact with Jane Hildegarde Clamp for as far back as I could check. Curious...

Back in my apartment, I figured out what my strategy should be. If the Shaws did find the message in the elevator, they would be there for only one reason: to return to the twentieth century, thereby using up their last trip on the elevator, the message might be useless. Therefore, they must be persuaded to read it before they took the irrevocable step.

I found a large manila mailing envelope and wrote on it with black crayon: SUSAN SHAW—MR. SHAW—DON'T COME DOWN UNTIL YOU READ WHAT'S INSIDE! Then I circled the Special Notice about Jane Hildegarde Clamp, to call the Shaws' attention to it; and put a question mark beside it to show that its significance was just a guess on my part. For a while I tried to think what it might mean to them, to figure out how it could possibly turn the tide of events where they were. But it was useless. With a sigh, I folded the sheet of newspaper and inserted it in the envelope, and went out in the hall to call the elevator.

The latest wisecrack about Mr. Bodoni's mechanical ability had been imperfectly scrubbed off, I noticed. I stuck the envelope to the rear wall with tape, and stepped back to view the effect. My message was as conspicuous as I could hope to make it. "Okay, old horse, do your stuff," I murmured to the elevator. It sighed, and the door trundled shut.

Well, it was out of my hands now. I went to bed. But the doubts flooded over me, I couldn't sleep. Had I done the right thing? How would I ever know? After an hour of tossing, I put on my bathrobe and rushed out to check the elevator. My message was gone. My heart lifted—and sank again. What did that prove, after all? Only that it was gone; perhaps to 1881, perhaps (just as likely) to the apartment of some nosy and not too scrupulous tenant...

How would I ever know...?

Saturday night was another sleepless one for me. At about nine-thirty Sunday morning I decided to go to the park; I thought that perhaps in the shade of a tree I might find some relief from the heat and from the questions that were still plaguing me. I pressed the elevator button and waited...And pressed again and waited. And waited.

Finally I took the stairs down. I ran into Mr. Bodoni at the front door. He was prepared for a Sunday outing too, in a black suit that made him look like a mourner at a gangster's funeral, and a straw hat, and a new (but of course unlit) cigar.

"Hey, Mr. Bodoni, what's the matter with the elevator?" I asked.

"Busted," he said with a huge smile. "Busted for good. Finished. I call the owners, they gonna replace. All brand-new parts—everything!" No more gestures of apology: Mr. Bodoni was a free man.

"Oh," I said.

"Whatsa matter, you crazy or someting, you don't wanna new one?"

"Well…I was kind of attached to the old beast. How did it go?"

"Hah?"

"How did it bust?"

"Boy oh boy!" he said, beginning to frown. "Some business! I don't even wanna tink about it!" His voice dropped to a confidential murmur. "You wanna know someting? Crazy lady in there!"

"What?"

"Yeah! Boy oh boy, I don't even wanna talk about!"

Nevertheless, I didn't have to prompt him to tell me the whole story.

In order to escape the heat late last night, he had gone down into the basement, where it was five degrees cooler than anywhere else. Settled in a camp chair, in his undershirt, a can of cold beer within reach, the early edition of the Sunday papers in his lap opened to the comics section, he slipped into a state of perfect contentment.

It lasted perhaps fifteen minutes.

A faint rhythmic banging began to intrude on his consciousness. It seemed to be coming from—from the elevator shaft…Oh oh! Had the elevator broken down at last? Was somebody stuck? He looked up at the arrow. No, it was moving; moving to the left. The banging became louder. It sounded as if someone were trying to do grievous damage. Indignation welled up in Mr. Bodoni's heart; he had no love for the elevator, but it was his responsibility. They shouldn't

do that! Thunderous blows drowned the sigh of the opening door. Mr. Bodoni stood up, prepared to defend his elevator against carousing delinquents or perhaps some tenant who had had too much to drink. "Hey!" he cried, taking one step forward, only to be stopped dead in his tracks by the most ferocious glare he had ever encountered.

It was not coming from a juvenile hoodlum or a drunk, but from a woman. She was awkwardly seated, as one entirely unaccustomed to such a position, on the floor of the elevator. Her stout figure was dressed in a red flannel robe. Her face, under a ruffled cap, was purple with rage, and her eyes glittered behind pince-nez glasses. The black umbrella with which she had been battering the elevator door was raised to strike another blow.

Mr. Bodoni managed another, and much more feeble, "Hey."

"I'll hey you, my man!" the woman shouted in a voice that was even more piercing that her eyes. "Who are you? What is the meaning of this outrage?"

"Outrage" had been a familiar word of late. Mr. Bodoni's wits rallied. "Not dangerous," he said, waving conciliatory hands. "A little slow maybe, yeah, but not dangerous. Don't hit, the paint job won't take it."

"Stop talking rubbish!" she shouted. "I demand an explanation!"

"No rubbish," Mr. Bodoni protested. "It's a little old, is all. Loose parts."

"I won't have any *more* of this lunatic raving!" she cried. "I am in severe pain. I require medical attention. Above all, I wish to return. And *you* stand there—!"

"Madame," a man's voice broke in, "there is nothing to be gained by shouting like that."

Mr. Bodoni tore his gaze away from the glittering eyes, and saw for the first time that there was another passenger within. It was a man with a bruised face and rumpled hair, wearing a very old-fashioned suit that was torn in several places and mottled with large wet stains.

The woman turned and jabbed at him with her umbrella, like a lion-tamer forcing an unruly beast back into its corner. "You, sir," she shouted, "are a scoundrel! I believe the most appropriate place for *you* is a police station. I intend to see you taken to one at the earliest opportunity." She turned to Mr. Bodoni again. "Don't stand there like an imbecile, my man! I have vitally important duties to discharge and I wish to return to them at once! Do you understand the mechanism of this conveyance?"

"Hah?"

"Look here, my good fellow," the man said from the corner of the elevator. He had been staring at the washing machines against the wall. "Just tell us where we are, will you?"

"Yeah," Mr. Bodoni said. "Here."

"No, no, what I mean is, where is this building—?"

"I wish to return!" the woman shouted at Mr. Bodoni. "Do what is necessary this instant, or I shall seek out your employer and have your wages stopped for a month!"

"Madame," the man snapped, "you are sorely trying my patience. Something serious is happening here, and I am trying to find out what, but you keep inter—"

"*Patience,* you scum!" she roared. "If I could stand, I'd show you patience!" she turned and slashed at him with her umbrella. The steel tip gazed his vest. A button fell to the floor and rolled over to Mr. Bodoni's feet. She turned back to skewer him with her glare. "I—wish—to—go—back," she said, enunciating each word like the crack of a whip. "I am waiting."

The message penetrated at last. Mr. Bodoni jerked his thumb toward the ceiling. "You wanna go back, hah? Back up there?"

She closed her eyes and inclined her head slightly. "*So* intelligent of him!" she murmured. "*Such* a firm grasp of what is required! *If* you will be so kind as to set me in motion."

Mr. Bodoni saw that for some reason she was waiting for him to press the button. He sidled toward the elevator, keeping his gaze fixed on her umbrella. Her mouth tightened, and she drew in the skirt of her robe as he approached. He dared not ask her which floor she wanted. He reached inside and pressed the first button his fingers found.

It was an emergency button. They all gave a start as the warning bell on top of the elevator burst into a deafening clangor. "Stop that noise!" the woman shouted, pounding Mr. Bodoni's paunch with her umbrella. He pressed three more buttons simultaneously and staggered back. The bell stopped. Its echoes could be heard bouncing about and dying away in the shaft.

"Look here!" the man said, appealing to Mr. Bodoni with a wild eye. "What do you know about this?"

"Not dangerous," Mr. Bodoni croaked.

The door trundled shut.

Mr. Bodoni sagged against the wall. Beads of sweat were trickling down his cheeks and neck. "Crazy!" he muttered. "Boy oh boy—crazy! Whew! Must be the heat." He found that his legs were shaking. He collapsed into his camp chair, took a deep swig of beer, and fanned himself with the sports section of his paper. Who? Who? Who...? They weren't tenants, he knew that. He hoped they weren't *going* to be tenants. Boy oh boy, with a crazy lady like that in the building he'd have to get a job somewhere else...Maybe they just wandered in from the street, crazy from the temperature. He hoped they would wander out again. He listened. All was quiet. Boy oh boy...He finished his beer in two more gulps, leaned over to retrieve the scattered comics—and froze.

Bang bang bang bang!

The elevator was coming down again. The shaft resounded like a huge drum to the blows of her umbrella.

Mr. Bodoni's spirit failed. "Nah," he bleated. His camp chair clattered over backward as he scrambled to his feet. He fled toward the stairs on the opposite side of the basement, shedding pages of newspaper as he went. Behind him the elevator door opened. Her shriek stabbed through his ears: "*Imbecile! Return me at once!*" He soared up the steps like a kangaroo.

He was standing out on the front sidewalk, panting and mopping his face, when a hand fell on his shoulder.

"Nah!" he cried, leaping halfway across Ward Street in one bound.

"Hey, Bodoni, whatsa matter with you? It's me!"

He turned, and saw that it was an old acquaintance, a man who lived on the sixth floor.

"Listen, the elevator's stuck down in the basement. I keep punching the button but nothing happens. It won't come up."

"Leave alone!" Mr. Bodoni cried. "Crazy lady in there!"

"What?"

Mr. Bodoni told him what had happened, and invited him to come see for himself. They crept silently a little way down the basement stairs, and peered across the room. The elevator stood open-doored, with only one occupant now. She sat on the floor with folded arms, an implacable presence, radiating fury in almost visible waves.

The two men sneaked back up the stairs.

"Oh boy oh boy!" Mr. Bodoni moaned. "What to do?"

"We better call the cops, Bodoni. She oughta be in a psychiatric ward."

It took three policemen to get her away. After the din was over, Mr. Bodoni discovered that the elevator had made its final trip.

"Crazy!" he said to me now. "Everything all at once! Motor shot! Circuits burnt out! Cable busted! Boy oh boy—zap!" He took a deep breath and grinned. "I'm gonna play bocce ball inna park. See ya!"

My mental turmoil of the last two days and nights was nothing compared to now. Because while Mr. Bodoni had been talking, a feeling that I can only call recognition had flashed over me. That "crazy lady," with her stout figure and glittering eyes and pince-nez glasses and umbrella, sounded so much like—like—! Why not? It wasn't impossible! And there was a man with her, too…Now who on earth—?

Oh lord, *what had happened in 1881?*

There was no relief in the park, no relief. I trudged back to the apartment building and hauled myself up five weary flights of stairs and mixed myself a cold drink. Susan's diary was on my bookshelves where I had put it day before yesterday. I looked at its spine and shook my head, almost wishing that the whole baffling business had never begun. There was something sticking up out of the top, like a marker. I couldn't remember having put any such thing in the diary. I pulled the book out to check. Yes. Something bulky between the front cover of the first page…Brown paper…

Funny! I stared at it and turned it over in my hands for a

long time before the meaning of it began to sink in. It was a large folded envelope of time-darkened brittle paper. The words on it were still perfectly clear: SUSAN SHAW—MR. SHAW—DON'T COME DOWN and on the other side of the fold UNTIL YOU READ WHAT'S INSIDE! Inside, darkened to a burnt orange-brown, was a fragile folded sheet of newspaper…

The back of my neck began to prickle. Now I really know how Susan and Victoria and Robert had felt when, after finding the treasure, they discovered that the front page of their newspaper had changed. My word! It's one thing to mention "time paradox" glibly, as I had to Charles, and another thing to *experience* it. I shivered. Here was the paradox in my hands, beyond explanation, beyond argument. The envelope had been in the diary for many decades. There was a straight-edged stain on the first page and the inside of the cover to prove it. But there had been no stain on the envelope in the diary day before yesterday, because I had not yet sent the envelope up the elevator to change the past…

Wait a minute—!

Mightn't that mean that the diary—that the diary also—that in the diary—?

My legs were doing funny things. I had to sit down. My mouth was dry and my hands shook as I turned to the place where—

Yes! There were now pages and pages of fast loopy scrawl after the word "despair"!

Mrs. Walker Weeps

It's happened! It's happened! We called up the elevator to leave and there was a sign on the back wall. At first we thought it was one of Mr. Bodoni's, but when my eyes got used to the light I saw it had our names on it! It said to read it before we came down, and because I tried to, it happened at last…

"Think an eagle will be enough?" Mr. Shaw said. "We never did find out what they charge, did we?"

"No," Susan murmured.

"Let's see…We've been here two days, more or less—oh, nuts! I don't know why I'm making a fuss about it. Let's just leave all we've got." The coins clinked as he laid them out on the little table by his bed.

He tiptoed over to the window and looked out. All the lights in the Walkers' house—all that were visible from here—had been extinguished for nearly an hour. That should be sufficient time for them to be settled into sleep over there. The Hollisters, who had retired about an hour ago, were well settled themselves; a throbbing chorus of snorts and snores from the back of the house attested to that.

"All right, chick," he said. "Time to go. Got everything?"

She picked up her diary and the farewell letter to Victoria and Robert, and nodded miserably. He blew out the candle, and when their eyes had become adjusted to the dark they crept down the stairs.

The stars seemed even more brilliant than night before last; the sky was luminous with them. 'I'll never see stars like this again,' she thought. They blurred. She stumbled along beside her father, blind with tears.

"Front door? Back door?" he murmured.

Her only wish now was to get the pain over with as quickly as possible. "Front," she choked.

Mr. Shaw stopped when they reached the porch steps. "Shoes!" he whispered, pantomiming the removal of his boots; he wasn't going to take any chances in the house. They sat down on the bottom step and took off their shoes—his genuine American articles, and the button-ups she had borrowed from Victoria. 'I'll leave them behind,' she thought. 'Nothing I can do about the dress, though.' Not so long ago she had daydreamed about going to town with Victoria and buying a whole wardrobe...The memory wrenched her heart.

They crept up to the front door in their stocking feet. Mr. Shaw opened it with extreme caution. Silence closed around them inside, broken only by their own breathing and the muffled ticking of the grandfather clock. They felt their way step by step among the dim shapes of parlor furniture. Here was the curtained doorway through which Maggie had made her appearance this morning. "Time—time—time" the clock dirged as they passed by.

"All right, Susie," Mr. Shaw whispered, "call it up."

She put her farewell letter on the table, propping it against the stuffed owl's glass bell, and placed Victoria's shoes side by side underneath. The lump in her throat felt as large as a fist. She turned quickly to the wainscotting of the outer wall, and pressed her thumb against the warm wooden surface. She could feel the vibration of the faraway mechanism lurching into life.

Her shoulders began to shake. Mr. Shaw murmured and put his arm around her. They waited. Behind the paneling sounded a hum, an approaching muffled groan...The wainscotting split, and rumbled apart. They flinched under the glare of the electric light.

There was a new sign attached to the rear wall of the elevator, but their eyes were so dazzled that they couldn't make out the words. Another one of Mr. Bodoni's notices, no doubt, about "smokking" in the elevator or dropping "liter" on its floor...

They got in.

Her aching eyes were beginning to accommodate to the light. SUSAN SHAW, she read on the new sign. Her mind was so numb with grief that she did not recognize these words for an instant. MR. SHAW...

"Daddy!" she whispered.

He already had his finger on the third-floor button. He had not looked twice at the sign.

"No!" she whisper-shouted, seizing his hand and pulling it away from the bank of buttons.

"What are you doing?" he muttered.

"Look, look, look!" She pulled him around by the arm so that he was forced to see the sign again.

SUSAN SHAW—MR. SHAW—DON'T COME

DOWN UNTIL YOU READ WHAT'S INSIDE!

They stared, too astonished to move.

"What's that all about?" Mr. Shaw murmured after a moment. "Inside what?"

"I don't know," she whispered.

"Do you think one of the Walker kids—?"

"No. The elevator wouldn't come up for them. It must be—" The idea was incredible, but she could think of no alternative. "It must be from the twentieth century!" And as she said it, the answer came to her.

Robert and Victoria had been successful after all.

She stepped forward and tore the sign from the wall. It was not a sign, but a manila envelope. Inside...She tried to force her finger under the glued-down flap.

The elevator door sighed, and began to trundle shut.

With a squeak of fright she hurled herself at the door, caught it just in time, and forced it back. It began to bunt against her hand with convulsive little leaps.

"Get out, get out!" she whispered to her father. "We have to read this."

"Why can't we read it going down?" he said.

"*No.* It says don't go down until *after* we read it!"

"But—"

"Oh!" she cried—tried to cry; her voice was too choked with urgency to sound very loud. She let the bucking door go, flung herself on him, and yanked him out into the hallway with the strength she had never suspected in herself. The wainscotting closed up again, the elevator groaned away down the shaft, and they were left clinging together and panting in the dark.

"Susan," he said in a low dangerous voice, "I am at the end

of my patience with you. I have had all the frustrations I am able to cope with. Call that elevator back."

"Daddy, I will, but I have to read this first!"

"Just how the *devil* do you propose to read anything in this dark?"

"I—" she began, casting desperately about, "I—Candles!" She started to back down the hallway. "There're candles on the mantelpiece in the parlor."

"Susan, you—"

"Daddy, just a minute, *please!*"

She turned and hurried as quickly as the dark permitted back to the parlor. Ooops! She found herself bending double over a hassock or something that had caught her on the shins; fortunately it was well padded. She looked about. Her eyes were adjusting to the darkness again. A shape loomed nearby. She touched smooth wood and plush—it was the sofa. And there, dimly gleaming a few yards away, was the white marble of the fireplace.

Somewhere at the other end of the house a door opened.

She whirled around toward the doorway and went rigid. Voices murmured and a light flickered on the other side, in the hallway where her father—He was going to be caught flat-footed!

Unless it was Victoria and Robert, in which case—

It was not Victoria and Robert. The voices were different. Two voices—one weeping, one murmuring…

They were almost in the parlor. Candlelight wavered through the portieres, shadows swayed on the parlor rug. Susan broke out of her paralysis. For some reason her father hadn't been seen. She mustn't be seen either. She scurried behind an armchair and crouched. But the urge to look could not be resisted, and she straightened up again until her eyes were just above the back of the chair.

Through the doorway came Mrs. Walker in a white peignoir, stumbling, weeping. "I can't bear it," she sobbed. "Oh, I can't bear it anymore!" Her loosened waistlength hair tumbled about her face, half hiding it. In candlelight it no longer looked chestnut, but dark, nearly black. The effect was both ravishingly beautiful and heart-breaking. Susan groaned to herself, and gripped the back of the sofa.

Maggie trotted along next to Mrs. Walker, supporting her with one arm. She held the candlestick in her free hand. "Ah, sure, sure now," she murmured. "It'll be all right, Mum. Sure, now." They slowly passed through the parlor into the front hall, and paused, out of Susan's sight now, at the foot of the staircase.

"Isabelle!" said Cousin Jane's voice from upstairs.

The candlelight flickered violently. Mrs. Walker murmured a wordless reply.

"We have much to accomplish tomorrow, Isabelle," Cousin Jane's voice crackled. "I suggest that you come up to bed immediately and obtain a full night's sleep. Wandering about at this late hour is not conducive to good health, and sets a bad example. Is Maggie with you?"

"Yes..."

"Have you locked up the house for the night, Maggie?"

The candlelight flickered again. "Sure, Mum, and wasn't I jist on the edge of doin' it when ye asked me."

"In other words, you have *not* done it. Lock up at once, and then get to bed! I hope I shall not have to tell you twice tomorrow night. Come up, Isabelle."

"Lock up, is it?" Maggie muttered. The bolt on the front door banged into place. "There, ye black-hearted she-divel! As for the rest of it, ye may do it yerself. I draw me wages for housekeepin', not guardin' a jail."

"Good night, Isabelle!" Cousin Jane said. It was not a wish, but a command. Doors closed. Maggie, still muttering in a fierce undertone, trudged upstairs. The candlelight faded, and all the downstairs was dark again.

Susan stood up and groped her way back to the hall. "Daddy?" she whispered.

The curtains by the window stirred. "Here!" he whispered.

"They didn't see you?"

"No, I zipped behind here and they went right by. I saw *her*, though. Good night!"

Something about him felt different. A kind of electric tenseness radiated from him; but it wasn't the anger and frustration of their recent quarrel over the elevator. Not now...

"Crying!" he muttered to himself. "Good lord! She was crying..."

She didn't know what to say. They stood there for several minutes. He seemed to be holding his breath, or caught up in a trance.

At last he breathed out with a sharp sound, almost a snort. He whispered, "All right, chick, let's go."

She became aware that she was still holding the manila envelope. "Daddy," she whispered, "we haven't read the message yet."

"Never mind that! Later!"

"But—"

He seized her arm with such a grip that she almost yelped with pain, and began propelling her toward the place where the elevator door was.

And past it.

And through the parlor.

And out the front door, whose bolt and knob yielded as silently and easily to him as if magic had been in his touch; and across the porch; and down the front walk.

"Daddy," she whispered, scarcely able to get the words out, "are we staying?"

"Absolutely!"

Then, in the middle of the Ward Lane, he stopped again, and let go of her arm, and fell into that trance-like state.

"By *George!*" he burst out after a moment. "I never even looked at her before! Never even saw her! I mean, all the time she was right in front of my eyes, and I never—Oh, good lord!"

Susan was in something of a trance herself. The smell of the night air, the brilliance of the stars, were too sweet to bear. Something inside her went *pop*, a warm bubbly explosion. Hello, stars! They blurred again—but this time through tears of happiness.

"Oh, Daddy…!" she choked.

"What?" he said, starting out of his reverie. "What's that? Oh, yes! Well, come on."

Again he seized her arm in that powerful grip. She let out a squeak. He paid no heed, but swept her back to the Hollisters' so rapidly that she had to half-run to stay on her feet. The symphony of snores changed its pace for a measure or two, as they crept up the stairs, and then continued *a tempo.*

She put her diary and the envelope down, and felt around

the bureau top until she found a match, and lit the candle. Mr. Shaw stood in the soft yellow light looking down with a puzzled expression at his boots—which were dangling by their laces from his left hand. She noticed now that she was in stocking-feet, too; her shoes—Victoria's—were still under the little table in the hallway of the Walkers' house…Not that it mattered. Not that anything mattered now!

"I never felt a thing!" she laughed. "We've been walking on air!"

"Ah," he said profoundly. He sat down on the edge of his bed, and was lost to the world again.

Susan tore open the manila envelope, and pulled out a folded piece of newspaper. Houses for sale. Houses for rent… She turned the paper over and saw a crayoned circle. *REWARD for info. leading to contact with Jane Hildegarde Clamp…* Question mark in crayon. Familiar name…Oh, she couldn't concentrate! A fit of giggles took possession of her. She kept looking at her father, who sat there muttering "By George!" to himself, with a dazed look on his face.

Suddenly he stood up, strode over to her, and kissed her on the forehead.

"Susie," he said, "thank you. Thank you very, very much. It all makes sense now. I mean, the whole thing. You knew it all along, didn't you? It's just that I couldn't see it until…But I mean it makes *sense* now. What I mean is—do you know what I mean?"

"Yes," she said, laughing up into his lunatic face. "I know what you mean."

Mr. Swingle States his Business

...tried to figure out what that notice in the newspaper meant. Was the name just a coincidence? While we were talking about it somebody came to call on us. He was a man with a beard, named Arbuthnot Swingle. The moment I saw him I knew he looked familiar...

Mr. Shaw's behavior at breakfast was so remarkable that even Mrs. Hollister forgot her shyness long enough to look at him directly, instead of out of the corner of her eye. At one moment he would be gay and laughing, delighted with everything. Abruptly he would plunge into a fit of abstraction; his eyes would glaze over, and with a look almost of gloom he would poke at his eggs and bacon. Just as abruptly, his eyes would crinkle into a smile again, and with a great laugh he would attack his breakfast like a man recently rescued from starvation.

Susan giggled, and choked over her toast, and stuffed herself, and giggled again. She was acting as loony as Daddy! Mrs. Hollister's lips tightened as she pushed the coffee pot to them. She looked as though she suspected them of having taken a pre-breakfast nip of spirits! Susan doubled over with uncontrollable giggling.

After breakfast they went upstairs. Mr. Shaw paused at the door of his room, and collapsed against the jamb.

"Susie," he groaned, "how can I ask her to marry me? I haven't got a thing to offer!"

"You have too! You're handsome and kind and—"

"And I'm flat broke, or right on the edge of it. Look!" They went into his room, and he pointed at the handful of coins on the night table. "There's our fortune—and we probably owe most of it to the Hollisters. We have what's left, plus the clothes we stand in."

"Plus our intelligence," she added. "We're both awfully smart, Daddy. And our knowledge! We know lots that people these days don't."

"Mmm...But that may not be the advantage you think it is. What I know best, for instance, is how to keep track of corporate finances. But I do it with machines that probably haven't been invented yet."

"Maybe you could invent them!"

"Oh, chick!" he laughed. "I'm not the Connecticut Yankee..." He sat in a wobbly rocking chair and put his chin in his hand. "The point is, I'm going to have to earn a living, but I don't know how to make my way around in this century. It's like being in a foreign country. I know I'm capable of learning my way around eventually, but it takes time; and while I'm doing it—" he pointed again at the money on the table "—that's what we have to live on...Sure wish I knew what happened to that treasure!"

"So do I," she sighed. "There's something funny about that. *I* don't think it was a tramp with a dog, or boys looking for nests."

"Well, whatever it was..." He lifted his hands and let them drop. "If I knew anybody here, I could borrow some money to tide us over. But I don't. And good night!" he cried, "all this is based on the supposition that Isabelle is willing to accept me in the first place. How are we even going to *see* her again, with that Clamp monster standing in the way?"

"Don't worry, Daddy. Bobbie and Vicky got around her yesterday, and so can we. Oh! Clamp! I almost forgot!" She ran into her room and brought back the piece of newspaper. "Here—Bobbie and Vicky asked the witch for help, and we got this in the elevator."

"What? What witch?"

She explained.

He began to laugh and shake his head. "You kids are—amazing! The way you accept...!"

"It's just a matter of getting used to it, Daddy. Here, read this. It's weird. I can't figure it out."

"Hmm," he said, after looking at the circled item for a while. "Is Cousin Jane's middle name Hildegarde?"

"I don't know."

"Who the devil would be looking for *her*, anyway? I should think almost anybody in the world would be happy *not* to know where she is."

"But look, Daddy—what's so weird about it is that it's a twentieth-century paper. I think."

"What! Mm—no date; top's been torn off. You're right, though, it does look like a—yes, see, it says 'blood plasma' here. That's twentieth century, all right. The name must be a coincidence, then—they can't be talking about *our* Clamp. Worse luck!"

"Why worse luck?"

"Because think how convenient it would be if she *were* in

the twentieth—"

There was a timid knock.

Mrs. Hollister stood squirming in the hall when Susan opened the door. "Gentleman to see you," she murmured at the ceiling.

"Me?"

"Well, no, both of you. He says it's kind of important, could you spare the time right now?" And Mrs. Hollister, looking hard at her own feet, handed Susan a card.

She studied it in bewilderment. Slowly untangling each Gothic letter from the thicket of ornament in which it lay concealed, she deciphered the name: Arbuthnot Swingle.

With a shrug she gave the card to her father.

"Who's this?" he asked Mrs. Hollister.

"I don't know, sir," she murmured at the door lintel. "Gentleman with a beard..."

It was Mr. Shaw's turn to shrug. "Beard...? Oh, well, all right, send him up.

Mrs. Hollister departed, and the Shaws frowned at each other.

There was a firm, quiet knock, and the caller stood in the doorway. He had an untidy, bushy black beard, and his suit was rumpled as though it had been slept in. By way of contrast, his hair was impeccably combed with oil or pomade, and glistened like the feathers of a blackbird. He was holding a derby in his white hands.

"I hope that my visit is not inopportune," he said. Susan started at the sound of that low, smooth voice. There was something familiar about it...

"No, no," Mr. Shaw said. "Come in, Mr., uh, Swingle. Have a seat."

Mr. Swingle laid his derby on the floor with care, then sat down, crossed his legs, and looked at Susan—and smiled. It was a curious smile, combining admiration with an undertone of irony. Susan squirmed a little, but could not stop staring at this unsettling stranger.

"Your daughter, sir?" Mr. Swingle enquired, turning to Mr. Shaw.

"That's right—my daughter Susan. My name is Shaw."

"Ah, yes, I was informed of that fact by your excellent landlady. Well, Mr. Shaw, I congratulate you: your daughter, sir, is an artist of the first rank. You yourself have a professional ability that is practically unbeatable. Practically—but not quite... Will you join me in a cigar, sir?"

"No, thanks, I don't—"

"I hope it will not incommode you if I indulge in one myself?"

"No, go ahead. I don't catch your meaning, Mr. Swingle. Will you explain?"

But Mr. Swingle, having lit his cigar, turned again toward Susan with that admiring and ironic smile. And as she noticed the way he held his cigar, lightly, fastidiously, between his fingertips, her eyes began to widen and her mouth dropped open.

"Ah, ah, ah!" he said, holding up his other hand and forestalling her gasp. "Such sharp eyes! Such lightning recognition! You are quite correct, my dear—we have met before."

And with an even wider smile than ever, he tore off his beard.

"Mr. Sweeney!" she moaned.

"Exactly! Or should I say, more or less? We know how convenient it is to have numerous names, don't we? Algeron

Sweeney will do—or Arbuthnot Swingle, or even Abernathy Swinnerton, if you prefer." Wrinkling his nose, he dropped the beard beside his hat. "Pah! What a tiresome apparatus! However, I did not wish to be recognized by the Walkers or by our good landlady. But I was sure that *your* keen eyes would not be deceived for long, my dear!"

"Will you kindly tell us what all this is about, Mr. Swingle—Sweeney—whatever?" Mr. Shaw said.

"With pleasure, sir. Your plan to exclude me from the kill was audacious and beautifully executed. It almost succeeded, but not quite. So I am here to congratulate you on a good try, and to inform you that it has failed. I am also here to demand my share of the spoils yet to come."

"Kill?" Mr. Shaw said. "Spoils? I don't—"

"Oh, come, come, my dear Shaw! I see that your acting abilities are almost equal to the young lady's. That air of innocent bafflement is marvelously well done! But why waste it on me? I believe we understand each other."

"The understanding seems to be more on your side than mine," Mr. Shaw said.

Mr. Sweeney blew a cloud of smoke toward the ceiling. "You need some time to think, don't you? Well, think away!—I'll give you all the time you need. Meanwhile, I will be as plain as I can. Through some coincidence we have settled upon the same mark, you and I. I do not intend to retire from the field. You do not intend to retire from the field. Therefore, we must share the mark between us."

"Mark?"

"Please don't be tiresome, Shaw! I refer to, or course, to our mutual victim, Isabelle Walker."

"Ah-h-h!" Mr. Shaw said. His eyes narrowed. "Victim? Good lord, man, you don't think that I—"

"No, I don't think," Mr. Sweeney said, waving his hand. "I know. And now that I know, I am not going to be put off the way I was last time. I confess that I was absolutely taken in by that little masquerade you arranged for me. It must have given you a good deal of amusement to see me fleeing from here under the conviction that Isabelle had already been picked clean and that I was in mortal danger of smallpox. Well, I don't begrudge you your little laugh. We know how to be philosophical in this game, don't we? And anyway, I had another little operation in town to fall back on."

"What do you mean by that?" Mr. Shaw asked.

"Another widow," Mr. Sweeney sighed. "Elderly, plain, grateful for a little attention—you know the sort of thing. Such a routine job that I could scarcely suppress my yawns as I relieved her of everything. A paltry fifteen hundred. So tedious...But, one must live, mustn't one?"

"You took—*every*thing?"

"My dear Shaw, what a curious question! Of course I did. After all, she has her house, and a large supply of leisure. She can take in boarders, or do laundry, or something."

"Oh. Yes, I see..." Mr. Shaw clasped his hands together until the knuckles turned white. "Well, ah, what brought you back here?"

"Why, I saw the two of you at the railroad station, just after the conclusion of my business with the widow, It seemed strange that the 'servant girl,' whom I had last seen in tears"—Mr. Sweeney smiled at Susan—"should now be so happily hob-nobbing with a gentleman. I thought it warranted further investigation. So I boarded the train, walked rapidly through the cars to the last one, disembarked, and took shelter behind a convenient coal bin. From there I watched the servant girl and gentleman being conveyed out of town by a citizen with a surrey. When the citizen returned, and I treated him to some beer—a great deal of beer—and learned some interesting facts: that the servant girl and gentleman were father and daughter, or at any rate passed themselves off as such; that they were boarding at Hollisters', right next door to the Walkers; and that the Walkers, far from having succumbed to smallpox, were in excellent health!

"Well, all this seemed to be worth looking into! I took a little stroll into the country, and sat down in the shade to observe the passing scene. And what an interesting scene it was! Here is the former servant girl, now a young lady, mixing on the closest terms with the Walker children. And, a little later, here she comes with her father, walking out to take the air and to commune with Nature. How absorbing Nature is to them! They listen to the songs of birds; they observe the flight of butterflies; they study the—oh, let us say 'minerals', under a certain blackberry bush—"

"Oh!" Susan gasped.

"Oh!" Mr. Sweeney echoed with a brilliant smile. "The study of Nature is so *rewarding*, isn't it?"

"Oh!" Susan ground out through clenched teeth. "You—!"

"Susan!" Mr. Shaw said, quietly but with such intensity that she turned toward him at once. He was trying to tell her something with his eyes. "Susan, my dear, Mr. Sweeney is right—we must know how to be philosophical in this game. Sit down, please, and be philosophical."

She subsided, wondering what he was up to.

"Well, Sweeney," Mr. Shaw continued. "We've had our little laugh, and now you're having yours. You are a dangerous man, I see."

"Permit me to return the compliment, sir. As soon as you had left, and I had discovered the gold, I did nothing but sing your praises for five minutes. '*What* a smooth operation!' I said. '*What* a pair of artists!' But a question began to nag me as I observed you further. A professional usually departs quickly after making such a kill—but here you were, showing every intention of remaining in the vicinity! What could be the reason for that? The answer staggered me, sir, and my admiration for your audacity soared beyond bounds. You could only be lingering here because there was even *more* to be gotten out of Isabelle Walker."

"Mmm," Mr. Shaw said. "You know, it's fascinating to watch your powerful line of reasoning unfold."

"You flatter me, sir. Well, enough of compliments. Shall we get down to business? I have a proposition to make."

Mr. Shaw raised his eyebrows.

"I propose to help you, if you wish, in finishing off Isabelle. Or, if you prefer, I will stand aside while you do it yourself."

"Very generous of you, Sweeney. You, ah, have a price, of course?"

"Of course. I expect half of what is to come."

"Oh, you do. And what about my gold?"

Mr. Sweeney smiled and shook his head. "I keep that, of course. If money is to be carelessly strewn about the countryside, then it must belong to him who finds it."

"I see. Now, let me get this straight—I'm having some trouble swallowing this. You propose to steal, and keep, all the money we have gotten so far; and you also propose to rob us of half of whatever *else* we can get. Is that it?"

"Your terms are crude, but their sense is correct."

Mr. Shaw's smile was incredulous. "Talk—about—audacity!" he said. "Sweeney, you flaming idiot, what on earth makes you think I'd ever consider a fool proposition like that?"

"My dear Shaw, let's not be obtuse, shall we? You don't have any choice. I've caught you red-handed, as they say in those lurid boys' novels. Isabelle may not know yet that her money had disappeared, or she may believe that you are 'investing' it for her; but in either case I can cause her to begin asking tiresome questions. It would be amusing to denounce you to the police, also. And while you are trying to calm their suspicions on one hand, and Isabelle's on the other, and failing, and finding yourself under arraignment on a very serious charge—*I* will be quietly traveling to distant parts with well lined pockets... Now, surely, forgetting what you have lost, and sharing a mere half of what is to come, must be more attractive to you than *that*."

Oh, the absurd, dreadful scoundrel, with his total misunderstanding of the situation and his silly, empty threats! Susan could no longer contain herself. She broke out in angry, disbelieving laughter.

"Susan!" Mr. Shaw snapped; and then, sending her that cryptic message with his eyes again, "Philosophy, my dear. Philosophy!" His shoulders slumped. He raised his hand to his mouth. "Well, Sweeney," he mumbled. "I—ah...I guess I—I need some time to think."

"Of course," Mr. Sweeney said smoothly. "I understand. Think as much as you need to."

There was a long silence. Susan wondered what her father was up to. He looked so beaten, sitting there with a glazed look in his eyes and his chin in his hands; as if all of Mr. Sweeney's assumptions were true! And yet Mr. Sweeney was wrong about *everything*, and in such an awful, hateful way. Oh, how she detested him! Look at him sitting there, so calm and easy, blowing his smoke at the ceiling with a little smile! She clenched her fists and bit the inside of her lip.

At last Mr. Shaw sighed and said, "Well, Sweeney, you seem to be holding a loaded pistol at my head...I guess I have to say yes to your proposal."

"I thought you would take a rational view," Mr. Sweeney purred. "Now, do you need my assistance or not? Where does your operation stand at present?"

Mr. Shaw leaned back in his chair and studied the cracks in the ceiling plaster. "Wel-l-l," he said at last, pursing his lips, "I think we'd better go ahead by ourselves, if you don't mind. Less complicated that way. You see, the fact is that we're on the verge of success. Your reasoning was correct, Sweeney. There *is* more where that gold came from—much more. And our hands are almost on it."

"Ah!" Mr . Sweeney breathed. "Cash? Investments? Property?"

"Uh, jewelry," Mr. Shaw said. He spoke slowly and carefully. "Mrs. Walker's late husband was extravagant, and used to—to shower her with jewelry on every occasion. Which, as you know, she never wears. She puts on a very, ah, modest appearance."

"Yes, she does, doesn't she?" Mr. Sweeney said, nodding. "I must say it made it difficult for me to assess how much she was good for. I never suspected jewelry."

"I wouldn't have, either, if it hadn't been for Susan. You see, we, ah, specialize in widows with children. You can get a lot of valuable information from children—if you're a child yourself. That's where Susan comes in. As you know, she's gained the complete confidence of Robert and Victoria. They put on little plays for their own amusement. They dress up in Mama's and Papa's old clothes, you know, and Susie suggests putting on jewels to make it more realistic. They can't resist that. It's so naughty—they have to, ah, borrow the key to Mama's jewel case without her knowing about it. But safe, too, because nothing gets lost it's all put away when the theatricals are over. And meanwhile, during the course of the play, Susan appraises the stuff—she's been to school for that—and when she gets the opportunity she makes a wax impression of the key."

"Ah!" Mr. Sweeney said. "*What* an artist! How much will it come to?"

Mr. Shaw assumed a reluctant expression.

"Oh, come, Shaw, don't drag your feet with me. I'm going to find out sooner or later, you know."

"Well, ah, we're pretty confident that it will be between, oh, forty and fifty thousand."

"Ah!" Mr. Sweeney breathed. His eyes were flittering, "I'll want to appraise them myself, of course, when we—" and he made a clutching gesture. "How soon do you think—?"

"Well…the situation over there is delicate. Mrs. Walker's cousin is visiting, and I'm sorry to say that she regards me with suspicion. I'm sure I don't know why!" Mr. Sweeney smiled his appreciation of this joke. "So we have to work a little faster than usually convenient. Susan rejoins her friends this morning, and she'll see to it that there are more amateur theatricals. If she can, she will make an impression of the key. We have a tentative plan to go on from there, but it will depend on what happens this morning, of course. Tell you what. Where are you staying? I could come and give you a progress report, say about twelve-thirty."

"Now, Shaw, you know I have no intention of divulging the whereabouts of my present lodgings. Let's meet in the Hollisters' stable. Twelve-thirty will be suitable. Have you anything else to say to me?"

Mr. Shaw shook his head.

"Very well." Mr. Sweeney picked up his beard, looked at it with an expression of distaste, and re-attached it to his chin. "This is the last time I intend to burden my face with this—excrescence. Hollisters' stable at twelve thirty, then. No, no, do not see me down the stairs. I prefer you to remain here. If you have any idea of following me, dismiss it; the minute I suspect myself of being spied upon, I will denounce you to the police. Good morning, sir; good morning, Miss Shaw. Remember!"

He paused in the doorway, pointed his fingertip at the side of his head, pistol-fashion, gave them a dazzling smile, and was gone.

In the Dragon's Lair

...so furious he scared me. After he got it out of his system he told me why he had put on that act with Mr. Sweeney and what he had in mind. The first thing was to get hold of Bobbie. We couldn't waste any time, so I had to sneak into the Walkers' house...

When they heard his footsteps on the veranda, Mr. Shaw jumped up and strode to the front window. His face was white, and as he watched Mr. Sweeney's retreating figure his jaw muscles twitched. He watched in silence for a moment, then turned, and with a roar fell on his bed and pounded it with his fists until the springs jangled and clouds of dust eddied throughout the room.

"Oh, the weasel!" he shouted. "The dirty cur! The slimy low-down cockroach!"

Gradually he subsided, and sat panting on the floor. "Oh, good night!" he groaned. "I think I could tear that skunk to little pieces and stamp on them! Calling her Isabelle! *Isabelle!* I don't know how I kept from grabbing his throat each time he said that. Oh, the rat!"

"That was an incredible act you put on with him, Daddy."

"Hunh! I could hardly believe I was doing it myself. Maybe some of your talent is rubbing off on me!"

"But what was it for?"

"To gain time. Say, we shouldn't be here. He's probably going to be spying on us again soon. I guess he hides in the trees across the road, but I don't know. Come on!"

He seized her arm and hurried her downstairs, through the kitchen and back shed, and out to the stable. Chickens fled before them, clucking. They sat down on a sack of oats.

"We have to get hold of Bobbie," Mr. Shaw muttered, biting his lip.

"Daddy, what are you up to with that fantastic story about putting on plays with Mrs. Walker's jewels?"

"I told you, I need time to think. That dirty swine has our fortune. If I didn't play along with him he'd vanish with it. It's just lucky for us that he has this greasy little fantasy about what we're up to. It means that as long as I tell him what he wants to hear, he'll keep coming back. Listen, we need Bobbie. Do you think you can penetrate the dragon's lair and get hold of him and bring him here?"

"I can try. Why do we—?"

"Oh, I'll explain later. It's just an idea I'm beginning to have...Now don't let yourself be seen from the road, chick, and tell Bobbie the same. The less Sweeney knows about our movements, the better. Got it?"

"Yes."

"Good luck, then. And listen—there's got to be a way out of this. I'm going to be thinking hard about it while you're gone. Bring 'im back alive!"

He hugged and kissed her, and she slipped out of the stable.

The thing to do, since she must not be seen from the road, was to approach the Walkers' house from the rear. Robert and Victoria had done it yesterday by following the hedge back. She walked behind the stable, wincing with each step. She was still in stocking feet.

Behind the stable was a weedy pasture. A huge grey-and-white barred hen looked at her with a malevolent eye, and sidled off, clucking. There the hedge rounded away toward the Walkers' side. She followed it, sucking air in through her teeth each time she stepped on a stick or stone. And here, finally, was a gate in the hedge, and on the other side was the back of the Walkers' stable.

She peered around the corner of the stable, and saw that a sun parlor window was open, probably the one Robert had used yesterday. There was no consistent cover between here and there. The only thing to do was make a dash for the hydrangeas under the window.

She dashed.

No one had seen her. She threw herself under the shrubbery, and crouched, panting. The soles of her feet throbbed.

A heavy greenhouse smell drifted out of the window. By standing on her toes she could just look over the sill into a bright room full of wicker furniture and potted plants. She listened. Somewhere in the house she could hear a clinking of plates and an occasional murmur of voices. They must be at breakfast, then; but where, she couldn't tell. Far enough from the sun parlor, anyway, to judge by the sounds.

She heaved herself up and slithered in, banging her knees as she passed over the sill, and landing on a basket-work chaise longue that creaked loudly under her weight.

The breakfast sounds continued without pause.

Peeking around the door frame, she discovered that she was looking into a hallway—not the one that contained the elevator, but the wider one on the other side of the house. A quick dash would take her to the stairs. She whisked down the hall. The thick pile of the carpet swallowed all sound—and how kind it felt to her feet after the lumps and bumps outside! Suddenly, before she could notice it and stop herself, she was opposite another doorway. Her horror-stricken glance through the door revealed a breakfast tableau: Maggie with a coffee pot bending over Mrs. Walker; Cousin Jane's stout, rigid back; a side-view of Robert hunched over and sullenly staring into his lap.

Then she was past the door. None of them had noticed. 'Oh, what a piece of dumb luck!' she thought, clutching her hands to her head as she flew up the stairs. 'I can hide in Vicky's room till Bobbie comes up.'

Victoria's door was shut. Could she still be sleeping? Susan knocked softly. There was a stir on the other side of the door, and Victoria whispered, "Bobbie?"

"No," Susan whispered back, "it's—" and then there was the sound of heavy slow footsteps on the stairs.

"Bobbie?" Victoria whispered again.

Susan turned the knob and pushed. The door would not open. The footsteps were ascending…Her eyes darted about the hallway. There was an open door! She scurried through it, dropped to the floor, and rolled under the bed. She had a glimpse in passing of maps and flags and a sword on the wall—it must be Robert's room, thank goodness!

The heavy footsteps came down the hall and into the room. She could see Robert's shoes coming up to the bed. She heard him groan. His feet vanished and the springs creaked as he threw himself down.

"Bobbie!" she whispered, scrambling out.

The springs gave a violent creak. "Vick!" he whispered. "What're you—?" Then he saw who it was. "Great Caesar!" he croaked. His face went white.

"What's the matter?" she whispered. "It's me!"

"But you—we thought—" he stammered. He touched her face with an icy hand. "Did you get another trip back on the elevator?"

"We never went!"

"But you left your shoes and a letter in the hall!"

"Oh!" she cried, slapping her forehead. She'd forgotten that letter!

"Not so loud!" Robert jumped to the door and closed it. "Oh, Sue! We thought you'd gone for good. We thought the wishing well had failed. Vicky's been crying her eyes out."

"Oh, I *am* sorry! I thought it was all over, too, when I wrote that letter, and then something happened and I forgot to take the letter with me when we went back to the Hollisters'. Why is Vicky's door locked?"

Robert made a face. "Cousin Jane...She's locked Vick up and put her on short rations. She didn't know we were out of the house yesterday, but just after I got back she ambushed me and asked where Vicky was. I said I was sure she was in the house somewhere, and she went searching, and I had to throw my arrowheads and Vick's mirror out the window. And when poor Vick came back from the wishing well, Cousin Jane pounced on her and just blew her up. And then Mama tried to defend her, and oh my, what a row! The punishment could be worse, I guess. Cousin Jane doesn't know it, but the key to my door fits Vicky's door, and there's a key to one of the closets downstairs that fits both of them. Vick and I found that out long ago when we were playing Prisoner of Chillon. So it means I can keep her in victuals. If her appetite were only better she'd be eating as well as the rest of us. I found your letter and the shoes this morning, by the way, while I was on a foraging raid for her."

"Could I have the shoes back? My feet are killing me!"

"Totus dexter. They're in Vick's room. Hey, what *did* happen last night?"

Susan brought him up to date on the events of last night and this morning.

"So now," she concluded, "Daddy's thinking about what to do next, and he wants to talk to you."

"We'll go right now!" He jumped up, then exclaimed, "Oh, your shoes! Mmm…I know—we'll smuggle a communication in to the prisoner." He ran over to his desk, and scrawled a note:

> *Mr. Shaw and Sue still here!! Mr. Shaw's heart smitten at last!!! Sue needs shoes, please hand them out. Destroy this dispatch.*

"Totus dexter! Now…" He carefully opened his door and beckoned Susan over. "You stand there," he whispered, "and keep a lookout down the stairs. Soon as you see or hear anything, give me a signal and retreat back here."

She nodded, and slipped over to the place he had pointed out. He crept to Victoria's door, knocked very quietly, and thrust the message underneath the door.

There was a moment of silence, and then a muffled squeak from within. Robert unlocked the door, and Victoria's head popped out. She looked wild, with rumpled hair and tear-reddened eyes. Her mouth dropped open with unbelieving joy as she caught sight of Susan. Susan waved, trying to say with that gesture, "Oh, Vicky, it's finally really happened, and I don't know how we're going to do it, but we are!" *"Shoes!"* Robert pantomimed.

Victoria vanished, and reappeared an instant later with the shoes. She blew a kiss at Susan. Robert closed the door and locked it, and he and Susan tiptoed swiftly back to his room.

She had no sooner stuffed her aching feet into the shoes when Robert murmured, "I think they're coming up, Sue. Quick! Back stairs!"

Footsteps were already sounding on the front stairway as they ran down the hall. Cousin Jane's voice crackled, "Isabelle, I would strongly suggest that you discharge Maggie as soon as you are in the city, if not sooner. People in reduced circumstances cannot afford—" and then Robert closed another door behind them, and they were in the darkness of the back staircase. These stairs were not carpeted, and their footsteps clattered and reverberated. Robert opened the door at the bottom, poked his head out, and called, "Maggie?"

"Sure and ye make enough clip-clap for two on them stairs!"

"Are you going to clear away the breakfast things now?"

"As soon as Herself's out o' the way, an' not before."

"She's upstairs with Mama now."

Maggie heaved a great sigh. "Ah, well...She's not after

plaguin' us much longer, there's a comfort."

"What do you mean?"

Maggie's voice sank. "Didn't I have a dream last night, as clear as ever was? Herself is goin' on a long, long journey when she least expects it. You watch! An' good riddance!" Her voice faded out of the kitchen.

"Don't I wish it, too!" Robert muttered. "Come on, Sue—quiet through the kitchen, and then run like blazes!"

Mr. Shaw's Plan

...in much better spirits after thinking about things. He had a really marvelous idea for taking care of Mr. Sweeney and getting our treasure back. The only thing wrong with it is that it's going to happen in the dark, so I won't get to see Mr. Sweeney's face when we spring the trap...

"Good, good, there you are!" Mr. Shaw cried when they burst into the stable. "I was beginning to wonder if you'd ever—How are you, Bobbie?"

"Corporal Walker reporting and ready for duty, sir!"

"At ease, Corporal," Mr. Shaw laughed. "I have some duty for you, all right. How is your mother? And Vicky?"

"Well...they're bearing up, sir."

Susan explained the situation in the Walker household to her father.

"By George!" Mr. Shaw said, clenching his fists. "I hate to say anything against a relative, Bobbie, but that—that cousin of yours really goes too far."

"Oh, I agree one hundred percent, sir! I think Mama's beginning to see through her, too. She pretends to be helping us, and maybe she is, a little; but it's mostly just an excuse for bullying us about."

"Well, she has no right to bully you about, and she *can't* bully me about, and when the time comes—Well, we'll deal with that later; right now we have other business. Did Susie tell you about Mr. Sweeney and his plans for us?"

"Yes, sir. Oh, I wish I were grown up! I'd give him such a thrashing!"

"Steady, steady! It's what he deserves, all right, but I've thought of something even better. Susie and I found a curious message in the elevator last night, and it's given me an idea." Mr. Shaw grinned and rubbed his hands. "Mr. Sweeney thinks he has plans for us, does he? Well, I have plans for *him*."

"Oh, Daddy, what?"

"Well, first I'm going to put a tail on him, as they say in detective stories."

Robert looked blank.

"Twentieth-century talk, Bobbie—it means I'm going to have him followed. Trailed. By you, if you're willing."

"Oh, absolutely, sir! What do you want me to find out?"

"All I want to know is where he's staying. He doesn't want me to know, so the chances are good that he's hiding the treasure there. You know the neighborhood, Bobbie. Where could he be living?"

"Well, there's the Knutsens and the Blalocks that way, and the Varnums and the Schultzes and the Besemers *that* way. He might be staying anywhere in town, for that matter."

"No, I think he'll stay away from town—he's been playing his dirty tricks there too, you know…Well, wherever it is, I know you'll find it. He's coming here for a progress report in a few hours. When he leaves, he's all yours."

"Totus dexter, sir! I know just where to wait for him, too—

the old apple orchard."

"Daddy, I still don't know what you're up to."

"Simple, my dear. We learn where Sweeney is living; we arrange for his prolonged absence; and we reclaim what he took from us."

"There's more to it than that," she insisted. "I can tell by the way you're smiling."

"You're right, there is more. It's Mr. Sweeney's prolonged absence that tickles my fancy at the moment. I have decided that if I am going to live in this world, I don't want Sweeney in it. Therefore, I am going to remove him—permanently."

"Oh, but, sir—!" and "*Daddy*—!" Robert and Susan said simultaneously.

He gave a shout of laughter. "Oh, the looks on your faces! No, I don't mean anything *that* drastic. What I had in mind was something harmless, but absolutely final. I want to give him a present—the last trip from here on the elevator."

"Ah-h-h!" Susan cried, clasping her hands.

"Oh, sir, that's magnificent!"

"I'm kind of pleased with the idea myself," Mr. Shaw laughed. "It should be simple enough to do, too—we just have to lead him on in the right way. When he comes for his progress report, I'm going to tell him that you've made an impression of the key, Susie—that's the key to your mother's fictitious jewel box, Bobbie—and that I'm going to have a copy of the key made. I'm going to tell him that the Walkers have invited you to spend the night, Susie, and that you'll take the key and do the dirty work as soon as everyone's asleep. I'm going to tell him that all we have to do, he and I, is to sneak into the Walkers' house at midnight and collect the booty from you. So he *should* walk right up to the elevator with his tongue hanging out, the rat. And we'll just—oh, assist him into it, and send him on his way with a long farewell! But of course, we'll have to make preparations...Bobbie, will you see to it that the doors to your house are unlocked?"

"Trust me, sir!"

"Good. Now, Susie, what you're going to do is creep into the house as soon as everyone's settled down for the night. When is that usually, Bobbie?"

"About ten-thirty, sir."

"A little after ten-thirty then, chick. I don't think Sweeney will be spying on us at that time of night, but he will be coming to meet me about eleven-thirty, so I want you out of sight well before then. Now, you should have a pillowcase with something fairly heavy inside, to represent the jewels."

"That's easy—Vicky and I can fix that up. You'll have her door unlocked too, won't you, Bobbie?"

"Leave it to me, Sue."

"Now, at eleven-thirty," Mr. Shaw went on, "call up the elevator, Susie. That's a lot earlier than we need it, but it's best to have everything ready beforehand. You'd better stick a wedge in the slot to keep the door open—you never know with that elevator when it's going to decide to close up again. Also, somebody down below might try to call it back, and we have to prevent that."

"What'll I use for a wedge?"

"Oh, a folded-up newspaper or magazine should do it. Bobbie, could you—?"

"Yes, sir. I'll have it all ready for her."

"Fine! Next step, Susie: turn out the light in the elevator. We'll want everything as dark as possible. If you can't find the switch, unscrew the lightbulb."

"All right. How do we 'assist' Mr. Sweeney into the elevator, Daddy?"

"That part will be up to me. He and I will come through the kitchen into the hallway. You'll be waiting in front of the open elevator with the pillowcase in your hands. Hold it out to the side, like this. When Sweeney puts out his slimy paws to take it, I will shove him into the elevator—hard enough, I hope, to take the wind out of his sails. The minute he goes in, chick, grab the wedge out of the door slot. I'll reach inside and press a button. And farewell, Mr. Sweeney!"

"Isn't there anything else that *I* can do, sir?"

"Yes. I think you and Victoria should be hiding behind the curtains in the hallway. I want you to be ready to come swarming out in case Sweeney needs more assistance than I can give him by myself."

"Oh, capital, sir! And in case he's going to be really troublesome, I'll have my cavalry saber—!"

"No!" Mr. Shaw said. "No. I'm sorry, Bobbie, but it's going to be dark, and there'll be too many of us bumping around in a small area to take chances with anything sharp. If he needs more persuasion, we'll apply it with our hands, and nobody'll get hurt."

"Isn't it going to be awfully noisy, Daddy?"

"That's the drawback," Mr. Shaw sighed. "Even at best there's going to be a pretty heavy thump...I hate the idea of alarming Mrs. Walker, and if Cousin Jane is aroused—!" He shook his head. "But I just don't know how we can avoid a certain amount of racket."

"I don't think a little noise will matter, sir. If Mama or

Cousin Jane do come down to see what's happening, we'll hear them. You and Susan can retreat out the kitchen door before they get to the hallway, and Vicky and I'll sort of fade up the back stairs and return to our rooms, and the whole thing will be blamed on Toby."

"Poor Toby!" Susan laughed. "He *is* handy that way, though."

"Well, I suppose that'll be all right, then," Mr. Shaw said. "If it is blamed on Toby, I'll see that he gets something he likes. Now, the only other thing that worries me is Maggie—she could spoil the whole plan just by making an appearance at the wrong moment. Does she wander around a lot at night?"

Robert grinned. "Only to catch me, sir. But we have an understanding now. As long as Vicky's locked up, I'm foraging for *her,* and Maggie said she'd stay in her room and let me."

"Ah! Well, if that's the case, then, I don't see how we can fail."

"Oh, we won't fail, sir! Mr. Sweeney's doom is sealed!"

They went over the plan once more, to be certain that each knew what was going to be done by whom, and when. Robert was to explain everything to Victoria that evening, as soon as it was safe to release her from captivity.

"Now, Bobbie," Mr. Shaw concluded, "you said you were going to lie in wait for Sweeney in the apple orchard? Fine! I think maybe you'd better take your station there right now. It's long before he's due, of course, but...well, I don't want to take any chances. He might just happen to come early, or he might spy around here for a while before he makes his appearance."

"I understand, sir."

"And listen—I can't impress this on you too strongly: *don't let him see you.* He's threatened to denounce me to the police if he finds out he's being followed, and I think he means it. Not that we have anything to fear from the police, but as soon as he tells on us he'll take the treasure and decamp, and there'll go our last chance of ever getting it back. So *don't,* for heaven's sake, even let him suspect you're on his trail."

"I won't, sir—trust me."

"And when you know for certain where he's staying, come back and report to me. And tonight—" Mr. Shaw smiled and pointed downward. "And then with *that* behind us, we can begin to consider how to deal with Cousin Jane."

"Yes, sir. Confusion to the enemy!"

"Exactly. Well, goodbye and good luck, Corporal."

"Goodbye, Bobbie. Be careful!"

"Goodbye, sir. Goodbye, Sue. I will."

They all shook hands. Robert gave them a final salute, and vanished out the door.

Waiting

...played his little scene with Mr. Sweeney to perfection! We had to spend the rest of the day waiting, and it was awful. At least Daddy could go to town and work off some of his nervous energy. I didn't have anything to do but worry. And there was plenty to worry about, such as the police visiting the Walkers, and the fact that Bobbie never came to make his report...

Mr. Sweeney gave a discreet cough. So quietly had he made his approach that Mr. Shaw, sitting on the sack of oats, yawning with nervousness and pretending to read a newspaper, never heard him. Susan had been caught napping, too—almost literally. She was in the loft, buried under some hay. The hay tickled her neck, but it was so warm that she had allowed her eyes to close.

The Shaws both jumped. Mr. Shaw lowered his paper, and Susan put her eye to a crack in the floorboards.

"Ah there, Shaw," Mr. Sweeney said in his smoothest tone. "Catching up with the wide world, I see."

"Yes, I, ah, thought I'd see what was happening." Mr. Shaw folded the paper, which happened to be two weeks old, and put it down.

"You did not pay your respects to Isabelle this morning?"

Mr. Shaw's jaw tightened. "Are you asking me, Sweeney, or telling me?"

Mr. Sweeney smiled. "My dear fellow, I keep my eye on what concerns me."

"All right, then, I did not visit Mrs. Walker this morning. Mrs. Walker believes that I am in town consulting with various gentlemen about the most profitable ways of investing the money she entrusted to me."

"How droll! Well, of course, *now* you can assure her that her fortune is in the best possible hands. Ah, ah, ah!—philosophy, my dear Shaw!"

Mr. Shaw glared and muttered something under his breath.

"Where is your gifted daughter?"

"Playing with the Walker children. Why?"

"Oh, I just found it curious that I didn't see her going there."

Mr. Shaw shrugged. "The children have their own ways of going and coming. Susan, as a matter of fact, has been to the Walkers' for more amateur theatricals, and has been in touch with me since. The results have been gratifying."

He pulled from his pocket and held out for inspection two lumps of beeswax which he had obtained from Mrs. Hollister. Impressed in them was the outline of a little key that he had found in a bowl of buttons, pins and other oddments on the chest of drawers in his room.

Mr. Sweeney shook his head in admiration. "That girl is—an—Artist!" he declared.

"Yes. I'll just stroll into town this afternoon and have a key made from this. Susan will find the key with her nightgown and robe and toothbrush when she comes to fetch them later in the day. You see, she's managed to secure an invitation to spend the night at the Walkers'."

"Ah!" Mr. Sweeney breathed.

"So the rest of the operation should be absurdly simple. Why don't you meet me here at midnight? We can proceed to the Walkers' house, and enter through the kitchen door—Susan will make sure it's unlocked for us. She will meet us inside, where she will hand over to us a cloth bag—a heavily-laden cloth bag." Mr. Shaw leered at this point so realistically that Susan could hardly suppress a giggle. "She will return to bed, while you and I go somewhere to divide the, ah, take. After that, I sincerely hope to say goodbye to you forever."

Mr. Sweeney rubbed his hands. "An excellent plan, Shaw. However, certain amendments will be necessary. For one thing, you and I will not by any means say farewell after our division of the spoils."

"Why not, for heaven's sake?"

"Oh, don't be tiresome, Shaw! I assure you it's not because I enjoy your company any more than you enjoy mine. But I know enough to watch out for my own interests. Why should I assume, as you obviously wish me to, that the bag is going to have the whole take in it? I know that Susan is cool enough to walk out of the Walkers' house tomorrow morning—right under Isabelle's nose, too!—with her overnight case bulging with booty that she somehow 'forgot' to put in the cloth bag. Obviously I can't say any farewells until she has reported back to you *in my presence.*"

"You intend to search my daughter's effects, sir?"

"Of course."

"Damn you for a scoundrel!" Mr. Shaw roared, stamping his foot.

'Well done, Daddy!' Susan thought. 'You're playing this

scene like a real pro!'

"Philosophy!" Mr. Sweeney laughed. "My concern is only to remove temptations from your path, Shaw! Now, I must insist on another change. We will meet in the Walkers' stable, not here."

"All right—but may I ask why?"

Mr. Sweeney looked at Mr. Shaw with unfeigned puzzlement. "*Why?* Shaw, sometimes you baffle me. The reason is, of course, that tonight there will be a horse in this stable, whose noise might betray our presence, whereas the Walkers' stable will be empty."

"Oh. Yes..." Mr. Shaw rubbed his face, and continued with a sigh, "I keep forgetting these little details."

Mr. Sweeney gave a superior smile. "Shaw, in this game there is nothing *but* detail. Now, one more amendment, and I'll have done. We will meet in the Walkers' stable at sundown, not at midnight. I want to keep my eye on you, frankly. There are just too many hours of darkness before midnight, during which you and Susan could—oh, succumb to temptation, shall we say? Sundown, then?"

Mr. Shaw pretended reluctance, but finally growled, "All right."

"Excellent. Just bear in mind that you have everything to lose if you cross me in the least particular. Have you anything more to say to me?"

"Nothing that you'd want to hear, Sweeney."

"Philosophy, Shaw! Next to a scrupulous attention to detail, that is the greatest asset we have in our profession. Good day, then—until sundown!"

Mr. Shaw strode to the door and watched him angle across

the pasture. "Come on down, chick!" he said quietly. She scrambled out from under the hay, and half climbed, half slid down the ladder from the loft. "Hold it, hold it," he muttered. "Not yet…All right, he's over the ridge. Run!"

They dashed for the Hollisters' back door.

"Our fish," he said when they were inside, "seems to have swallowed the bait."

"Daddy, you were marvelous!"

She got the giggles as they went upstairs. As soon as they were in his room she declaimed, "Are you going to search my daughter's effects, sir?" and fell into a chair, helpless with laughter.

Mr. Shaw grinned. "It did go off pretty well, didn't it? All except that part about forgetting Hollister's horse. Well, that's all right—the more superior he feels, the more relaxed he'll be. The unctuous creep! Well, it's Bobbie's show now. All we can do is wait."

"I *hate* waiting."

"Don't blame you. Oh! I guess I have to keep up the masquerade and go to town to have a key made. It'll be a nice walk, anyway."

"I can't go for a walk or anything, can I?"

"No! You sit tight—Weaselface might be watching."

She groaned.

In a little while he left. She brought her diary up to date, putting in plenty of detail in order to pass the time.

The afternoon grew hotter as it wore on. She paced her room. She threw herself on the bed and tried to nap. She picked up a copy of *Harper's Bazar* ('Is that the way it's spelled?' she wondered), and leafed through it. "Paris Fashions," she read. "[From our own correspondent] It may be affirmed that the article most worn in Paris is fur. This fashion is imposed by the severe winter which we are undergoing…" Winter? She turned to the cover and looked at the date: February 7, 1880. Oh, foo! She dropped the magazine and began pacing again.

Mrs. Hollister scuffled and made mousey housekeeping sounds below. Flies buzzed against the window…

Mr. Shaw came back at four o'clock.

"Hello, chick! How're you doing? Did Bobbie show up yet?"

"No. Oh, what a beautiful hat!"

"Had to get it," he said, taking off a shiny new straw hat with a black ribbon, and mopping his brow. "Everybody was giving me funny looks. Bare heads are definitely out of style this year. Well, I hope Sweeney is watching—he can now conclude that we have a key to Mrs. Walker's jewel box."

He sat down with a sigh by the front window, and they had the waiting fidgets together.

At five after five Mr. Shaw gave a start and said, "Oh oh! There's Maggie out in the road. She's got a bonnet on. Walking fast. Looks like she's going to town. Maybe they gave her the evening off."

"Or else she's been fired by Cousin Jane," Susan groaned.

There was another hour of waiting and fidgets, and muttering by Mr. Shaw over Robert's failure to report. They heard the sound of hooves and wheels on the road.

"Here comes Uncle Sam Windbag," Mr. Shaw sighed. He glanced out the window. "Oh oh! No it isn't. It's—a policeman, by George! Badge on his hat, anyway. With Maggie. I wonder what...Oh—good—*night!* Sweeney's done it!"

Susan's heart constricted. "You mean he—?"

"He must have caught Bobbie trailing him, and suspected we were behind it, and so he's told the police.—There they go, into the Walkers'. Oh, the dirty dog! There goes our fortune..."

"Wait, Daddy!—Maggie went out a while ago, and now she's come back with a policeman. It looks like the Walkers sent her to get one. Mr. Sweeney might not have anything to do with it!"

"Oh, lord!" he groaned. "I guess I'll have to go find out for sure."

When at last the policeman could be seen coming out of the Walkers' house and climbing into his buggy, Mr. Shaw ran out to intercept him. Susan peeked through the curtains and watched with a pounding heart. The policeman—he wore a derby!—pointed over his shoulder with his thumb at the Walkers' house. Mr. Shaw nodded. The policeman leaned forward. Mr. Shaw shook his head. They exchanged a few more words; then each raised a hand in farewell, and the buggy moved off down the road. Mr. Shaw came hurrying back to the house. He had no sooner gotten inside when Mr. Hollister's buggy appeared.

"Almost got caught by Uncle Sam!" he panted, bursting into the room and banging the door shut. "Phew! Narrow escape from a fate worse than death! Well, the fuss over at the Walkers' is that they think Bobbie's run away! That's Cousin Jane's conclusion, anyway. The policeman thinks she's called him into it just to create the maximum pain for everybody. He's probably right. He had a few words to say about her that express *my* sentiments exactly."

"Where do you think Bobbie is?—still trailing Mr. Sweeney?"

"He must be..." Mr. Shaw rubbed his chin for a minute. "You know, what's probably happening is that Sweeney is over there somewhere spying on us, and Bobbie is over there somewhere spying on *him,* and—oh, good night! You know what that means? It means Sweeney probably saw me out there talking to that cop!" He slapped his forehead. "What's he going to conclude from *that?* It might just make him nervous enough to run!"

Susan didn't know what to say. She chewed her knuckle and resumed her pacing. Their dinner came up a short time later—Mr. Shaw was "indisposed" again—but they had little appetite for it. Mr. Hollister brayed below. Mrs. Hollister murmured. A group of birds had hysterics outside, presumably over Toby. The light turned golden, and then ruddy. The Shaws waited.

Robert did not come to make his report.

And then at last it was sundown. Mr. Hollister was delivering a monologue to his wife out on the veranda; his nasal bray went on and on without interruption, like a waterfall. Mr. Shaw stood up with a great sigh.

"All right, chick—it's time for me to go. If Sweeney doesn't show up soon, it means he's gone for good—with our fortune. In that case, I'll be back within an hour. If he does show up, we'll go through with everything as planned. I guess you and I can bring it off by ourselves, can't we? Just be sure to take a loaded pillowcase and a newspaper with you. Here, take my watch, too. If I don't come back, go to the Walkers' about eleven. Use the front door—the back door can be seen from the stable. Are you all straight now on what you're going to do over there?"

"Yes." An anxiety that had been building up in her for hours finally burst forth. "Daddy, what if something has happened to Bobbie?"

"Oh, hon, he probably just forgot that he was supposed to come make a report."

"But what if something *has* happened to him?"

"We'll go looking for him as soon as we're free. All right?"

She had to be satisfied with that.

He hugged her. "Goodbye, chick. Slow and easy, now. It's all going to turn out fine."

She couldn't bring herself to say anything. They blew a kiss at each other, and Mr. Shaw slipped out, leaving her to wait alone.

Mr. Hollister Defends the Widow's Hearth

...awful night! About the only thing that went right was that I got out of the house safely. I was worried sick about Bobbie. I waited in the back yard and then in the hedge until after eleven and went to the Walkers'. Everything began to get out of control...

Mr. Shaw did not return. Mr. Sweeney must still be in the picture, then, and the plan would proceed.

It was a warm night with a nearly full moon alternately shining and hiding behind clouds. From the veranda came the creak of rocking chairs and Mr. Hollister's everlasting bray. She glanced at the watch again: only a few minutes until ten. 'They're *never* going to turn in!' she thought, chewing her knuckle. But it suddenly came to her that she didn't have to wait until the Hollisters were safely snoring in bed—she could go now. She could walk out the back door and sit under a bush or something until it was time to go to the Walkers'.

It was done in a minute. She slipped the watch into her pocket, blew out the candle, and crept out of the house. She carried a rolled-up copy of *Harper's Bazar* to jam the elevator door, and a pillowcase weighted with all the small heavy objects she could find.

The hedge would be the best place to wait, but she couldn't

get to that part with the hole in it without the risk of being seen by the Hollisters. She decided to wait in the back yard for the time being, and made herself comfortable under a small tree.

As comfortable as she could, that is, considering her state of mind. What had happened to Bobbie? Could he have just *forgotten* about coming to report to them? That didn't sound like Corporal Robert Lincoln Walker. Was he injured or stuck somewhere out in the fields or woods? Her heart failed her.

Some time later Mr. Hollister's voice ceased braying and turned into a huge yawn. Mrs. Hollister's voice murmured something. "N-yas, n-yas," Mr. Hollister trumpeted. There was a sound of footsteps on loose floorboards, and protesting door-hinges.

Susan jumped up and slipped across the yard to the hedge. A light went out on the third floor of the Walkers' house. 'Well, there's one of them down, anyway,' she thought. She peered at the greenish glow of the watch hands: ten-thirty-five. "Go to bed, please!" she hissed at the house. There was still a faint glow of light in the downstairs windows...

She waited.

The glow vanished from the downstairs windows and reappeared in two of the upstairs windows in the back of the house.

She waited.

Ah! There went the upstairs light. She looked at the time: ten to eleven. She would wait until a quarter after.

She waited for twenty-five minutes, and then for a few more to allow the moon to go behind a cloud.

Now she could go! She scurried across the yard to the front porch, slipped off her shoes, and padded up to the door.

It was locked.

'Oh, good grief!' she thought wearily. Robert was supposed to have taken care of the doors. If they were still locked, it meant that he—oh, she couldn't worry about that now! She crept down the steps and put her shoes back on. She'd have to try the kitchen door. And if *it* was locked—? Well, check first and ask questions later…

But no—she *couldn't* try the back door. Her father had told her not to, because it was visible from the stable…

Windows, then—how about windows? Back on the porch she went, and crept up to the window closest to the door.

What was that?

She froze and listened. Out on the road there was the faint rhythmic sound of hooves and wheels. Her instinct was to slip away from the porch and hide. But no—the road was far from the house, the porch was in shadow—no one would notice her. She turned back to the window and pushed up on its unyielding frame.

The hooves clopped, the iron-rimmed wheels crunched on the gravel, past the Hollisters', past the hedge, past the—no, *not* past the Walkers'. The sounds stopped at the front gate. The horse gave a flubbery snort and shook its harness. There were voices. There were lights. "Oh, no!" Susan gasped. Dark figures with bull's-eye lanterns were coming up the walk.

She scurried to the end of the porch, threw her leg over the railing, and slid down into the hydrangeas.

A rumbling voice said, "All right, young-feller-me-lad, *now* we'll see."

"Why'ncha lea'me alone?" a boy's voice whined. "I never been here in my life."

"Dunno, Frank," another man's voice said. "I don't think

he's the one. Lady distinctly told me brown hair. This kid—"

"She wants a runaway," Frank rumbled, "and we *got* a runaway. Up to her to say if he's the one or not."

"I ain't no runaway. I was just goin' to visit my Cousin Florrie. Lea'me alone."

Boots clomped up the steps and across the porch. Circles of light darted about. There was a thunderous knocking at the door.

"She a reg'lar fierce 'un, Frank. I wish you'd—"

"Dooty is dooty," Frank rumbled. "She reported a runaway, and we—"

The house echoed to a renewed application of the knocker. Then came the sound of the bolt being hurled back, and the door opened with a crash.

"What is the meaning of this?" Cousin Jane snapped.

"Police, ma'am. We—"

"What is it—what is it?" Mrs. Walker's voice cried from within.

"Go back to bed, Isabelle. I will deal with this."

"You're looking for a runaway boy, I believe."

"I am not. *You* were supposed to be looking for him, but he has returned. Who is this? You were not seriously going to present *this* vagabond as a candidate, were you?"

"Ma'am, you reported a runaway boy. We had a runaway boy. We—"

"No one with half an eye in his head could possibly imagine that *this* grimy little heathen could belong to this house. You are bunglers, sir! I shall lodge a complaint with your superiors in the morning. Good night to you."

The door shut with a crash that set the glass a-rattle, and

the bolt snapped home like a rifle-shot."

Told you, Frank," said an apologetic murmur. "We should've—"

"Well, melt—my—badge—for—a—revolving—rat-trap!" Frank rumbled on a rising note. "All right, my high and mighty hoity-toity Duchess, just you—"

"Ow!" the boy yelped. "Leggo my ear!"

"—just you come crying to us again with your runaways, or your arson, or your robbery—" their boots thumped down the steps, down the walk "—or your bloody *murder* even, and see if I don't show you the broad side of my—" His voice went on indistinctly through the gate. The buggy creaked. "Gee yup!" he roared. His whip cracked, and the horse went cantering down the lane with the sound of a massed cavalry charge.

'Well,' Susan sighed to herself, 'at least Bobbie's safe... *Why* didn't he ever come to tell us what he found out? Good grief, it'll take everybody forever to settle down in the house now... Wonder if Daddy and Mr. Sweeney heard all that?' She looked at the watch: three minutes till midnight! Her stomach flopped over at a new thought. What if the two men had *not* heard the disturbance? The whole house had been between them and it, after all...In that case, they would be coming to the back door in a few minutes! And here she was, still outside...'

There was no more time for caution. She scrambled back on the porch through the clutching branches of hydrangea, and leaped to the window. The lower sash would not go up. Maybe the upper sash would come down? No. Next window, then. She pushed and panted at its sashes without result.

"Stop, thieves!" a voice shouted from the Hollisters' house. Susan gave a start that lifted her feet clear off the porch floor.

"Horse thieves!" Mr. Hollister bawled. *"Cutthroats! Don't move—I've got you in my sights, you Republican sneaks!"*

An instant of silence, then: *"Oh, you will, will you?"*

BALOOM! said a very large gun. Echoes bounced between the two houses and their stables: *whap whap whap whap whap...*

The echoes died away into a dreadful waiting quiet.

Susan cowered in terror. A door slammed at the Hollisters'. Footsteps pounded down the Hollisters' walk, on the road, through the Walkers' gate. The moon revealed Mr. Hollister, dressed in boots and white nightshirt, and carrying a gun nearly as long as himself.

Once more Susan threw her leg over the railing, and

dropped down into the hydrangeas.

Mr. Hollister thumped up on the porch, pounded the door, and waited, breathing heavily and muttering "N-yas, n-yas," to himself.

The door crashed open, and Cousin Jane shouted, "Are we to have no peace tonight?"

"N-yas, ma'am!" Mr. Hollister brayed. "I believe the customary tranquillity of our rural—ha—nocturne has been restored. Hiram W. Hollister at your service, ma'am. I—"

"This is an outrage!" Cousin Jane cried.

"It is indeed, ma'am!" Mr. Hollister trumpeted. "I share and endorse your sense of abomination! Perilous times, ma'am! But for my alertness and quick action, you and yours might have been murdered in your very beds, ma'am!"

"What?"

Mr. Hollister's voice sank four tones. "Night prowlers, ma'am. I was awakened from my peaceful slumbers by the sound of their horses and vehicles. Looking out my window, I espied a gang of them creeping out of your stable and toward your house with sinister intent. I did not falter, ma'am! I addressed them in no uncertain terms, and fired a warning shot over their heads. My resolution took the heart out of 'em, ma'am! They have dispersed, and I believe I can safely say that our accustomed—ha—serenity reigns supreme."

"Well, sir, I suppose we must thank you," Cousin Jane said grudgingly. "You will be suitably rewarded in the morning."

"Oh, no, ma'am!" Mr. Hollister brayed. "With all respect, allow me to tender my refusal. The knowledge that I have successfully defended a widow's hearth and home, ma'am, is reward enough for—"

"Very well, sir. Thank you and good night. Pray do not raise your voice or discharge your weapon again. I assure you that this house is securely locked. If any ruffian manages to gain entrance notwithstanding, I shall make him regret it. Good night, sir."

The door closed smartly, the bolt clicked into place, and Mr. Hollister stumped away, muttering "N-yas,n-yas," as he went.

Susan chewed on her knuckle and pondered her next move. What were her father and Mr. Sweeney going to do now? How far had they been "dispersed" by Mr. Hollister? Would they give up, or would they wait and try to enter the house when all was calm again? 'Oh, good grief!' she thought. 'I guess I'd better try to find out what they're up to. If I stick close to the bushes, I might be able to get a look at them that'll tell me something. *If* they're still back there…'

She crawled out from under the hydrangeas, and began to creep around the right side of the house—the side away from the Hollisters'. There were two bays jutting out on this side. She had just reached the second one when she heard a stealthy sliding sound over her head.

Corporal Walker's Ordeal

...have to go back and tell what happened to Bobbie first. When we were comparing stories later he said he almost ruined his special mission right at the beginning. The rest of what went wrong wasn't really his fault...

Robert's lying-in-wait station was a gnarled Northern Spy on the edge of the orchard. Sitting with his back against its trunk, he could just see the Hollisters' stable through a waving screen of grass. He raised his face to the sunlight, closed his eyes, and thought about the day ahead.

There would be a row with Cousin Jane when he got back, of course. She would probably want to lock him up in his room. He would have to put his key in his shoe before he returned home, so that when she asked for it he could say that he had lost it, turning his pockets out for verification. Then if she did manage to lock him up anyway, he could still escape, and let Vicky out, and have everything ready for the execution of the plan.

As for the plan itself, he considered it brilliant. If there was any flaw at all, it was that he, Corporal Walker, would not be able to bring his cavalry saber into the action. It would really be capital if only—if only...A scene began to take shape in his mind: Mr. Shaw lay on the parquet floor, unconscious through some mishap; Susan and Victoria cowered in the shadows, wide-eyed with admiration; Mr. Sweeney, snarling with rage, backed into the elevator, quailing under the fearless frown of Corporal Walker. Blood trickled from a picturesque wound on Corporal Walker's forehead, and the razor-keen blade of his saber gleamed...

He awoke with a start, just in time to see Mr. Sweeney in the flesh disappearing over the ridge in Hollisters' pasture. "Great Caesar!" he sobbed. He leaped up and dashed toward the pasture, pommeling his head with both fists. Two more seconds of slumber, and his special mission would have failed utterly...He demoted himself to Private on the spot. 'One more little mistake like that, Private, and I will drum you out of the regiment altogether!' he raged.

He popped over the ridge in the pasture too quickly. 'Look out, you idiot!' his mind shouted. Mr. Sweeney was halfway to the woodlot, but had paused and was turning around. Robert dove into the grass. 'Oh, look here, Private!' he roared inside. 'This won't do *at all!* Going too fast is just as bad as falling asleep. What kind of a scout *are* you?' If there had been a rank lower than Private, he would have demoted himself to it immediately.

After a while he raised his head very slowly. Mr. Sweeney was striding into the elephant-grey beeches and shaggy hickories of the woodlot. Robert slunk after him at a half-crouch, ready to drop instantly. His heart was beating high, but his head was steady now.

Mr. Sweeney led him through the woodlot, slantwise down the next meadow, across Ward Lane, and then behind the Ward Lane hedgerow until he came to a place opposite the Walker and Hollister homesteads. Here, in a thicket of sumac and elderberry, he could watch the houses without being seen from them. He sat down and made himself comfortable with his back against a boulder. Robert crept up as closely as he dared, ending under a clump of hawthorns about fifty feet behind and to the left of Mr. Sweeney. He carefully stretched himself out, rested his chin in his hands, and watched.

It slowly, painfully, maddeningly became clear that Mr. Sweeney intended to sit there for the rest of the afternoon, with only an occasional recess behind a willow thicket to take a few quick puffs on his cigar. Robert sweated in the heat, and shifted his weight, and blew at the wasps and bees and flies that hovered in front of his face, and crushed the spiders and other fauna that wandered into his sleeves and down his collar, and stifled the sneezes that bulged in his nose, and tried to ignore the hunger pangs that pinched his stomach with growing insistence, and shed tears of vexation, and yawned, and fought against the desire to lower his head and close his eyes for just a minute, and bit his lip, and lectured himself on the duty of a scout…and endured.

Only a few events punctuated the endless afternoon. Mrs. Hollister came out on her veranda and flapped her dust rag. Maggie appeared with a bucket and mop to sluice down the Walkers' front porch. Mr. Shaw came walking back from town in a new straw hat. Mr. Sweeney made an ironical salute toward his back as he went up the Hollisters' walk. Maggie set off townward in her bonnet. That was strange, Robert thought; it seemed too late in the afternoon for her to go strolling...A buggy came from town with—great Caesar!—a policeman and Maggie in it; they went into the Walkers'. Mr. Sweeney became as tense as a watchspring, and a sick anxious fear crept through Robert's heart. What was the matter at home, what could have happened? Ah, here came the policeman again, alone. And here came Mr. Shaw out of Hollisters' to talk to him. Mr. Sweeney's back went rigid. Then the policeman drove on, Mr. Shaw ran back into the house, Mr. Hollister drove into his stable, and all was calm again—except Robert's wildly speculating mind.

Mr. Sweeney retreated behind the willows and smoked the remainder of his cigar in quick, short puffs. Obviously his mind was in a turmoil of speculation, too.

But he calmed down again, returned to his watching place, and kept a lookout for another hour. Then he got up and went behind the willows for—no! He was walking away.

'Ah!' Robert thought. '*Now* we'll find out what we want to know.' It was dinnertime—as the painful state of his own interior told him—and Mr. Sweeney must be going to his lodgings to fortify himself for the night's villainy. Robert heaved himself up, clenched his teeth against the pain in his stiff joints and muscles, and began to stalk his quarry.

But Mr. Sweeney did not go to the Knutsens', or the Blalocks', or anywhere else that Robert had mentioned to Mr. Shaw. He went by devious ways to the great beechwoods that crowned the hill some three-quarters of a mile distant from the two houses, and plunged in. Presently he could be heard breaking sticks.

Robert crept with exquisite care between the trees to the edge of a small glade. There was Mr. Sweeney in his shirtsleeves, crouched in front of an improvised stone fireplace, touching a match flame to a small heap of sticks. His coat and hat were hung on a nearby snag; underneath, a blanket was spread out on a pile of dead leaves; and beside this bed, lined up with mathematical exactness, were a calfskin valise, a box of cigars, an extra pair of boots, and shaving tackle.

'A camp!' Robert thought. Of course—it made more sense than lodging with people who might snoop or ask questions... Suddenly he had an idea. Mr. Sweeney would surely want to gloat over the purloined treasure before the light failed. Why not watch until that happened? *Wouldn't* it be a triumph to report to Mr. Shaw that he had discovered the exact place where Mr. Sweeney had hidden it! Above and beyond the call of duty...

He hugged himself, and settled down to watch.

There followed a very bad half-hour, during which Mr. Sweeney slowly and fastidiously dined on toasted muffins and cheese, and drank tea. 'Ah, you scoundrel!' Robert thought, while his mouth watered and his stomach rumbled. Well, enjoy it while you can, you villain—it's your last dinner in this century.'

'Now!' he told himself when Mr. Sweeney had finished. But Mr. Sweeney was not in a gloating mood yet. He laid himself down on his blanket, and luxuriated in a cigar. Then for a long time he did nothing. Then he smoked another cigar.

'Oh, thunderation, come *on!*' Robert groaned. Daylight was beginning to dim...

Ah! Now! For Mr. Sweeney suddenly started out of his reverie, glanced skyward, and jumped up. He threw his cigar butt into the embers, put on his coat and hat, slipped something from the valise into his coat pocket, and strode away—passing so close to where Robert lay hidden that Robert could have touched him.

Now what? Robert followed with a rapidly beating heart.

Mr. Sweeney led him, in the gathering darkness, across fields and meadows, over fences, through hedgerows, across Ward Lane—and to the Walkers' own stable!

Robert's head whirled with puzzlement. He crept up to the side of the stable. Voices were murmuring inside. He laid his ear against the weathered boards. Mr. Sweeney and Mr. Shaw were talking inside.

They were speaking in such low voices that he couldn't hear what they were saying. He crept to the shelter of a mock orange bush where he could see the stable door, and crouched. Several windows in his house were lighted. It occurred to him for the first time—his heart gave a guilty lurch—that his mother might be seriously alarmed about his absence by now. He'd been gone almost the whole day...He'd better get back. But he was supposed to report to Mr. Shaw. How could he if—?

He waited, tense with anxiety, for more than an hour. Neither Mr. Shaw nor Mr. Sweeney reappeared. Well, he couldn't make his report, then. He *had* to go back and get the scene with Cousin Jane over with, so that everyone could calm down and go to bed. They simply had to be asleep before he could let Vicky out, and bring her up to date, and make everything ready to carry out the plan.

He sighed, and stood up. So much time wasted for nothing…!

"I insist on knowing where you have been!" Cousin Jane snapped.

"Oh, Bobbie, Bobbie!" Mrs. Walker sobbed. Her haggard, tear-stained face cut him to the center of his soul. "I can't tell you now, Mama," he wept. "All I can say is, it was all for the best. You'll see."

"For the *best!*" Cousin Jane snorted. "You were expressly forbidden to leave this house, and yet you have been gone for twelve hours. We have been sick with worry. We have been put to the trouble of calling in the police. Do you say that is for the *best?* What have you been up to?"

He shrank under the glitter of her eyes, but remained silent.

"You've been associating again with that Shaw girl, haven't you? With the daughter of a scoundrel, whom I forbade you ever to see again!"

"Bobbie," his mother wept.

"I'm sorry, Mama. Please believe me."

"Very well," Cousin Jane snapped. "We shall see about leaving this house 'all for the best.' Where is the key to your room, sir?"

"I—I lost it," he mumbled. It suddenly came to him that he had never put the key in his shoe after all. What if Cousin Jane demanded that he turn out his pockets—? He forced his hands to hang slack.

"*Lost* it? Have you no respect for anything? Very well,we shall see if this key fits." She took from her neck the string loop on which Victoria's key dangled, and pointed toward the stairs.

"March!" she snapped.

"No," Mrs. Walker said. Cousin Jane turned. "I beg your pardon, Isabelle?"

"I said, no!"

"You said *what,* Isabelle?"

"You are turning my house into a prison!" Mrs. Walker cried. "You lock all the doors. You have locked up my daughter. You are threatening to lock up my son. Why don't you lock Maggie up? Why not lock me up, too? Oh, you are a monster! I won't have it, I won't have it!"

"You wrote to me, Isabelle," Cousin Jane said in a deadly calm voice. "You urgently requested my advice and my aid. You knew that I could not be spared from my duties with the Tropical Islands Civilizing Mission, and the United Gentlewomen's Crusade for the Suppression of Infamous Literature, and the Lady's Society for the Moral Instruction of the Laboring Classes. And yet you called on me; and I, without hesitation, hastened to your side. And what did I find, Isabelle? I found you keeping a sullen, hysterical and incompetent servant. I found your finances in total collapse. I found you entertaining—and *in the morning!*—an obvious scoundrel, a *man!* I found your children disrespectful and disobedient. But did I shrink? No. I have stood by you unflinchingly. I have tried to make your servant see her duty. I have attempted to order your affairs. I have patiently endeavored to guide your children's footsteps back to the path of civilized behavior. And at every step, Isabelle—" Cousin Jane's voice had been getting louder and louder, and was now crackling like a fusillade "—at every *turn,* Isabelle, you oppose me; argue with me; try to thwart me! IS THIS GRATITUDE?"

Mrs. Walker was weeping too wildly to answer. Robert felt such a desire to hurl himself headfirst into Cousin Jane's stomach that he almost swooned. 'Steady!' he heard a voice commanding him through the buzzing in his ears. 'The plan must proceed!'

"I—I am ready to accept—my punishment, ma'am," he choked.

"Come up!" she snapped, heading for the stairs. "In deference to your mother's demoralized state, I shall release you and your sister in the morning. But if you try to take advantage of my clemency in any way, you will regret it for a long time to come."

She marched him upstairs, holding a candle in one hand and the key in the other. She tried the key in his door, and gave a little grunt of satisfaction on finding that it worked. She gestured him in with a nod, and snapped, "You will bring your sorrowing mother untimely to her grave, young man. Mend your ways, sir!" The door closed behind him, the key turned with a click, and he was alone in the dark.

He was shaking, but his heart was jubilant. 'Not bad,' he thought, 'not bad! You carried out your mission without getting caught, and you held firm in the face of the enemy.' He patted himself on the upper arm, restoring himself to rank. 'Not bad at all, *Corporal!*'

"Bedtime, Isabelle!" Cousin Jane commanded from the head of the stairs. "Your nerves are overwrought, and I am feeling somewhat fatigued myself. We must restore ourselves for the tasks of tomorrow."

All would be quiet soon. He would unlock his door, creep into Vick's room, tell her about the plan of campaign—

His hand froze for an instant, then clutched wildly in his pocket. A hot flash surged through his body. There was a hole in the bottom of his pocket, and the key was gone.

He collapsed on the bed, sobbing. In his mind's eye he tore the Corporal's stripes from his sleeve, snatched the decorations from his breast and trampled them underfoot, snapped his sword in half, and drummed himself out of the regiment forever.

The Plan in Ruins

...from bad to worse. Our "cat fight" saved us and we got into the house finally, but I couldn't go to the elevator because Maggie came downstairs to fill her pitcher. Bobbie set Vicky free, but they were surprised by Cousin Jane. Bobbie got away. Everybody ended up downstairs. I was found by Cousin Jane. I knew it was all over when I saw Daddy and Mr. Sweeney come in...

Susan shrank into the bushes and looked up. A second story window was being opened, inch by inch...

Whose? In her mind's eye she surveyed the inside of the house. When you went up the stairs, Vicky's room was here, Bobbie's was here; which meant, from the outside of the house, that—that she was now crouching under Bobbie's bay window. Ch...ch...ch...Bit by bit the window sash slid up, until there was a gap of nearly two feet between it and the sill. For a few minutes Susan thought she could hear rustling sounds. These were followed by a quiet thump. A white shape materialized over the sill, and slithered groundward in a series of little jerks. It was a knotted bedsheet. Another thump...Out of the window came a pair of legs. The legs kicked. Then there was a gasp, a scrape of buttons over wood, and the rest of Robert appeared with a rush. His feet thunked against the carved wooden arch of a downstairs window.

'Good grief!' Susan thought. 'He'll put his foot through the glass in a minute! She must stop his swinging. She squeezed into the shrubbery, grabbed the end of the sheet, and pulled it to one side. His startled white face looked down on her over his arm.

"Bobbie!" she whispered. "It's—"

There was a ripping noise.

He gave a stifled yelp. The sheet went slack in her hands. She tried to throw herself aside, but it was too late. His weight struck her right shoulder, and they toppled into the shrubbery. The crash was like a forest tree collapsing.

She spat out a mouthful of leaves and twigs, and whispered, "You all right?"

"Think so. My ear hurts."

High above them came the sound of a window being thrown open.

"Cat fight!" Susan whispered. "Quick!" She rounded her lips and crooned, "Ow-w-w-w-w-w-w-w."

Robert caught on at once. "Oooo-oooo-oooo-oooo," he sang, *glissando*.

"Yow-wow-*wow!*" Susan shrieked, thrashing in the shrubbery with her legs.

Maggie's voice floated down through the darkness. "Wisha! Wisha! Get on out o' that, ye divels!" Something heavy clunked against her windowsill, and a stream of water cascaded down into the bush next to them.

"There's more o' that if ye want it," Maggie threatened. "And divel a drap o' milk will ye be gettin' from *me* in the mornin', Toby! Ye black limb o' Satan!"

The window slammed shut.

Susan let out a tremulous breath, and whispered, "Where've you *been?* Why were you climbing out the window?"

"Oh, Sue, I made such a mess of everything! Cousin Jane locked me up and then I found that I'd lost my key. What're you doing here?"

"I can't get in! Oh, it's all so awful—the whole plan is falling apart!"

"There's still a chance to make it work, Sue! Your Papa and Mr. Sweeney are hiding in the back yard! I saw them for a second over by the pond after Mr. Hollister fired. I'll bet they mean to carry on as soon as everything calms down again. We have to get ready for them!"

"How? We're locked out!"

"Nil desperandum, Sue. There's more than one way to get into the house. Come on!"

They extricated themselves from the wreckage of the shrubbery, and crept around to the other side of the house.

"Here," Robert whispered. "There's a broken pane in the cellar window. I can reach through and undo the catch." He dropped to his hands and knees to crawl under the hydrangeas. She crouched to follow him, but he whispered, "This is a hard way in, Sue. Go to the front door. I'll have it open in a jiffy."

"All right."

She trudged back to the porch, and leaned against the door frame. Good grief, what a night! Once, long ago—it seemed years ago now—she had had a lovely vision: strolls in the country, picnics by a babbling stream, her father and Mrs. Walker gazing into each other's eyes, while she and Victoria and Robert played tag and laughed in a meadow full of flowers and sunlight... How had that dream turned into this nightmare of frustration and panic and scurryings around in the dark? She sighed. 'If I just survive tonight,' she thought, 'nothing will ever faze me again.'

The bolt slid back with a stealthy scrape, the door opened, and she was inside.

"All set!" Robert whispered. "I unlocked the back door, too. Here's the closet key, so I can let Vicky out. It doesn't *exactly* fit, but if you kind of lift it at the same time you turn it, it usually works. I'll go up and tell her what the plan is."

"Good! I'll call up the elev—"

"Great Caesar!" Robert hissed, clutching her arm. "Somebody's moving around up there!"

They crouched and listened. There were quiet shuffling footsteps somewhere on the second floor, and a wavering glow of candlelight was approaching the top of the stairs.

"Into the parlor!" Robert whispered.

They ducked behind the sofa and watched. It was Maggie, padding downstairs in carpet slippers, a robe several sizes too big for her, and a frilled cap tied under the chin. She was carrying a candlestick in one hand, and a large gleaming china pitcher in the other. She yawned as she passed by the parlor entrance.

"Going to fill her pitcher," Robert whispered. "I'll charge upstairs while she's in the kitchen. Get the elevator ready as soon as the coast is clear. We'll be down as soon as we can."

"Right! I'll be waiting for you."

He tiptoed to the parlor entrance, glanced down the hallway, and then silently vanished up the stairs.

"Klunk-ump, klunk-ump," the pump in the kitchen complained.

Susan took a step toward the other hallway, the one where the elevator was, and hesitated. Could she risk it yet? Maggie might come back that way…

Oh—good—*grief!* Her hands were empty—at some point during all the hurly-burly outside she had lost her pillowcase and her *Harper's Bazar. Now* what was she going to use to wedge the elevator door open? She was going to have to find something, quick! Her trembling hands felt along the surfaces of plush, brocade, polished wood…This box wouldn't work, this vase wouldn't, wasn't there *any*thing—?

Oh, oh, Maggie was coming back—candlelight was wavering down the hallway by the stairs. Susan dove behind the sofa, and peeked over the back. Maggie shuffled into view, leaning a little to the right under the weight of her pitcher.

Crash! A door was hurled open upstairs.

Both Susan and Maggie jumped. Maggie's candle dipped so wildly that it almost went out, and a dollop of water from her pitcher splashed on the floor.

"Robert!" Cousin Jane's voice snapped. "What are you doing out of your room? How did you open that door? Answer me, sir!"

Another door banged open.

"Isabelle! Will you kindly look at this? Do you see what comes of relaxing discipline even for an instant? Oh! *Oh!* Victoria! What are *you* doing with your door open? Isabelle, this is an outrage! These children are *defying* me! I will not have it! Robert! *Robert!*"

Robert came bolting down the stairs like a rabbit. His momentum carried him into the front door with a glass-rattling smash. He rebounded, dodged around Maggie—another dip of the candle, another splash of water on the floor—and disappeared down the hallway.

"Mer-r-ciful hivvens!" Maggie exclaimed.

"Come back here this instant, you ruffian!" Cousin Jane shouted. "Return at once or I shall come down and fetch you! If you put me to that trouble, I promise you that you will never forget it!"

"Jane!" Mrs. Walker's voice cried. "I have reached the end of my tether! Don't you dare touch that boy!"

"I see my duty and I intend to do it!"

"Jane—!"

"Interfere with me at your peril."

Down the stairs Cousin Jane stormed, in a red flannel robe and a nightcap. She carried a candle in one hand and brandished her umbrella in the other. Even in the soft candlelight her eyes and pince-nez glasses seemed to glitter. Mrs. Walker and Victoria came running down behind her.

"What are you doing here, you nincompoop?" Cousin Jane shouted at Maggie. "Why didn't you stop him?"

"Sure, Mum, with both me hands full? And himself passin' by like a cannonball?"

"Imbeciles!" Cousin Jane raged. "I am surrounded by imbeciles! Where did he go?"

"Sure, Mum, how could I tell with him skinnin' out so fast he was gone before I could turn me head?"

"If you touch that child, Jane," Mrs. Walker said quietly, "I shall—I don't know what!"

"Sure," Maggie said, lifting her chin, "and whatever it is, Mum, I'll help ye!"

"Your wages will be stopped as of this instant," Cousin Jane snapped. "As for *you*, Isabelle, I shall deal with you later." Suddenly, with amazing agility for one of her stoutness, she pounced into the parlor, raising her candle as she did so. Susan was completely taken by surprise, with her face lifted above the back of the sofa. She shrank with a squeak of dismay.

"Aha!" Cousin Jane cried. "You thought to outwit *me*, did you? Stand up, you heathen! You insubordinate—Oh! It's that Shaw baggage! *What are you doing here?*"

Her umbrella was poised to strike. Her glasses glittered like the eyes of a serpent. Susan began to back away on legs that threatened to buckle under her. "I—" she croaked.

"This is a plot," Cousin Jane hissed. "I can smell it. And Robert is implicated too, isn't he? You have corrupted him, haven't you? Oh, I saw right through you and your father the minute I laid eyes on you. A precious pair of scoundrels and thieves! Where is he? What are you up to? What are you doing in this house? Where is Robert?"

Susan, backing away, stumbled over a hassock, staggered a few steps, grabbed out with both hands to keep from falling, and seized something that bore her weight. Fringed portieres... She was in the doorway of the hall. She continued to retreat before Cousin Jane's implacable advance. The grandfather clock ticked and tocked as though nothing were passing but time.

"*Out* with it! *Out* with it!" Cousin Jane cried, slashing with her umbrella. The steel tip whistled in a downward arc one inch from Susan's face. The door at the other end of the hallway opened.

"What's that? Who's that?" Cousin Jane snapped. She stopped, lifted her candle, and peered past Susan into the shadows. Maggie came up by Cousin Jane's left side; she was moaning, and her round eyes were fixed on Susan. Mrs. Walker stopped one pace behind. Victoria, waxen-faced, stared over their shoulders.

"Aha!" Cousin Jane said. "Exactly! That scoundrel Shaw! And another villain! Oh, yes, quite a little plot, isn't it?"

Susan turned. Her father, looking very strange, was coming into the light, followed by Mr. Sweeney. He was soaking wet. His hair was plastered down over his skull, his boots made squelching noises, his lovely suit was dark and clinging and festooned with water-weed. And oh!—oh!

Did Mr. Sweeney have in his hand what she thought he had?

Yes…

Susan's legs would not hold her up any longer, and she collapsed against the wainscotting.

Mr. Shaw Goes Under

...told us that his part of the plan went pretty well at first. Mr. Sweeney was suspicious, but Daddy calmed him down until the police came with that runaway boy. Mr. Sweeney insisted on going to the house to find out what was happening. Mr. Hollister fired as they began to cross the yard, and from then on everything got out of hand for Daddy too...

"Sweeney? Sweeney?"

There was no answer. The stable was empty.

"Good night!" Mr. Shaw muttered. He groped through the dimness until he came to a manger, where he sat down.

Was Sweeney going to show up, or had the plan miscarried? Mr. Shaw rather hoped the latter. Throughout the afternoon his original enthusiasm had been slowly giving away before the onslaught of doubts and scruples. He was a law-abiding man, after all, with small taste for either violence or deceit. Sweeney would come to no physical harm in the elevator; but still, to be snatched from your own century and hurled into another was a serious matter.

So was taking the law into one's own hands...

But then the vision that had been haunting him ever since last night suddenly glowed in his imagination again: Isabelle Walker, her tumbled hair glinting in candlelight, her cheeks wet with tears...His heart leaped. And yet the man he was worrying about could pretend to pay court to her for the purpose of stealing every last thing she had! And without a qualm! Mr. Shaw could hear that smooth voice saying, "Why, she has her house and plenty of leisure. Let her take in boarders, or do laundry, or something..."

Ah, the dog! Feel scruples about *him?* His fists clenched. At that instant a quiet footfall sounded, and a low voice said, "Shaw?"

Mr. Shaw, trembling with rage, had all he could do to keep from hurling himself on Mr. Sweeney. "Here," he grated.

Mr. Sweeney crunched over the straw until the pale oval of his face was visible. He leaned against a post. His voice was intense and quiet. He said, "Look here, Shaw, I want an explanation!"

"About what?"

"That business this afternoon with the policeman."

"Oh. It's nothing to do with us. Robert disappeared for a while, that's all."

"Why? He was supposed to be playing with the girls."

"They, ah, had a quarrel, and that cousin who's staying with them lectured him about manners. So he went off to sulk, and the ladies thought he'd run away, and called in the police. And then he came home again, and it all blew over."

"I didn't see the boy going anywhere," Mr. Sweeney said. "Or coming back either."

"Well, you can't watch everywhere at once, can you?"

"But I did see you consulting with the police!"

"Sweeney, don't be a flaming fool. I know you've been watching me. If I wanted to bring the police into our business, I wouldn't do it right in front of you. I spoke to that policeman simply to find out what he was doing here. In fact, I suspected *you* were behind it. I thought maybe you'd changed your mind and denounced us after all."

There was a short silence. Then Mr. Sweeney said, "That won't do. If you really thought you'd been denounced, you wouldn't have walked out into the arms of the police like that. You'd have made your escape."

"Sweeney," Mr. Shaw sighed, "your suspicions bore me. I've given you my explanation; you can take it or leave it. If you think something funny is going on, why aren't you making *your* escape?"

"Ah!" Mr. Sweeney said. "Ah! You were just hoping I'd do that, weren't you, Shaw? That's your game, isn't it? And then you'd have the jewels all to yourself, wouldn't you? Well, abandon that hope, Shaw. I'm staying right here. We will proceed as planned."

"You know, Sweeney, one might be led to conclude that you don't trust me."

"Oh, perish the thought, Shaw! I trust you implicitly—mainly because I know that *you* know how hot I can make it for you if you try to betray me. That means in *any particular*, Shaw. Do we understand each other?"

"I guess we do."

"Excellent!" There was a rustling noise as if Mr. Sweeney were taking something out of his pocket, and then the faint tinkling of a little bell.

"What's that?"

"My repeater," Mr. Sweeney said impatiently. "What's the matter with you, Shaw? Nerves?"

"No, it just, ah, took me by surprise." 'Repeater...?' he wondered.

"Mmm. After nine. We have some waiting to do, Shaw. We might as well do it comfortably." And Mr. Sweeney threw himself down on the straw.

Repeater! Of course—it was a watch that struck the time when you pressed a button...Mr. Shaw sighed, and sat down on the straw himself. Yes, they *would* proceed as planned. He felt no more doubts, no more scruples. The very tone of Mr. Sweeney's voice had cured him of those.

They waited.

"Hullo!" Mr. Sweeney said when they heard the horse and buggy stop out in front of the house. They held their breath and listened. There was a long silence; then the faint snap of a whip and the sound of the horse cantering away.

"Something peculiar here, Shaw," Mr. Sweeney muttered.

"There certainly is. They wouldn't be having visitors at this time of night, would they? What time is it, anyway?"

Mr. Sweeney's repeater tinkled. "Almost twelve!" he exclaimed. "Look here, Shaw, you didn't arrange to have someone drop in on us, did you?"

"Oh, don't be an idiot!"

Mr. Sweeney breathed hard for a few minutes, then said, "I want to know what's going on."

"So do I. What do you suggest we do?"

“I believe we’d better go to the house and investigate. This could seriously affect our plans, Shaw.”

“I know.”

They stood up. Mr. Shaw bit his lip. What *was* happening at the house, anyway? His heart hammered against his ribs as he reflected that any kind of disturbance could upset the plan completely. They stepped out of the stable. Good lord, how bright the moon was! Mr. Sweeney nodded toward some ghostly white bushes, and they headed for the nearest one.

“Stop, thieves!”

They froze.

“Oh, good night!” Mr. Shaw muttered. “It’s that flaming fool, Hollister!”

“Horse thieves! Cutthroats!” Mr. Hollister bawled from the second floor of his house. *“Don’t move—I’ve got you in my sights, you Republican sneaks!”*

Mr. Sweeney soundlessly melted behind a bush. “Down!” he whispered.

“Oh, you will, will you?” Mr. Hollister brayed.

Mr. Shaw, still immobile in his tracks, staring at Hollisters’ house, saw a bright orange flash erupt in an upstairs window. There was a terrific blast. Mr. Shaw felt an urgent desire to be on the other side of something solid. He jumped for the nearest bush. Too small, too thin! A hedge loomed nearby. He hurled himself into it, through it. Something glimmered in front of him. His foot caught on a low stone parapet, and he fell, clawing the air for support. Then he struck—but not moonlit turf as he had expected. Down he went, with an involuntary gasp that half filled his lungs with water. He was drowning! He touched mud, gave a mighty kick, shot up into the air, and

found himself standing waist deep in a pond. He gagged and spat out a stream of stagnant-tasting water.

Mr. Sweeney hissed "Imbecile!" and seized his hands and hauled him out. They crouched behind the hedge that bordered the pond, and listened. Silence had returned to the world.

It was broken by a door banging open at Hollisters'. In a moment they heard a faint braying in front of the Walker house; then another interval of silence; then Hollisters' door again.

"Hail, the conquering hero," Mr. Sweeney sneered. "I expect they're all going to be up now, appreciating his heroism. Awkward…I know your daughter will be keeping cool during the uproar, however."

"Oh, I'm sure she, ah—"

"She's such an artist, she could even turn it into an advantage. No opportunity like a moment or two of confusion for dipping into the jewel box, eh? Well, let's give them a little time to settle down, and then carry on with our investigating."

"Ah, all right."

"I detect a certain lack of conviction in your tone, Shaw. One might even say, an outright reluctance."

"Oh—oh, no. It's just that I, ah—all this noise and so forth has—shaken me up a bit."

"Perhaps your little aquatic excursion has had, shall we say, a *dampening* effect? Well, these things will happen. One must exercise one's philosophy, Shaw."

'Oh, go this, that, and the other, you weasel!' Mr. Shaw raged to himself. 'What the *devil* am I going to do now?'

The plan just couldn't work now that everyone in the house was aroused and on edge. Oh, *blast* that idiot Hollister! Of course he had told them what he had seen in their back yard; and even if they went back to bed immediately, their nerves would be stretched tight. The slightest sound in the house would have them all up and about instantly…Maybe he should call off the whole thing until tomorrow night.

"Come along, Shaw," Mr. Sweeney murmured, standing up. "Once more into the breach."

"Look," Mr. Shaw began, "how about—?"

There was a crash in the shrubbery beside the house. Cats began to yowl and thrash about in combat. A window was thrown open. Maggie's voice could be heard shouting in reproof. Water spattered down on leaves. The cats disengaged.

Mr. Sweeney sat down again. "More alarums and excursions. You know, Shaw, it all begins to take on a faintly comic aspect, don't you think?"

"I don't see the humor of it," Mr. Shaw muttered. Blast the man, anyway! He actually seemed to be enjoying all this! "Look," he began again. "It occurs to me that Susan may not have gotten the chance to, ah, do it, what with all these interruptions. Don't you think we—?"

"Oh, I have complete faith in that daughter of yours, Shaw."

"Well, ah, I do too, of course. It's just that everybody will be so nervous and jumpy in there that—And if we don't show up, she'll know just what to do. Then tomorrow night we can—"

Mr. Sweeney laughed quietly. "Shaw," he said, "the trouble with you is that you are so childishly transparent. I've been in this profession a long time, my dear fellow, and no one can catch me twice with the same tricks."

"What?"

"I will admit that these disturbances have been very competently staged. Of course, while you were in town today you might have made arrangements for a brass band and a fire brigade, too—or did you? Perhaps they're in the wings now, waiting for their cue. And I must say that your own acting is first-rate—all this pretense of reluctance and nervousness."

Mr. Shaw was having difficulty catching up. "Now wait a minute," he said. "Staged? Do you actually think that I—?"

"Come off it, Shaw," Mr. Sweeney sighed. "You and Susan frightened me away once with a rigged-up scene. Now that I know how you operate, it's not going to work a second time. I am *not* coming back tomorrow night only to find that you two have flown the coop—with the jewels, of course. And since you are so reluctant to share, I might as well confess that I don't enjoy sharing, either. I want those jewels myself, Shaw. All of them."

Mr. Sweeney took his hand out of his pocket. There was a chilling *click*. Mr. Shaw found himself looking into the muzzle of a revolver.

"Forward march, Shaw! No use tempting Hollister into any more acts of heroism, so we'll just take a roundabout route until the house covers us, and then double back. Now please don't oblige me to shoot you, my dear fellow—it's so unprofessional and unphilosophical."

The Battle of Elevator Hall

...turned into a terrific struggle after Bobbie tipped the scales. I guess all that water saved us, really, because it made everybody skid and fall so much. Otherwise Mr. Sweeney might have gotten away and Cousin Jane wouldn't have "sealed her own fate," as Vicky puts it...

"Mer-r-cy on us!" Maggie quavered. Her candle performed wild figures in the air. "It's them Shaws! And that Mr. Sweeney!"

"Steady, Maggie," Mrs. Walker said in a quiet voice. "There's nothing to be afraid of."

"Sure and I'm stiddy as I can be, Mum, with me second sight tellin' me them Shaws are a sign."

Mr. Shaw looked at Susan and lifted his shoulders in a gesture of despair. "I'm sorry, chick," he muttered. "Everything went to pieces out there. Mrs. Walker, I hope I'll have an opportunity to explain, or *try* to expl—"

"Your explanations are not wanted," Cousin Jane snapped. "You are a scoundrel, and that is all *we* need to know. I thought I had made my prohibition clear. And yet I find your daughter creeping about in the dark like a thief, and subverting the Walker children; and I find *you* up to who knows what villainies, prating meanwhile of 'explanations.' There can be no explanations under these circumstances. You are to leave this house instantly. *And* your daughter. And you too, whoever you are!"

Mr. Sweeney raised his derby and said, "I have not had the pleasure of making your acquaintance, Madame."

"And I have no wish to make *yours*, sir! You are an impertinent scalawag! Leave this house at once, all of you! And be assured that I intend to notify the police about your actions immediately."

"I am trembling in my boots, Madame," Mr. Sweeney said in his smoothest voice. His lips twitched as though he were suppressing a smile. He turned his eyes to the others. "Well! Quite an *omnium gatherum!* How are you, Maggie? Please accept my apologies for any lost sleep this may cause you. Isabelle! I didn't think I'd have the pleasure of seeing you again. Such a pity that we have to meet under these awkward circumstances! Ah—that fiery light in your eyes—enchanting!"

"I know what to think of you, sir," Mrs. Walker said.

"Quite so. Victoria, my dear! You look frightened. There is no need to be apprehensive, you know. As long as you all behave, no harm will come to any of you. Now, who is missing? Oh, yes, Robert! Still sleeping after the rigors of the day, I presume. Such an active little fellow!"

"My patience is at an end!" Cousin Jane shouted. "I have

undergone shouting and shots in the night and impertinences and disobedience and base ingratitude and loss of sleep. This effrontery is the last intolerable straw! Get out!" She took a step forward and raised her umbrella.

"Madame," Mr. Sweeney said with venomous intensity, "my patience is no more elastic than yours. Do you see what I have in my hand? If you don't step back and hold your tongue, I will shoot this gentleman. And if *his* life is of no consequence to you, *yours* will instantly follow."

"Jane!" Mrs. Walker said. "I'm afraid that Mr. Sweeney means exactly what he says. Please do what he asks."

"Very well, Isabelle—for your sake, not for mine. I have nothing but scorn for his threats." Cousin Jane stepped back beside Maggie and lowered her umbrella. Her face was dark with rage. *"Scoundrel!"* she hissed.

"That I am, Madame," Mr. Sweeney said, flashing his most brilliant smile. "It is my calling in life, and I glory in it. But I take no pleasure in forcing my company on those who don't welcome it, so I shall detain you no longer than absolutely necessary. Susan, my dear, where is it?"

"What?" she croaked.

"Oh, come, girl—you know what I mean. The cloth bag!"

Good grief, what was she going to do now? "Cuk—cuk—cloth bag?" she stammered, shrinking back against the wainscotting. Something in the wall gave way under the pressure of her shoulder blade.

"Sweeney, let her alone," Mr. Shaw said. "There isn't any cloth bag. There aren't any jewels. The whole thing was a—"

"Still trying to put me off, Shaw? Your persistence is admirable, but I'm beginning to find it tiresome."

"Sweeney, you flaming ass, don't you understand? There *isn't—*"

"Shut up, Shaw. Susan, bring me that bag. If the jewels aren't in a bag yet, bring me the box—and your key, too. You have two minutes. If you are not back by then, your father is a dead man."

'I can fix up another pillowcase!' she thought. 'I can throw some of Vicky's things in. At least it'll give us some time to—' "I'll—I'll get it," she said, staggering forward a step.

Behind her the wainscotting split open with the old familiar rumble and sigh. A harsh glare of electric light flooded the hallway.

Everyone gasped.

"Oh, good night!" Mr. Shaw muttered at the ceiling. "That's all we need!"

"Mer-r-rciful hivvens!" Maggie moaned. Her eyes turned up in their sockets, the candle and pitcher fell from her hands, and her body toppled over backward. Mrs. Walker caught her by the shoulders just in time, and, staggering under her weight, eased her to the floor.

Maggie's pitcher landed on Cousin Jane's left foot with a crunchy thud, and fell over, sending a gush of water across the parquet floor. Cousin Jane shrieked and doubled over. Her candle fell to the floor, and her pince-nez glasses, popping off her nose, bounced at the end of their black ribbon. She shrieked again, a long soaring crescendo that made the glass front of the grandfather clock rattle, and hopped backwards, putting out her free hand for support. Mrs. Walker's shoulder was the first thing that came within reach. She seized it and leaned. Mrs. Walker, still in the act of kneeling by Maggie, dropped suddenly to her knees under Cousin Jane's weight, and for an instant it looked as if both of them would collapse in a heap.

Victoria scurried forward and lifted Cousin Jane upright again.

"Ooooooh! My foot! Send for the doctor! Get me to a chair!"

"There're chairs in the parlor, Cousin Jane," Victoria quavered. "If I hold you up, do you think you can hop—?"

"No!" Mr. Sweeney said. "No one will leave this hallway but Susan. The rest of you will stay exactly where you are."

"You are a heartless villain, sir!" Victoria flashed out. "She is in pain!"

"She may endure it standing as well as sitting. You are not to move."

He turned to Mrs. Walker with that familiar smile of ironic appreciation. "Well, Isabelle! What a consummate deceiver you are! I knew you were wealthy, but I would never in a thousand years have suspected that you possessed electric lighting. And a closet with self-opening doors! That's affluence on a grand scale! Well, my dear, this excessive wealth must be a burden to you, so I am going to relieve you of some of it. Susan, why are you dawdling? Fetch me that jewelry, girl. One minute left, and your father's life hangs in the balance!"

"I—I'm going," Susan gulped. She was rooted to the spot. She was trying not to look directly at what was happening, trying not to betray to Mr. Sweeney the fact that—that—

"Push, somebody," Robert said.

He had crept down the hallway from the kitchen, quiet as a moth, and had gone down on his hands and knees just behind, and broadside to, Mr. Sweeney's legs. Mr. Sweeney turned his head with a little snort of surprise. For an instant the muzzle of his revolver was not pointed at Mr. Shaw's ribs. Susan, feeling as though she were in a dream, as though she were moving under water, as though she were someone else watching a stranger named Susan doing something that was more dangerous than anything she had ever done in her life—Susan stepped forward one long step, and laid both her hands against Mr. Sweeney's chest, and shoved.

Mr. Sweeney toppled backwards over Robert in an almost leisurely arc, his mouth opening and his eyes widening as he went. There was a loud explosion from his pistol. Two of the paper flowers in the vase (on the marble-topped table with the carved lyre-shaped legs) leaped up and turned into fragments, and a windowpane in the parlor shivered out of its frame with a sweet silvery tinkle.

Mrs. Walker and Victoria screamed.

Mr. Sweeney hit the floor with a crash and a grunt, and his derby flew off. Mr. Shaw pounced on him, and snarled in a high choking voice, "Call her *Isabelle*, will you, you slimy rat!" He grabbed Mr. Sweeney's right wrist in one hand, and pommeled his face with the other. Mr. Sweeney said "Aagh!" and seized Mr. Shaw's cravat. They grappled and rolled together.

"This is an outrage!" Cousin Jane shouted. She pounded the floor with the tip of her umbrella. "Why has no one fetched me a chair? Why has no one gone for the doctor? Isabelle, turn those ruffians out of the house at once, and attend to my needs!"

But Mrs. Walker paid no attention. Her lower lip was crushed between her teeth, and her eyes were fixed on Robert. He was lying face down on the floor, trying to protect his head with his arms as the battle-locked forms of the two men rolled and grunted on top of him.

"Mmf fm mumpf!" came his voice from the melee.

"What?" Susan cried. She hovered on the edge of the fight, looking for her chance to jump in and help her father, but aware that if she jumped at the wrong instant she would only hinder him.

"Umm!" Robert said.

"Gun!" Mr. Shaw gasped by way of translation. "Get—" and then his voice was cut off as they rolled over again. But here was Susan's chance. Her father was forcing Mr. Sweeney's hand, the one that held the pistol, down toward the floor. She stamped on it with her heel. Mr. Sweeney shouted, and the pistol came loose.

Then Robert's knee appeared out of the scrimmage and struck the pistol, and sent it spinning across the floor toward the red velvet window curtains. It created a confused wake as it plowed through the puddle of water from Maggie's pitcher. Susan leaped for it—tried to leap for it. The wet floor was as slippery as ice. Her feet shot out from under her, and she landed on her back with a jolt that knocked most of the breath out of her lungs.

A kind of buzzing roar filled her ears for a moment as she gasped air back into her chest again. She raised her head, and looked around in time to see Mr. Sweeney staggering to his feet. Her father, balanced shakily on one knee, was drawing back his arm for another blow.

His fist flashed through the air. Mr. Sweeney, either intentionally or because his feet were skidding in the water, dodged the blow. The momentum of Mr. Shaw's swinging arm carried him around in a semicircle; he lost his balance and went down on his chest with a grunt. Mr. Sweeney lurched forward, stumbled over Susan, got to his feet again instantly, and took two great slippery steps that brought him close to Victoria and Cousin Jane.

"Stop or I'll shoot!" Robert squeaked.

Mr. Sweeney glanced back, and froze.

Robert was on his knees by the window curtains. He held the revolver in both shaking hands; and even as Mr. Sweeney turned his head, one of Robert's thumbs pulled back the hammer.

All was silent. Slowly, slowly, Mr. Sweeney turned around. "Well!" he said quietly, with a slight smile on his lips. "What do you wish me to do, Robert? Perhaps Mr. Shaw could make a suggestion."

Without thinking, Robert turned to Mr. Shaw. Mr. Sweeney hurled himself on Victoria—but his foot slipped in the water as he pounced; and instead of seizing her firmly as he had intended, he fell toward her, saving himself from going down only by clutching her shoulder with both hands. She screamed and twisted away from his grasp; her feet skidded backwards; she fell to her knees. Deprived of their support, Cousin Jane and Mr. Sweeney toppled toward each other, and embraced. They swayed for a moment, dancing around Victoria, frantically trying to maintain balance. Their gyrations carried them forward a few steps. Cousin Jane cried out as her injured foot momentarily took her weight. Then Mr. Sweeney regained control. He spun Cousin Jane in a half-circle so that he was behind her; hugged her tightly, pinning her arms to her sides; then heaved her about to position her stout body between himself and Robert.

Robert lowered the pistol.

"Let me—*go*, you cur!" Cousin Jane gasped. She still had a grip on her umbrella; but without the use of her arms, she could only tap Mr. Sweeney on the leg with it by waggling her wrist.

"With pleasure—Madame," Mr. Sweeney panted. "But only—when we—reach—the parlor. Backward—march!"

He tried to pull her backwards. It might have worked with Victoria, but Cousin Jane was too heavy. "Wretch!" she cried. "Let *go!*" and she flung her whole weight forward.

The locked forms swayed, and went down in a slow arc, Mr. Sweeney on the bottom, Cousin Jane on top, through the elevator door. The impact of their bodies on the floor made the elevator jangle and bounce in its shaft.

The wainscotting sighed, and began to rumble shut.

"Hey!" Mr. Shaw shouted. "Stop it! *Get* it!"

He and Susan lunged for the elevator on hands and knees. Susan was closer, but even so she was almost too late. The door nipped her hand in its rubber-edged bite; then the safety device wheezed, and the door recoiled.

"Hold it open!" Mr. Shaw panted. He struggled to his feet and skidded toward the elevator.

Cousin Jane rolled away from Mr. Sweeney's prostrate form, sat up, and replaced her pince-nez. "Out*rage*ous!" she hissed through clenched teeth. "I'll make them pay for this!"

Susan threw herself against the folded-back door. It bunted against her palms, protesting: *wheeze-grumf, wheeze-grumf.*

"Miss Clamp!" Mr. Shaw cried. "Get out of there!"

"Scoundrel!" she shouted. "Leave this house at once! And

take your gutter-brat with you!"

"You don't understand! You have to get *out!*" And Mr. Shaw reached forward to pull her clear.

"Don't touch me!" she spat. Her umbrella whistled through the air and struck him squarely in the face. With a cry he staggered back, and fell.

"Daddy!" Susan screamed. She scrabbled over the floor toward him.

The door began to trundle shut again.

Mr. Sweeney struggled to his feet, gasping for air, and lurched toward the narrowing exit.

Cousin Jane roared, "Don't you *dare* close this door!" and began to pound a deafening tattoo on it with her umbrella.

"Back!" Robert cried, leveling the revolver.

Mr. Sweeney, supporting his weight with his right hand, which had unknowingly come to rest on the control buttons, paused groggily for an instant—a fatal instant.

The wainscotting closed, plunging the hallway into darkness, and the resonant *bang bang bang* of Cousin Jane's umbrella faded away into silence.

For a long time nothing could be heard but the ticking of the grandfather clock and the sounds of heavy breathing. The smell of gunsmoke still hung in the air.

"Are you all right, Daddy?" Susan quavered.

"Think so... Whew, what a clout! Is she gone?"

"Yes."

"Oh, lord..."

In a low, shaking voice Mrs. Walker said, "Have we all gone

mad, Mr. Shaw?"

"Oh no, oh no! It's all explainable, sort of." They could hear him struggling into a sitting position. "Mrs. Walker…I guess this is going to sound irrelevant. Please forgive me. Did your cousin have a middle name?"

"Yes: Hildegarde."

"Ah! Hmm…"

"Where has she gone, Mr. Shaw?"

"Well, ah, it's hard to explain, Mrs. Walker. She's gone very far away. I don't believe any harm will come to her, but she won't come back. Ever. I'm sorry."

"Oh." Mrs. Walker was silent for a while, and then said in a very low voice, "Perhaps it is wicked of me, but—but if it is true that she will come to no harm, then I cannot bring myself to feel sorry that she won't return."

"Nor can I," Victoria said shakily.

"Me neither!" Robert declared.

Click whirrr, said the clock, and its sweet melancholy chime announced that the new day was three-quarters of an hour old.

"Vicky, dear, you're closest to the parlor. Will you please bring in a candle?"

"Yes, Mama."

For a long time they listened to Victoria bumping around in the dark, and the *skritch skritch* of her shaking hands striking one match after another in the attempt to light a candle. At last she succeeded, and a soft orange glow came wavering back into the hallway, and they could all see each other again.

Mrs. Walker still knelt by Maggie, and was chafing her wrists. Mr. Shaw sat leaning back on his arms, with a smile dawning on his face—the smile of a man who realizes that all obstacles have been removed from his path.

"By George!" he murmured. "By *George!*" He got to his feet, shuffling to keep his balance in the water slick. "Corporal," he said, catching sight of Robert, "we'd better lay down our arms, don't you think?" He took the revolver from Robert, uncocked it carefully, and laid it on the marble-topped table. "That gun might have been the end of me. Corporal—no, I think from now on we should say 'Sergeant.' Sergeant, you saved my life, I think. Thank you."

Robert blinked solemnly and reddened as they shook hands.

"Vicky, Susie, you were both enormously courageous. Good work, and thank you!"

Susan and Victoria slopped and slid toward each other, and fell into each other's arms, and began to laugh and cry at the same time.

"Great Caesar!" Robert muttered, trying to look disgusted, but swallowing hard.

"As for me—well, you may all take turns kicking me. How *could* I have concocted such an asinine plan?"

"Oh, it was a capital plan, sir! It's just that the unexpected always happens during a battle."

"Well, thank goodness you kids knew how to take advantage of the unexpected! Mrs. Walker, I owe you an explanation."

"An explanation would be most welcome, Mr. Shaw."

"Oh my, oh my! It's such a long story!" Despite his soaking clothes and plastered-down hair and a raw contusion on his forehead, Susan had never seen him looking so handsome and happy. He glowed with excitement, like another candle. "I don't think you're going to believe it. I don't think *I'm* going to believe it. You see, we—but before I tell you all that, I want to tell you something else. And *then* I'll tell you why we—what we—oh, good night, where do I begin?"

"Begin with the elevator, sir!" Robert cried. "It goes through time, Mama! It travels to the *future!*"

"It really begins with Mr. Sweeney!" Victoria said. "It was Susan who unmasked him, Mama! We suspected he was a scoundrel, but she's the one who really proved it!"

"It really begins with the witch," Susan put in. "At least our part of it. You see, Mrs. Walker, we couldn't even have come here if she hadn't given me three trips—"

"But I had to go to the wishing well before she did that. And I had to go *again*, yesterday—no, day before yesterday—"

"And we had a treasure map, Mama, and it was from a newspaper in *1960!*"

"And we found the treasure!"

"Only we lost it again."

"But I know where his camp is, and I'll bet it's there! That's why I was away so long, Mama, but I couldn't tell you in front of Cousin Jane."

"Goodness!" Mrs. Walker said, looking from one face to another. "The more you tell me, the less I understand. You seem to have been up to a great deal behind my back!"

"Oh, yes!" Mr. Shaw laughed. "It's a regular conspiracy. Our children are deep-dyed plotters, Mrs. Walker. I didn't know anything about it myself until they had it all settled among themselves what our fate was to be."

"*Our* fate, Mr. Shaw?"

Victoria and Susan glanced at each other and began to giggle.

"Yes, our fate. Believe me, I resisted as long as I could. You may resist too, but it'll be useless. You can't win against these three!"

"I am more confused than ever, Mr. Shaw."

"Oh, I can understand it. I'm trying to un-confuse you as fast as I can. That's why I started to say what I started to say a few minutes ago. I'll say it again. I'm going to warn you, now, that I am *going* to say, later—I mean, so it won't be so much of a shock then—later, that is—What I *mean* is, after all the explanations are explained, and everything, I'm going to ask you to marry me."

Susan sucked in her breath and looked at Mrs. Walker.

But Mrs. Walker did not recoil, or faint, or scream. She said, "Oh." Perhaps she flushed a little—it was hard to tell in candlelight. She kept her gaze steadily on Mr. Shaw. She said, "I think I'd better put on some water for tea. Vicky, will you take care of Maggie, please? Bobbie, we'll need the smelling salts again—they're in my room." She stood up.

Mr. Shaw offered his arm and said, "The floor is awfully slippery."

She looked at him gravely for a moment. "Well, my children trust you implicitly, it seems. I believe I can, too." She gave him a little smile, and laid her hand on his arm, and said, "The kitchen is that way. Lead on, Mr. Shaw."

An Old Photograph Reviewed

Susan's diary doesn't end with her father helping Mrs. Walker along the slippery floor of the hallway. There is more. I'll get back to it as soon as I've mentioned some other matters.

For instance, there is the question of what became of Mr. Sweeney. All I can do about that is to report my speculations and, in a moment, a wild surmise.

I assume that when the elevator stopped again after Mr. Bodoni sent it up from the basement, Mr. Sweeney escaped. He would have had to come within range of Cousin Jane's umbrella to do so, and I'll wager that she gave him a couple of good thwacks as he scrambled out. Perhaps he brushed against the basement button in passing, and thus sent the elevator on its final descent. Very likely he lurked about in the building for a while, wondering where he was. Eventually he must have wandered out into the street, to encounter all the surprises that the twentieth century had in store for him. I hope his philosophy was equal to the occasion...But then, the Sweeneys of this world usually land on their feet; and I conjecture that it didn't take him long to discover that he could make use of his professional talents as well in this century as in the last.

Cousin Jane, I regret to say, came into the twentieth century a wealthy woman.

Although Mr. Shaw and Mrs. Walker were not sorry that she was gone, it did bother their consciences that she would be plunged into the twentieth century without any means of support. So after some careful thought, Mr. Shaw set up a small trust fund in a bank that he knew would be reliable—the Tri-City Guaranty and Trust Company—and deposited sealed instructions in their vaults. The envelope was to be opened on a certain Tuesday of March, 1960—that is, three days after the Shaws had disappeared in the elevator. Mr. Shaw could not know, of course, that matters at this end would be delayed a year and a half. (More about that delay in a moment.) But the Special Notice did make him realize that for some reason Cousin Jane might be difficult to locate. So the instructions were that on the following day, the bank should look for Jane Hildegarde Clamp (carefully described as to physical appearance, dress, and state of mind) in the Ward Street apartment building; and that if she were not found, the bank should advertise for her whereabouts. That was why the Special Notice had been running in the papers for so long.

It fell to me to give the Tri-City Guaranty and Trust Company the information it had been seeking, and to claim my reward. Cousin Jane was rescued from the Ward Street police station, and put in possession of her trust fund. It was an impressive amount of money after eighty years of growth.

I have mentioned that I don't subscribe to a newspaper, but I do look at them in the news-stands, and buy one when the occasion warrants; and as Cousin Jane's new career was of the kind that journalists delight in, I was able to follow it in some detail. It did not take her long to decide that she disapproved of the twentieth century, and that her duty toward it was clear. With her fortune she established a foundation, the Mission for the Elevation of Contemporary Moral Tone. The Mission sent workers to remote tropical islands to bully the inhabitants into wearing more clothes and improving their table manners. It showered the Laboring Classes with moral instruction in the form of tracts and pamphlets—all of which ended up as litter in the streets. It strove mightily to suppress Infamous Literature, making a serious nuisance of itself among publishers and libraries and booksellers...

But Cousin Jane finally met her nemesis in the form of a gentleman whose dedication to moral tone seemed as relentless as her own. He became the Mission's treasurer. Two months later he vanished with a large part of the Mission's money. He was arrested at the Mexican border, and brought to trial, and given a stiff sentence; but the money was never recovered. Cousin Jane was forced to retire into a frugal private life, leaving contemporary moral tone to shift for itself. The ex-treasurer's picture in the newspapers showed a fastidiously dressed and combed man with a beard. His name was reported to be Adelbert Swinderby; a name which suggests to me—But as I said, it is only a wild surmise on my part. I can't prove anything.

Why did the witch wait so long before bringing me into the case? I don't suppose I'll ever know for certain, but my tentative solution is that the matter simply slipped her mind for a year and a half. She *was* vague and absent-minded—Susan and I both noticed that. I think of her as one day suddenly putting her skinny fingers to her mouth and exclaiming, "Oh, dear! I was going to do something about little what's-her-name back in 1881, wasn't I? How careless of me! Well, now, let—me—see..." Practically speaking, it didn't matter that she was late, since the elevator could travel in time as flexibly as you or I can travel in space. Just as we can get to the Historical Association's headquarters from any point in the city, so could the elevator take my message back to the Shaws from any point of time in the twentieth century.

As for my friend Charles, he was more skeptical than ever when I posted him on all the new developments; although he did admit that my "story," as he persists in calling it, was a "good yarn." But his disbelief no longer irritates me. If it pleases him to think that he is right, then it pleases me even more to know that he is wrong; so our friendship is unimpaired.

And lastly, the elevator.

Late Sunday night I went down into the basement to pay my final respects. I patted the poor old battered conveyance, and thanked it for all it had done, and asked for one final favor. The favor was granted; or at any rate, not denied. I borrowed a screwdriver from Mr. Bodoni's workbench, and reverently took down the metal plate that says *Capacity 1500 Lbs.* It is one of my favorite keepsakes.

A crew of brisk and efficient men in green coveralls arrived Monday morning, and set to work. By the time they had finished on Wednesday afternoon, nothing was recognizable any more. The old arrows and dials had given way to lights that blinked the number of the floor. The new mechanism made very little sound—mostly a kind of discreet and well-lubricated *zzzzz*. It hurled you up or down with a speed that seemed to separate your stomach from the rest of your body. The interior of the car was grey and pastel blue, and there was a thick wall-to-wall carpet. A vent chilled you with a blast of conditioned air. Music, the kind you hear in dentists' offices and supermarkets, poured without interruption from a concealed loudspeaker.

Mr. Bodoni was delighted. "Real class, hah?" he said to everyone he met, grinning around his dead cigar. All the tenants seemed to agree.

I guess I'm a crank. I've used the stairs ever since.

Susan's diary goes on to record that early in the afternoon of the day after the Battle of Elevator Hall (as Sergeant Walker called it) everyone, including Maggie and Toby, fared forth on a treasure hunt. Maggie went because her second sight had been so triumphantly vindicated, and she was confident that her occult powers would enable her to find the gold, no matter how well it was hidden. Toby went because he was the kind of cat who becomes anxious when he sees all his people leaving the house at the same time. Sergeant Walker led the way to Mr. Sweeney's camp, and Toby brought up the rear with a series of rushes and skulks and an occasional yowl.

It turned out that Maggie's second sight was not up to this kind of work. They spent several fruitless hours poking through Mr. Sweeney's things, and under logs, and in leaf drifts and thickets. Toby turned kittenish, and dashed among them sideways with his back up, and finally capped their vexation by scooting up a tree and getting stuck. Robert had to climb after him. While he was aloft he noticed what looked like rope-ends draped over the lip of a tall hollow stump. They *were* rope-ends, although from ground level they looked like pieces of frayed bark. Everyone took hold of a rope, and hauled, and heavy bundles came up from inside the stump...They tried to carry Toby home in triumph, but he would have none of it. Cats don't understand that kind of ceremony.

The problem of evading Mr. Hollister's garrulity became troublesome, and eventually the Shaws went to town and followed up an advertisement in the newspaper for rooms and board. Their prospective landlady had no sooner shown them around when she collapsed on a horsehair sofa in the parlor and burst into hysterical weeping. Bit by bit they learned that she had recently been bilked of her life's savings. She could not bring herself to say how it had happened; but the name "Abernathy Swinnerton" came out between sobs and hiccups. Mr. Shaw and Susan exchanged glances over her head. They took the rooms at once, and Mr. Shaw made arrangements at his bank for full restitution.

He also hired a horse and trap from the local livery stable, and took driving lessons, and practiced on daily trips to and from the Walkers'.

Five days after the Battle of Elevator Hall, Mrs. Walker said yes to Mr. Shaw. Victoria claimed that *her* sharp romantic eye had already detected the state of her Mama's feelings as early as the first hour of the treasure hunt. In any case, there were proprieties to be observed, and the engagement period proceeded in the approved leisurely fashion of the time. There were long strolls and rides through the countryside, some by moonlight, and shopping expeditions, and picnics on the grassy banks of streams, and tea and cakes and ices in the garden at dusk: everything, in short, that Susan had dreamed about and yearned for.

So the summer passed, and autumn came; and on a bright blue-and-gold day in October, Mrs. Walker became Mrs. Shaw.

Susan's interest in her diary begins to taper off after this. The entries become shorter and farther apart in time. They mention sleigh rides and snowball fights; magic lantern shows; the purchase of a family mare, named Lady Jones at first, and later, when her true character began to come out, Lazy Bones; Mr. Shaw's provision for Cousin Jane in the twentieth century (a long entry here: the solution obviously intrigued Susan. I'm glad she never knew about the dreadful Mission); Maggie's betrothal to the policeman who had brought her back from town that afternoon when Robert was stalking Mr. Sweeney; school-days; the restoration of the garden around the house; the birth of a little brother…

The last entry is dated September 30, 1882. It mentions various small matters, and tells about the visit of a photographer. She must have been interrupted while writing, because the final sentence says, "He also took some pictures of" Of…? The house, maybe, or Lazy Bones, or Toby—I don't suppose I'll ever know. But I know it was this visit that resulted in the old brown photograph that formerly hung in the reading room of the Historical Association. I say "formerly" because one day Charles remarked, "Well, Edward, there aren't many eccentrics left these days, so I suppose we should encourage the few we still have;" and he made me a present of the photograph. It hangs above my desk as I write. Thanks to Susan's diary, I know much more about it now than I did when I first saw it.

For instance, I know now that Robert is a cadet in the Colonel Andrew Belcher Stump Military Academy; and that he is scowling in order to keep from laughing, because a schoolmate of his (an older boy whom he worships, here on a weekend visit) is making faces at him from behind the photographer.

I know now that the bundle of blanket and lace that Mrs. Shaw looks down upon so tenderly contains John Thomas Shaw, Jr., who is fifty-one days old. (I also know that both Susan and Victoria were disappointed when he was named. Susan—perhaps with tongue in cheek—wanted him to be called George Bernard. Victoria was set on Robin Adair Beauregard.)

I once described Mr. Shaw's smile in this picture as "happy but faintly bewildered." I thought the faint bewilderment might be there because he was still having trouble believing what had happened. But there could be a simpler reason. One of the items in Susan's last entry is, "Daddy's repeater still missing." You can get a lot of bewilderment out of something like that. As for the happiness—who wouldn't be happy married to someone as beautiful as Isabelle? And who wouldn't be happy with investments in two young but thriving inventions, the telephone and the electric lamp?

I previously thought that Victoria had that faraway musing look because of general romantic tendencies. I was only partly right. The main reason for her expression in the photograph happens to be Robert's aforementioned schoolmate. He is tall, and comes from Virginia, and has courtly manners (when he is not standing behind a photographer) and his name is Talbot.

As for why Susan smiles—well, we know why. There is nothing more to add. But I must confess something. That smile, delightful as it is, irks me a little at times. It's so—smug; as though everything were *her* doing.

Sometimes I long to be able to say to her, "Susan, my dear, *I* had a hand in bringing about your happy conclusion, you know. And although you may think that your fortune is unique, I suspect that perhaps it isn't. Because I have a note from an old acquaintance of yours; a note written in a spidery hand on thick creamy paper. It begins, 'Reservations for this year are filled.' Do you see the implication, Susan? *For this year...*"

But I suppose it's just envy that makes me want to tell her that. She smiles because one year she was chosen. Whereas *I* can only hope. I keep telling myself that there are grounds for hope. The writer of that note knows me. This year, perhaps, or next year, or sometime—

Author's Note to Time at the Top

Like Susan, the heroine of this book, Jill Morgan of Purple House is a time traveller. She ventures into the past to rescue books that are stranded there, and brings them back to the present, and gives them new life. Now she has rescued and revived *Time at the Top*. I can't say how grateful I am, and how pleased; because, of all my books, this one is closest to my heart.

The writing of it was the most enjoyable experience I've ever had as an author. Not that it wasn't a struggle! Working out the story involved a great deal of mental turmoil, and setting it down was slow and frequently laborious. Writing never comes easily for me: I stare out the window a lot, and throw away half a dozen pages for every one I keep—and in the end, like as not, I'll throw that one away too. But in spite of that, or maybe because of it, the making of this book was a joy from beginning to end.

The greater part of the pleasure came from creating, or in some cases merely finding, my characters. I fell in love with them all. I loved quick-witted Susan and slow-witted Mr. Bodoni; Victoria the romantic and Robert the commonsensical; Mr. Sweeney, the smooth talker and Mrs. Clutchett, the chatterbox. I loved my bag lady witch and her driver, Nicky—who most likely (this just occurred to me now!) was really a black cat inside that smart motorcyclist's outfit. I had a special affection for my other black cat, the undisguised Toby, having borrowed him from my little daughters, Beth and Kitt, whose pet he was. And the elevator, of course—how could I not love the conveyance that takes my unsuspecting heroine back in time? I gave it as much personality as I could, and convinced myself to the extent that when, in the sequel to this book (*All In Good Time*) the elevator dies of its exertions, I felt that I was saying goodbye to a beloved and eccentric friend.

When I reread *Time at the Top* now, the memory of that pleasure comes rushing back. What a gift and a blessing it was! The exuberance I felt seems to me to radiate from the pages still. It is my hope that you, my new readers, will feel the glow of it too. May my pleasure become yours as you read!

Edward Ormondroyd
2003

EDWARD ORMONDROYD grew up in Swarthmore, Pennsylvania, and Ann Arbor, Michigan. During WWII he served on board a destroyer escort, participating in the invasions of Okinawa and Iwo Jima.

After the war he attended the University of California at Berkeley, where he received a bachelor's degree in English. Later he went back for a master's degree in library science. He lived in Berkeley for 25 years, working at various jobs while writing children's books, including *David and the Phoenix.*

He and his wife Joan moved to upstate New York in 1970. They live in the country near Ithaca, in a house designed and partly built by Edward. Their seven children are all grown and independent. They have two grandsons and a granddaughter.

Edward's interests include studying piano, gardening, books, birds, flowers (wild and tame) and listening to classical music.